The Mongoliad
Book Two

The Mongoliad
Book Two

BY

NEAL STEPHENSON, GREG BEAR,
MARK TEPPO, NICOLE GALLAND, ERIK BEAR,
JOSEPH BRASSEY, COOPER MOO

47NORTH

The characters and events portrayed in this book are fictitious. Any similarity to real persons, living or dead, is coincidental and not intended by the author.

Printed in the United States of America.

Published by 47North
P.O. Box 400818
Las Vegas, NV 89140

ISBN-13: 9781612182377
ISBN-10: 1612182372

To the spirits of Charles Dickens and Robert E. Howard

CAST OF CHARACTERS

In Hünern

Andreas: Shield-Brethren knight initiate
Rutger: Shield-Brethren knight master, quartermaster of the Rock
Styg: Shield-Brethren initiate
Eilif: Shield-Brethren initiate
Maks: Shield-Brethren initiate

Hans: orphan of Legnica, member of the local gang known as the "rats"
Father Pius: Roman Catholic priest
Dietrich von Grüningen: *Heermeister* of the Livonian Order
Sigeberht: the *Heermeister*'s bodyguard
Burchard: the *Heermeister*'s bodyguard

Onghwe Khan: Ögedei Khan's dissolute son
Tegusgal: captain of Onghwe Khan's personal guard
Ashiq-temür: second in command of Onghwe Khan's personal guard
Zugaikotsu no Yama: Nipponese *ronin*
Kim Alcheon: Korean Flower Knight

In Rome

Ferenc: a young Magyar hunter
Ocyrhoe: orphan of Rome
Matteo Rosso Orsini: Senator of Rome
Master Constable Alatrinus: keeper of the Septizodium
Father Rodrigo Bendrito: a priest of the Roman Catholic Church
Robert of Somercotes: Cardinal of the Roman Catholic Church
Sinibaldo Fieschi: Cardinal of the Roman Catholic Church
Rainiero Capocci: Cardinal of the Roman Catholic Church
Giovanni Colonna: Cardinal of the Roman Catholic Church
Rinaldo de Segni: Cardinal of the Roman Catholic Church
Tommaso da Capua: Cardinal of the Roman Catholic Church
Romano Bonaventura: Cardinal of the Roman Catholic Church
Gil Torres: Cardinal of the Roman Catholic Church
Goffredo Castiglione: Cardinal of the Roman Catholic Church
Stefano de Normandis dei Conti: Cardinal of the Roman Catholic Church
Riccardo Annibaldi: Cardinal of the Roman Catholic Church

In the East

Feronantus: Shield-Brethren knight master, the Old Man of the Rock
Percival: Shield-Brethren knight initiate
Raphael: Shield-Brethren knight initiate
Roger: Shield-Brethren knight initiate
Finn: Germanic hunter, Shield-Brethren companion
Yasper: Dutch alchemist, Shield-Brethren companion

Istvan: Hungarian horse-rider, Shield-Brethren companion
Cnán: Binder, Shield-Brethren guide
Eleázar: *Matamoros,* Shield-Brethren initiate
Taran: Irish gallowglass, Shield-Brethren knight initiate and *oplo*
Rædwulf: English longbowman, Shield-Brethren initiate
Illarion: Ruthenian noble, Shield-Brethren companion
Haakon: Shield-Brethren initiate
Vera: leader of the Shield-Maidens
Alena: Shield-Maiden
Benjamin: Jewish Khazar trader
Kristaps: the First Sword of Fellin, Livonian knight
Alchiq Graymane: Mongolian *jaghun* commander

Ögedei Khan: *Khagan* of the Mongol Empire
Yelu Chucai: Kitayan advisor to the *Khagan*
Gansukh: Mongolian hunter, emissary of Chagatai Khan
Munokhoi: *Torguud* captain
Lian: Chinese slave and tutor
Toregene: Ögedei Khan's First Wife
Jachin: Ögedei Khan's Second Wife

1241

Haverfest

CHAPTER 1:

QUOD PERIERAT REQUIRAM

Rome was not the first city Ferenc had ever seen. As a child, he had lived in Buda, where the clustered buildings were strewn like squat boulders along the banks of the slow-moving Danube. His memories, though, were but vague shapes in a fog compared to the reality laid out before his eyes.

Rome lay below them, wrapping itself around the River Tiber like a jealous lover. The light was strange here too. It was brighter and brisker than his memories of Buda, as if the sky over the city had cracked open and scattered celestial sparks upon the peaked rooftops, creating a dazzling spray of illumination.

Ferenc glanced at the priest slumped on the horse next to him. He was draped over his horse's neck, his knuckles intertwined in the animal's mane so tightly they were white. The light from the city was reflected in his eyes, making him look almost blind. A ropy strand of spit quivered in his tangled beard.

His fever was back. The disease had gone into hiding deep within the priest a week ago, and then he had insisted they ride farther and harder each day. Ferenc had tried to hold him back, knowing this relief from the burning infection was temporary. He had been right: this morning, it had returned. The skin around the wound on the man's hip was still angry and red, even though the gash was closing. If it closed all the way, it would seal the fever inside, and he would never heal.

With a groan that made Ferenc shudder, the priest pushed himself upright. His right foot slipped from the stirrup. He grabbed at the horse's mane to keep from falling, and the animal tossed its neck back, as if protesting his clumsiness. Father Rodrigo shook his head, and the spit flew from his beard. "Rome," he croaked. "We made it."

When he looked at Ferenc, his eyes were still filled with the wild, reflected light from the city below. The young hunter made the sign of the cross on his chest, as the priest had taught him, and whispered the holy words that would protect him from possession. His mother had taught him other charms against evil spirits—the warding eye, the sign of the forest—but he didn't want to enrage the priest. He didn't want the madness in the priest to know he was afraid.

Ferenc had come to realize the strength of the priest's magic. Father Rodrigo had one sign he used for everything. He didn't have to remember the prayers to the wind or the rain or the spirits living in the forests. He didn't have to know the hymns to sing before and after a hunt. He didn't have to memorize the glyphs and sigils used by mothers to protect their houses and children. The priest had one sign only—such a simple gesture, so easily taught to children, so easily remembered—and one god to call upon. Followers of such magic asked only for strength and guidance; why they needed either was left unspoken. *God knows,* the priest had assured Ferenc, *God knows everything in your soul.*

"Yes," the priest said, crossing himself as Ferenc did. "Praise His mercy." He returned his attention to the city. "He has carried us this far, and He will only need to sustain us a short while longer."

The last few days had been filled with the same sort of fear that had chased them away from Mohi. An army lay around the hills of Rome, a discordant mass of unorganized men that had none of the terrifying precision of the Mongols, but had been foreign occupiers nonetheless. The two companions had fallen into old routines—traveling by night, moving slowly across unmarked terrain, avoiding all contact—and only this morning had they sensed they were through the cordon of soldiers.

The priest swayed, and Ferenc again feared Father Rodrigo would fall. But he caught himself—somehow—with a hand across the neck of his horse and his head thrown back in a wild, wordless plea to Heaven.

Father Rodrigo's horse, used to hours and days of the priest as near deadweight, seemed spooked at his unexpected shifting in the saddle and sidestepped irritably. If his horse grew any more agitated, Father Rodrigo would surely be thrown. The priest claimed his god watched over fools and idiots, but he'd also said, *Thou shalt not tempt the Lord thy God.* Ferenc had seen enough men thrown from their horses on the plain near Mohi to know what would happen. He nudged his mount toward the priest's and leaned over, patting the horse's flank. Sweaty—and now twitchy. Which made his own exhausted mount suddenly twitchy too. They'd been pushing the horses too hard, and the animals were becoming choleric. It wouldn't take much for both of them to bolt.

Me too, Ferenc thought. He settled his weight in his saddle, quieting his own horse with a firm hand on the shoulder and soft words. They had gotten these horses just inland from Venice, in the flat plains of the western Veneto; they were spindly-legged nags, not at all suitable for climbing mountains. They didn't understand Ferenc's Magyar, but they understood his voice. They knew his tone. As he spoke to them, they calmed.

Father Rodrigo hadn't noticed the moment of unrest. The city held him enraptured. "There," he said, pointing. "Santa Maria Maggiore. That tall spire there. That is where I received my confirmation." He expelled a sharp laugh. "Twenty years now, I've been gone for twenty years." He moved his hand slightly, referencing another landmark that Ferenc could not separate out from the forest of towers and domes. "Over there is the Basilica of St. Peter's. Across the river, Ferenc. Do you see the house of holy light?"

But the light is shining on all of them, Ferenc thought, although he kept his tongue still. The priest seemed to be shaking off some of the malaise that had bound his bones. For a while now, perhaps as long as it would take them to descend this hill and join the flow of travelers entering the city, Father Rodrigo might remain lucid. Perhaps even long enough for them to reach the river. Perhaps.

"Come," the priest said, rapping his heels against his horse. "We have a little farther to travel." The horse snorted and picked its way downslope, toward the broad, paved track of the road.

Ferenc remained for a moment, idly rubbing the itching skin on the front of his left shoulder. Most of their nicks and cuts from last spring had healed, nothing more than thin, pink lines of new skin on their sun-darkened faces and arms. The most grievous of his wounds had been an arrow to the shoulder, and it was the last to heal. Fortunately, the enemy archer had been very strong and Ferenc's gambeson had not been very thick. The arrowhead had gone through, missing the bone; it had been simple to break the shaft and draw the two pieces out. Simple, yes, but taking the arrow out had hurt worse than getting shot. At least the wound had been clean—easily dressed and cared for.

He'd also cleaned and bound Father Rodrigo's wounds, and cleaned and rebound them often during their journey from the death fields at Mohi. But the Father's infection ran too deep for Ferenc's skill. They needed to reach the sanctuary of which Father Rodrigo spoke so longingly. Here they would find more priests and also, Ferenc assumed, healers—men who could save Father Rodrigo both from his infection and his madness. Ferenc did not quite understand what was in this great basilica of Father Rodrigo's—this *house of holy light*—but he imagined it as a gleaming fortress of strength, beauty, and an omnipotent magic born of pure faith.

Ferenc nudged his horse forward, following Father Rodrigo's. As they wound their way toward the bottom of the narrow hill, the sounds of civilization rose up to meet his ears: voices calling out, metal ringing against metal, the groan and creak of an old wagon as it rumbled down the dusty track, and in the distance, the steadily growing buzz of the city. They had avoided settled areas for so long that all these noises, the cacophony of city life, created an undifferentiated tumult in Ferenc's ears. It reminded him not of his childhood memories of Buda, but of the sound that had swept across the fields of Mohi shortly before dawn on that ghastly spring morning months ago. That crackling noise of men's fear. The sound of thousands of men babbling to themselves as they waited for their turn to die.

Ferenc hunched his shoulders, ignoring the twinge below his clavicle, trying instinctively to protect his head, to shelter his ears from possible screams and wails—sounds he was more likely to hear in his mind.

This morning, on the open road to Rome, he had heard only the sounds of travelers: children laughing or singing tunelessly, oxen lowing as they pulled carts toward the city, men calling hesitant greetings to one another. While these travelers were aware of the presence of a nearby army, they did not have the same fear. No one fretted whether or not they were going to be the first to die. Of all the people on the roads to Rome, only Ferenc—and Father Rodrigo too, judging by the tension in his jaw and the faraway look in his eye—were haunted by the distant disaster that had befallen Christendom on the banks of the Sajó River.

The harbingers of the Apocalypse—horse riders from the East—had come to Christendom. Those who survived the horrifying battle at Mohi—who were to bear witness to the rest of the West—were forever marked.

◆◆◆

Ferenc's resolve failed when they reached the market. He had girded himself for the sensory onslaught, but the noise still buffeted him like the winter wind screaming through the rough passes in the Carpathians. He was surrounded by the clucking cries of distraught poultry, the bleating of terrified pigs, the cacophony of vendors shouting and arguing with customers over the prices of their wares, the whistling din of pipes as musicians tried to play loud enough for street performers to dance. And always the smell of unwashed bodies, rotten fruit, pig shit, cow shit. The turgid atmosphere of too many people living in too small a space.

It was all Ferenc could do to keep his terror in check. He wanted to jerk at his horse's reins until the animal reared back, then plow through the crowds and flee Rome entirely. The dumb beast already sensed his fear and didn't know what to do except be frightened as well. *Run,* Ferenc thought, *we're close enough.* He eyed the priest. Someone would find him and take him across the river. Someone else. It didn't have to be him.

Whatever lucidity Father Rodrigo had up on the hill was gone now. The priest slumped forward again on the neck of his horse. His eyes were unfocused, and while his lips were moving, what came out of his mouth was nothing but nonsensical syllables. Ferenc had heard enough Latin over the last months—both feverish and liturgical—to learn the shape of the words; what was spilling from Father Rodrigo's mouth were only fragments, gutturals, fluttering sibilants—as if his tongue were a dragonfly's wing and couldn't slow itself enough to alight on a full word.

The hunter nudged his horse even closer to the priest's and leaned over to tug at the knotted rope around Father Rodrigo's waist. Two sharp tugs, enough to get his attention. Father Rodrigo slowly and laboriously hauled his head around as if it were a stone block. He stared at his shorter companion. His eyes were again filled with fever light.

He's blind, Ferenc realized. *All he can see is the past.* "Holy man," he said, and when Father Rodrigo didn't react, he said it again, louder. "Can you help me, holy man?"

After the Mongol army had swept across the plains at Mohi, those who hadn't been killed outright lay broken on the battlefield, waiting for the scavengers to come and finish them off. It was the rain that had brought Ferenc back, the cold and bitter taste of the water dripping down his face and into his mouth. He lay curled in a heap of dead men, directly under the brute who had tried to crush his skull with a club. The flies were undeterred by the rain, crawling across the Mongol's bloodstained face and over his one remaining eyeball. Ferenc's knife stuck out of the man's other socket.

Ferenc couldn't reach it, nor could he pull himself free from the pile of dead men. He could only lie there, watching the rain sluice off the corpses in streams of pink and red, watching flies crawl in and out of his assailant's gaping mouth.

And then the priest had stumbled past, dirty and bloody. Ferenc had filled his chest as best he could under the crush of bodies and called out. *Holy man,* he had cried. *Can you help me, holy man?* In that moment their fates became bound.

His mother had taught him about the endless cycle of the seasons. *Every year we start again,* she had told him. Before he was old enough to hunt, she would lead him by his small pink hand into the garden as the frost fled and the ground became soft. There, she taught him how to dig up what was dead. *This is what was,* she had said, shoving the twisted roots into his hand; *this is what will be,* as she planted the new crop and had him pat down the soft soil. When he was older, he had asked her why she repeated the same phrase every year. *Because that is how we remember,* she had told him. *That is how we bind ourselves to the world.*

Ferenc repeated his question one last time. He needed Father Rodrigo to remember that moment on the field of Mohi. It was how they were bound together.

Father Rodrigo blinked, and his mouth slowed, articulating more clearly the words in his throat. "*In...intende in adjutorium meum,*" he whispered. "*Deus salutis meae...*" He lifted his head and appeared to realize where they were. His fingers moving awkwardly, he fumbled with the drawstrings of the satchel tied to his waist. When he got it open, he shoved his hand inside and rooted around for a long time until he found what he sought. He thrust his hand toward Ferenc, nearly falling off his horse in the process; clutched between two fingers was the dull metal shape of a flat-topped ring. "*Educe me...*" He shook his head and tried again, this time in Ferenc's native tongue. "Take me to the palace," he said.

Ferenc leaned toward him, reaching for the ring. His fingers brushed the cool metal.

"*Caput orbis terrarum—*" A fresh bout of shivering overtook the priest, and he let go of the seal so that he could grab the pommel of his saddle. "Go to where St. Peter rests," Father Rodrigo urged when he could speak again. "Show them. They will know what to do…"

Ferenc examined the ring in his hands. He had seen it before. The priest had taken it out of his satchel occasionally and peered at it, but he had never explained its significance. The top was flat, inlaid with a cross, and raised letters ran along the outer edge. They meant nothing to Ferenc—other than the now familiar shape of the cross—but Father Rodrigo thought someone at the cathedral would know. Ferenc glanced around the bustling marketplace. Soldiers. The city's militia. Perhaps the soldiers would know.

Clutching both the ring and the reins of Father Rodrigo's horse, Ferenc began to ride slowly through the square. He owed the priest his life, and his debt would only be repaid when they reached their destination. The chaos of the market frightened him, and he'd faltered. He had turned to the priest for aid, and even in his fevered state, the priest had responded with a message, a sign. This was how his God worked, after all. When you lose your way, you prayed to Him for guidance and He would send you aid. He would tell you what to do and where to go.

Ferenc made the magic sign—forehead, sternum, left shoulder, right shoulder—and behind him, swaying drunkenly on his horse, Father Rodrigo did the same.

✦✦✦

They were clearly foreigners, and not just because they were stones in the natural flow of the market. It was closing in on midday. The blockade surrounding the city had reduced most of the itinerant vendors to barely a trickle, and those farmers who were able to set up their stalls had already come and gone, their wagons picked clean by the early morning residents. The pair stood out, not by virtue of their ragged appearances or because they were on horseback, but because they didn't have a clear destination in mind. They wandered aimlessly, moving at odds with the rest of the people in the square. One of them, the elder, appeared to be drunk. The other was not a local youth. Nor was he a simple farmer, though he had that wide-eyed, skittish, wondering look Ocyrhoe had seen on many a lad the first time they came to Rome. She sensed he was only a few years into manhood, but his beard and hair were thick and long, his face dark and lined from exposure.

She had been watching them since they came in through the Porta Tiburtina. The Via Tiburtina wasn't a major thoroughfare like Via Appia, but it was the only open road into Rome for those coming from the east.

Each morning, she climbed one of the churches on one of the seven hills of Rome and took stock of the city. There was too much of it for one person to cover; she couldn't hope to watch over it all, and so each morning she had to make a choice. Which gate? Which district? Which road? Where would she go? This morning, what little wind there was at dawn had been from the east, and so she had come to the market square next to the Porta Tiburtina to watch and to wait.

She was the only one left. She had to be careful.

Rome was caught in the throes of two crises. There were those who were still mourning the loss of the Bishop of Rome; others stood in the shadow of the walls and looked for signs that Frederick, the Holy Roman Emperor, was losing his taste for the blockade. Ocyrhoe wasn't privy to most of the political and religious machinations, nor did she profess to understand all of them, but she understood the rhythm and the pulse of the people, and in it she sensed a great deal of unease and danger.

And this had been true even before her kin-sisters had begun to disappear.

Two weeks ago, she had spotted the white pigeon on the statue of Minerva. When it had still been there the next morning, she had dared to climb up and retrieve it. The message on its leg had been written in the secret language, and without her sisters to help her, Ocyrhoe had spent most of the day deciphering it. The message was nothing more than a simple question, and she knew instinctively that it was meant for her: *Where are my eyes in Rome?*

The others were gone, taken—or driven off—by the Bear's men, or they had fled before the Emperor's armies had set up their camps outside the city. She was the only one left—too small to be noticed, too young to flee the city that had reared her—and so the task fell to her: to watch, to wait, to learn what was happening. And when the time came—when another bird appeared on Minerva's shoulder, as she knew in time it would—Ocyrhoe would be ready to report on everything she knew, on everything she had seen.

Today had brought these two: the drunken priest and the wild man-child.

The younger one wasn't very tall or broad, but he was more square than round in the chest. His shaggy hair had been bleached blond by the sun a long time ago, and what was left of his natural brown persisted as shadows and stripes through his beard. A rustic, homemade bow and quiver were slung across the withers of his horse. A small knife was thrust through his belt. The older man was trying to be a nondescript traveler, but Ocyrhoe sensed he was a priest. His hooded robe—stained and worn from travel—was a simple garment and gave no hint as to what sort of priest he might be. But the thin cord wrapped around his waist—from which a plain satchel was hung—was a rosary. He had cut off most of the long tail, but the short stem still had a few knots.

They were strangers, and she only had to watch them clumsily navigate the flow of people, carts, and draft animals through the market to know that, but there was something else about them that drew her attention. She had been training with Varinia—before her kin-sisters started to vanish—and the older girl had marveled at Ocyrhoe's instincts. *You read patterns too readily for an orphan,* she had told Ocyrhoe. Ocyrhoe hadn't understood what she meant and only shrugged. There was nothing *that* mysterious about her ability; she kept her eyes open, watching, and just knew when something wasn't right.

She tagged along after the pair, staying two horse-lengths back in the crowd. She knew the local cutpurses well enough to avoid their closeness, and little else distracted her focused attention.

The priest swayed on his horse, dependent on his companion's guidance. His head rolled loosely on his shoulders, and his pale, greasy hair stuck damp and matted to his forehead. His cheeks were flushed, and his eyes couldn't stay still. As Ocyrhoe slipped closer, she revised her assessment of the man's condition. He wasn't drunk; he was sick.

She kept at arm's length to one side of the young man's mount, not to be kicked, as they navigated the tangle of stalls and carts. The youth had a purpose but didn't know his destination. Ocyrhoe read the frustration on his face as he pulled his elder into an impassable clump of vegetable sellers. She feigned interest in some apples as the youth confusedly turned the horses around—eliciting shouts of derision and annoyance from the surrounding merchants—and pushed back toward the center of the square.

The gimlet-eyed merchant whose apples she was appraising regarded her with suspicion; she raised her left fist and shook it as if clenching a coin tightly between her fingers. The man crossed his arms over an ample belly and continued to stare, wordlessly calling her bluff. She actually did have a few coins in a tiny leather pouch that hung from a strap around her neck, but she wasn't about to waste one here.

As the two horses passed behind her, she made a display of mock outrage that this peasant would think she'd deign to steal from him.

"Run along, rat." He laughed at her.

She did, falling in behind the pair, ducking her head slightly to use the horses themselves as cover from the riders. As the youth nudged his horse, directing it to their left, the priest's horse—caught off guard by the sudden change in direction—stopped and pawed the ground. Ocyrhoe came to an abrupt halt as well, close enough to touch the priest's horse. The urge to reach out and put her hand on the animal's flank was strong, and she wrestled with the desire. As the priest's horse tossed its head and stepped after the young foreigner's horse, she let out the breath she had been holding. She stood still and let them get some distance.

Too close. Before she could castigate herself further, the priest twisted around and looked straight back at her, as if he knew she was there. As if he knew what she had almost done.

She panicked and did exactly what she shouldn't have: stood rooted to the spot by the intensity of his gaze. There was a light in his eyes, a glitter of some fire beyond the burning distress of fever. She shivered despite the hot sun beating down heavily on the square. Her skin turned cold, gooseflesh racing up her arms and chest. A procession of images flickered in her head like bits of a half-remembered dream. The two men had traveled a great distance, she knew this instinctively: through a dense forest, across the stark terrain of a high mountain pass, over a trampled and bloody field.

When she blinked, it was as if a cloud flew in front of the sun, and when it was gone, so was the priest's attention.

She swallowed thickly, the back of her tongue tingling. As she tried to make sense of the flash of insight, she noticed a squad of the local militia, rough stock sporting the white and purple of the Bear. Their path was going to intersect that of the riders. The leader was a thick-necked man with a round face and tiny eyes—he reminded Ocyrhoe of a hungry pig—and the confusion sown by the pair of riders had caught his attention.

The squad leader raised his hand, open palm directed at the horsemen, and his men-at-arms slapped their bracers against their leather jerkins. The sound broke the cacophony of the market, as the market-goers instinctively pulled back. A bubble opened up around the soldiers and the foreign horsemen, and a hush fell over the square.

"What is your business in Rome?" the squad leader asked, his eyes flicking back and forth between the two newcomers. He stood in front of the youth's horse, feet planted apart, looking like a dun-colored boulder.

The young man said something in a foreign tongue, pointing at the priest, who was swaying in his saddle, his focus elsewhere. Ocyrhoe stepped behind a vendor's cart, out of the priest's line of sight. She didn't think he was looking for her, but she was still spooked by that prior moment of clairvoyant connection. She wanted to slip away into the crowd and vanish. But she stayed, dropping to a squat so that she could still see what was going on from beneath the cart.

When the squad leader repeated his question, his men punctuated it by loosening their swords in their scabbards. The rattle of metal made the foreigner talk more rapidly, his strange words tripping over one another like the chorus of a child's chant. Ocyrhoe picked out the one familiar word before the soldiers, but finally it dawned on them too: "Peter," he was saying. "St. Peter."

"St. Peter. The basilica? Do you wish to see a priest?" the squad leader asked. "There are many priests—many churches—in Rome."

Ocyrhoe crept forward to get a better angle. She couldn't see the young foreigner's face—but she could see the reaction of the soldiers as the boy held something up. In unison, their eyes widened and their brows furrowed.

"St. Peter," he repeated, and pointed at the priest on the other horse. Ocyrhoe saw he was holding a ring. He hadn't understood the squad leader's words, but the gist of the man's question had been plain. Likewise, the visual aid of the ring and the swaying priest were enough to make his response clear.

The priest gasped like a fish, finding a moment of lucidity, but his voice was so ragged and strained that Ocyrhoe could barely hear it. "The Pope," the priest rasped. "I have urgent news for His Eminence."

"What news?" the squad leader demanded.

The priest shook his head, lapsing into the babbling cant of his scripture. "*Quod perierat requiram,*" he sighed. "*Et…et quod abjectum erat reducam, et quod confractum fuerat alligabo, et quod infirmum fuerat consolidabo, et quod pingue et forte custodiam…*"

The squad leader crossed himself, then stepped closer to them, gesturing for the ring. The young stranger leaned back in his saddle, the metal ring clutched desperately in his hand. The squad leader grimaced as he closed his own hand and raised his fist toward his men, who quickly responded with another noisy rattle of their swords. Instantly terrified, the youth tossed the ring to the leader.

The squad leader caught the ring and brought it close to his face so he could squint at it. Without turning his head, he called to his men, and one of the taller ones leaped forward. A hushed conversation followed. Ocyrhoe strained to catch their words, then took a few steps forward, just in time to see the leader drop the ring into the open hand of the tall soldier, who saluted, spun around, and trotted off through the crowd.

The foreigner had spotted the transfer too, and he cried out in protest. The priest was so startled by the sound he fell off his horse and landed with a thump on the stone paving and dirt. As the crowd surged forward, the youth pulled hard on the reins of his own horse and leaned forward, signaling—*accidentally?* wondered Ocyrhoe—the animal to rear up and paw at the air. One hoof struck the squad leader with a glancing blow to the head. The soldier flinched and ducked, crying out in pain, and behind him, his men drew their swords.

For Ocyrhoe, the world unraveled in that instant. The crowd became an undulating mass of bodies: some resisting being shoved forward, faces contorted with fear at the sight of weapons and flailing hooves; others pulling back, arms raised to protect their heads.

The priest lay sprawled on his back in a cloud of dust—slack-jawed, eyes flicking left and right, hands twitching—caught in the grip of fever-born phantoms. The squad leader gawped, the open cavern of his mouth making him seem like a dull-witted buffoon; his men flanked him, staunch-shouldered, arms flexed for a fight, their expressions a mix of ferocity and fear.

The foreign youth's horse pulled back its lips and flared its nostrils; the wild boy himself was the only one who appeared calm in the sudden fracas. It was now clear to Ocyrhoe that he had perfect command of his mount and had deliberately set off this chaos. She made her decision in that instant.

With an ease that belied the confusion and tumult of the marketplace around her, she fixed her eye on a spot on the young man's horse. As she moved, the noise of the crowd faded to a distant growl, like thunder dying across the hills. Her feet hardly touched the stones as she sprang up and dashed forward, and she barely registered the presence of the semiprone merchant whom she used as a vault to achieve a place on the foreigner's horse—right behind him, so close she pressed against his back.

Her arm, around his shoulder. He tensed.

Her mouth, next to his ear. "Ride," she whispered, then pointed, her finger tracking the tall soldier with the ring as he neared the edge of the square.

"Peter," she said, knowing it was the only word he would understand. He did.

She felt his legs clamp around his horse. The animal snorted and charged, diving toward the shining blades of the approaching soldiers. Her heart leaped into her throat, her skin flushed and heated at the thought that she had made a terrible mistake. But the foreigner had given his horse the freedom to run, and run it did, scattering soldiers and commoners alike.

Ocyrhoe held tight as the market became a blur. The soldier with the metal ring had disappeared around a corner; he did not know they were chasing him, and even if he did, he couldn't outrun this horse. She had never ridden a horse before, and the powerful thump and heave of the animal beneath her was both terrifying and exhilarating.

CHAPTER 2:

BOY MEETS GRUEL

Every day in the cage was another day of freedom.

Haakon's prison was a rough enclosure of wood and bone and metal, too small to allow him to stand upright, and if he lay down and stretched his arms over his head, he could just touch the metal bars with both his fingers and his toes. The roof was made from long planks, mismatched and warped. The cage sat in the back of a weather-beaten cart. A pair of stolid oxen pulled the cart—one brown, one black—at a pace always too slow for the liking of their handler. At first, Haakon was inclined to agree—the scenery passed with agonizing slowness—but in time, he realized every day they traveled was another day he would not have to face whatever fate the Virgin had in store for him. Another day of life. Another day of freedom.

The caravan was heading east. It had left Legnica the morning after his bout in the arena against the "demon" Zug. Haakon had walked into the tunnel of the Red Veil, expecting—naively, he now realized—some manner of reward ceremony, perhaps even an audience with Onghwe Khan himself. Instead, he had been accosted by a dozen Mongol warriors wielding pole-arms with weighted ends. He had instinctively blocked the first guard's jab, and had soon realized that defending himself was only going to increase how much they would hurt him when they finally knocked away his sword (and he did not suffer the illusion that he could best twelve men with pole-arms).

They had driven him into a tent beyond the arena, and once inside the tent, they had forced him to strip out of his armor. As long as he complied with their gestures, they only prodded him with the weighted staves; they did not want to hurt him, and Haakon—biding his time—did not relish the idea of trying to escape with a broken arm or leg. Once he had removed his armor, his arms and legs were bound. A crude leather sack was forced over his head. Only then had he panicked.

Some creature had perished in the bag; he could smell—and taste—the taint of its blood. He tried to shake the bag off his head, but as he thrashed about, he only managed to force the rough hide more firmly against his mouth and nose. He could hear their laughter, and as he struggled against a black tide that threatened to overwhelm him, their laughter became the last thing he remembered.

When he came to his senses, he was in a cage, buffeted by the cart as it bounced over muddy ruts of a wide track through the Polish forest. Since then, the only thing that had changed was the landscape. The trees, shorter and fewer in number, gave way to rocky terrain and then gently rolling plains covered with silky, tall grass.

The caravan was long, though much of his immediate view was blocked by similar cages on the carts in front and behind him—other prizes from Christendom.

The man in the cart just behind Haakon's was huge. His red hair and beard overflowed his tiny head, and his body—wedged against the cage's bars and in the cramped corners—was covered with a layer of fine red hair. *A wrestler,* Haakon thought. He fervently hoped their destination was not another gladiator-style arena. He did not wish to fight this man.

The captive in the next cart forward lay on his back and did not move overmuch; Haakon suspected he would not survive their journey.

And so Haakon waited. In time, his body grew accustomed to the shifting motion of the wooden cart; he listened to the Mongols as they shouted at the oxen, slowly absorbing the sounds of their language; he could tell when the cooks shifted from green wood to dried dung for their fires; when it rained, he would roll against the bars of his cage and let the bitter water sluice down his grimy face and into his mouth. He slept as often as the rattling motion of the cart allowed. At night, he studied the sky, trying to find the shapes he knew: the eyes of Thiassi, thrown into the heavens by Odin after the All-Father plucked them from the *jötunn*'s head; the deer (Duneyrr, Duraþrór, Dvalinn, and Dáinn) who cavorted in the branches of the World Tree; and the trio of bright stars that represented the distaff of Frigg. Below the horizon, he watched the passage of the caravan guards, memorizing the schedule of their shifts. Even if an opportunity presented itself to escape, he was not inclined to take it. Where would he run?

His captors were taking him someplace, for some reason. He'd know soon enough. Perhaps too soon.

The rhythmic creaking and jolting of cage and cart, the guttural curses of the handler and his assistant, the infrequent lowing of the oxen, the mournful sighs and whispers of wind over the endless grass, filled Haakon's mind and brought him a strange, contemplative peace. He had many, many hours to remember his training…and to prepare for whatever ordeal awaited him.

Your enemy will arrive when he is ready. At Týrshammar, Feronantus had been their *oplo*, and the elder veteran's style had been much different than Taran's training at the Legnica chapter house. Haakon had struggled with winning the first crossing of the swords, and while he knew his greatest weakness was committing too heavily to his initial strike, he had not been able to come up with a better tactic. *Learn to wait,* the old master of Týrshammar had told him. *Even though it may seem impossible, when your blood is hammering in your ears and your hands are eager to bury the sword point in your enemy's skull, hold back. Watch. Wait!*

For the following month, Feronantus designated Haakon as the defender in every practice. He could never initiate an attack; he could only respond. At first, Haakon had chafed at this role, thinking he was being punished, but gradually, he came to realize the defender was actually the one who *controlled* the exchange.

✦✦✦

A week or two into their journey, the caravan paused at an enormous camp that stretched as far as Haakon could see. His field of vision was limited by other carts and cages, now circled and bunched, but through them, in every direction, he saw nothing but the rounded peaks of Mongolian tents—*ger* was the word they used—and a fluttering profusion of standards and tiny flags.

Haakon's legs failed him as he realized this was the true Mongolian Horde that threatened Christendom. The force sprawling across the plain near Legnica had been a gnat compared to this gigantic assembly, and he shivered uncontrollably as he tried to imagine how many men the Mongol generals had at their disposal.

On his knees, he pressed his head against the rough floor of his cage, seeking sanctuary in a childhood prayer to the old gods of his forefathers.

Eventually, someone rapped against the bars of his cage with a baton. A thin man with a wispy strand of hair hanging stiffly from his chin stood beside the cage and jabbered in the Mongol tongue, smacking his baton repeatedly against the bars. Haakon looked up from his prayers and blearily focused on what the man was directing his attention to: a wooden bowl and, beside that, a strip of dried meat. The Mongol rapped the bars once more, indicating that he should eat.

Haakon scrambled over to the food, ignoring the Mongol's cackling laugh. He was familiar with the meat; once a day, a piece much like it was thrown into his cage. It was salt or sweat cured and had the texture of untreated leather. Eating was a time-consuming process of flexing and softening the meat with his hands before forcibly ripping it up and putting small pieces in his mouth; then he worked the dried meat more with his teeth and what saliva he could muster. To eat it too quickly was to be stricken with stomach cramps later. The first time, the cramps had lasted a full day and he had not been able to move his bowels for another two days afterward.

Occasionally, he could catch a guard's attention, and through pantomime at first—but more recently, using some of the Mongol words he had learned—he would ask for water. Once in a while, they would bring him a small amount in a crude cup, barely enough to lessen the drudgery of eating the meat.

The bowl, to his surprise, contained a watery rice gruel. Still a little warm, even. It was, Haakon decided, a reward from the Virgin for his patience. He meant to savor it, but his fingers scooped it quickly into his mouth.

For the next hour, until the man returned for the bowl, he sucked at its rim, making sure he got every last drop.

The following morning, the thin man arrived again with both meat and gruel. Haakon ignored the bowl at first, beginning the laborious project of softening the meat instead, and his stomach cramped. His body yearned for the watery rice paste, but the change in routine had made him wary. Why were they feeding him better? Had he reached the end of his journey?

There was more activity along the line of carts this morning, and he pressed himself against the bars to get a better view. Several groups of men were slowly moving down the line, assessing the cargo. They were dressed in much finer clothes, colorful silk jackets instead of the heavy and plain garments he was used to seeing.

Leading them was the largest man Haakon had ever seen.

Though tall and broad shouldered, the man's greatest bulk lay in an enormous midsection, wider than a *karvi,* or a *snekkja,* even, longboats that could carry up to two dozen warriors. Haakon reckoned it would require the strength of two, maybe three men to lift this giant off the ground—and more to push him over.

Unlike the others, the giant wore armor of overlapping leather plates—the entire skin of at least one adult ox, Haakon reckoned. Around his neck and over the armor, he wore many necklaces—gold and silver—and a huge gold medallion glittered at the shallow hollow of his throat.

The gold had been worked into the snarling visage of a wolf.

One of the caravan guards, in awe of the giant and his retinue, nervously gibbered as the group paused near Haakon's cage. Haakon listened to the guard's stammering speech, catching a few words. The large stranger stared at

Haakon all the while, grunting occasionally in response to the guard's story, and Haakon realized the guard was telling the giant about the fight in the arena. With a wild cry, the guard launched into a clumsy impression of Haakon's final assault on Zug with the demon's pole-arm. The giant—who, Haakon guessed, was one of the Mongol generals, perhaps even one of the other Khans, a relative of the dissolute Khan who lorded over Hünern—glanced briefly at the guard as the nervous man finished his exhibition, before returning his piercing gaze to Haakon.

Haakon shrugged. "I fight," he said, hoping that he had learned the word correctly from the caravan drivers and that he was not claiming to be a farm animal.

The giant laughed, and Haakon reasoned it made no difference if he had gotten the Mongol word right or not. His life was entirely in this Mongolian's hands, and as long as the man appeared amused by his words, then whatever he had said was the best response. Haakon realized the general's visit was probably the reason he had been given the gruel—if the prizes were to be inspected, it followed they should be somewhat healthy. He picked up the bowl of uneaten gruel and raised it in a gesture of thanks.

The general grunted in response and took several ponderous steps closer to the cart. His round face was oddly childlike, but his eyes were too quick and focused to be mistaken for a youngling's innocent gaze. His retinue darted around behind him, like a pack of scavengers waiting for the larger predator to finish with its kill.

Not knowing what else to do, Haakon sat down and started to eat the gruel. The general watched, studying Haakon not as a curiosity but as a warrior would carefully watch the simple movements of his enemy in order to learn something of how he might carry himself in combat.

When the bowl was empty, the general pointed at himself with the forefinger of his right hand. "Soo-boo-tie," he said. He said it again and then pointed to Haakon.

"Hawe-koon," Haakon replied, touching his chest.

The Mongolian general nodded and tried Haakon's name several times, sounding as if he were trying to speak around a stone in his mouth. Haakon decided to not undertake the same effort, fearing the general's humor might dissolve should Haakon display a commensurate clumsiness with the Mongolian name. Instead, he saluted with the bowl again, and as it was empty, he offered it to the general.

He had wanted to show some deference to his captor, the sort of noble gesture that Feronantus would have expected of him. Even though he was a prisoner, he was still a member of the *Ordo Militum Vindicis Intactae.* The bowl was the only thing he had to offer. His fealty was not available.

Soo-boo-tie stared at the crude bowl for a moment and then plucked it from Haakon's grasp. He spoke a few words to his retinue, and they scattered, rushing to continue their inspection of the caravan's prizes. Soo-boo-tie lingered for a moment and then laughed once more as he turned to depart, waving the bowl at Haakon.

The caravan guard stared at Haakon, open mouthed, and when Haakon met his gaze and shrugged, the guard spooked—jerked back, dropped his jaw, and raised his hands in deference. Then he recovered, straightened, snapped his mouth shut, and ran bandy-legged after the general and the others, leaving Haakon to wonder what had just transpired.

The next morning, the caravan moved on, and no more gruel was offered. The caravan masters returned to throwing a single strip of dried meat into his cage, once a day. But the pieces were bigger and not quite as hard.

◆◆◆

Haakon dreamed about the bowl. In the dream, he had not given it back, and the general had let him keep it. During the day, he hid it beneath his ragged shirt, tucking it against his side and holding it in place with his arm. On the nights when it rained, he pushed it out of his cage to catch the rainwater.

The shallow bowl of his dream was turned from a piece of knotty wood, and he could feel the tiny divots in its center where the woodworker had finished his work with a chisel. Was its maker still alive, or had he been killed when the Mongols had conquered whatever city he lived in? Haakon and the bowl had that much in common: they were spoils of war.

During the endless caravan ride, he had seen, firsthand, the aftermath of Mongol victories. From the older Shield-Brethren who had gone to the Levant to take part in the Crusades, he had heard stories about the atrocities perpetrated by the conquering armies (with the exception of the legendary Salah-ad-Deen, whose name Haakon could barely pronounce, though Raphael had spoken it several times). The reality, however, was much starker than his imagination.

Everything and everyone in these dying lands seemed to have become a prize to be split up, argued over, and ultimately taken away, killed, or enslaved. A Mongol commander's worth became measured in how much treasure he controlled, and Haakon could imagine how the constant lure of fresh conquests would be irresistible to those hungry to prove themselves to their generals. One bowl was not much in and of itself, but when wagons laden with such prizes returned to the *Khagan*, the wealth became substantial. One man made little difference, but cart after cart of prisoners made the victory all the greater.

In Haakon's dream, he imagined using the long-lost bowl to escape, beating a guard who came too close to his cage, smashing it over the Mongol's head until bone broke. The bowl itself was too knotty to break, a twisted piece of an ancient tree that was older than any living Mongol today.

Haakon dreamed even while awake. Once free of the cage, he would find a blade. How many could he kill with blade and bowl before the Mongol archers filled him with arrows? Could he steal a horse and ride away?

How far from Legnica was he?

Free of his cage, surrounded by dead Mongols, he found himself in possession of a map, a yellowed piece of parchment like the old map of the known world the Shield-Brethren kept in the great hall at Týrshammar. The eastern edge of the map was the great winding length of a Ruthenian river. The Volga? That name sounded right, but he wasn't sure. He had only seen the map once after word of Onghwe's challenge had come to Týrshammar's cold rock. Feronantus had used it to show the Shield-Brethren where they were going, but had only gestured at the eastern edge of the map to show where the invaders were coming from. None of them had imagined they would ever actually go there.

Still free of his cage, the bloody bowl clutched in one hand, he found himself riding one of the squat Mongol ponies, his body rocking back and forth as the pony galloped free. Did it know where it was going? In Haakon's other hand the parchment map streamed out like a banner; he tried to look at it as the pony fled through the sea of grass. The moon was a pale sliver in the dark sky, and the markings on the map were faint lines in the ghost light. Here was a river, there a mountain range, and then—the rest of the parchment rippled out like an endless ribbon of moon-white blankness.

Still, Haakon kept riding, hoping the pony was going in the right direction, toward the river and the mountains.

Otherwise, he was going to tumble over the edge of the map, into the endless, frozen depths of Hel's terrible domain...

◆◆◆

A voice.

Haakon opened his eyes and stared at the cage's slatted ceiling for a few moments, then shivered to toss off the fleeting, terrible fragments of his dream. Hel herself had gripped him with hideous claws of icicles and bone. Her tangled gray-white hair had been crusted with the frozen brine of mourners' tears...

He lurched and cried out in abject misery. Such a fool he had been, riding that stupid pony over the edge of the known world! Why hadn't he checked the stars? If he had put the Dvalinn, the sleeping deer, on his right, then he would have been heading west.

He looked away from the cage ceiling, trying blearily to recall the open night sky.

"Wake up, fool," the voice said again. Something banged against the bars, and Haakon turned his head. One of the Mongolian short-legged ponies trotted alongside the slowly rolling cart. Its rider was leaning over and banging a bowl against the bars to get Haakon's attention. White liquid slopped out, and Haakon scrambled up to the bars, his throat constricting in panic at the sight. The rider grinned and let his horse drift away from the cage so that Haakon had to squeeze himself against the bars and strain to reach the bowl.

The horseman finally relented, with a grunt. Haakon grabbed the bowl and tugged it into the cage, where he held it in wonder for a few seconds. The bowl contained thickened rice paste, a strip of meat, and a residue of sweet rice water. Using the piece of meat as a utensil, Haakon scooped the paste into his mouth. His belly, shrunken to almost nothing, filled quickly, so he chewed the piece of meat slowly, taking his time with it, and made sure to suck down every drop of rice water—and then to lick the bowl clean.

Gruel *and* meat. And the rider did not come back to take away the bowl. Something had changed. The caravan was going to halt soon.

The terrain had changed again. A few days ago, they had passed within sight of a small village nestled in the crook of a long and glittering track of river, and since then, isolated patches of pasture had started to break up the endless expanse of steppe grass.

During his long journey, Haakon had come to understand just how nomadic the Mongolian people were, and the familiar signs of civilization struck him as oddities on the steppes.

At first, they had passed through regions conquered by the Mongol Horde, savaged lands that had been stripped of any value by the voracious appetite of the raiders. And then came the desolate places, lands too sere or remote for any people to find hospitable.

His belly full, Haakon wedged his shoulder against the bars of his cage to brace against the motion of the cart, steadying his eyes to watch these strange scenes pass by. They had certainly gone off the edge of any map he knew, of any map anyone he had ever met might have known—with the exception of the Binder girl, perhaps.

He stared at the wandering clumps of herd animals—sheep, goats, camels, the occasional yipping dogs and shaggy cows—and the tiny clusters of *ger* that sprouted from the grasslands like gray mushrooms. He was the first of his brothers to come to this place, and for the first time in many days, he found himself looking forward to what lay beyond the horizon.

Does Zug's home lie out there? he wondered.

When the rider returned for the bowl, Haakon asked him if this place had a name. The Mongol answered brusquely, and Haakon repeated the single word to himself for the rest of that day, trying to dispel the unease it left in his belly.

It sounded like the noise ravens made. *Kara-kora-hoom.* He couldn't stop thinking about the black birds he had seen on the ruined walls of Legnica. Ominous harbingers.

The Shield-Brethren swore their oaths to the Virgin Defender, a warrior maiden whose face they would never truly see until they died. She was *Skuld,* and yet she was not. Some of the other boys from his tribe clung tenaciously to the stories they had absorbed from their mothers' breasts, but Haakon had looked on the vastly different faces of the students at Týrshammar and understood each knew the Virgin in his own way. When the priest in the Christian temple spoke of "Mary," he was talking about the same goddess.

Even back then, before Haakon had learned how to hold a sword and how to carry a shield, he suspected the world was larger and more mysterious than he could ever truly imagine.

Hearing the raven-squawk name of the place where he was being taken, he found comfort in the idea that the world, in all its cruel vastness, was but a grain of sand in the Virgin's palm. It did not matter where he died. As long as he died in the Virgin's service, he would finally see her glorious face.

After his inevitable and bloody warrior's death, the icy fingers of Hel would twitch empty, and the queen of the dead would scream in disappointment.

The Virgin herself would be waiting for Haakon. She would garland his neck with a wreath of cornflowers and clasp him to her spring-sweet bosom.

This he knew, and it gave him strength.

CHAPTER 3:

THIRSTY WORK

Before the Battle of Legnica, Hünern was little more than a collection of farms clustered haphazardly around a blacksmith and a church. A small hamlet that grew, almost by accident, out of a desire for farmers to have a place where they could pray and drink without having to travel to the city of Legnica. When the Mongol army assembled to fight Duke Henry II of Silesia, Hünern was abandoned and then overrun. The church remained, its awkwardly tilted spire rising over a landscape of crooked and broken walls, like eggshells scattered across a chicken coop after a fox's rampage.

When the Mongolian engineers began to build their arena, mercenaries, fighting men, traveling merchants, and other vagabonds summoned by Onghwe Khan's challenge reclaimed the ruins of Hünern.

Invariably, the first structures rebuilt after the sacking of a city were one or more churches. The dead must receive absolution before they could be interred, and the survivors—in the absence of strong battlements and armed soldiers—had only their faith to protect them. A house of prayer meant they had not been abandoned; within the sanctuary of the church, they could open their hearts in prayer and hope to be sustained.

Inevitably, an assortment of dilapidated taverns followed, because laying stone and raising walls—especially those of a church—was thirsty work. In the absence of salvation, what else could a man do but drown the pernicious voices that whispered incessantly of one's coming damnation? If God had abandoned you, what use was prayer? Drink was better.

In Dietrich's opinion, the closest approximation of a real drinking house in Hünern was a battered, slant-roofed shanty with only two real walls, two tables, a few benches, and a handful of wobbly stools. Known as The Frogs—after the amphibians that hid in the cracked rubble and called to one another in high peeps and groans at dusk—the tavern was permanent enough to warrant a staff of three.

If God had abandoned his Church and his Faithful, at least He had left them a place that served real ale and not the horse's piss the Mongols guzzled. A few hours in the afternoon at The Frogs quenched both thirst and burning soul.

Dominus custodiat introitum meum et exitum meum, he thought, hoisting his dented tankard. Foam slopped over his arm and onto the floor. *Sanctuary is all we have ever sought. I will confess to this blasphemy,* Dietrich assented after he quaffed half the contents of his flagon, *the next time I am in Rome.*

Dietrich had brought a full squad with him to The Frogs this afternoon. Usually he was only accompanied by Burchard and Sigeberht—he never left the Livonian compound without his bodyguards—but the incident at the bridge required the Livonian Order to show its strength. Rumors needed to be silenced; the people needed to see the power and presence of his knights. They needed to be *reminded.*

The man who ran the tavern, a Hungarian with a whistling voice and a tongue that he couldn't keep fully in his mouth, had managed to acquire an oak chair—a heavy piece with a tall back, much like a lord's seat at the head of the table. He allowed no one else to sit in it, and he always made a fuss when Dietrich showed up, running a rag over the seat and arms before letting the Livonian Grandmaster sit, asking him several times if he was comfortable enough, providing him a barrel on which to rest his tankard.

Gratitude and obedience. At The Frogs, the relationship between a knight and the people was clearly understood.

Dietrich and a company of *Fratres Militiae Christi Livoniae*—nearly a dozen knights and twice that number of men-at-arms—had arrived in Hünern the first week of June, to establish their presence among the Western fighting orders at the Mongolian Circus.

Dietrich had at first considered taking over the church, but after a brief examination of the field of tents and flimsy shelters huddling close to the walls of the church, he opted for a more defensible location. On the southern verge of the camp, near a muddy pasture—a field of tenacious grass poking up through the mud and ash—he found a barn with half a roof. The occupants, a band of squatters, mostly elderly or crippled, had taken one look at the host of warriors with their white surcoats and red markings, and fled.

In that rout, one gray-bearded old man with a bloody stump for an arm had passed quite close to Dietrich and roundly cursed him. Dietrich had turned aside and let him live. The smell of gangrene would have haunted his sword.

Since then, more of the Livonian Order had arrived, doubling the number of knights. They overflowed the barn, and Dietrich had set his men to erecting a rudimentary perimeter. The walls wouldn't stop a halfhearted attack from the Mongol host camped to the east, but they would present deterrent enough to thieves and scavengers. The small compound was a haven for his order within the pustulant chaos of the carrion eaters who trailed after every invading army.

The Mongolian army was dispersed in many camps to the east, the largest occupying a great Romanlike square-beamed fort. Mongols and their lackeys were a permanent presence that no one would entirely forget, but by virtue of their number and their organized encampment, the Livonians found themselves the recipients of a certain largesse from the Christian population of Hünern.

Gratitude and obedience. From the people to the knights who protected them. For the knights, such behavior was demanded of them by the men they served—kings and popes.

For more than thirty years, the *Fratres Militiae Christi Livoniae* had crusaded on behalf of the Bishop of Riga, cleansing the trade routes and converting the pagan tribes who were scattered throughout Livonia. The Pope had even taken notice of their work, calling upon them to bring Christ to the Novgorodian lands. But the order had been abandoned by God. The pagan tribes had realized they shared an enemy and, putting aside their petty differences, had fallen together into a large host. They had attacked Master Volquin's army at Schaulen, and over the course of a night and day, the pagan army decimated the order. The Livonian Brothers of the Sword fled, and would have vanished utterly if the Pope had not granted them refuge in the ranks of the Teutonic Knights.

Was it better to survive as subjects of another master than to be scattered and lost? At first, many of Dietrich's brothers would have said sanctuary was preferred, but after wearing the Teutonic cross for a few years, they began to chafe under their new banner. What was the cost of their salvation? Some wondered if they would ever truly find God again.

Two years after the Battle of Schaulen, Dietrich had been summoned to Rome for a private audience with Gregory IX. The meeting had occurred during a time when His Eminence and the Holy Roman Emperor had not been at each other's throats, before the supreme Pontiff had fallen ill. Dietrich did not know why the Pope had granted him an audience, but held out a dim hope that the Pope was going to offer him—and the remnants of his order—a commission to lead a new crusade to the Levant.

The Pope, however, had had other plans.

God has not abandoned anyone, least of all those who are willing to fight and die for Him, Gregory IX had said during his first audience with the Pope after being elected *Heermeister* of the Livonian Order. *His design is too vast and too subtle for us to comprehend. All we need to trouble ourselves with is faith and obedience; in return, He will grant us not only eternal life in Heaven, but also eternal life in this world. All He asks in return is that you serve Us.*

I do serve, Dietrich had replied. *My duty and my life are devoted to the Church.*

Not enough. Clutching the gold keys of his office, the Pope had offered his left hand to Dietrich. On his finger was a gold ring, and its seal was a fragmented Greek letter, an omega cleaved in twain by a stick—or a *fasces,* an old Roman weapon used by the lictors. *You must serve Us,* the Pope had reiterated.

Dietrich had pressed his lips to the ring and had been shocked to find it cold. The Pope's fingers were like ice, his palm stiff and waxy—as if he were already dead.

Dominus custodiet te, the Pope had blessed him. *Dominus protectio tua super manum laevum tuum.*

The Lord will protect you.

The servingwoman appeared at his elbow, rousing him from his reminiscence, the pitcher of beer perched on her wide hip. "More, *Heermeister*?" she asked in German.

Dietrich grunted and raised his tankard. She poured adroitly, and the foam rose to the edge of the tankard but didn't slop over. Her movement was supple and simple, the sort of deftness that came with practice. Was she married to the Hungarian tavern master, or was she his daughter? He glanced up, his gaze lingering on her breasts.

"What's your name?" he asked.

"Flore," she replied, her eyes downcast. "Flore di Mantua, *Heermeister.*"

Italian, he thought, taking another look at her shape. "That's enough, Flore," he said. "For now." She gave him a short bow, and he watched her walk away, considering how he might spend the evening once he was done parading his men around Hünern.

As Flore stopped to refill the cup of a bearded man with a wide mouth, Dietrich let his gaze move on, reexamining the other patrons of The Frogs: a sad assortment of drunk mercenaries; a few priests, more interested in drinking than tending to their flock (though Dietrich couldn't blame them); a trio of Italian merchants, loudly telling lies about the bulk of their cargo; several groups of vagabonds and ruffians who clutched their cheap mugs as if they were the most precious possessions they owned.

Worthless wretches. He lifted the tankard, inhaling the slightly acrid scent of the ale. He watched Flore laugh at something the bearded man said; she pushed hair back from her face and cocked her hip flirtatiously.

Dietrich grimaced as he drank. *All you had to do was show some gratitude in return for our protection.*

The incident at the bridge still galled him. Two of his knights had been summarily beaten by a single opponent. One said it was a Mongolian; the other man argued it had been someone else—one of the other Easterners who were part of the Khan's menagerie of fighting men. Either way, the soldiers' mission had been simple: escort the priest to the Shield-Brethren chapter house, look suitably menacing along the way to advertise their strength, and return. The soldiers had opted to not take their shields and to ride a few of the more swaybacked nags the order had at its disposal—decisions that, in retrospect, were ill-advised.

During his interrogation of the pair, one of them—Tomas, a Curonian—had tried to plead his case, but Dietrich hadn't been interested. A swift backhand to the mouth had been enough to silence the man's whining.

The very reason you were unhorsed and beaten by a lone man with a stick, Dietrich had explained very precisely, *was because you failed to properly equip yourself.*

Tomas had not been at Schaulen. Had he been, Dietrich was fairly certain he would have been killed in the enemy's first sortie. Probably while looking for his shield.

And the priest—Father Pius—appeared to have grown a backbone in the interim. In contrast to his obsequiousness prior to the skirmish, he had become taciturn and close-mouthed—as if the Livonian Grandmaster's foul mood no longer frightened him. Pius remembered more of the incident than he let on, but the priest was only too quick to lay hands on his cross when faced with Dietrich's ire. *Qui custodit mandatum custodit animam suam,* the priest had said, pointing to the same symbol on Dietrich's surcoat. A man's soul was only secure as long as he observed the commandments of the Lord.

Testis falsus non erit impunitus. There had been some satisfaction in watching the priest's reaction when he had quoted the other half of that Biblical proverb—*he that speaks falsely imperils his soul*—but the implied threat hadn't loosened the man's tongue.

Dietrich knew he should have taken the first note from the priest, and some of the fury directed at his defeated knights stemmed from his own failure. Still, the more he thought about the situation, a process assisted by several flagons of beer, the more he started to see how both notes falling into the hands of the Shield-Brethren might be less of a catastrophe than it seemed. The conflicting notes, should God deem it so, might even be an opportunity.

Discord and confusion among one's enemies was always a primary goal of any successful strategy, and if the *Ordo Militum Vindicis Intactae* had managed to get their hands on both letters, it was very likely they suffered more confusion than insight from these missives. The Korean's letter was innocent enough—nothing more than a request for a meeting—but the false letter claimed that the Mongols had killed their missing champion.

Dietrich knew the Shield-Brethren weren't fools—unlike some of his men. They would see the second letter as the inflammatory lie that it was, but it would cast doubt on the first one, simply because it offered so little. Even if they wanted to ignore both, they could not afford to. After the First Crusade, they had retreated to their remote fortress—like a mortally wounded animal that crawls off to die. Cutting themselves off from the civilized world, they became more and more insular, fading into dusty obscurity. Even here, they set themselves apart from the rest of Christendom, hiding out in the ruined monastery north of Legnica. *Like lepers.*

The confusion of the letters would only serve to remind them of their self-imposed exile. They didn't know what was going on in the camp around Hünern. They had no tactical advantage; their actions were going to be *reactions*, and while their martial art may be wound around ideals of humility and patience, they had fought in enough battles to know the army that was always on the defensive was rarely the victor.

Once, the slightest mention of the Shield-Brethren had been enough to cause a commander to reconsider his plan of attack. The sight of an armored troop of knights had sent more than one army fleeing. A single warrior would have been more than a match for a barbarous stick-wielder; attacking two would have been a fool's errand.

Dietrich chuckled as he regarded the few sips left in his tankard. *That's what they've become—diseased lepers, hiding out in the shadows, afraid to show their faces.*

Mollified, he finished his beer and banged his tankard on the table. *One more,* he decided, *and the woman too.*

CHAPTER 4:

PRISONS WITHIN PRISONS

As he approached the *Khagan*'s private quarters, Gansukh considered how he was going to talk his way past the guards. He doubted Ögedei would see him if he simply walked up and asked to be presented to the *Khagan*. It was quite possible that Ögedei's reaction might be less restrained than it had been at the dinner celebration, though the lingering bruises on the young man's face spoke otherwise. It had been several days since he had presented the cup to Ögedei, and he had bided his time before attempting to seek the *Khagan*'s audience once more. He felt he was making progress in his efforts to curb Ögedei's drinking, but he was still cautious. The *Khagan* was not unlike a wounded mountain lion.

The two guards outside the *Khagan*'s chambers looked even more nervous than he did. They stared past him, refusing to acknowledge his presence, and Gansukh paused, his conviction wavering.

"I..." He cleared his throat. *Tell them what you want,* he thought. *Do not spin a story.* "I need to see the *Khagan*."

Neither guard replied. The one on the left rested his hand on the hilt of his scimitar, while the other blinked several times and licked his lips. *Being ignored is better than being assaulted.*

Their behavior was odd, though; he would have expected them to take joy in telling him that the *Khagan* had expressly commanded them to treat him like this, like a worm not worthy of notice. After a month at court, he knew well the delight the Imperial Guard took in reminding visitors of their lower station.

"I have an important—"

He was cut off by a loud wail from inside the room. At first, he thought he had imagined the sound because the guards did not react, but then he caught the nervous twitch of their eyes—toward the door, at him, and then back to the empty hallway.

"Sounds like someone in pain," Gansukh said. "Shouldn't we investigate?"

The lip-licker's tongue darted several times, and he glanced at Gansukh, then intercepted a hard stare from his companion. "The *Khagan* is not to be disturbed," he said gruffly, as if none of them had heard the scream from within the room.

He's afraid.

The shriek again rent the quiet hallway. Gansukh looked between the guards, whose decorum was fraying rapidly. This time, they refused to meet his eyes.

"I think that's the *Khagan*," Gansukh said.

"No it isn't," the man on the left said. The other guard nodded fervent agreement. He wanted to appear stern and threatening, but the slackness of his jaw only made his face quiver, defeating his attempt to appear menacing. "We have strict orders," the left-hand guard continued. "We are not to enter, nor are we to allow anyone else to do so."

"Is that wise?" Gansukh stepped closer to the door, and while both guards tensed, neither took action to stop him. "Is that what you are going to tell Master Chucai when he finds out that the *Khagan* has…*impaled* himself on a dagger or slipped and broken bones…or something worse…?" Gansukh leaned in toward the door and cupped his hand to his ear, almost enjoying himself, pretending to listen intently for any noise from the suite. "He could be dead…"

"He's not dead," the second guard said doubtfully, his face pale and damp.

"No, no. Of course not. I was just suggesting that it was *possible* such a calamity had occurred," Gansukh replied. Moving his hands slowly so as to not alarm them, he innocently indicated the door. "But we don't really know, do we? Are you going to take responsibility for the *Khagan*'s death, if indeed that is what has happened and he bleeds out while you stand here? Is that the sort of Mongol you are? The kind who follows *orders* blindly without ever thinking for himself? Maybe you should be *thinking* that this situation has changed…"

With a muttered oath, the left-hand guard stepped aside. "You check," he snapped at Gansukh. "It is your head she will take. Not mine."

She. Gansukh pretended to not have heard the guard's slip, and he inclined his head as his hand found the latch of the door. "I accept the responsibility," he said. "May the Blue Wolf take pity on me." Before the guards could change their minds—or locate their courage—he opened the door a crack and slipped through.

Inside, he pressed his back against the door panel and shut it as gently as he could—trying not to draw anyone's attention while he surveyed the chamber and figured out what was going on.

A white haze of incense smoke curled about the ceiling, making the room seem larger than it was. On the far side of the chamber, Ögedei lay prone on a couch, his body wracked with heaving sobs. The *Khagan,* conqueror of the world, reduced to a frightened child. One of his wives—Toregene, Gansukh recalled—knelt on the floor beside the couch, leaning against his shaking bulk. She was stroking his back, speaking to him in a low voice, her words plaintive and comforting. "...such a *strong* speech. They loved you. Did you not hear how they cheered for you...?"

She caught sight of Gansukh, and her face became wild—vicious, like a cornered wolf intent on killing as many as it can before it dies. "Get out!" she shrieked. "How dare you disturb the *Khagan*!"

Gansukh stood his ground. "How drunk is he? During his speech, the *Khagan* could barely stand. Have you let him drink since then?"

"The *Khagan* does as he pleases," she snapped.

"And what does the *Khagan*—the Great Khan of Khans—have to say, then?" Gansukh approached the couch. If he stayed back near the door, he feared his courage would fail. *Do not let them see your fear. Be stronger than your enemy.*

Hearing Gansukh's voice, Ögedei raised his head. His eyes were wide and bloodshot, his face bloated and red. When he spotted Gansukh, he scowled and briefly looked more like the *Khagan*—the leader of the Mongol Empire—than a tired old man. "Get out of my sight, whelp," he barked. "Run back to my brother and tell him I will drink as I please."

Toregene smiled, and the sight of her cold diplomacy chilled Gansukh. "The *Khagan* is pained by the death of his younger brother. He simply wishes a reprieve from the weight of those memories."

What she felt for Ögedei was not love, Gansukh realized. She was devoted, but not to the man. She was devoted to her position. She had given the guards their instructions. She wanted Ögedei weak and malleable, susceptible to her whims and desires. The wine gave her that power. Lian had warned him, hadn't she? So long ago, that day in the garden. *Who is closest to the Khagan at court?* Not his generals. Not his warriors. *His wives.*

"I…I only…" Gansukh's head reeled as he struggled to see a solution to this new puzzle. If there was any hope of sobering up the *Khagan*, it had to be away from Toregene's influence. Away from the court and its revelries and dinners, away from everything. "I only wished to bring the *Khagan* a message," he blurted out in desperation.

"There is no message," Toregene snarled.

But Ögedei heard him—and not only heard him, but wanted to hear more. To Gansukh's surprise, the *Khagan* motioned his wife to silence. Grunting, he pushed himself upright on the couch. "Tell me," he sighed.

Thinking quickly—this was his only chance—Gansukh tried to piece together a plan. He had to get the *Khagan* out of his chambers, had to get him to where there were more people. When the *Khagan* fell into his drink's dark grasp tonight—and Gansukh was now certain that he would—he would need someone to slow his descent, or at the very least pull him back.

"M-m-master Chucai requests your p-presence," Gansukh lied, his tongue stumbling at this audacity. "Your warriors were inspired by your speech today. They want to show you their devotion. You should be seen, my Khan."

Toregene gave him such a hateful stare that Gansukh's skin itched as if she had drawn a bow on him.

I just have to get him away from her. Away from all of them…

◆◆◆

The dancer twisted and swayed like a tree in the wind. Firelight made the gold threads in his belt twinkle, and the fabric of his red robe seemed to crawl and writhe on his body. He jigged a merry circle, his arms undulating to the rhythm of the horse-head fiddle. A crowd surrounded the pair, enraptured by both song and dance, mesmerized by how the two twined together.

All the tribes were demonstrating their traditional dances this evening. Chucai had said it had been his decree—this demonstration of tribal heritages so that all Mongols would learn each other's history and character—but he could not recall making such a noble resolution.

Ögedei slumped in his gilded chair and stroked his beard. In fact, he could not even recall leaving his chambers. Yet he had, and now he was out here, in the open courtyard of his palace, trying not to be sick. *All this motion and noise. I wish they'd all go away and let me be. Let me drink…*

The fiddler's tempo increased, his bow skillfully gliding along the strings, and the dancer kept perfect pace. The fire behind him cast a long shadow over the ground, a tall partner matching and exaggerating each gesture. A breeze, stirred up by the energy of the revelers and the bright fire, lifted the plaintive melody aloft, making it run free, like the wild horse in the heart of every man.

Ögedei could not move his limbs, and his head felt as if it were packed with earth. *Trapped—prisons within prisons.* The words kept repeating themselves in his head, and he tried to understand them. He tried to figure out where they had come from, what they meant, and why they frightened him so. He couldn't walk, but he could raise his arm. Raising his arm was easy. It came up like so—and with it, a cup of wine. The big vessel rested against his lip naturally, and without any more effort, he could tip it back and let the wine flow into his mouth. Some of it escaped, dripping down his chin, and when he lowered the cup, he saw drops had stained his robe, a dark blotch just above the embroidered dragon's claw. He tried to flick it away, and when it didn't vanish, he rubbed it harder, which only served to make the stain bigger. *Trapped*, he thought, scraping his fingernail across the silk. *I just have to get it out.*

The crowd was not paying any attention to him. They stared at the dancer, rapt, swaying unconsciously to the music. These two caste-men were all they cared about, while he, the *Khagan*, was invisible. He jerked the cup to his lip, drinking deeply; the wine stung his mouth, but when it flowed inside him, it warmed him, an insulating blanket that kept him safe from all the noise and light of the world.

He focused, blearily, on the dancer.

…dare he…do… Ögedei thought, or had he said those words aloud? Inside was blending with outside. His spirit was being crushed beneath the enormous weight of his robes, of what they represented, of who he was supposed to be. *Prisons within prisons.* Only a faint persistent nausea reassured him that he even still had a body. "I'm…rullr of…" No one paid him any attention. Maybe he had just thought the words this time. *Rullr…* What had he said or thought he had said? Everything was running together, the way blood and mud ran together in the rain.

He stood, or he thought he stood; it was getting so very hard to tell. He felt like a child's toy, or worse, like he was watching someone play with a child's toy.

The crowd had lost interest in the dancer, finally turning their attention toward him. *Look at me.* He stretched, growing taller than his skin allowed, and lurching unsteadily, he stumbled toward the red-robed dancer.

The man's face was long where it should be narrow, pitched where it should be open. His arms spread like bird wings. Ögedei snorted, blowing snot out of his nose, and then giggled. *How could this man even pretend to be a dancer? Could they not see how ugly he was?* The man stumbled toward the edge of the crowd, flapping his bird wings in alarm. Ögedei laughed, and flapped his arms too. *Watch me fly. Watch me dance.* The ground tilted beneath him, and watching from a vast distance, he grew worried about that child's toy. It was about to fall over—

He caught himself at the last second and spun around. The faces of the crowd swirled past, a crazy panorama of heads, lips, eyes—laughing, shouting, smiling, crying. They loved him. He could see the glow of adoration on all their faces, and the energy of their affection made him spin faster.

He was dancing. He could see it quite plainly—his movements had neither rhythm nor tempo, almost comic and yet almost horrifying. The fiddler kept playing—*yes, like he should; play for your Khagan*—and the birdman who thought he was a dancer flew away. Ögedei threw out his arms and flailed them wildly, chasing his opponent away with his wild display of avian aggression. He threw back his head and brayed a great laugh. *They are all watching me.*

"This's how da-da-dancing is." It was difficult to speak and move at the same time, and he pitched back alarmingly. Whirling his arms—*I am not a bird!*—he arrested his fall and remained upright. Chest heaving, he stared at the crowd and realized they were silent. They were not shouting and cheering. They stood and stared, as if what they saw horrified them.

"What's it?" he cried. "Not enough f'r you?" He tottered as he whirled, not to dance, but to glare at all of them. If he spun fast enough, he could see them all at the same time. "I'm the…greatest. Youuu're worms. In dirt."

The crowd began to shrink, folding back on itself with each of his rotations. Fewer and fewer faces stared at him. They wouldn't even look at him. *Cowards,* he raged. *I am Khagan of an empire of cowards.*

A hand grasped his arm, and he turned to strike the man foolish enough to lay a hand on him, but he was still spinning and his legs crossed themselves. He would have fallen on his face, a discarded child's toy, but the hand holding him was strong and it kept him upright. He grasped the hand that held him and traced his eyes up. Forearm to elbow to shoulder to head. To a face.

A young face, with eyes that did not look away. Nor were they filled with fear or disgust. There was a bruise on the cheek and a thin line—red and scabbed. *I know this face.*

Ögedei smiled and fell into the embrace of the man who had caught him. *Friend,* he thought, *you did not run away.* After that, he remembered nothing.

CHAPTER 5:

CUSTODI ANIMAM MEAM, QUONIAN SANCTUS SUM

It is always the sound of the tree falling that wakes him—a cracking and tearing as if the sky is being torn apart by God—and it snaps him upright, gasping like a fish thrown out of the sea. His heart is pounding so hard in his chest that his whole body quakes. He can't see anything. God has hidden the world from his eyes. All he hears is the sound of wood splintering and shattering. When the bulk of the tree hits the ground, he feels the impact in his bones, and his heart skips.

What comes next, in the wake of the thunderous collapse of the tree, is always different, although he knows he is trapped in the same nightmare: sometimes it is rain, sticky and heavy like blood; sometimes it is a howling wind; sometimes thunderous echoes that roll back and forth like an approaching storm, one that never arrives.

The echoes are too rhythmic for thunder this time, too much like drums or hooves.

He sees them coming. At first, they are tiny dots of light, like fireflies in the distance. But they grow too large to be fireflies, the pinpricks of light blossoming into balls of dancing flame. He sees the faces next: mouths, leering and screaming;

eyes, filled with distorted gleams of Hell. The ghosts ride short-legged horses, almost ponies, and the sight would be comical if it weren't for their number and the death they bring.

Behind the riders looms the rest of the nightmare, a landscape that swells and opens like a malevolent flower blooming. It makes his stomach twist, seeing the world come back from nothing. It is like watching a parchment thrown into a fire come back to life, blackened ash transforming into a fire-gnawed page. The riders pass over him, the horses leap deftly over his supine form, and the world slams into him, not as ephemeral as the ghosts of the Mongol army.

He knows this place: the battlefield at Mohi, near the Sajó River, where the Mongol armies met King Béla's forces. The Mongols sprang a trap on the Hungarian forces, crushing them between two lines, like a blacksmith crushing a fly between calloused palms. Around him, scattered in clumps and piles, are the bodies of the fallen. They aren't dead; the field is twitching and writhing with the mortally wounded. He realizes that every one of those who fell at Mohi is trapped with him in this nightmarish limbo, caught between death and reality. All they crave is release from the pain.

Nearby, a man tries to hold his stomach closed, but he is missing the lower half of his left arm, and he doesn't understand why he can get no grip on his skin with his left hand. On his left, two men who are both skewered on the same lance struggle to pull themselves free of the pole, but they keep moving in opposite directions. They bump each other or strain at the lance, and the motion only pulls at the other man. They haven't come to blows, but they will soon. They don't know any other way to free themselves. A man wanders by, the naked stump of his neck weeping a steady stream of blood down his back. He carries a head under his arm. It isn't his, and it directs the body across the field, looking for its lost body.

What is he supposed to do? Is he supposed to save them all? The one with the missing hand—is he supposed to find it and return it, and would God's grace reattach the hand to the arm? What about the mortal slash across the belly? How is he supposed to close that wound? He has no needle, nor any thread. His hands are empty, and his satchel is gone. All that he has is his robe and his rosary.

A man with his throat cut stares at him, and he looks away, unable to bear the sight of the soldier's suffering, the desperate plea so plainly visible in his eyes. "I cannot help you," he whispers. He walks away, his bare feet sticking to the damp ground. It is the only gesture of compassion that he can think of; any other action would give the wounded man hope, and he knows there is no hope in this nightmare.

On his left, he spots a bony ridge of crumbling rock that rises out of the bloodied plain. There are five horses standing there, and four of them—each a different color—are clumped together, standing shoulder to shoulder. Sprawling across their backs is an enormous figure, a man so wide his bulk overflows the quartet of horses. Black shapes crawl across his skin. A man in armor sits on the fifth horse, and his armor is untouched by battle, neither marred by blade nor discolored by blood. His visor is down, hiding his face. There is something in his hands—

A voice draws his attention away from the vision on the hill. Someone is shouting his name. There, on his right. "Rigo!" The figure gestures him over, and after a final glance back, he picks his way, stumbling, through the maze of bodies, to the man who knows his name.

"I do not know you," he says when he gets close to the other man. He is both familiar and not, like a distant relative of a close friend.

The man smiles. He is young, though there are lines around his eyes and on his cheeks. His beard is neat and groomed, and his robes are unmarked by passage through the field. "Not like this," he agrees. "No, you do not."

"And how do you know my name?" Rodrigo asks. "Are you an angel?"

The man shakes his head. "No more than you."

Rodrigo looks back over his shoulder. On the distant hill, the figure sprawling across the four horses seems larger, and the shadows flow off him now, coursing down the hill and onto the field like the tumultuous spring runoff of mountain streams. Rodrigo covers his face with his hands. "I am damned," he says. "I cannot be saved."

"*Salus,*" the young man says. He gestures for Rodrigo to come closer. "It is the secrets of your heart," he whispers, ducking his head, when Rodrigo has taken three more steps, "that will save you, my friend. The burden asked of one man may seem impossible to bear, but God believes your heart is strong enough. He hears your pain; He hears all their pain. Is the burden He asks you to carry less than His?"

He looks past Rodrigo's shoulder for an instant, his eyes losing their focus. "Remember, Rigo, we are all His children, and He welcomes all of us back into His embrace." He returns his gaze to Rodrigo, and there is a deep sadness in his eyes now. "Regardless of how or when we might return to Him."

A light flares behind Rodrigo, the sudden glow driving all the sorrow out of the young man's face. His eyes vanish, and his smile transforms into a shining line. Rodrigo looks over his shoulder, squinting against the glare. A ramshackle hut appears behind him, and amber light floods from the open door and through the cracks and gaps in the walls.

"No," Rodrigo says, shaking his head. The young man has turned into a phantom, a fading wisp of smoke that curls away from him as he tries to grab it. He doesn't want to look at the hut again—he knows it too well—but he can't help himself. Shoulders hunched, he peers around slowly.

There is someone standing in the doorway, blocking the light. The figure is small, a child, and it raises a hand to Rodrigo. Other figures appear behind the child. Taller figures, limned in red, and they drag the child inside. "No," Rodrigo shouts, and when he tries to run toward the hut, his legs are bound. Hands have seized his feet and calves, hands of the dying. He struggles, loses his balance, and is pulled to his knees.

More of the dying grab him. "Save us," they whimper and beg. "Save us all."

"I can't," he sobs. He strains against the mob, trying to break free. The hut's door is still open, but the light inside is flickering. Guttering. Going out. Hands tear his robe, and cold fingers scrabble against his skin.

When the light goes out, he's fairly certain the scream that fills the void is his own.

◆◆◆

The last thing Father Rodrigo could recall (other than this half-forgotten, fading dream) was sitting on his horse outside of Rome, looking down at the play of light across the rooftops of the city. Now everything was flush with shadows, lit only by the glitter of dust in the moonbeams. He lay on a ragged straw-filled pallet, though the straw was little more than chaff. The air was dry, choked with dust and the scent of something desiccated and moldering. He did not know where he was or how he'd gotten here…these were dangers, he knew, but he sensed there was some other danger, more sinister, that he could not consciously remember.

The knuckles of his outstretched hand brushed a stone wall, and he was reminded not of the safety that a stone wall can offer, but of the dry darkness in the tombs beneath the churches in Paris, where the saints lay buried. A maze of narrow passages, with tiny niches carved out of the walls for the wrapped bodies. This place wasn't cramped, and the ceiling was much higher than the close confines of the tomb—yet something about it was equally unsettling. Moonlight filtered through cracks and gaps in the ceiling. Rodrigo rolled onto his side to examine the rest of the room and realized he wasn't alone.

A man sat slumped against the wall on the bench opposite, some ten paces away. At first, Rodrigo thought he was dead. His head was tilted back, and his mouth gaped open, as if he had died of a horrible thirst. A heavy book lay in his lap, open but forgotten. But then a breath hiccupped out of his chest, and his mouth snapped shut. He grimaced, tasting something foul on his tongue, and his eyes opened.

Rodrigo's breath hissed noisily out of his mouth before he could clamp his lips shut. The figure heard him and leaned forward, peering into the cold gloom of Rodrigo's corner. The motion moved his face into a streak of illuminating moonlight, and Rodrigo had to bite down on the inside of his cheek to keep from crying out.

It was the man from his dream.

Older, most of the gold in his hair was rust now, and there were more lines on his face, but the intensity of his gaze hadn't faltered. If anything, it had only gained strength as the body had aged.

"You are awake," he said. In the dream, Rodrigo hadn't noticed an accent, but now he heard a rough edge to the man's Latin, as if someone had taken a hammer to the ornate scrollwork of a building and knocked all the grace out of the marble.

"Perhaps," Rodrigo replied warily. Again, some part of his mind whispered an alarm to him.

"This is disconcerting, I know," the man continued. He noticed the book in his lap, and quietly closed it, running his hand over the thick leather and inlaid stones of the cover. "Please do not be frightened. You are safe. Well, relatively. More than you were a few hours ago, but..." He glanced up at the ceiling, and his mouth worked around the edges of a smile. Then he glanced back down at Rodrigo with an expression of weary compassion. "You are in Rome, my friend. Near the old temple known as the Septizodium. I am Robert, of Somercotes. Once I was the chaplain to the English king, Henry III. Now"—he shrugged—"just one of God's devoted servants, I suppose."

Rodrigo sat silently, growing accustomed to the dim light. His companion was apparently very used to it, for he did not have even a candle with him. Rodrigo pulled his robe snugger, absently worried the extra fabric near his heart, and leaned his weight onto his right hip. "I am Rodrigo Bendrito," he said eventually. "Lately of Buda, at Béla's court." It was his turn to shrug. "Which is no more."

Somercotes made the sign of the cross and left his fingertips at his lips. "*Salvum fac servum tuum, Deus meus, sperantem in te,*" he murmured. "Were you there?"

"Where the armies of Béla and Prince Frederick met the Mongol Horde?" Rodrigo said.

Somercotes nodded. "Yes," he confirmed.

He shifted his weight again and realized what had been bothering him. His satchel was gone. Hoping he was not being too obvious, he released one hand from his cloak and felt around in the straw for it.

"You've come a long way," Somercotes said, and Rodrigo grunted vacantly. "Not quite what you expected, is it?"

Rodrigo found the wall near his pallet and put his back to it. Still no sign of his satchel, but not far from the head of the straw-filled bed was a tray and small bowl.

"Please, eat," Somercotes said, noting Rodrigo's interest. Investigating the two containers, Rodrigo found water in the bowl and, on the tray, three small pieces of bread, a handful of nuts, and some round objects. *Olives,* he realized as he tentatively ate one. It was enough to wake up his stomach, and he proceeded to devour the food. His fever was gone, replaced by a ravenous hunger. The sort of hunger he hadn't felt in a long time. *I'm going to live,* he thought with genuine surprise as he tipped back the bowl and drank the water noisily. *God does save those who believe in Him.* He felt a little twinge of guilt for having *doubted,* but that emotion was quickly set aside as his fingers scrabbled for the food on the tray, shoveling it toward his eager mouth.

"Thank you," he said to his benefactor when he had finished the meal. His brain knew it had been a meager amount, but the handful of nuts and olives and bread filled his shrunken belly painfully full. The bowl of water had barely slaked his thirst—yet still it seemed like the best meal he had ever eaten.

Somercotes inclined his head. "A small repast does a great deal to restore a man, does it not? More so, perhaps, than a banquet."

Rodrigo found a laugh in his chest, and he let it out as he eased himself against the wall, the straw-filled pallet beneath his legs. "I would have gorged myself," he said. "I would have eaten like a starved dog until my stomach burst."

"Hunger sharpens a man's spirit."

"And his curiosity," Rodrigo noted. "Where am I? You called it—"

"The Septizodium," Somercotes supplied. "It's an old pagan temple, devoted to a number of the old gods. The only virtue remaining in its walls is their thickness. It is a simple yet effective prison. One that has the added benefit of its obscurity."

"A prison? Why?"

"To keep us focused, to keep our spirits and minds hungry. We are fed, as you can see, but many other comforts have been taken from us." Roger smiled. "It stays hot. All this stone. The walls soak up the sun during the day, and it takes so very long for the heat to fade. Some of us have had some experience with fasting and prayer. Being sequestered isn't that much of a hardship. But the heat? The heat will break all of our spirits eventually." Somercotes shifted on his makeshift bench. "But as to why we are here, is that not self-evident to you?"

Rodrigo shook his head. "Self-evident? No. Such truth is obscured both by these walls and the darkness in which I find myself."

Somercotes was silent for a moment, and when he spoke again, his voice was much softer. Almost conspiratorial. "Why have you come to Rome?"

"I have a message for the Pope," Rodrigo said. "As well as news from the north."

"Which Pope?"

"The Christian Pope. The only Pope there is—Gregory IX," Rodrigo replied. "I don't—"

"Gregory is dead," Somercotes interrupted. "There is no Pope in the Vatican." He indicated the room around them. "And we are imprisoned here until we elect a successor."

CHAPTER 6:

AN AFFABLE EXCURSION

Andreas took three of the Shield-Brethren initiates and went overland, eschewing horses in favor of being able to move more stealthily through the wooded terrain. Eilif had previously scouted the river that rambled across the fields north of the ruins of Koischwitz, and he led the squad to a low spot in the fields where the stream was shallow. The water was warm, and with their boots and gear clutched in their arms, they waded across.

Squatting behind a scraggly hedge not far from a mound of burned timber, they dried off and donned their disguises. Over linen undershirts, they wore brigandines—sleeveless vests fitted with stiffened leather and thin plates of metal. They wouldn't protect one's vitals as well as a maille shirt, but they weren't as bulky and made less noise. Over the armor, they wore loose gambesons and cloaks—the most threadbare and patchwork ones they could find among the brothers at the chapter house. Andreas opted for a fustian robe instead, one he had dragged through a fresh pile of horse shit before they had left, much to the dismay of the others. To further his disguise as a nomadic priest, he wore a wooden cross he had made earlier that morning from two pieces of wood, freshly cut from an ash branch, and a long leather cord.

Eilif, Styg, and Maks had bows in addition to their arming swords and knives; Andreas tucked a knife into the belt he wore under his robe, and since it would be difficult to draw the blade quickly should he need to protect himself, he also had a crooked walking stick. It was shorter and not as straight as he would have liked, but it was in keeping with his disguise.

Once dressed, Andreas put his hand over his heart and gave a quick nod of farewell to the others. With a jaunty spring in his step and whistling a half-remembered Genoan sailing song, he strode off toward the hazy smudge on the southern horizon that was the tent city of Hünern. He walked like a man who did not care what lay behind him, and should he have looked, there would have been no sign of the others.

They had vanished, like the morning mist under the gaze of the warm sun.

It is going to be a warm day, Andreas noted as he walked. He could smell the pungent effluvium of the makeshift city already—the miasma of unwashed bodies, offal, fermenting ale, and cook fires rolling across the fields like a slow-moving wave.

Moisture from the previous night's rain darkened his robe as he walked through the weeds and brush, and the ground squelched here and there beneath his feet. The ground was only going to get muddier as he got closer, and he was reminded of the long walk up Mount Tabor more than a decade ago.

It had been in the fall, a turning of the season that had been ushered in by a week of torrential rain. They would have all drowned in the mud had they not gained the high ground and taken the citadel. *Was the rain a gift or a warning from God?* the more pious of them had wondered.

Andreas thought they worried too much about God's design.

Rutger, the grizzled quartermaster who oversaw the Shield-Brethren chapter house outside of Legnica, was one of those earnest thinkers. He had argued with Andreas for several hours last night about sending a party to Hünern. Andreas understood the man's position; after all, it was the same rhetoric he had heard many times from the *Electi* at Petraathen. *It was our duty to guard and protect, to take no side in a conflict.*

To be invisible.

To what end? Andreas had asked. The answer had been hollow, empty words that had been repeated so often they had lost their meaning. To Andreas, the true answer had been clear enough, and he had not stayed in Petraathen overlong after his return from his pilgrimage. Perhaps it was his own wanderlust that put his feet on the road again, his own inexperience and youthful exuberance that made him yearn for the company of more open-minded men, and perhaps what drove him out was his hubris as well—his dissatisfaction with the concept of *hiding* as a viable defensive strategy.

He had hoped that his northern brothers from Týrshammar were different, and he had been disappointed when he had arrived at the Legnica chapter house to find those who might have been like-minded had already left, gone on some secret mission.

Rutger, to his credit, had shown that he could change his mind. Eventually.

The other day, a messenger had arrived from Hünern, a young boy with *two* letters from a man who claimed to be a Flower Knight—an order of knights whom none of the Shield-Brethren had any familiarity with. The letters were conflicting, and as they learned from the boy, very likely the result of some mischief by the Grandmaster of the *Fratres Militiae*

Christi Livoniae. One stated that Haakon, the young Shield-Brethren who had disappeared through the Red Veil in the arena following his victory, had been slain by the Mongols; the other asked for a meeting between the Shield-Brethren and the Flower Knight. Andreas's argument with Rutger was that the Shield-Brethren needed to discern which was the true message—though it was not hard to guess which one was most likely crafted by the Livonians.

Volquin, the last *Heermeister* of that order, had been an arrogant prick, and more than one flagon had been raised at Petraathen when they heard of the Livonian defeat at Schaulen. The death of any knight was a loss, but no one shed any tears when the *Fratres Militiae Christi Livoniae* were scattered. Andreas was no stranger to stupid brutality in leadership—he could list Cairo, Jerusalem, the assault on Mount Tabor, and at Cortenuova, even, as examples. In most cases, it was a wasteful tragedy when men were sent to their deaths by their ignoble commanders, but all of the knights serving Volquin had actually chosen to stay with the man. Their deaths were…just. And the Livonians, a blight upon the history of the martial fighting orders, had been dissolved.

Or so they had thought.

We cannot be blind, he had argued with Rutger. *We have to know whom we face.*

And Rutger had finally acquiesced. *Take three men,* he had said. *Find out their intent. Do not engage them.*

Of course not, Andreas had replied.

✦✦✦

Shortly after wandering into the sprawling outskirts of the city that surrounded the Mongolian arena, Andreas spotted a grimy boy watching him. He was a scrawny lad, and he lacked a shirt—though, judging by the sun-darkened color of his skin, he was not concerned overmuch by its loss. Andreas first spotted him perched on a cracked rain barrel near a pair of tents that had once been blue; shortly thereafter, he saw the boy again, crouching behind a block of rubble next to a misshapen oven cobbled together from cracked brick and charred stone.

Andreas bargained with a fruit vendor for a couple of apples, offering muddled Latin phrases and an exaggerated wave of his wooden cross as a blessing in exchange. The fruit was mealy and riddled with worm-sign, and he threw one of the apples at the boy, who snatched it from the air like a bear grabbing a fish from a river. As soon as the boy had devoured the fruit, Andreas held up the other apple and beckoned the youth over.

"I'm looking for a boy," he said. "His name is Hans."

The boy scratched his head and shrugged, seemingly unable to understand the Shield-Brother's Latin. His eyes flicked back and forth, though, betraying him. When he reached for the second apple, Andreas tucked his hand into his sleeve, making the fruit disappear. "I want to find Hans," he said. "Help me, and then you can have the apple."

The boy chattered at him in some pidgin tongue that was part German, part Latin, and a scramble of something that Andreas assumed was the Mongolian tongue.

It was possible the boy didn't know whom Andreas was talking about, but the lad reminded him of the youth who had come out to their chapter house. There was an alert watchfulness in his expression, and even as scrawny and ill fed as he appeared, he wasn't afraid—a sort of brusque defiance that Andreas read as *ownership.* They might be orphans, but this was *their* city. If this boy didn't know Hans personally, he knew someone who would.

"Hans," Andreas said one more time, and he flicked the tip of his staff, catching the boy in the shin. "Now."

The boy hopped back, clutching at his ankle. He howled at Andreas, his face screwing up in an overblown rictus of pain and anger. Andreas shrugged; adjusting his sleeve to reveal the apple, he brought it up to his mouth and made to take a large bite.

"No! No!" The boy changed his mind, and his hands were now entreating Andreas to stop. "Hans," he said, nodding, when Andreas lowered the apple. He took off, sprinting down the muddy street.

Andreas smiled and looked over his shoulder. Maks was arguing with the same fruit vendor he had gotten the apples from. There was no sign of Eilif or Styg, but he knew they were nearby.

Andreas wandered on, no real destination in mind. There were three matters he sought to accomplish on his jaunt into the city, and making contact with Hans was the most critical. The boy would provide him intelligence about Hünern, and thus educated, he could complete his other tasks. Until he made contact with Hans, he wanted to get his own sense of the city.

The battle of Legnickie Pole had taken place just a few months ago, and Duke Henry's army had been broken and scattered. The orders had lost men too; more than a hundred Templar and Hospitaller knights had fallen. It had been a slaughter, a brutal decimation that should have left a permanent stain on the landscape. And yet, not more than a few *verst* away, a gladiatorial arena had been erected, and to it had flocked tens—if not hundreds—of combatants, all eager to prove themselves against each other and the most relentless force Christendom had ever seen.

They came willingly, filled with that same burning zeal he had seen time and again on the ships bound for the Levant. They wanted so badly to take up arms against the foreign devils who had invaded their homelands. They knew there was no hope on the field of battle—the piles of skulls outside the walls of Legnica were a constant reminder of that fact—and yet they came anyway.

Andreas could remember that incendiary desire to fight, to rage against a world that seemed to have been forgotten by God, to raise a sword against an enemy that seemed to be both faceless and everywhere. To slice, to cut, to kick, to bite—to blindly lash at the very existence that inflicted so much pain.

Nothing ever changes, does it? he mused. *We fall into this world, and all we do for the duration of our miserable lives is fight.* He touched the ragged cross that swung on the cord around his neck. *What else do we know how to do?*

✦✦✦

When the scrawny boy returned, he attempted to haggle with Andreas over the terms of their deal. *Apple first,* he had insisted, *then Hans.* When Andreas laughed and stood firm, the boy had screwed up his face and stuck out his tongue. But he relented, beckoning for Andreas to follow him.

The boy led him down a narrow alley filled with vats of fermenting ale. Brewers, wearing aprons and gloves stained with their work, glared as Andreas passed. He was both an outsider and a priest as they saw him—doubly unwelcome—and the only reason they didn't run him off was because of his escort. The boy ducked under an ash-streaked tarp that was stretched over a frame of rough-cut lumber, beckoning with a pale arm for Andreas to follow.

Warily, Andreas lifted the edge of the tarp with his stick. Beyond was a narrow space—stark in its emptiness and open to the sky at the top. A tree stood in the center, though it was so strangely twisted and warped that Andreas could not tell if it aspired to provide shade with its foliage—should it ever grow any—or if it was a nut-bearing tree that had already shed its leaves in preparation for winter. Scattered around its lumpy roots were scraps of wool and linen—blankets, Andreas realized, as he spotted a boy with a face streaked with mud and ash sleeping with his mouth open under a haphazard bundle.

It was the equivalent of a walled garden, a hidden sanctuary that offered respite from the ravages of the world. They were common enough at monasteries—secluded places where the monks could withdraw and meditate without too many distractions. At Petraathen, the contemplative garden was a sheltered slab of stone that looked out over the mountains—there were no trees or flowers, just the endless expanse of the majesty of God's creation to take in.

In Hünern, God's majesty was expressed in the defiantly interwoven limbs of a single tree.

Beyond the tree, several stools were grouped around a crate, and Andreas's guide perched on one of the stools, eagerly waiting for his reward. There were a couple of wooden cups and a pitcher on the makeshift table, and as Andreas entered the hidden sanctuary, he caught sight of another boy, whose face lit up at the sight of the Shield-Brethren knight.

Hans.

Hans picked up the pitcher and poured a libation into a cup as Andreas walked past the tree and the sleeping child nestled in its roots. "Welcome, Knight of the Rose," the boy said in his oddly accented Latin.

Andreas tossed the second apple to the boy who had brought him and accepted the cup from Hans. He inhaled the aroma of the freshly poured ale. *Sage and thyme,* he noted. "Thank you," he said after he tasted it. "Your hospitality is most gracious."

"This is our…" Hans tried to think of the correct word. He put his hands together in a ring and held it over his heart. "Our *protection.* Our sanctuary."

Hans smiled, and his expression was so guileless—filled with such innocence and hopeful naïveté—that Andreas was filled with an intense desire to crush this boy in an embrace as if he were a long-lost son. In a flash, he knew what his father felt every time he came back from the sea and was bowled over by a young Andreas. He knew why his father had hugged him so tightly.

He surprised himself by giving in to this desire. He swept Hans up in a crushing bear hug. The boy fought him for a second, squawking unintelligibly. He relaxed quickly enough and let Andreas hold him, and somewhat tentatively, his own arms stretched around the big man's frame.

"This is the best ale I've tasted in a long time," Andreas offered as an excuse when they released each other. "I had thought to never taste such nectar again, and…" With a shrug, he drank the rest of the cup and held it out for more.

"Ernust—my *uncle*—makes it," Hans said as he filled Andreas's cup. His hesitation and stress on the word *uncle* made it clear that the relationship was one of convenience and not blood.

"Your uncle Ernust has been blessed with a God-given talent," Andreas said. "Does he produce such elixir with an eye toward the marketplace in this growing city?"

"He does."

"And I would assume there are a number of alehouses which seek to acquire his spectacular libations."

Hans scratched the side of his nose and looked askance at Andreas for a moment and then nodded. He offered Andreas a third cup, which the knight considered refusing, but then relented.

"In addition to inquiring how I might acquire a barrel or two of this fine ale for my brothers, I also seek more immediate assistance from you, my young master." Andreas smiled. "There is a man I need to find, and I think you know him—either by sight or by reputation." When Hans nodded, Andreas swallowed half the contents of his cup before continuing. "I would like to see more of this city, and I do not wish to be distracted or befuddled by its confusing array of unmarked streets and chaotic marketplaces. Would you be my guide?"

Hans bowed. "I would, Sir Rose Knight."

Andreas laughed. "Please," he said, laying his hand on the young man's shoulder. "Call me Andreas. Brother Andreas, if you must. Let there be no more talk of titles."

"Very well," Hans agreed. He hefted the pitcher. "Would you?"

"No, thank you." Andreas took one last sip from the cup and poured the meager remains out among the roots of the tree, careful to not splash the sleeping boy. *In memoriam,* he prayed. It was an old ritual, one rooted in a time before the Shield-Brethren founded Petraathen. Much of the world had changed—both outside the walls of the ancient citadel and within—but the intent of the gesture still had truth and meaning. The chain of brotherhood remained unbroken. With a lingering glance at the twisted branches of the tree, he followed Hans out of the hidden garden.

✦✦✦

As they walked, Hans described the geography of Hünern. There were two landmarks that pulled at the inhabitants—like lodestones, Andreas pointed out, and Hans only shrugged, unfamiliar with the word. *The arena,* he pointed, *and the church.* The Mongol camps lay closer to the arena, the heavy tents peeking over the mud-brick walls like shy clusters of mushrooms; the tents, shanties, fortified compounds, and half-raised walls of the assembled Christian encampments were a circular labyrinth with the leaning spire of the church in the center. Roads and paths became narrower and more infrequent as one got closer to the church; in their zeal to be close to the beacon of Heaven, desperate pilgrims claimed nearly every inch of open ground.

The arena was not at the center of the new city, Hans explained as they approached an open commons. Wooden scaffolds and a jumbled mass of crates and sloppily connected pieces of wood made for a crude parody of the more refined construction of the arena, visible on their left. Stakes and ropes marked off three areas, and while they were currently empty, their function was clear. A pole stood beside each fighting ground, a pair of rings and posts jutting from either side. A wooden triskelion separated the arenas from each other, and each leg of the platform was a honeycomb of narrow slots.

"It's called First Field," Hans said. "This is where they start." He pointed at the platform in the center. "They bring their flags and place them there."

Andreas nodded, understanding how the system worked. Each fighter entered in the competition by putting his flag in one of the open slots. When all the holes in a leg of the triskelion were filled with standards, the fights would begin. A pair of standards would be moved to one of the circles, and their owners would enter the roped-off arena and compete. It was a system not unlike the one used by knights throughout Christendom in their tournaments of arms.

"Win here; go there," Hans said, pointing at the arena.

"How often are the fights?"

"Every three days." Hans shrugged. "But no one goes to the arena anymore, and so they don't fight as much."

Andreas nodded. The Mongolian champion whom Haakon had fought had gone crazy when the young Shield-Brother had spared his life, and a number of Mongolian guards had died in the ensuing riot. Onghwe Khan had closed the arena, and there hadn't been any word when—or if—he was going to start the fights again.

The temporary residents of Hünern were waiting, and after a few weeks, they were starting to lose their patience. Andreas assumed the same was true for the Mongolian army. How long would they simply sit and wait for their Khan to regain his interest in the competition? How long before tempers frayed to the breaking point?

The situation was not unlike a siege, and Andreas had seen the way madness crept in men's minds when they thought they were trapped.

"The Mongol camps are there." Hans waved his hand. With the arena on his left and the church on his right, Andreas guessed the general direction of Hans's wave was to the south and east of First Field. Hans pointed to the west. "Knights there, and Christians." His hand moved to indicate the church and the area to the north and west of it. "Hünern, before…" Hans trailed off with a shrug. "Some call it that now too."

"And where we came from?"

"Rat," Hans said. "That's where the rats live." There was a hint of pride in his voice.

"Rat," Andreas echoed. "Do you have names for the other quarters as well?"

Hans indicated each section again as he listed their names. "Wolf, lion, and eagle."

Andreas liked the simplicity and the descriptive names the boy had given the areas of the city. He doubted a reasonably accurate map could be made of Hünern, but Hans's basic divisions against the two perpetually visible landmarks made it easy to know where one stood in the sprawling maze. If you were closer to the arena than the church, you were closer to the enemy; safety meant putting the church between you and the Mongols—a rule any good Christian could remember.

"The Livonians are in the Lion Quarter, then?" Andreas asked.

"Mostly," Hans answered. He brought his hand up to his mouth, and Andreas realized he was miming a specific action. "The *Heermeister* likes to drink," the boy said.

Andreas chuckled. "Having tasted your uncle's ale, I can't say that I blame him." He clapped the boy on the shoulder. "Lead on, young scout. I want to see everything. Show me the Mongols, the Livonians—I want to see where they sleep and keep their arms—and then we'll go find their master and have a drink with him."

An idea was beginning to form in his head—a simple plan that Rutger would, no doubt, find entirely unacceptable. Yet, there was an elegant purity to it that was appealing. *Yes,* he thought, looking at the honeycombed triskelion, *at some point you cannot hide who or what you are.*

✦✦✦

In the Wolf Quarter, the Mongolian presence was overwhelming. Andreas had expected to see an armed presence, but the sheer number of roving four-men patrols astounded him. They got as far as being able to see the gates of the Khan's compound, but Hans would go no closer. Nor could Andreas blame him. At least three groups of Mongolian guardsmen had taken interest in the two of them already, and to stand around and stare at the gates would only attract more attention.

Marching up to the gate and asking if one of the guards would mind delivering a letter to the Flower Knight wasn't an option. Andreas hadn't really thought it would have been that simple, but there was no reason to not be sure. At the very least, he had gotten a glimpse of the Mongolian defenses and had found them strong and sound. Nothing larger than a squirrel or a rat was going to sneak into the Khan's camp.

He and Hans swung west, scurrying back across the invisible line that separated east from west, losing themselves in the unnamed and unmarked alleys that snaked across the city. Soon thereafter, he spotted the Livonian standard, raised over a dilapidated barn, the white flag snapping in the wind. The red cross surmounted the red sword, its tip pointing down as if to signal to any passersby, "Here be righteous knights."

Slightly north of the Livonian camp, Hans led Andreas through a half-collapsed arch and up a charred beam. The wood groaned and shifted under their combined weight, and Andreas crouched low, keeping both hands on the beam. A jumble of masonry jutted out from a ruined wall, obscuring their view of the camp. They couldn't be seen, either; Hans, crouching at the top of the beam, indicated that Andreas should creep up the last few feet and peek over. Andreas did and found he had a bird's-eye view of the Livonian camp.

They surrounded a run-down barn that was missing half of its roof. A lazy curl of gray smoke from within the barn indicated the barn was used as the communal mess. Andreas guessed the *Heermeister*, the Livonian Grandmaster, had sectioned off a private space for himself underneath the portion of the building that was still covered.

A corral of rope and logs kept the horses sequestered on the eastern side of the compound, and several pieces of sailcloth had been stitched together to make a clumsy shelter and windscreen. Andreas would have set aside part of the barn for the horses—that was its original function, after all—and let the men sleep in their tents, but the Livonians clearly thought differently about their mounts.

The entire compound was protected by a fragmentary bulwark made of debris piled behind hastily dug trenches, clumps of rubble, and stacked logs. It wasn't defensible, not like the Mongolian ramparts, but it was enough of a barrier to grant the knights the illusion of being fortified and entrenched. *Half of the winning strategy in any battle is making your enemy believe you are stronger than you are,* Andreas thought, glancing back at Hans, who was perched—perfectly still—on the wooden beam like a hunting bird, waiting to be loosed.

"How many knights?" Andreas whispered. "Men with armor and swords."

Hans shrugged and, without losing his balance, held up both hands, fingers spread. He opened and closed his hands.

"More than twice ten?" Andreas interpreted. Hans nodded.

Andreas peered over the lip of the barrier hiding them, trying to get a count of his own. There were nearly three dozen horses—near as he could tell—which didn't conflict with Hans's number. Each knight had more than one horse. And there were more than twenty men milling around. Some were men-at-arms; some were squires and craftsmen retained by the order—noncombatants. Not all of them were knights. Still, more than twenty was as good a guess as any.

There weren't twenty full knights at the Shield-Brethren camp. Some of the young ones might be ready in a few years, but most—like the boy Haakon had been—had not been tested. Their swords were plain and their pommels were blank. They had promise, but they weren't ready.

A group of Livonians was drilling in the northwest corner of the compound, and Andreas settled down on the beam to watch. After a little while, he shook his head and sat down, letting his legs dangle off the wood.

"Their drillmaster must be blind in one eye," he explained in response to Hans's quizzical glance. Seeing no change in the boy's expression, he tried to explain and then gave up after a minute or two. "Clumsy," he summarized, miming dropping his weapon and cutting his fingers off. "Not very dangerous."

Hans nodded and smiled. "Very clumsy," he said. "And noisy."

"Some things never change," Andreas chuckled. "Okay," he nodded, "I've seen enough. Let's go find that drink house of the *Heermeister*'s."

Hans dropped off the beam and made for the gap in the rubble. Andreas was right behind him, but he paused when he caught sight of the church spire framed in the gap. "Wait," he said. He stared at the church for a moment, thinking fiercely, and then a large smile broke across his face. "Do you remember the priest who was supposed to bring the message from the Flower Knight?" he asked, and when Hans nodded, he continued. "Let's stop by the church, then. I may be in need of...confession." He smiled. "Yes, let us call it that. I have something to confess. If I remember how that works."

I can't get into the Mongolian camp, he thought, *but I don't need to. Not if they opt to come out.*

✦✦✦

An hour later, after walking past the front of The Frogs—noting the Livonian presence in the street—Hans and Andreas ducked around the building and found a sheltered spot along the back wall. Hans showed him one of several peepholes, and while they waited for the three Shield-Brethren who had been shadowing them all day to catch up, he looked for the Livonians inside.

There had been seven horses in front of the drinking house—three hobbled and four whose riders were milling about aimlessly. The escort, unsure how long they were going to be left waiting.

Andreas felt the presence of other people behind him and turned his head slightly to acknowledge the arrival of his shadows. "Seven," Eilif said in way of a report, confirming Andreas's count.

Andreas nodded at the hole in the wall. "The *Heermeister* is inside, with a pair of bodyguards."

"Rutger said to not engage them," Maks reminded Andreas.

"I think he was referring to their entire host," Andreas suggested.

Styg choked, caught trying to laugh and inhale at the same time. Andreas glanced at him, trying not to dwell on the pale stippling of a beard the young man was trying to grow.

Rutger, for all his caution, was right, Andreas reminded himself. Starting a fracas with the Livonians would only end up getting one of his charges hurt—or killed, even. They were his responsibility, and he needed to be sure they got back to the chapter house alive.

He put his eye to the hole again. The Livonian Grandmaster—based on his position directly between the two other men sporting white surcoats—was a short man with thick-hewn features and stringy brown hair that hung to his shoulders. He was leering at the servingwoman as she refilled his tankard. It was fairly obvious what was on his mind. The two bodyguards seemed alert and proficient soldiers. They'd react quickly to any threat, and he'd have to deal with them decisively if he was going to get close to the *Heermeister*.

If I had three veterans, this would be easy, Andreas sighed. They'd walk in the front door, just a bunch of armed men—unemployed mercenaries hoping to find a source of coin in this urban wilderness. Then one man to watch the door, one man for each bodyguard, and Andreas to deal with the Grandmaster. It'd be all over before anyone knew what was happening, and if they were lucky, none of the Livonians would be dead. A quick chat with the head of the order, and they'd depart, vanishing into the chaos of the Eagle Quarter before the men outside even knew their master had been ambushed.

Quick and bloodless. And none of the witnesses would really know what had just happened, he thought, *but they'd tell the story to anyone who would listen.* By the end of the day, the entire city would be talking about the incident, and not in a way that would be flattering to the Livonians.

But with just these three, he wasn't sure they could overwhelm the bodyguards on their own. If he had three more men, he'd be more confident, but singly, it was too risky. Especially against men who were tasked with being ready for any sort of surprise attack. It would be very difficult to catch them unaware.

Andreas watched the Livonian Grandmaster slouch in his chair and brood. The man wasn't in any rush to leave.

He'd stay and drink until his mood changed. If he stayed long enough, maybe his bodyguards would tire and their attention would wander.

He sat back on his haunches and laughed quietly. "The men outside," he explained to the others, "they're already bored. We don't have to wait." He swept his hand across the ground, clearing away the loose rock and grit. Drawing his knife, he started marking a crude map in the dirt. "This is The Frogs. We're here; the Livonians are here..."

CHAPTER 7:

A KNIFE IN THE DARK

When Percival, Vera, Roger, and Raphael understood that men-at-arms were moving through the caverns near them, their shared instinct was to think of how they might defend themselves. This was not a reflection upon their courage or their martial spirit; they simply assumed, at first, that the Livonians—for these were almost certainly the Livonian Brothers of the Sword—must be coming for them.

On a moment's reflection, however, they all understood the same thing at once, which was that these interlopers must have been intending to take the Shield-Maidens' fortress from within by erupting from the cellars and overwhelming the surprised defenders.

Directly on the heels of that came the realization that the invaders had no idea that Percival, Vera, Roger, and Raphael were down here.

They all moved toward the chamber's exit at the same moment. Percival happened to be closest, but Roger was quickest, shouldering his way rudely past the larger knight and getting into the passage before anyone else. "Begging your pardon," he muttered over his shoulder, "but what is about to come is not shaping up to be a swords from horseback kind of fight. It is going to be daggers in the dark."

Raphael—bringing up the rear—could see Percival's chest expand as he drew breath to lodge some objection. But then the breath went out of him without a word being spoken. No one could question Roger's command of close-quarters fighting. His knowledge of grips, locks, and throws was almost Talmudic, and all who had sparred with him knew better than to try to resist once he had laid a hand on one's wrist or gripped a fistful of garment.

They had left most of their weapons and all of their armor above, as it seemed foolish to go clad in heavy maille, carrying a three-foot-long sword, when creeping through a cellar to look at an old saint's bones. The men were all carrying rondel daggers, and Vera had a single-edged knife in her belt. Thus armed, they would go into combat against knights. Aboveground, in the light of day, it would make for long odds. At close quarters in the dark, however, the Livonians would be hindered by the length of their swords. And piercing maille was precisely what rondel daggers were made for.

Still, it was a desperate venture, and during the helter-skelter rush through damp and darkness that followed, Raphael had time to understand that the fight that was about to take place in the tunnels beneath Kiev would be marked down, in the annals of the Shield-Brethren, as a suicidal last stand—supposing any news of it ever reached the surface. Just the sort of fight, in other words, that they had all been trained to undertake at a moment's notice without hesitation. Raphael was not certain that he was equal to it. The quest to find and slay the Great Khan was at least as hopeless, but the nature of that undertaking gave him much more time to prepare himself for the fate waiting at its end. This, though, had been sprung upon him and promised to be much more ignominious.

And so he was thankful in a way when he tripped over something heavy and soft on the tunnel floor, fell down full-length, and realized that he was lying on top of a dead Livonian knight. Roger had taken him from behind and shoved his rondel into some part of the man's anatomy that had brought about instantaneous death.

Running his hand down the front of the dead knight's body, Raphael found a belt buckled over his maille shirt, then followed that to the man's left hip, where he felt the cold steel pommel of a sword still in its sheath. Raphael drew this out as he clambered to his feet, and knew from its weight and the size of its handle—big enough only for a single hand—that it was an arming sword, relatively short bladed and not too out of place in these cramped settings. Thus fortified, he stumbled forward toward the sound of the fighting. He had fallen well behind the others as the result of his discovery of the dead Livonian. The candles had gone out. It was impossible to make any sense of what was happening. Then—his foot encountered another body. He nudged it, heard the soft jingle of its maille, and stepped over. A few more paces and he found another corpse. Roger had taken down at least three of the Livonians before they could even become aware of his presence.

Others, sensing that something was terribly wrong, were now calling out in alarm to their brethren farther ahead. Percival, seeing that the advantage of surprise had been lost, now bellowed out the war cry of the *Ordo Militum Vindicis Intactae* in a voice as loud and clear as the blast of a trumpet, its final syllable collapsing to a deep grunt as he hurled himself into some hapless defender. A similar cry erupted from Vera's throat, from which Raphael guessed that the two forces had smashed together in a space up ahead that was wide enough for two or three to fight abreast.

Caroming around a slight bend in the tunnel, he came in view of a chamber, dimly illuminated by the guttering, hissing flame of a torch lying on the floor—apparently dropped by one of the Livonians. It was only a few paces ahead of him, its light partially eclipsed by the silhouette of a man, clad in maille and a helm, moving crabwise. Raphael immediately understood that this man was trying to get around behind Percival or Vera.

Raphael flexed his wrist, bringing the tip of the arming sword up, and at the same time brought his left hand across his body to grip the flat of the blade between the heel of his hand and the balls of his fingers. The technique, called half-swording, enabled finer control of the weapon's tip, and a moment later, Raphael took full advantage of it to insert the blade beneath this Livonian's aventail and ram it up into the base of his skull. The man's head snapped backward, which Raphael found odd until he realized that Vera, whipping around, had backhanded the pommel of her knife into the bridge of the fellow's nose at the same instant.

The Livonian crumpled to the floor between them, and Raphael's eyes met Vera's for an instant. Then they returned their attention back to the chamber, a wider space where at least three passageways came together. Raphael gathered quick impressions: Roger collecting a downward stab with his right arm and turning it into a hammerlock, bending his foe to the ground and prying the dagger from his hand in one fluid motion; Percival, having locked up another man's sword arm, sweeping around like a compass tracing an arc while shoving his hands downward to dislocate the shoulder. A bobbing light approached from up the leftmost tunnel—other Livonians hurrying back to help their brethren. Raphael hefted his stolen sword and hurled it like a spear in that direction.

At the same moment, Percival's foe collapsed to the ground, snuffing out the only torch in the chamber. The left tunnel went dark as well. Raphael's thrown sword seemed to have found its mark.

"Vera! It's me," he called, groping through the dark until he felt her hair beneath his hand. She spun toward him and he felt a momentary apprehension that she would put her blade into his heart—but instead, she gripped his elbow, patted his chest with a strong hand, and said, "You aim well, sir."

"I stand here," Percival called from off to their right. But Roger's plight they knew only from his war cry, as he went into combat with one who had, it seemed, emerged silently from the tunnel—a more formidable foe than the others, since Roger was unable to instantly dispatch him. The combat was turning into what sounded like a grappling duel, both men going to the ground, gasping and grunting as they struggled to achieve dominance. Raphael scarcely had time to wonder what sort of man could challenge Roger in that kind of fight when he felt Vera's grip shift on his arm, and a moment later, she spun about and slammed up against his back. Other Livonians were entering the dark chamber. A voice—not one Raphael recognized—let out an unearthly shriek as Percival did something terrible to him. Perhaps warned off by that sound, other foes shied away, instinctively seeking the silence around Raphael and Vera—a quiet space, but hardly empty, as they quickly discovered.

A long, exquisite confusion followed—a shifting scrum of bodies, flick after flick of Raphael's dagger blade, the press of Vera defending his rear as they circled around each other, the clang and spark of swords striking the roof of the cave, shouts of pain, piglike grunts as blades struck home—finally broken by a light bursting into the chamber. Raphael and Vera looked up to see Yasper holding a torch and Finn brandishing a lance, and in the dimness behind them, Cnán darting left and right, trying to peer around their shoulders.

"They are with us," Raphael said, laying a steadying hand on Vera's knife arm, which was covered with blood to the elbow. He looked up into her face, fearing she might have been wounded during the struggle in the dark. She was blood-spattered but seemed unhurt and resolute. She gazed curiously at the newcomers, but Yasper and Finn were staring aghast at something on the other side of the chamber. Following their gaze, Raphael saw Percival—but there was no sign of Roger.

Percival was kneeling, intent on a body slumped on the floor, and there was no aggression in his posture. In that moment, Raphael understood whose body Percival knelt over. Roger was dead.

Raphael, unwilling for the moment to accept such a loss, turned his attention to the scene. Dead or dying Livonian knights almost covered the stony floor. One of the latter managed to push himself to his feet, but his leg gave way immediately, and he collapsed against the wall. Frantic, he tried to roll along the wall and feel his way toward the entrance of a narrow side tunnel.

For a moment, he glared at them from stark white eyes set in a bloody face. Then he toppled into the passageway, pushed himself up onto all fours, and began to crawl. "Kristaps!" he called. "Kristaps! Take me with you!"

Raphael saw now a faint gleam of firelight reflected from the walls of that passageway. Kristaps was making good his escape—leaving his dead and dying fellows behind.

They all reacted at once, and in the same way, but Finn happened to be closest and entered the tunnel first, hefting his lance onto his shoulder as if he might hurl it at the retreating Kristaps. He planted his foot on the collapsed and wounded Livonian's back and slammed him down onto the ground, then trod up and over him.

"Finn!" Percival called. "Hold!"

Had he said it in anger, or in a voice of stern command, Finn might not have heeded him. But Percival spoke in the pleading tones of a man whose heart was breaking, and this was so shocking that it spun the hunter around. He, and all the others, gazed in astonishment at Percival's face, which was streaming with tears.

"Were it our purpose to seek revenge," Percival said, "none would burn for it nor pursue it more ardently than I. Perhaps I shall have it one day. But duty calls us upward into the sunlight. Even now, the Shield-Maidens may be under assault. We must go to stand by them in the defense of their hospice."

◆◆◆

The whole struggle had lasted but a few moments. Raphael's impressions of it were now as dim and blurred as one of last night's dreams. And yet, a month later, he was still unable to purge it from his mind.

For many days now, they had been riding over the steppe, surrounded by a sameness of grass and low hills, topped by swifting clouds, or by nothing but eye-draining blue sky. Raphael's mind, seeking stimulation, rooted around in his memories, perversely hunting out those that were freshest and most troubling—the circumstances surrounding Roger's death.

There had been no fixed boundary, no moment when they had crossed over a river or a ridge and seen the steppe stretching before them. Rather, during the weeks that they had ridden east in the company of Vera and a dozen other Shield-Maidens, the land had insensibly grown flatter, the rivers more widely spaced, the patches of forest smaller and sparser. Cultivated fields, which earlier in the journey had been packed up against one another like stones in a rubble wall, spread apart, dwindled to isolated farmsteads like islands in a sea, and then vanished altogether.

One day, it occurred to Raphael that he had not seen a farm or a forest in nearly a week, just the occasional lonely tree or dugout shack, swallowed up in grass—endless grass, creeping up over the horizon, then falling back behind them.

Out here, only the grass had a voice. Human sounds seemed to fade to whispers, and the whispers were swallowed in turn by the rustle and hiss of the grass in the steady, slight winds. The thought of months of this steady, low hiss depressed him, drove him back again and again to the awful memories...until, in desperation, Raphael finally decided that he would listen closely to the hiss and study the voice of the grass as he might a foreign language.

He became sensitive to different varieties and listened to what they said about the weather and the soil. Closer to Kiev, where the climate had been moist enough to support farms, the wild places had been dominated by feather grass, a robust and luxuriant species that, at this time of year, was topped by silky blond fibers that purred in the wind. Mixed in with it was a good deal of wild rye, wheat, and barley—not such as could sustain human life, but enough to give Raphael an idea of how the descendants of Adam had first come to cultivate such plants and learn the art of making bread. As they went on, making their course a bit south of true east, the climate became more arid and the fur of grass became mangy, with patches of bare earth showing through. The grass here was stunted, with finer shafts and less luxuriant tops, growing in stiff clumps instead of a carpet. Rising above these spiky tufts from place to place were fragrant shrubs, thigh high, which elicited some interest from Yasper at first: he identified them as wormwood and seemed to know something of their properties. After he had seen a thousand, then ten thousand of these go by, he no longer found them remarkable and stopped taking samples.

Vera was their guide. She had traveled in these parts before. Her order maintained old maps and manuscripts, compiled by travelers of yore, which she had studied since the nuns had first taught her to read. Many of them told tales of a great empire, the Khazars, who had once controlled this territory, holding at bay the Mahometans and Persians in the south, the Turks in the east, and the Slavs in the west, until the great Sviatoslav, at the head of an army bolstered in part by Vera's predecessors, had broken their power. Now surprisingly little trace of them remained. Or perhaps the landscape was actually dotted with ruined cities, which Vera was taking care to avoid. Some days the only signs that humans had ever inhabited these places were the occasional *kurgans*, the burial mounds left by the steppe people as monuments to kings, heroes, and—to judge from the size of some of them—fallen armies. It was these, more than anything, that troubled Raphael's mind. For the last thing they had done before riding out of the gates of Kiev had been to bury Roger in the churchyard at the top of the hill, and like all fresh graves, this one had looked like a long, low mound—a small *kurgan* that would, in time, sink into the earth like all the others.

When he thought of this, his hand would sometimes stray to the dagger in his belt. Not to its hilt, but to the blade, which he could feel through the leather scabbard. His fingers would trace its outlines and he would wonder whether this steel had been responsible for Roger's death. For there had been a moment, during the fight in the dark, when Raphael had collided with someone—someone armed and moving with a purpose—and his arm had lashed out unthinkingly and driven this blade home in a body. He was sure of that. He had not struck a limb, but a torso. He could remember how the grip had twisted slightly in his hand as the blade found its way between ribs. Raphael's fist had thumped against the torso as the blade had gone in to its hilt. And that torso, he was quite certain, had not been protected by maille.

During this endless ride across the ruins of the Khazars' empire, it happened a hundred times that, while ostensibly thinking of something else, he would glance down to find his fingers tracing the outline of that blade and realize that some part of his mind was reliving the fight in the tunnels yet again. When this happened, he would always tell himself the same thing: it meant nothing. Not all of the Livonians had worn maille. They had been accompanied by local monks, who, of course, didn't even *own* maille.

Had they not been so worried that the Shield-Maidens above were being attacked, they might have stayed down there and sorted through the bodies, and Raphael would have found one, unarmored, with a small but fatal dagger wound in the ribs. But it had not happened that way. They had rushed up through the cellars of the priory to find nothing amiss and Feronantus and the other members of the party awaiting their return. Others had gone down later to retrieve the bodies. The thought that he might have slain Roger in the dark had not fully entered Raphael's mind until late that night, when he'd seen it in a nightmare, and by that point, all of the corpses had been put under the ground except for that of Roger, who was allowed to lie in state in the church while they prepared a proper burial. Raphael had succumbed to what he freely admitted was a species of moral cowardice: he had not inspected the body, not looked for the wound that had done his friend in, because he was afraid of what he would find. The image of that hypothetical dagger wound was now burnt into his mind like a stigma.

CHAPTER 8:

NAKED UPON THE STEPPE

Nothing but a vast emptiness, as if he lay naked on the steppes and the stars had all gone out…

Ögedei sat up with a gasp and then immediately fell onto his side, retching and puking. His head was caught in the grip of a horrid demon, squeezing his brain like it was wringing juice from a piece of fruit. His skin was hard and brittle over bones that seemed to smolder. Breathing was both painful and thrilling, as if he were stealing each inhalation, past the number he had been allotted for his life. He gasped and spat, trying to rid himself of the sour-tasting bile on the back of his tongue. His cheeks ached, and his vision was filled with dancing motes.

"You're awake." A voice from Heaven, proclaiming a great truth that he now had to live up to. Ögedei managed a guttural groan and rolled onto his back, fighting a wave of nausea that threatened to send him to the edge of the bed again.

"I have died," Ögedei whispered.

"Not quite," the voice replied. "Though, for a while, I was not certain you would ever wake."

Ögedei turned his head slightly and peered around for the source of the voice. The speaker had admitted uncertainty, a lack of all-seeing knowledge. The voice could not be divine in origin; it came from a man's throat.

He lay in a *ger*, the air around him heavy with smoke. A censer hung from the ceiling, seeping a hazy fog from a smoldering patch of herbs. The fog made the air fragrant and pleasing, but harder to breathe. Other braziers glowed, dull red splotches that cast dull shadows on the rough hide of the *ger* walls.

Sitting on a low stool near his bed was the young whelp of Chagatai's.

Ögedei's eyes drooped, suddenly heavy, and with a great effort, he forced them open again, forced himself to focus on the face of Gansukh.

"Where am I?" he demanded.

Gansukh roused himself at Ögedei's question, sitting more upright. "My Khan," he said, "you were not yourself last night. I had to escort you away…to someplace safe. Where you would not be disturbed. While you recovered from the—"

Ögedei squeezed his eyes shut and winced as sharp jabs of pain lanced back through his head. He dimly recalled a dancer—*no, he had been the one dancing*—and let out a long sigh as he realized there could be any number of indignities that Gansukh was not telling him.

"My Khan…" Gansukh tentatively broke the silence. "The path you have chosen for yourself. It goes nowhere. It—"

Ögedei smacked his hand against the bed. "You dare to lecture me?" His mouth moved uncontrollably, trying to swallow away the acrid taste of his saliva.

Gansukh said nothing, but in the ruddy light of the *ger*, the dark bruise on his face said enough.

Ögedei fumbled for another stinging accusation, but all he could think of was *I'm grateful.* Someone had come to his aid; someone had given him shelter and succor. *Boroghul,* he thought. He was seventeen again, back at Khalakhaljid Sands, lost and dying. "I made a spectacle of myself in front of the entire palace, didn't I?"

Gansukh shrugged.

"You are right, young pony," he sighed. "What path is this that I am on? This is not the road my father saw for me. This is not the path of the Empire." He held his hands over his face and tried very hard to hold back the tears. "I've been so weak, haven't I? I've been lost for so long."

"The hardest thing," Gansukh said, "is to admit you're lost."

"No," said Ögedei, lowering his hands. "It is harder to find your way back."

✦✦✦

The *ger* belonged to a nameless shaman. As the old man mumbled and shook a deerskin rattle, Gansukh explained that he couldn't have taken the *Khagan* to either of their chambers. They had to go somewhere where no one would find them, for as long as it took for Ögedei's senses to clear. At first, Ögedei had bristled at the young man's audacity, but he soon realized Gansukh had done the right thing. If they had been found, they would have been unable to have this moment of calm clarity. Ögedei, grudgingly, realized it was exactly what he needed, and what he never would have been able to find for himself, because no one in his court would have truly listened when he asked for such privacy.

The shaman stooped slightly under the weight of his cloak, made of thick blue-dyed wool and strung all over with dangling pieces of copper, eagle feathers, scraps of pelts, and dried herbs. His face, nearly buried beneath an elaborate feathered headdress, was leathery, almost skull-like, cheekbones sharply jutting and dark eyes twinkling. Behind him, crudely carved wooden puppets of men with animal features dangled from the ceiling, their heads hanging lifelessly.

When he spoke, the shaman's voice was hoarser than Ögedei's. "You seek guidance," he wheezed.

Gansukh nodded. "We seek the insight of your wisdom and power, Wise Master. There is a weakness in our *Khagan*'s spirit. One we must purge."

The shaman scrutinized Ögedei, muttering an inaudible chant in time with the rhythm of his rattle. "Your soul is an empty waterskin," he said after a lengthy examination. "When you fill it, you fill it with poison."

Ögedei swallowed heavily. "Yes," he admitted.

"Why do you not fill it with life, with power?"

"I do not know."

"This warrior who sits beside you, who speaks with the voice that should be yours—does he know?"

Gansukh started slightly, though he hid his surprise well. "I…I don't…" he stuttered.

"Yes," Ögedei interrupted. "He knows."

"The poison lies within you too. Even if you filled your soul with life and power, your body would still be diseased. Do you understand?"

"I…I think so." But he wasn't sure. "What must I do?"

"You must free yourself from this poison—not just your soul, but your body as well." The shaman cocked his head, his ear pointed in the direction of his puppets, as if listening to something normal men could not hear. "It is not enough to fill your waterskin with water, for the water of this valley carries all the filth that is washed from the city by the rain—by the tears shed for your pain. You must go to a place where the world is still pure, wild, and unbroken by man. You must go to the sacred grove, near the Place of the Cliff." He pronounced its name slowly, reverently.

"Where is that?" Gansukh asked.

"It is the birthplace of our ancestors," Ögedei said. "The home of the Blue Wolf and the Fallow Doe. The burial ground of my father."

The shaman grinned. What teeth he had were yellow and sharp. "A powerful place where the primal spirits still live—the spirits of all the animals you have hunted and will ever hunt. There is one there, one great spirit that will truly test the soul of a warrior. A great bear. Thrice as tall as his mortal kin, with claws and fangs of iron, and the strength to cleave valleys in the earth."

"And I am to hunt this bear?"

"If you are a true warrior, you will emerge from the forest victorious." The shaman shrugged, as if it were a simple thing he was pronouncing. "If not, you are unworthy of being *Khagan.*"

A simple thing. Ögedei nodded. *Prove yourself.* There was nothing else to say, and so he bowed to the shaman and prepared to get up.

"Wait." Gansukh dug inside his *deel* and produced a small bundle of silk. "There is something else. Something about which I need your guidance," he said, slowly unwrapping the silk. He plucked the small item from its nestled wrappings. "Can you tell me what this is?"

It was a sprig, a tiny twig cut from a tree. Ögedei stared at it, a vague unease moving in his stomach. Should he know what it was?

The shaman took the sprig from Gansukh and brought it close to his face, alternately squinting and peering at it with wide eyes. Having examined it, he clasped his hand tightly around the twig, closed his eyes, and began to chant nasally, in the fluid language of spirits. He rocked back and forth, jangling the metal on his cloak, and began to shake his rattle. His face scrunched in on itself as the rattle clattered faster and his chanting became louder and louder. Then, opening his eyes violently, he vented a mighty shout.

"It is a powerful thing," he said casually, as if nothing had transpired in the last few minutes. "A thing that will be reborn." He thrust the sprig at Gansukh, as if he were eager to part with it.

"Is that all you can tell me?" Gansukh asked. "What powers does it have?"

The shaman shook his head. "Beyond my seeing," he whispered.

Ögedei snorted, more to hide his own unease than from derision. "It is so small. Is it not just a twig?"

"Perhaps *it* is just a twig." The shaman stared at him with wide, unblinking eyes. "And perhaps *you* are just a man."

"Where did you get this?" Ögedei demanded of Gansukh and then belched—unease blooming in his stomach, flowing up into the back of his throat.

"The thief who came to your palace, the one I chased onto the steppes. The one..." Gansukh swallowed heavily and dropped his head toward Ögedei. "She stole this twig from you or"—his brow furrowed—"maybe she was trying to bring it to you. I don't know which, and I regret not having brought it to you before now, but I did not know whom to trust." He held out his hand, offering the sprig to the *Khagan*. "I should not have hidden it from you."

Ögedei stared at the sprig but made no move to touch it. "Perhaps you were right to hang onto it, pony." He shook his head slowly. He did not know what it was—he certainly had never seen it before this moment—but he felt as if he should know. As if the tiny sprig should be the most important thing in his life, but he could not fathom why. "If it was mine, Gansukh, I lost it," he said. "I am a drunk, while you are a Mongol warrior. Maybe it is exactly where it should be—in your hands."

He glanced at the shaman, who was slumped over as if asleep. "Perhaps it is just a twig," he mused. *Perhaps I am only a man.* "But for now, it should stay in your care."

✦✦✦

Transformation swept across the plain outside Karakorum. Under the watchful eyes of the *Torguud*, an army of craftsmen worked at assembling axles and wheels, laying long platforms upon which they erected massive tents. Long lines of carts were being loaded with provisions, and countless heads of oxen milled about in makeshift corrals that threatened to burst. Surrounding this frenzy of construction was a bustling population of like-minded merchants and tribesmen, assembling their own caravans and *ordu*.

Master Yelu Chucai strode through the confusion, overseeing the proceedings. As he passed, men averted their eyes and bent to their tasks with extra enthusiasm, not wanting to draw his attention. Everyone knew of the chief advisor's mood.

During the first night of the festival, the *Khagan* had lost control—dancing drunkenly out in the main courtyard—and before the *Khevtuul* had been able to assist him back to his chambers, he had been spirited away. He knew Gansukh had taken Ögedei, and he put off the increasingly aggravated captains of both the *Khevtuul* and the *Torguud*, saying that the *Khagan* was indisposed and not to be disturbed. The ruse had worked until someone—and he suspected Toregene's hand in the rumor—let slip that the *Khagan* was not in his chambers.

As the *Khevtuul* were on the verge of marching on the palace, the *Khagan* had reappeared, striding through the palace gate as if just returning from a pleasant walk, acting as if he always left the palace without a retinue of guards. He had refused to speak of what had happened or where he had gone, ordering only that the remainder of the festival be canceled. He instructed Chucai to make immediate preparations for his departure from Karakorum, without the slightest flicker of awareness of the headache his disappearance had caused.

Their destination—he blithely informed Chucai—was not to be the winter palace. They were going to Burqan-qaldun.

My Khan, he had argued, *you cannot seriously expect your entire retinue to follow you across the steppes.*

I don't, Ögedei had responded. *But I am not just* your Khan. *I am the* Khagan. *What else can they do?*

Chucai had pressed the *Khagan*, possibly more than he should have—the man had, after all, being drinking heavily the last few days—but the *Khagan* had cut him off. *I have made so many concessions to civilized ways,* Ögedei said with an unexpected fervor. *Now it is time for civilization to make a concession to the Mongol ways.*

"Master Chucai—"

A small man stood in Chucai's path, fearful that the tall advisor would not notice him and stride right over him. "What is it?" Chucai snapped, rocking on his heels.

The man pointed. "A caravan has arrived from Subutai, and the *Khagan*'s son. Gifts from the campaign in the West."

Chucai stared at the plain, trying to pick out the one caravan among the dozens being assembled. He spotted the likely one and noticed what looked like cages on several of the wagons. He began walking toward the wagons, causing the small man to leap out of his way and then run to keep up with him. "Prisoners?" Chucai asked.

"Warriors," the small man panted. "From Onghwe Khan's..." He didn't finish, not knowing if Ögedei's displeasure about his son's predilections extended to gladiatorial fights.

Chucai looked over the cages on the weathered oxcarts. They were filled with a ragtag assortment of men, spoils of war from the distant corners of the world—places he would never visit. One man, exotically dark-skinned, squatted in a corner of his cage, gnawing on his knuckles; another, a Southerner from the looks of him, glared murderously at Chucai, his expression so marred by malnutrition—toothless gums, crusted lips, chancres on his face and hands—that the glare was more entertaining than terrifying. A third was so enormous he barely fit in his cage.

"What should we do with them, Master?"

Chucai understood the man's confusion. The festival celebrating Tolui had been scheduled to last a week, and while the caravan of Onghwe's *gifts* was late, it should have arrived in time for the final ceremonies. The *Khagan*, however, had unexpectedly changed his mind about his departure date from Karakorum.

"Take them with us," Chucai sighed, and waved off the small man. "We will need entertainment on this journey."

The small man nodded and ran off to shout orders at the weary caravan master.

Chucai paused. One of the prisoners revealed little concern about the bustle around his cage. In fact, he seemed fascinated by the strange world in which he now found himself.

The prisoner sensed Chucai looking at him and openly met the tall man's gaze, showing neither fear nor aggression.

He was lean and muscular, with hair so pale it was almost white and light-blue eyes.

CHAPTER 9:

ENTER THE BEAR

Ocyrhoe knew the general layout of the Orsini palazzo. When the man she'd been following passed the pair of guards at the gate, she knew where on the back wall she could slip unseen into the grounds. There was enough moonlight to spot the shadows made by handholds on the rough stone wall. She climbed the wall, hung off the other side, and dropped into the shadows. An ancient apple tree leaned drunkenly toward the main house, and she clambered up its sprawling branches until she could leap lightly to the roof of the main building. The master of the house—Orsini, the Bear of Rome—usually met his visitors in a large room that looked out over the terraced ponds in the back. The moon was high in the sky, round and gravid, and its pale light revealed the long expanse of the city that lay below Orsini's estate.

The roof here was well maintained, the tiles firmly interconnected, making it easy to move quickly and quietly. Ocyrhoe scampered like a squirrel across the angled peak of the roof, past the rim of stones that lay around the hearth's smoke hole, and then launched herself at the stone railing of the balcony above.

A pair of lions, one on each front corner of the balcony, rose out of the worn stone balusters, mouths wide in frozen roars. Their backs and rears vanished into the railing, but the sculptors had carved every detail of their heads, chests, and forelegs, down to their clawed feet. Ocyrhoe grabbed one of the lions' open mouths, her hands wrapping around its stony lower jaw, and her feet swung, scrabbled for a moment, and then found the top of the lion's claws. She pressed herself against the granite beast, trying to catch her breath. She hadn't stopped moving since this afternoon. Not since she had leaped onto the back of that horse.

The rest of the day had been a whirlwind. The strange sensation of flying as she clung to the hairy foreigner and his horse. The earthy smell of the young man. The soldier's blade and the foreigner's knife. The stone in her hand and how much it hurt her palm when she smashed the soldier's head with it. The stranger's alien language, a lilting song that was frustratingly familiar yet completely incomprehensible. His name—Ferenc—which he repeated over and over and over again until she figured out what he was trying to tell her. How immediately he fell asleep once she found a safe place for them to hide.

She had tried to lie down too, but her body was too wound up. Too much energy coursing through her. Too much she didn't know. As much as she hated to leave the young man by himself, she couldn't sit there and watch him all night. She had to find out what had happened to the priest.

That mystery hadn't taken long to solve. An inn near the Porta Tiburtina market was still reliving the incident from that afternoon when she slipped in. The stories being bandied about the smoke-filled room were outrageous, and more than one storyteller was arguing that his version was the true one because he had been there. *I saw it with my own eyes! This is the way it happened!* The only thing all the tales had in common was the whispered destination of the priest: *Septizodium.*

A clink of metal—like a knife against a plate, or a decanter against a cup—returned her attention to her moonlit surroundings. Ocyrhoe shifted her weight and found a place for her foot on the curve of the lion's shoulder. She pushed herself up so that she could see over the edge of the balcony's railing. The balcony was long, running nearly the length of this side of the palazzo, and there was a set of double doors off to her left. Directly in front of her was a window. Its shutters were open, letting out light and sound; her line of sight wasn't very good, but she could hear voices. Two men, she guessed, though she couldn't make out their words.

She pushed up more and got an elbow on the top of the railing. The muscles in her arms protested as she pulled her body up. She was getting perilously close to complete exhaustion; she wouldn't be able to do much more running and climbing before her body gave out. As quietly as possible, she slipped over the railing and hid in the shadows along the side of the house.

Inside, a line of oil lamps hanging along the inner wall created dancing patterns of illumination—gloom and half-light. A wooden table sat in the center of the room, and there were two stools placed nearby. There were indeed two men: one standing, one sitting. The man she had followed was sitting, eating; the other man was the Bear.

The Bear—Matteo Rosso Orsini—watched his visitor eat. Orsini was a big man, prone to wearing big robes—even in this heat—and his smooth face was ruddy in the firelight. Ocyrhoe had seen him laugh once, and the sight had terrified her. He'd thrown his head back and opened his mouth wide, and she couldn't help but think of a snake unhinging its jaws to swallow its prey. But what had really terrified her was all the teeth. His mouth seemed to be filled with more teeth than the human head should possibly hold. And his laugh. It came from deep in his belly—a roiling sound of thunder.

"All this way for a plate of meat." Orsini shook his head, bemused by the way the other man attacked his plate. "Perhaps I should offer to provide more food for your friends."

The man from the Septizodium paused, his tongue touching a blot of grease on his lower lip. "No," he said. "I don't want them to become comfortable."

"What of you? Are you going to sneak out every night to feast at my table? That isn't wise. Someone will see you eventually, someone we don't control. They will talk to the wrong people, and—"

"The city isn't yours?"

The Bear didn't take the bait. "It's not the city that concerns me. It's the people in it."

The man gestured at his companion with his knife for a second before returning to cutting his meat. "They're simple. Like cattle. You spook a few of them, and the rest will follow. And the ones that wander away from the herd are lost, and they know it. They only want to return to the comfort of the herd."

"Yes, dear Sinibaldo"—the Bear leaned on the table—"but what happens when someone else spooks the herd?"

The man called Sinibaldo shrugged and kept eating.

He looked familiar to Ocyrhoe, and she moved closer to the light, trying to get a better glimpse. This was the first chance she'd had to see his face. When she had first spotted him near the base of the Palatine Hill—near the old facade known as the Septizodium, the place where the rumors said the priest had been taken—he had been a hooded figure, ducking through the shadows.

She had been prowling cautiously, conscious of more than a usual number of guards guarding…nothing. This mysterious man had suddenly appeared in front of her, stepping out of a deep shadow in the wall that must have hidden some manner of secret doorway. His hood had been pulled close about his face, reducing his peripheral vision; otherwise, he would have spotted her. But she had held perfectly still, and he hadn't noticed her.

In fact, the whole way here, he hadn't seemed terribly concerned about someone following him. Ocyrhoe had found such inattention odd, but it made the job of shadowing him easier.

He was wearing a plain brown robe. Such a common vestment among the clergy told her nothing about his identity. She knew him, but she couldn't place where. She bit her lip in frustration. She should be able to place him even without the trappings of his office. She'd been practicing recently, sitting at the edge of the Porta Appia market in the morning and picking out faces from the crowd. When she reached twenty, she would leave her spot and try to find them in the throng. She could find ten of them easily, and the other day she had made it to sixteen, but the rest of the faces faded too quickly, and she hadn't been able to find all twenty yet. Varinia could do thirty, and the older girl impressed upon Ocyrhoe that a true kin-sister never forgot a face.

"So," the Bear said, "if you aren't here for the food, then why have you come?"

"We have a new visitor," Sinibaldo said around a mouthful of food. That must be her priest; Ocyrhoe was pleased with herself for making a correct assessment of the mystery man's involvement.

"Yes," Orsini said. "So I have heard. There was quite a commotion near the Porta Tiburtina earlier today. One of my men was assaulted."

Sinibaldo put aside his knife and poured himself more wine. "Tell me everything."

The Bear poured wine into his own glass. "The priest and his companion came from the east, along the Via Tiburtina. On horses. Looking like they've been on the road for weeks. The priest was spouting nonsense—gibberish, most likely, though a few of them swore that it was Biblical verse. The other one was speaking some tongue no one knew. They appeared to be lost—or rather, uncertain of how to get to their destination."

"And that was?"

"The Papal Palace."

Ocyrhoe sucked in a noisy breath as she finally recognized who "Sinibaldo" was; she ducked back into the shadows, hands flying up to cover her mouth. He was one of the Pope's men, the ones who wore crimson. *A cardinal.*

She crouched in the dark, straining for any sign that the men were aware of her presence. Somewhere, out among the apple trees, an owl hooted, and a few moments later, there was a rustling in the branches as the bird took flight. Ocyrhoe turned her head and nearly leaped out of her skin.

The Bear was standing right there, just inside the room. Not more than two paces from her. He was looking out across the terraces, his wine goblet held loosely in his hand.

Ocyrhoe tried to quiet her heart, which was racing in her chest like a wild animal. It sounded so loud to her that she couldn't believe he didn't hear it. He was toying with her, pretending not to notice she was there, and in another instant, he was going to whirl on her, reaching out with his big hand. His left hand dropped to the hilt of the dagger stuck in his belt, and she nearly screamed. For a moment, she thought she had, but then the sound cut off abruptly, and she realized it was the death cry of a small animal caught by the owl.

The Bear grunted, belched, and then took a long pull from his goblet. His hand fell away from his dagger, and he turned away from the open door. "The companion tried to communicate with some of the city militia who were there. He offered them a ring. Like the kind—"

"The kind that a cardinal of the Church would wear?" Sinibaldo interrupted.

The Bear didn't say anything, and Ocyrhoe, her courage returning, leaned forward slightly, peering up at the Bear's large bulk. He was staring at the man at the table, a frown on his face. "I suppose it could have been," he said.

"Why don't you know?" Sinibaldo asked, his voice tightening.

The Bear shrugged and took a long pull from his cup. "I haven't seen it," he said.

Sinibaldo slammed his hand against the table, and the sound sent Ocyrhoe huddling against the wall. She wanted to turn into a mouse and scurry away into a crack in the walls.

"I don't have time to play games," Sinibaldo said, and when the Bear didn't say anything, he continued. "Where is it?" he demanded.

"I don't know," the Bear said. "It was taken from my man as he tried to bring it to the captain of the watch. The priest's companion went wild and chased the soldier down. He had help, too. When the confusion all started, someone leaped out of the crowd and came to the foreigner's aid. One of our own citizens. A young boy."

He turned back toward the window. "Or a girl," the Bear mused.

Ocyrhoe pressed herself closer to the wall, remembering the events Orsini was retelling. The boy had driven his horse into the man, knocking him down. She had slipped down, grabbed the man's helm from where it had fallen in the dirt, and hit him hard on the head. He had been dazed, his hands slack and open. She had scooped up the ring, ran to the boy and his horse, and they had made their escape.

The room was quiet, a silence that stretched on for a long time. Ocyrhoe's legs were starting to itch from the sweat running down them, and her heart wouldn't stop fluttering in her chest. Finally, Cardinal Sinibaldo Fieschi—the most powerful man alive in the Catholic Church—cleared his throat. Ocyrhoe heard the distinct sound of wine pouring into a cup.

"A *girl?*" Fieschi asked. "One of those—I thought we agreed that you would clear the city of *them?*"

"I have," the Bear countered, his jaw tight and locked.

Ocyrhoe screwed up her courage and raised herself closer to the open window. She had to hear this. She had to know what had happened to her kin-sisters.

"My men have scoured the city," the Bear said, his tone becoming more like the growl of his namesake with each syllable. "They've been driven out of their hiding places. A couple were killed, I have others in chains, and the rest ran like rabbits, abandoning the city. They are gone. Their network is broken."

Fieschi's tone was quiet and dangerous. "Who is the girl, then?"

The cup creaked in the Bear's hand, whining with distress from the man's heavy grip. "Who is the priest?" he countered.

There was a whisper of cloth, and the thump of items striking the table. The Bear vanished from the window, and Ocyrhoe risked a quick peek to see what had drawn him away. Fieschi had produced a satchel from beneath his robe—after a moment, she recognized it as the one the priest had been carrying—and had strewn its contents across the table. "I don't know who he is," Fieschi said. "But I know *what* he is. He is another vote."

Ocyrhoe shifted to her left to get a better look at Fieschi. He was slouched in his chair, his attention on the contents of the priest's satchel. His fingers idly drummed on the table.

"In which case you can quit that hellhole so much sooner," Orsini said, interrupting the cardinal's reverie.

"Can we?" Fieschi snapped. "He evaded the Emperor's blockade into the city, which means that the Emperor *wanted* him to get into the city. Why? Because he is one of the Emperor's men—the very sort of man we do not want voting in this election."

"We do not know that he is Frederick's man," Orsini insisted defensively. "He might be just the opposite, in fact." He rifled roughly through the contents of the satchel as if somehow seeking proof of this. His jaw tightened and lines creased his forehead. Ocyrhoe leaned forward, nearly putting herself in plain sight. Her eyesight was sharp, but she couldn't see much. On the table, in addition to the Holy Bible, there was a large piece of parchment with writing on it, a short knife in a plain sheath, several tiny purses (one that made the musical sound of coins as the Bear dropped it on the table), and a few other items the Bear dismissed.

"He's sick," Fieschi said. "Weak from infection and delirious. There are wounds on him that have not healed well. Combat wounds. Not recent ones." That got Orsini's attention, and Ocyrhoe's as well. "Yes, he has seen battle in the last six months." Fieschi leaned forward. "Now where would a man such as this see battle?"

The Bear picked up the knife again and pulled it out of its sheath. "There are many places," he said carefully. "The roads aren't safe."

Sinibaldo laughed, and the sound made Ocyrhoe flinch. Realizing how exposed she was, she drew back. "Very few places are safe anymore," the cardinal said. "Which is why few travel alone. The only ones who do are those who have the protection of the Holy Roman Emperor." He emphasized this last phrase impatiently, clearly wanting some kind of reaction from Orsini.

Orsini resheathed the knife and put it down, refusing to give Fieschi the satisfaction of an emotional response.

Sinibaldo slammed his hand against the table. "Orsini! Your men threw him in the Septizodium without bothering to learn who he is, where his loyalties lie. They picked him off the street and tossed him inside like he was a common criminal. And now we're stuck with him. Now he has a voice in the election—*the decisive voice,* given our stalemate." His voice was hard, and the words flew out of his mouth in a rush, as if they had been held in him too long. "For all we know, those halfwits of yours have just effectively offered up St. Peter's throne to Frederick. We don't know who this man is, and if he is Frederick's man, then he will guard himself well. We won't know anything about his allegiances until we take another vote—"

"You are a guest in my house, Sinibaldo," Orsini snapped, cutting the other man off. "I would suggest some care with your tone. I agree the circumstances are unfortunate, but based on your inflated sense of your own powers, I advise you to use his confused state to your advantage. If he is indeed delirious, find a way to make him yours." It was a challenge.

They stared at each other for a moment, and then Fieschi looked away. He picked up his knife and returned to eating. "Very well, let us allow the possibility that he might be something other than Frederick's tool," he said around a mouthful of food.

Orsini picked up the piece of parchment and held it up to the light. "What's this?"

The Bear was too intent on squinting at the page to notice the other man's reaction, but Ocyrhoe watched Fieschi. She saw his hands stop moving; she saw him slowly put the utensils down. "That? It's nothing," the priest said. "A scrap from an illustrated manuscript. A book not unlike—"

"And this?" The Bear pointed to something on the page. "Here, in the margin."

Fieschi picked up his cup and drank slowly. "The scribbling of a madman," he said. "Translate it if you wish, but I can tell you what it says. It is heretical nonsense, a prophecy filled with astrological prattle—references to the influences offered by Saturn and Jupiter. Naturally, it talks of the downfall of the Church, and it intimates that everything will come to an end in less than twelve years. This is the very sort apocalyptic rabble-rousing that will inflame the citizens should it find its way into the hands of the wrong sort of miscreant."

The Bear put the page down. "Who is he?" Orsini asked.

Fieschi waited for a long moment, and when the larger man started to fidget with the items on the table, he smiled. Orsini noticed the cardinal's expression and his face tightened. He picked up the wine flagon in an effort to draw attention away from his grimace, but he poured the wine sloppily, splashing some on his hand and the table.

The cardinal let out a low laugh. "As you suggested, as long as he's delirious and confined with me, I can control him, so why should you fear anything?" He leaned forward. "But the girl and his friend. And the ring. Those are out of my control. Are you certain you shut down the witch network?"

Orsini's face colored. "They're gone," he insisted. He gulped his wine. "I'll find the ring," he said. "You do your work."

"Of course," Fieschi said smoothly. "As you said, he is another vote, and perhaps he could be convinced to help us.

Even if he did set out on his journey as the Emperor's man, if he is deranged enough now, he might not understand what he is to do. Perhaps the fact that he isn't in his right mind might be useful."

An owl hooted close behind Ocyrhoe and she started forward, her hand accidentally tapping against the frame of the window. She threw herself flat on the balcony floor, and a second later was hustling over the railing and back down the stone lion. She had been too noisy this time. They must have heard her. She dropped down to the lion's feet and hung on, her legs dangling over open space. She couldn't see the window, but she could see the play of shadow and light change as Orsini came to the window again.

She held on, her fingers cramping, but the light didn't change. *He was still there.* Her arms started to scream with exertion. *How long was he going to stand there?*

Her left hand slipped, and she bit down on her tongue to keep the fear in. The stone was warm and slippery. She wasn't going to be able to hang on much longer. The fall wasn't that far; she would be able to land easily. But she couldn't do it quietly. He was bound to hear the sound of a body hitting the tiles of the roof below. He'd raise the alarm, and the palazzo grounds would fill with soldiers and torches. She'd be caught, killed on the spot most likely. *They're gone,* he had said. She was the only one left. No one was going to save her.

The owl hooted again from the nearby tree. Orsini grunted, and something flew over Ocyrhoe's head. His cup, trailing a rain of red wine, struck the trunk of the tree and clattered through the branches, startling the owl.

As it clattered, Ocyrhoe let go.

CHAPTER 10:

INTO THE LAND OF THE KHAZARS

The first week, they had covered ground quickly on European horses taken from the Livonians. They had carried some fodder with them. When this ran out, they slackened their pace and gave the horses leisure to forage in abandoned farm fields where wild grain was richly interspersed with the native feather grass. A fortnight into the journey, Vera had guided them to a market town on a great river where they had traded for steppe ponies, which were smaller but capable of traveling indefinitely on nothing but fresh grass—and in fact rejected provender as unpalatable. That was the last place they had seen that could answer to the name of city or town. Vera knew where it was that Raphael wanted to go, but rather than guiding them along a straight course to that destination—a range of low hills east of the Volga—she allowed the horses to trace the invisible boundary between the tall feather grass of the north, where they could enjoy level footing and richer forage, and the spiky bunchgrass that prevailed farther south.

A subtle shift in the ground, the patterns of birds in the distance, a fragrance on the breeze told them that they were descending into the watershed of the great river—the last river of any consequence that, Vera assured them, they would be seeing for a very long time. There were no bridges and no fords; they would have to be ferried across, a fact that obliged them to gather round the fire one night and hold a council of war. The fire was a feeble glimmer, reflecting the lack of trees hereabouts, and Raphael hoped that this was not an omen of what might emerge from the discussion.

It had been surprisingly long since they had all gathered in a circle and faced each other in this way. Proper campfires had been few and far between. The openness of the steppe invited the group to spread apart; at times, their caravan might be stretched out over a mile, while their camp might occupy an acre. Since they could all see each other at great distances, this did not occasion the same concerns about getting lost as would have applied in the forests of the north. A spread-out camp made it easier for the horses to forage. A strung-out caravan would make it more difficult for a Mongol raiding party to surprise and surround the entire group. The Shield-Brethren had had quite enough of one another's company during the journey from Legnica and felt no need to bunch up. The twelve mounted *skjalddis* under Vera's command provided a welcome change in company, and many long marches and evenings in camp could be whiled away in conversation—frequently somewhat halting, given the language barrier—between these two long-sundered branches of the lineage of Petraathen.

At first, Raphael had been dismayed by the number of *skjalddis* whom Vera had brought, worrying that their numbers would have diminished the ranks of those who remained behind in Kiev, but she had scoffed at his concern, pointing out that thrice this number of Shield-Maidens remained in Kiev. And there was only ever room enough for a dozen on the walls at any given time.

For the purposes of this evening's council, the twelve Shield-Maidens were posted as sentries, forming a large and loose ring around the fire, about a bowshot in diameter. Only Vera joined the Brethren to discuss the next day's maneuvers. She sat to the left of Cnán. The Binder had, at first, found the Shield-Maidens impossibly strange and had pointedly avoided their company, but as the weeks had gone by, she had adjusted to their ways and been drawn into their society.

On Vera's left side was Feronantus. Even more so than usual, the old man had kept to himself during the weeks after Kiev, and Raphael had often noted him riding far out in front of the others. Not, he suspected, out of an intention to scout the way, but because he enjoyed the illusion that he was alone on the steppe. He carried Taran's sword always, as Percival now carried Roger's. Cnán had remarked on this during the journey, and Raphael had explained to her that each man was honor-bound to bring his fallen comrade's weapon back to the hall of arms at Petraathen to be mounted alongside those of other Brethren who had fallen in battle over the ages. "Then we had best stop losing people," she had remarked, "or the survivors will have to carry an insupportable burden across half the world."

Percival sat left of Feronantus. Small sideways movements of the latter's eyes reminded Raphael of the strange tension that had existed between these two men since the vision, hallucination, or angelic visitation that Percival had experienced on the day of Taran's death. Percival himself was oblivious to this. For a fortnight after Roger's fall, he had spoken barely a word to anyone, ranging far off to the caravan's flanks, staring into the distance, mourning and thinking.

Thinking, as Raphael could easily guess, about his quest, and the folly into which it had led him, and the consequence of that folly.

Of the surviving Brethren, only Raphael knew about Percival's quest. Percival had first mentioned it in the presence of Vera, Raphael, Roger, and Illarion. Roger was now dead. Illarion had decided to stay behind in Kiev. His health had not fully recovered. His country was calling to him; he felt that he could strike a harder blow against the Mongols by remaining there, regaining his full strength, and confronting them directly rather than taking a chance on surviving the trek to the Great Khan's capital. So the only witnesses to Percival's odd behavior concerning the quest were now Raphael and Vera, and since Vera had not known Percival before, it meant little or nothing to her.

Continuing around the circle leftward, then, the next was Eleázar, who was relaxed and happy, as he had been enjoying the company of the Shield-Maidens almost too heartily for a celibate monk. Then Yasper, bored and morose. In the aftermath of the cave fight, they learned that the Livonian leader—the one named Kristaps—had escaped from the tunnels by returning to the monastery near the river, emerging from the well house, and stealing Yasper's horse, which had been laden with all of the scraps of metal that the alchemist had been patiently assembling for his still-making project, as well as a jug of *aqua ardens*. Since then, of course, they had seen nothing except open countryside, and Yasper had been reduced to the status of a mere herbalist. Next to Yasper was Istvan, somewhat pointedly placed directly across the fire from Feronantus so that the two men could look each other in the eye over the flames. Then Raphael, then Finn, then Rædwulf.

Finn and Rædwulf had only just arrived back in camp with the gutted corpse of a small antelope slung over the back of a spare pony. They had been absent for two days. Finn, never one to sit still during a solemn discussion, busied himself butchering the animal. Raphael tried to prevent his mouth from watering as he thought about the roasted meat they would be enjoying later. The steppe was replete with small burrowing animals that were hardly worth the effort expended in catching them. It was becoming increasingly obvious why the Mongols derived so much of their diet from mare's milk. Antelope meat, stringy and gamy though it might be, was a delicacy.

"We are pleased to help you eat your bycatch," Feronantus said, "but this is not the game you were hunting for, is it?"

Finn, perhaps not trusting himself to interpret the dry humor, pretended not to hear, and so eyes moved to the face of Rædwulf.

"I saw him clearly," the Englishman announced. "As you all know, I scoffed louder than any of us when Finn told us, a fortnight ago, that he had seen a man tracking us and recognized him as the grizzled Mongol who eluded us after the fight that killed Taran." For they had made a habit, all during the journey, of letting Finn range across the countryside in their wake, secreting himself in covert places to look for any who might be pursuing them. "But I have seen him now, and there is no mistaking his gray hair. It is the same man. I have apologized to Finn for doubting him."

"How close did you get to him?" Feronantus asked. The others were all letting out exclamations of surprise, but he still needed convincing. Or perhaps, Raphael realized, that was what a leader must do: play the role of skeptic even when—*especially* when—all others had swung round to a shared opinion.

"Well within a bowshot."

"A Mongol's bowshot, or—"

"Mine." Rædwulf could shoot an arrow a long way.

"Did you consider taking the shot?" Feronantus asked, with the faintest trace of a smile.

"Of course," Rædwulf said, "but he knew where I was."

"Still, you could have shot him!" Istvan blurted.

Rædwulf's eyes swiveled to study the Hungarian. "It was odd, to my mind, that the man allowed himself to come within my range."

"Have you an explanation for this oddity?" Percival asked.

"I do," Rædwulf said. "I think that he is unfamiliar with the characteristics of the Welsh longbow and the arrows that we use."

"He thought he was safe," Feronantus said.

Rædwulf nodded. "I could have disabused him," he said, "but the wind was swirling, and—"

"If you had missed," Percival said, completing his sentence, "you would never have been given another chance."

A silence ensued, broken only by the snap and hiss of the fire and the swift, slick movements of Finn's knife through the antelope's carcass.

"What are we to make of this Graymane and his dogged pursuit of us?" Raphael asked finally.

Feronantus looked mildly annoyed and did not answer immediately. Of course, this was precisely the question on his mind.

"He is a man of some authority," Feronantus said, "or else he would have gone immediately to his superior and handed the matter off to him. Instead, he devotes weeks to following us, studying us. Why?"

"He wants to know what we are about," Raphael said. "We have aroused his curiosity."

"And perhaps he has his own reasons for traveling to the East," Eleázar suggested.

"Further evidence, if true, that he is a man of some consequence in the councils of the Mongols," Feronantus said.

"It is a fine riddle," Vera said, "and pray enjoy it at your leisure. I must know whether you wish to cross the Volga tomorrow or not."

"If we cross over," Rædwulf pointed out, "then Graymane will suspect that our errand must lie far to the east."

"Oh, I think Graymane knows that already," Feronantus said. "No. The journey already drags on far longer than I had hoped. We cross over with no further delay. And if Graymane follows us, then we set a trap for him—and this time Rædwulf lets his arrow fly."

✦✦✦

It did not happen as quickly as Feronantus had hoped. The larger settlements along the river, where ferries were easy to come by, were garrisoned by the Mongols, and so two days were lost in scouting up and down the Volga's bank to find a way across. Vera's second-in-command, Alena, located a fishing village whose inhabitants were willing to ferry the party and their horses across the river in exchange for a tariff that Feronantus claimed to find shocking. But the Shield-Brethren had made it obvious that they were trying to hide their movements from the Mongol authorities, and so it was inevitable that they would end up paying dearly. Rather than paying double to ferry the Shield-Maidens over as well, and then paying yet again to bring them back a few days later, they made the decision that Alena would remain with the other women on the river's west bank and await the return of Vera.

In truth, Vera was of little use to them once they had reached the eastern bank. Her fluency in Slavic languages had, of course, been indispensable near Kiev, and her expertise in the geography of the steppes had seen them to the great river more quickly and safely than they'd have been able to manage on their own. But she and Alena had been able to communicate with the fishermen only with great difficulty, and they had finally resorted to drawing figures in the dirt. The few locals on the eastern bank who were willing to come anywhere near them were of another race altogether and did not speak a single word of Russian, Greek, Latin, or indeed any of the languages of Christendom.

Cnán identified them as a sort of Turk and found a way to talk with them. Her skills had been of little use to the group during the journey from Kiev, and she had become little more than a shadow following in the wake of the company. Now, once again, they were unable to continue forward without her assistance. Raphael found himself to be inordinately pleased by this turn of events, realizing he had come to enjoy Cnán's presence when she was an active part of the company.

"You know what I am looking for," Raphael told her as they approached a small settlement of such Turkic-looking people, "so feel free to ask whenever you sense that the time is right."

A long conversation followed, in the hut where the headman of the village lived. Cnán served as translator for Feronantus and Raphael. Or that was the plan going in. But after a few initial pleasantries, she stopped translating altogether and would sometimes speak to the headman for as long as a quarter of an hour without bothering to turn round and say a word to the knights. It was obvious, however, from tone of voice and facial expressions, that she was busy satisfying the chief's curiosity and assuaging his concerns about this armed band of Frankish interlopers who had just presented themselves on his doorstep. So Feronantus did not bristle, but merely sat still, looked formidable, and behaved himself.

Raphael, with nothing better to do, doodled on a blank page of the book that he carried with him as a sort of diary and sketchpad.

Finally, Cnán turned and addressed them. "I think it is safe now to ask him."

She spoke in Latin, and her words—as Raphael saw, when he looked up from his sketching—were directed at him. Surprised, he gave a little shrug and glanced at Feronantus, who nodded.

Cnán turned back to the headman and spoke to him for a little while, and in that speech, Raphael thought he heard words very like *Khazar* and *Jew*, *Ibrahim* and *Musa*—words that he had been hoping would be known to the natives of this land.

The chief responded immediately. Cnán turned to Raphael. She almost never smiled. But she was smiling now. "He says that they are not all dead yet," she announced, "and that he can show us the way to where they live. In exchange for a small consideration, of course."

"Of course," Feronantus said.

◆◆◆

At a certain point, perhaps three centuries ago, the Khazars had converted to Judaism. Lacking rabbis, they had sent some of their young men down into Jerusalem, Baghdad, and Cairo to study at the great yeshivas. The intention, of course, was that they would return home once they had completed their studies. And, indeed, that was how it happened during the first century or two, when the Khazars' empire had stood at its zenith. But the decline of their power had led to gradually increasing emigration and reduction of the populace.

Jewish Khazars, dispossessed of land by the empire's shrinkage and decline, or simply feeling insecure about the stability of the place, had traveled south with what possessions they could carry. The tiny colonies of Khazari rabbinical students in the great cities of the west and south had swelled into neighborhoods, clearly defined at first, but growing more diffuse with time as the descendants of the first waves of emigrants had intermarried with the indigenous Jews. Still, they could be identified, if you knew what to look for, as a small but distinct minority.

During his travels through the Islamic world, Raphael had seen traces of them as far west as al-Andalus. In Toledo, he had befriended a young man of Khazari descent named Obadiah. Raphael's curiosity about the Khazars' past had earned him an invitation to Obadiah's home for a Passover *seder* at which he had plied Obadiah's incredibly ancient great-uncle with endless questions. From this and other researches, he had learned that the Khazars' wealth and power had derived largely from their position astride the Silk Road and that, during their heyday, it had been considered no great thing for a Khazari trader to range over a territory bounded on the east only by the ocean that washed the shores of China and on the west by the capitals and trading cities of Christendom. They had been so pleased to meet a young Christian who actually cared about their history that they had, in truth, burdened his mind with far more information than he really desired. For Raphael, in those days, had been curious about *everything*, not just the Khazars, and Obadiah had been only one of a number of friends he had pestered with innumerable and sometimes impertinent questions.

Recently, though, he'd had cause to wish that he'd consumed a little less wine at that *seder* and listened more carefully to Obadiah's great-uncle. For the company of Shield-Brethren had a problem, which was that summer was already drawing to a close, and still they had a vast distance to cover and little time in which to cover it. Without Cnán's guidance, of course, they would have traveled even more slowly. But even with her help, they were not moving nearly fast enough. Raphael had conceived an idea that they might get across the steppes more quickly and more safely if they could form some sort of alliance with traders going into the East to trade for silk. People, in other words, who actually knew what they were doing—who took those routes routinely, for a living.

So it was that, the day after the conversation in the hut, they rode up a winding path into dark hills that brooded over the east bank of the Volga. They were dark because they actually had trees on them—not everywhere, but in their declivities and on sheltered slopes. The few people eking out livings in those hills were a far cry from the generally prosperous and well-fed urbanites Raphael had known in his youth, but certain details in their appearance, their clothing, and their language made it clear to him that he was looking at the last of the Khazars and that this godforsaken range of hills was the rump of their empire, the final refuge into which their beleaguered ancestors had retreated hundreds of years earlier. Like everyone else, they must be paying tribute to the Mongols, but the Mongols seemed to be leaving them alone, and no wonder, since the wooded hills were not well suited to their ponies.

Vera pointed out that she had ceased to be useful to them some days ago and was about to become a positive impediment, since if these Khazars knew anything of their own history, they would remember that women of her order had marched in the invading army of Sviatoslav.

Feronantus reluctantly agreed and detailed Finn, Rædwulf, and Eleázar to escort her back to the bank of the Volga so that she could buy passage across and be reunited with Alena and the others. The rest of them said their goodbyes, and Raphael found himself powerfully affected, knowing how unlikely it was that he would ever again look upon this handsome woman with whom he had fought back-to-back in the tunnels. They embraced front-to-front, and then he turned away from her before the pain in his face became too obvious.

That contingent rode away in the company of their guide, who had been paid the agreed-on amount by Feronantus.

Feronantus, Raphael, Istvan, Yasper, Percival, and Cnán now began what they assumed would be a slow and halting project of making themselves known to, and trusted by, these last remnants of the Khazar Empire. Even Raphael, who had come up with the idea, gave long odds that it would work. But they had to cross through this territory, or other territory like it, in order to get where they were going anyway, and they could not move too quickly lest they make it impossible for Vera's escort to reconnect with them. No harm in being friendly with the locals en route.

They came upon a hill-bound village of scattered huts and even a few grand log houses, with great central halls, the moss and decay of which spoke hauntingly of lost glory. Cautiously, they made their way to a central square and arrayed themselves around a stone-faced well, to be unavoidable and yet demonstrate they meant no harm. For a time, the inhabitants kept their distance, perhaps remembering the Varangians who had once harried their towns—but need finally drove them in.

They were a picturesque lot, with broad, flat faces not unlike the Mongols themselves, though wearing long black robes with gray-and-silver embroidery over gray loose pants, and broad-brimmed fur hats. The women wore white-and-gray and dun skirts, long and full, and their blouses were adorned with luxurious sable—thick, well cured, and neatly sewn. Some were bold enough to display, as they drew water from the well in wooden buckets, ornate gold torques and other jewelry that Raphael recognized as Greek in craftsmanship but Scythian in design.

Working in concert with Cnán, who knew how to make herself understood (for the Khazar language was yet another Turkoman dialect), Raphael began attempting to strike up conversations with old men whom he guessed were rabbis, showing by various gestures of respect that he knew a little of these people, their history, and their religion and that he'd had friendly dealings with some of their long-lost cousins in the Diaspora. At first, he received very little response, which was to be expected, but on the third night of their sojourn, he was at last invited into the well-kept home of a rabbi of some importance, who had traveled to Jerusalem and Baghdad and who could speak Hebrew and Arabic. Raphael spoke a few words of the former and was reasonably fluent in the latter, and so it was now possible to have something like an actual conversation. The great bulk of this was given over to pleasantries and chitchat, but at the end, Raphael was able to make some allusion as to their errand: they sought assistance in traveling far into the East, preferably as quickly as could be managed.

The rabbi seemed to find this interesting but had little to say about it. Which was to be expected, and which Raphael considered to be excellent progress for one evening. More importantly, they were now offered hospitality, and some social presence, for this rabbi presided over the synagogue and invited them to make themselves comfortable in an old disused house. Some great family had abandoned it centuries ago and moved to Antioch or Jerusalem, and the locals had been using it as a barn. After their many nights under the sweeping starry sky, having a log-and-wattle roof over their heads—even though knocked through with holes and packed with starlings, who peppered them with droppings—seemed like luxury.

The next day, Finn and Rædwulf and Eleázar caught up with them and reported that they had seen Vera to the river and observed her journey to its opposite side in a fisherman's boat. A prearranged smoke signal proved that she had reconnected with the other Shield-Maidens. They had retraced their steps up into the hills with care, leaving Finn behind in places of concealment to look for any persons who might be tracking them. Finn had seen nothing.

That evening, a longer discussion took place, with Raphael now serving as an interpreter between Feronantus and the rabbi—whose name was Aaron. Again, much time was expended on pleasantries, and Raphael had to bridle his impatience by reminding himself that if they could strike some sort of deal that would get them into a Silk Road caravan, it would save them many weeks of aimless travel in bitter country. They crept infinitesimally closer to explaining what it was that they really wanted. But it was plain from the look on Aaron's face and the nature of his questions that he was baffled by these Franks and their inexplicable desire to range far into the East.

The next day was spent as they always spent rest days, in mending their equipment, looking after their horses, and obtaining the necessaries for the next leg of the journey. Rabbi Aaron had gone on a journey of his own—since rabbis were scarce, he had to range across a fair territory—and so they dined in their house on food purchased from local hunters and went to bed early.

The following day, Aaron came back to town in the company of a relatively prosperous-looking Khazar merchant and let it be known that they would continue the discussion that evening.

The affluent merchant—it was too much of a stretch to describe him as rich—seemed to be just what they were looking for in the way of someone who knew his way around the caravan business. Little happened during their first encounter, the purpose of which, evidently, was to give this man—whose name was Benjamin—an opportunity to size up the mysterious Franks. But it was clearly a propitious sign that the rabbi had bothered to summon such a person, and so they bided their time and redoubled their preparations the next day.

That turned out to be the Sabbath, and so nothing at all happened, but on the morrow, Rabbi Aaron and Benjamin turned up at their house in the middle of the day, seemingly eager to continue the discussion.

And that discussion went quite well for about an hour. At which point Vera, covered with blood and bandages, staggered through the open door, lurched into their midst, and collapsed on the floor.

Once they had recovered from their astonishment, all rushed toward her to see what was the matter. On her shoulder and arms and one leg, she was swathed in mud-spattered and bloody bandages. She waved them away, though, and insisted they go outside first and tend to Alena.

Alena was sitting on an exhausted Mongol pony, hunched over, shivering uncontrollably, though the afternoon was warm. Percival and Eleázar carried her down as gently as they could, then brought her inside and laid her on a pallet so that Raphael could get a look at her. She too had been wounded in several places, and the wounds crudely bandaged. Raphael was disturbed by one in particular, a deep puncture of the arm, obviously made by an arrow, which had suppurated. Alena's skin was marked by three distinct red lines that originated at the wound and ran up toward her armpit. Raphael had seen such marks before. They did not bode well.

"What are you doing on this side of the river?" Cnán was asking Vera. "Where are the other Shield-Maidens?"

"They are all dead," Vera muttered, her jaw aquiver, and so exhausted she could barely force out the words. "As soon as we began the journey west, we were ambushed by a force of Mongols."

"How many?" Istvan asked.

"A *jaghun*—one hundred men," Vera said. "Though they are fewer now."

"Do you think it was an unlucky chance?" Feronantus asked. "Or…?"

Vera shook her head. "They were lying in wait for us," she said. "And their commander was the one you call Graymane."

CHAPTER 11:

A GOOD STRATEGIST

It is easy to overthink, Andreas had told his three charges. *A good strategist does not try to anticipate his enemy's every move; he simply plans to have his men prepared and in reasonably good position for any possible action. As when Taran taught you one-handed sword techniques, your opponent might attack in a variety of ways, but why complicate your response by trying to anticipate all of them? Make him come for you; be ready.*

Much of training is challenge and repetition, and he knew they had had enough of those. The next task of a good leader is to instill confidence, and in the last few weeks, Andreas had seen how Taran's labor had brought forth that strength as well. All these warriors needed for their final tempering was real combat.

Which had brought him to the last aspect of the trinity of exemplary leadership: leading men into battle. Though, in this case, it was his hope that the conflict would not be fatal for anyone; he wanted to get his opponents' attention, not earn their enmity.

Andreas strolled around the side of the alehouse, walking with stick in hand; none of the four Livonian knights left outside The Frogs seemed terribly concerned about his presence—or anything else. Whatever obedience Dietrich von Grüningen had meant to implant in them had not taken root in their hearts, and as their *Heermeister* sat inside the alehouse, drinking his fill of the local brew, his escort sat in the sun, bored and sleepy.

They had taken up their positions across the muddy track. Their horses, hitched in a line along the low remnants of a brick wall, stood with heads down, ears forward, eyes heavy lidded, alternately lifting a hind leg or a foreleg, tails swishing at flies.

Two of the four knights were close to dozing off; another, closest to Andreas, leaned against the wall, his eyes dull from having checked the blade of his arming sword for nicks and divots over and over in the last hour. He looked up as Andreas approached. At first, his interest was fleeting, but as he realized something was amiss, he met Andreas's gaze, his back straightened, his right hand firmly clasped his sword's hilt, and his left hand fell away from stroking the blade.

Andreas ignored this and let his eyes pass over the seven horses. "Those are fine horses," he said, then slowly returned his attention to the Livonian.

The Livonian eyed Andreas, examining his robes, then loosened his stance a bit and offered a grunt in response. Andreas's disguise—the dusty, smelly robe, the crooked walking stick, the wood and leather cross—revealed no immediate threat, but the Livonian was not entirely convinced.

"I think I'll take them," Andreas finished, and slowly, he tightened his grip on the crooked stick.

The Livonian snorted. "They are not for sale, old man."

Andreas shrugged. "I was not offering to buy them."

The second Livonian, overhearing this exchange, found it interesting enough and peculiar enough that he roused from lethargy and dropped his hand to his hilt.

The first Livonian was shoving himself away from the wall when Andreas snapped the end of his stick up toward the knight's stomach. Off balance, the knight swung his sword wildly, trying to block Andreas's strike. Steel struck dry wood, and chips of the staff splintered off with a dusty crackling sound. Andreas let the stick's tip rotate back and whipped the butt around in a hard, whip-crack strike at his opponent's helmeted temple. The Livonian so struck dropped to the packed dirt, letting go of his sword and clutching his head. The ornamental ridge across the top of his helmet was deeply creased. This sound, unlike the parry, was more alarming—a sharp, loud *whang* that startled the two napping Livonians.

The second Livonian was in the process of drawing his sword when Andreas backhanded him in the face. His nose spurting blood, he forgot all about his sword and collapsed, like a man falling to his knees during a particularly moving sermon. With a sharp snap of his wrist, Andreas whipped the stick around. He struck the man on the side of the helmet, and the soldier bounced off the wall, his helmet absorbing most of the impact—but giving his head a good, rattling shock.

Andreas stepped over the fallen man, focusing on the two remaining knights. They were now on their feet, swords drawn, and regarded him warily. All surprise was lost; Andreas was clearly a serious threat, and they were deciding how best to rush him. Andreas paused as well, but for an entirely different reason, and their momentary impasse was broken up by the sudden appearance of an arrow in the shoulder of the third Livonian, on Andreas's right.

Eilif, from a hidden position behind Andreas, upsetting the balance of power between the combatants with a single well-placed arrow.

The Livonian grunted in pain, staggered back several steps, and looked down and sideways at the deep-sunk shaft, confusion writ on his face as he tried to figure out how a man dressed as a priest, armed with only a crooked walking stick, could make an arrow suddenly sprout from his arm.

The fourth Livonian's attention was also drawn to the arrow, and Andreas took advantage of that drift in the man's attention to step in and smack his wrist. He followed with two sharp blows—one to the face and one to the forehead—and his opponent crumpled like a sack of loose bones.

Keeping an eye on the Livonian with the arrow in his shoulder, Andreas whistled for his companions, and they were at his side in an instant. Eilif had a second arrow laid across his bow, in case one of the stunned Livonians had any fight left in them.

"The horses," Andreas said, nodding toward the line of mounts, heads raised now, ears perked, curious but not yet alarmed. "Take all but one and ride out."

The arrow-shot Livonian scuttled toward the front door of The Frogs, yelling for his *Heermeister* inside. Andreas scooped up one of the arming swords and flung it at the fleeing man. It bounced off his shoulder, knocking him over, and he shrieked as the shaft of the arrow was shoved farther through the meat of his arm.

"I'll be along shortly," Andreas said, shooing the others with a quick gesture. "After I deliver a message."

✦✦✦

Having drained the bitter dregs from his tankard, Dietrich von Grüningen stared morosely at the damp stains on the warped table beside him. One more, or should he take his leave from this rat-infested place? Sigeberht would stay to collect the serving wench; she might provide enough entertainment to alleviate Dietrich's darkening mood.

He was spared any further consideration of this quandary by the sound of a man's scream. The cry was muffled by the misshapen door of The Frogs, but as several patrons began to jostle one another in an effort to rush out of the dim alehouse, the cries of alarm from the street rang more clearly. "*Heermeister!*" someone was screaming for his attention.

He struggled to stand, but his feet slipped on the rough dirt floor of the alehouse. Nearby, Burchard was already up and charging toward the door; Dietrich slapped his hand against the wobbly table, trying to brace himself. The damned table kept moving; his tankard fell over and rolled off the edge. He felt Sigeberht grab his arm, but shook off his bodyguard's help. "I can damn well walk out of this noisome place myself," he snarled. "No one is going to assist me."

The sun lanced his eyes as he stepped out of The Frogs, and he raised a hand to cover his face. Forced to squint, he wiped sun-dappled tears from his eyes.

Burchard had drawn his sword and was standing beside a mewling man with an arrow sticking out of his shoulder. Dietrich blinked heavily, realized that the wounded man was one of his knights, and somewhat blearily, he swept his gaze across the street and took stock of the rest of his men. It took him a few seconds to realize what was missing from this wavering, dismal scene.

The horses were gone. The men he had left guarding them lay sprawled along the wall, not dead—though it might be better for them that they were—but clearly overwhelmed and beaten. They had been neatly and precisely bludgeoned; there was no blood on the wall or in the mud.

Recalling the trouncing his men had received at the bridge, Dietrich felt his face flush. His unsteadiness forgotten, he stalked over to the wounded man and kicked him heavily in the ribs. The man cried out and curled in on himself like a worm. The fletching of the arrow in his shoulder bobbed up and down.

"What happened?" Dietrich snarled.

"*Heermeister*," Burchard said quietly, calling Dietrich's attention away from the stricken man.

A little ways down the street, a man in a stained and thread-bare robe sat on a horse.

"*My bay stallion!*" Dietrich exploded.

"*I* happened to them," the man said. "Do I have your attention?" There was a chiseled look to the big man: expressive eyes, smile lines darkened by the grim set of his mouth, and a fierce defiance in his bearing. He held the stallion's reins in one hand and, in the other, one of the arming swords that had formerly belonged to Dietrich's knights.

"My *undivided* attention," Dietrich replied. He rested his hands on the hilt of his sheathed sword, adopting a stance that suggested he was unimpressed. He heard a creak of leather at his side as Burchard shifted. *Very well*, he thought, *every word that comes out of this braggart's mouth is only going to increase his suffering.*

"The sins of your order have not been forgotten," the man said, "and you would do well to remember those are debts as yet unpaid."

Burchard spat in the mud and began walking toward the horseman. The man shook the reins of the horse, and the animal took several mincing steps to one side. "Hold," Dietrich called to his bodyguard, and when Burchard came to a stop, Dietrich continued. "I owe you nothing," he sneered, "and it is you, having done violence to my men, who owes *me* a blood debt."

The man laughed. "A blood debt? I have but given them a few knocks to remind them of what happens to sluggards who fall asleep while on duty. Surely you would discipline them similarly yourself, *Heermeister*."

"I might," Dietrich acknowledged, "but that decision is mine, and not yours."

"Was it also *your* decision to send the priest with a false message?"

Dietrich stared hard at the rider, the fog now completely lifted from his eyes and thoughts, fingers lightly fondling the hilt of his sword.

The man returned his gaze, equally unflinching, daring him to reply. Fuming, Dietrich considered his response. This man was undoubtedly one of those arrogant Shield-Brethren bastards, and his question was nothing more than a blatant trap. *He already knows the answer,* Dietrich thought. *If I agree with him, then I will be confessing to sowing discord. If I deny his words, then he will call me a liar in front of my men.* The net result would be the same either way: the Shield-Brethren would have an excuse for enmity between the two orders.

This trap aggravated Dietrich more than the theft of his stallion. He raised his shoulders, took in a bored, long breath, and then dropped them, as if vexed by a wayward child. Then he struck a nonchalant, almost careless pose. *How is that for an answer, you sanctimonious bastard?* Despite this, however, his eyes darted about, searching for archers. He liked swift arrows no better than the next man.

The rider smiled, as if he had anticipated such a response. "A word of advice, then, *Heermeister,*" he called. "Pick your battles more wisely than did your predecessor."

Dietrich clenched his sword's pommel and pulled the blade a finger's width from its scabbard. "You presumptuous whore's son," he spat.

The rider laughed. "Look to your men, *Heermeister.* I think we are done exchanging pleasantries." His arm snapped forward, quick as a willow branch, and the arming sword flew through the air and embedded itself in the earth at Burchard's feet.

The man then dug his heels into the barrel of his newly acquired mount and pulled the reins, bringing the horse about. "My thanks for the fine destriers," he shouted as the stallion leaped into a gallop, mud and grime spattering in the horse's wake.

"*Heermeister—*" Sigeberht had come up behind him. Dietrich whirled on his bodyguard with such violent motion that the tall Livonian took a step back.

"Let them go," Dietrich snarled. "All of you will walk back to our compound, and that one"—he pointed at the man lying in the mud—"keeps that arrow in his arm until he arrives." *Perhaps the shock of the walk will kill him,* he reflected bitterly. *It would be the only excuse I'd need.* As it was, this incident was only further humiliation.

He stalked toward The Frogs, rudely shoving past his bodyguard. "I will be here," he said, "awaiting your return."

"But," Sigeberht began, "what of your safety?" He stood awkwardly in the street, hands hanging loosely at his sides.

"If the Shield-Brethren had wanted me dead," Dietrich pointed out, "I question whether you would have been able to defend me. So why don't you do something *useful* and *fetch me a horse?*"

He slammed the door behind him, cutting off the sight of his worthless men. Sinking into his private chair, he pressed his fingers against his forehead and massaged his hot skin.

Without a word, the tavern owner scuttled over and rooted around on the floor for Dietrich's discarded tankard. Finding the vessel, he put it on the table, and with a trembling hand, he poured a full measure. Dietrich waited until the man had finished before he swung his arm and knocked the tankard flying. Ale spattered the nervous man, and his tongue flickered against his flaccid lips.

"Do you really expect me to drink from a dirty tankard?" Dietrich inquired, a deadly stillness in his voice. Shivering with fear, the tavern owner darted off to find a more suitable drinking vessel. Dietrich sank back in his chair, fingers on his forehead again.

◆◆◆

Returning to the chapter house on horseback was both swifter and more exhilarating than a slow trudge through the woods, and Andreas caught up with the younger members of the *Ordo Militum Vindicis Intactae* not far from the ruins of Koischwitz. *This* was what they were meant to do, and what the order excelled at: decisively besting better armed or armored men in combat, riding wild across open lands on the horses taken from their defeated enemies, and reveling in the intoxicating freedom that came from openly defying a foe who thought their order weak and complacent. Such a victory as they had accomplished would restore the morale of the others and would serve to remind them all what their roles in this world were. The assembled mass of their enemies could rise against them, and all it would take to beat them back was a strong arm and a strong will. *We have been idle too long,* Andreas thought, laughing into the wind. *We have forgotten who we are.*

Passing into the sanctuary of the woods, their horses slowed to a steady trot as the track became narrow. Andreas inhaled deeply, sucking in the scented air of the woods to calm his racing heart. Though the thrill of besting the Livonians was still bright in his blood, it was dangerous to let such enthusiasm guide him completely. He must retain some clarity as to what might follow from this victory. It was a minor skirmish in a much larger campaign, and his enemy—for all his clumsy senselessness—would adapt to his plans.

As his heart's rapid drumbeat slowed, Andreas took in the richness of the forest. An endless number of drifting motes outlined beams of sunlight that cut between the trees like blessings from Heaven.

We are these specks of dust, he reflected, *and it is the design of the Divine Light that brings us together. We cannot see the whole of the Light, but in our passing, we give it form.*

It was an idea not unlike an old story he had once heard at Petraathen, one of the oft-told tales that spoke of the Shield-Brethren's origins.

Andreas paused near the jagged trunk of an old tree, felled long ago by ill weather. Even from the height of his saddle, the place where the crowning branches had been snapped off rose well above his head, and the stump carved a gnomon's shadow out of the sunlight flowing through the hole in the forest canopy above. Even dead, the old tree seemed eternal, and Andreas was a minute speck drifting in its sheltering shade.

Folk legends made the forest a fearful place, home to evil spirits, and only the truly capable or the desperate braved the woods. In daylight, staring up at the ragged trunk, Andreas was reminded of the wonder and the fear he'd not felt for years; the tree, though no longer growing, was still alive, covered in a stippled pattern of moss, its jutting, broken heartwood the host to all manner of small creatures. Insects buzzed in the shade, a low thrum beneath the celestial chorus of hidden birds. Andreas closed his eyes, and this world of faint voices opened up to him, a mystical realm that could only be heard when all the voices spoke at once.

Styg's horse ambled past him, the young man's leg brushing his as the horses jostled, and Andreas put aside his meditative calm. As he flicked the reins, his eyes fell on the roots of the jagged tree. They lay exposed, contorted like a mass of thick vines around a piece of aged granite too massive to be sundered by their persistent and perpetual grip. He saw the tree now as a pillar of stone, retained by loyal roots. In his thoughts, stone and tree coexisted.

As they rode on, he locked away the image in his heart.

They would soon be at the chapter house. Perhaps he would tell Rutger about the tree and the stone—maybe even speak of the hidden sanctuary that belonged to Hans and the other ragged boys of Hünern. Though, he suspected Rutger would be more intent on castigating him for the encounter with the Livonians and the horses.

But they were very nice horses.

CHAPTER 12:

PREPARATIONS

Ögedei stirred and opened one eye fully. His hand unconsciously started to grope for the low table on his immediate right. The enormous cup Gansukh had given him stood on the table, half full of pale wine.

"You wanted me to tell you about the caravans from Onghwe," Gansukh reminded the *Khagan.*

Ögedei sat up, licking his lips. He squinted at Gansukh as his questing hand found the cup. "What did my son send?" Ögedei's hand shook slightly as he gulped the wine. Gansukh ignored how the *Khagan*'s eyes twitched in his direction. *I am making him aware of his weakness.*

"Tribute," Gansukh said. "Spoils from the lands of Rus and…" He hesitated, unsure how the *Khagan* would react to the news. "He sent fighting men, captives from some competition that he holds."

Master Chucai had given him a brief explanation of the arena that Onghwe would erect during the months when the Mongol army was laying siege to foreign strongholds. While he understood the strategy of such an activity, and part of him was even curious as to what it would be like to compete in such a tournament, he found the idea unbecoming of a Mongol. A sure sign of the Empire's increased dissolution and its departure from the true path given to the Mongolian people by the Blue Wolf.

"How many men?" Ögedei asked.

"Twelve, and the guards say the red-haired one is bigger than two men. Bigger than General Subutai, even."

"Not likely," Ögedei laughed. "And even if he were, his talents would be unlike the General's. Subutai's genius is not in hand-to-hand combat." He raised the cup again, but then he changed his mind and lowered it without drinking. Stealthily, he glanced at Gansukh's hand, the motion of a nervous and guilty child. Gansukh's hands were empty; he hadn't brought a bottle with him. "What of the others?" he sighed, sinking his chin into his chest.

"Christians and one Muslim. I do not know what countries they call home. One has yellow-white hair and very pale eyes. A Northerner."

"Fighters?"

"Yes, my Khan, that is my understanding. Some of them were victorious at your son's arena."

"Fights to the death?"

"All but one." In response to Ögedei's raised eyebrow, Gansukh explained. "The Northerner fought Onghwe's *ronin.* At the end of the fight, the Northerner had taken the *ronin*'s *naginata* and could have killed him with it, but chose to spare his life instead."

Ögedei stared at the Spirit Banner. "Interesting," he murmured.

Gansukh had heard stories of the warriors from the islands that lay beyond China. More demon than man, the stories went, so impervious to fear that even the Chinese would think twice about facing even a modest army of these skilled swordsmen. A *ronin* was a disgraced warrior, a man who had lost his lord and who wandered those islands like a ghost, beholden only to his blade. That Onghwe had such a man in his stable of fighters was almost too incredible to believe; that the pale Northerner, almost a ghost himself, had apparently bested the man further beggared belief. Gansukh was inclined to dismiss everything he had heard from the caravan guards as wild rumors, the sort of exaggerated storytelling to which men, bored into foolishness by the tedium of their long journey, would fall prey.

However, the detail that the Northerner had shown mercy to the *ronin* had piqued his curiosity as well.

"What else?" Ögedei said, his attention drifting. "What other tribute has my son sent? Wine from foreign lands?"

Gansukh nodded, his heart sinking. "Yes, my Khan." As far as he knew, Ögedei was honoring his wish about the cup—restricting himself to but a single full vessel a day—but he worried that such self-control was a tenuous arrangement, one that could be put aside in an instant. Gansukh wished they would leave Karakorum already. The journey to Burqan-qaldun would offer many distractions—including these fighters. While they remained here, Ögedei had nothing to do but brood.

Gansukh did not know how to fight *brooding*. Nor, he feared, did the *Khagan*.

✦✦✦

Lian sat on her sleeping platform, knees pulled to her chest, arms wrapped around her knees. On the floor of her room was a large leather bag, half filled with clothing and other items she should take. But the task had become overwhelming, and she had retreated to the safety of her bed. She stared sightlessly out the tiny window of her room, oblivious to the changing colors of the clouds as the sun set.

She was reliving the night of her failed escape. Everyone had been swept up in the celebration of Tolui's memorial, and she had tried to slip away. But she had run into the guards in the alley, and the experience had made it all too clear to her that her plan had been incredibly foolish.

Running into the guards had been a fortuitous accident. Only after she had escaped them and returned to her chambers had she realized how much a blessing their drunken advances had been. Had they been less—or more—besotted, she could have been raped; had they realized her plan, they probably would have killed her. While her quick thinking and courage had played a large part in saving her from such a horrible fate, she could not ignore how the threat of Master Chucai's displeasure had helped as well. If she did escape to the steppes outside Karakorum, she would lose the privilege of that security. She would be even more vulnerable, and in some ways, being attacked by marauders would be the most *pleasant* fate she could hope for.

Lian let her chin drop to her knees. The memory of the men in the alley had vanished, swept aside by a tumbling flood of older memories. Sights and sounds and sensations from when she was a child, when her family was still alive. She wiped angrily at her eyes, shoving aside the memories and the tears that threatened to spill. *No, I must think. I must plan.*

She needed an accomplice, a warrior who could protect her. But could she convince Gansukh to help her? Could she convince him to betray his *Khagan* and his tribe? He was fiercely proud of being a Mongolian warrior, and she admired how fervently he clung to the hoary principles of his culture, but she had seen flaws in his devotion. He was beginning to wonder what part he played in the changing Empire. Could the sparks of his discontent be fanned into outright rebellion? How far would he be willing to go for her?

Could she…seduce him? Would that be enough? There was a certain amount of pleasure in that idea—pleasure that had little to do with the actual necessity of her plan—and she toyed with the idea for a moment.

The *Khagan*'s trip to Burqan-qaldun would take several weeks. The immense caravan of the *Khagan*'s entourage would distract the Imperial Guard; it would be her best chance to escape. *This time, I cannot falter. I must do whatever it takes.*

Her resolve restored, she returned her attention to the tedious task before her—packing. Chucai had provided her with a large travel bag, and once it was fully packed, it would be far too large for her to carry by herself, one of Chucai's little reminders: she enjoyed a great deal of freedom, but that freedom was also a burden. She could, if she so desired, divest herself of a number of her robes as well as many of the lotions, oils, and powders she relied upon, but to do so would be to give up the tools she needed to be something other than a simple chamber slave. Her value to Master Chucai could be readily accounted in the profusion of silks that overflowed the travel bag.

If I left everything, I *could fit in this bag,* she thought, idly stuffing a poorly folded green silk robe into the gaping mouth of the bag. She had a vision of Gansukh riding away from the *Khagan*'s caravan, the leather bag thrown across his saddle, her bare feet protruding from the gathered mouth of the bag. *I would be free.*

Absently toying with the partially packed robe, she let her gaze roam about the room. What was more important? All the trappings of her prison, or freedom? She could earn money—somehow—and buy new robes. They wouldn't be as fine as these, but what did that matter? The oils and lotions she would miss, but she had lived without them before. When the Mongols had conquered Qingyuan, she had lost everything. She had been just another frightened prisoner, a foreign woman to be shared among the rapacious Mongol warriors until she was nothing more than a dry and broken husk. She had caught Master Chucai's attention, and it hadn't been because of fine clothes or her painted face or the way she smelled. It had been her bearing and her tongue that had saved her, two things that could not be taken from her.

If she left everything, she would still be *Lian*, and that had been enough to save her once before.

Her roaming gaze fell on the small satchel she used to carry her teaching materials. It had a shoulder strap, a critical necessity, as it would leave her hands free. Could she climb or ride a horse or fight if she was carrying a bag? Shaking her head, she started to sift through the detritus of her belongings. She could leave it all, but that was what a terrified slave girl would do. She was not that girl. *Sturdy shoes, a waterskin, food.* She started to assemble a few critical things. *Jewelry can be traded.*

◆◆◆

Dawn began to recolor the peaks of the palace roof, and Master Chucai watched the light drip down the glazed tiles. It would be another hour before the light warmed the glade in the *Khagan*'s gardens where he stood. He was not chilled, however; he had begun his *qi* exercises when the roosters in the camps outside the palace walls had started crowing, and he would be done long before sunlight reached the balconies on the upper floor of the palace.

He had slept very little in the past few weeks. The *Khagan*'s decision to go to Burqan-qaldun presented a number of logistical problems, and all of his time was devoted to organizing the expedition so that it could leave as soon as possible. Three weeks had passed already, and the *Khagan*'s patience was starting to become very brittle.

The *Khagan*'s drinking had lessened, and Master Chucai had congratulated Gansukh on his small victory, but neither man wished to lose the ground he had gained.

Chucai folded his long frame in half, bending impossibly far forward while keeping his legs stiff. His outstretched arms slowly scooped out and up as if he were gathering a large tiger in his arms. His fingers stiff, hands pointing toward the dawn-painted palace, he slowly lifted one foot and stepped under the imaginary tiger in his hands as if he were shifting it to his shoulders. His *qi* extended deep into the ground, balancing him as he shouldered the imaginary weight of the full-grown tiger. He rotated his hips, lifting his other foot and stretching it toward the southern wall of the garden. He held the pose until the muscles in his lower back quivered, mentally reciting several sets of the questions and answers that the Yellow Emperor put forth in his *Inner Canon*—questions that were meant to facilitate a cleansing of his mind and body in conjunction with the *qi* exercises.

After thorough consideration of the Yellow Emperor's insights, he turned his shoulders and raised his arms. The tiger became an enormous stork, and he stretched to his full height in a stiffened parody of the bird's own motion as it leaped into flight. He inhaled until his lungs were swollen with air; as he exhaled, he relaxed his arms and let his leg come back to the ground.

Only then did he acknowledge the fidgeting slave who had been standing nearby since before dawn had breached the eastern horizon. "Yes?"

"Master," the slave bowed, "Mistress Lian has given me her travel trunk, and I have loaded it with the rest of your household."

Chucai undid the ties on the sleeves of his robe, letting them down. "Did you examine it?"

"Yes, Master. Nothing but clothes and all the other things a woman carries with her."

Chucai nodded absently. *No food or money. No sign that she was harboring a plan to flee.* He waved the slave away. Nevertheless, he would keep an eye on the Chinese woman. She had been in his household a long time, and he knew all her moods. She was hiding something from him, and while he suspected it was nothing more than a foolish infatuation with Gansukh, he was not entirely confident there wasn't something else on her mind.

She was an intelligent woman, and she had a certain animal cunning that he knew better than to dismiss. If he were in her place, he would consider escaping during the trip to Burqan-qaldun. It would be the best time.

Chucai left the pastoral embrace of the garden, his mental energies restored by the rigors of his *qi* meditation. The garden was a placid calm within the swollen chaos of the palace grounds. Walking toward the main courtyard, he reentered the bedlam of the court's preparations.

The activity that filled the courtyard was not unlike a city marshaling for war.

Hundreds of people swarmed the courtyard, jostling and yelling at one another. What had once been an orderly attempt at a long column of carts had collapsed into a confused mass. Supplies were being thrown, hauled, shoved, and haphazardly stacked in a frenzied effort to get everything packed on top of something with wheels. Crates of dried fruit and meat; barrels of *airag*, *arkhi*, and wine; bags of clothing and furnishings; medical supplies; the heavy bundles of dismantled *ger*; weapons—all manner of goods needed to sustain the hundreds of travelers who would be going with the *Khagan*.

Six hundred and four. Chucai knew the exact number, just as he knew how many barrels of *arkhi* and crates of dried meat were being loaded as well.

Six hundred and nine, actually, if one were to count the prisoners from Onghwe, but the *Khagan*, in a moment of lucidity a few days ago, had reminded him that these men would not be traveling any farther than Burqan-qaldun.

At the center of this activity was the *Khagan*'s wheeled *ger*. The hides stretched tightly over its wooden frame had been painted white, and the morning light made them glow. A team of eight oxen shifted impatiently, and behind the *ger*, six supply carts were being frantically readied.

Late the day before, Chucai had given the order that all preparations be completed by sunrise. Though he doubted Ögedei would emerge from his quarters until late morning, he wanted the caravan ready to depart the instant the *Khagan* climbed onto the platform of his movable tent. The caravan masters knew they would be left behind were they not ready, and none of them wanted to face the shame of having to chase the *Khagan* across the steppes.

In a rough line to the north of Ögedei's *ger* and supply carts were three smaller wheeled *ger*: two for Ögedei's wives, followed by one to be utilized by Chucai and a few other important advisors.

Ögedei had casually mentioned that he expected Gansukh to be given space in this tent, and Chucai had simply nodded. He had no intention of allowing Gansukh and Lian to sleep in the same *ger*. For a while, he had been incensed at the idea, more so when he realized his reaction was that of a protective father more than the *Khagan*'s senior advisor. Fortunately, Ögedei had mentioned the same expectation to Gansukh, and the young man had come to him to ask the best way to decline the *Khagan*'s suggestion. *I need some…space,* Gansukh had said. *I would prefer my own* ger.

Staring at the mob of Imperial Guard lined up behind the three *ger*, Chucai understood the need. Three *jaghun* of mounted soldiers, Munokhoi's elite troop, and two companies of a hundred men each. Their supply train stretched out of the palace gates—cooks, doctors, livestock drivers, wagon masters. A small group of acrobatic entertainers caught Chucai's eye as they performed up and down the supply line. Mukha had shrieked for half a day when she had been told they couldn't come along; Chucai had relented finally, only to get her to shut up, and he secretly hoped a Chinese raiding party would confuse them for an unguarded supply caravan.

There was no sign of Gansukh or Lian. He was not concerned yet, but he kept an eye out for them.

CHAPTER 13:

SIGNA HODIE LUMEN VULTUS TUI SUPER ME

Gregory is dead.

The three words staggered Rodrigo. From this simple statement spun a maelstrom of confusion. *The Pope—dead.* To whom would he deliver his message? Why had God sent him here when there was no way for him to be relieved of his burden? The Church would be consumed with discord as the factions vied for dominance, and he couldn't wait until a new Pope was elected. Christendom was under attack. A vast threat was coming out of the East, and he had been sent to warn the Church.

Robert of Somercotes tried to continue their conversation—speaking of cardinals, their duty to the Church, and of the *sede vacante*—but Rodrigo could grasp nothing of what the other man was trying to tell him. The news of the Pope's death was too overwhelming. Not even food and water could completely lift the burden of his exhaustion—the burden of his duty. The weight crushed him, and he lay back on the pallet. Sobbing gently, he collapsed into a dreamless stupor—not sleep, but a complete senselessness of both mind and spirit. His body demanded rest. His journey was not done yet, and if he was going to survive, he needed strength, both in body and spirit.

When he woke, the three words still churned in his head—*Gregory is dead*—but somewhere in his senseless slumber, he had located a hidden reserve of strength. God would not abandon him, not as long as he continued to believe his burden was just. Not as long as he had faith.

By the warm tint of the light in the tiny, high-ceilinged room, he knew it was day—by the relative cool, still morning. Rodrigo felt his stomach rumble and almost chuckled at it, as if it were some sickly child that had finally grown healthy enough to complain.

Gingerly, sore all over and still feverish, the priest staggered to his feet and took a few uncertain steps toward the open door. He could walk, perhaps even for some distance. *Praise God.* He shuffled carefully down a stone hallway. Doors at irregular intervals opened on either side into other rooms like his, although several, at a glance, had more furnishings, or at least boasted places to hang clothing—cloaks and robes, the vestments of religious men.

As he approached the end of the corridor, he realized it was a ruinous mass of stone and masonry, the result of the upper floor having collapsed. Leaning against the wall, he cast his eyes back on the series of doors he had passed. One of the rooms must have another exit, a door that would let him out of this corridor. There must be another way.

Unless his recent visitor was a figment of his feverish imagination, much like the young man he knew to be part of his dream. Had he imagined the visit from the older version, along with the meager meal he had been given? Such thought troubled him, for it meant he was still in the grips of his nightmare. Even the sensation of food in his belly was part of his fever dream.

A dark corner of the collapsed hallway—which he had assumed to be nothing more than a niche of shadows—turned out to be a narrow opening. Keeping one hand on the wall, he lurched toward the gap, frantic for the possibility of finding a way out—a way of verifying that he was awake, that he no longer dreamed. He had to turn sideways to fit, putting both hands on the wall now, and he sidled past the fallen rock. He pressed close to the heavy stones, and he focused on his hands: on moving his right to touch his left; on moving his left away, drawing his recalcitrant body forward.

The walls on the other side of the collapse were a different color, the stone more pink than gray, and the general condition of the ceiling was much better—no gaps through which sunlight could peer. Nor were there any doors in this hall; it ran for several dozen paces and then terminated at a large hole in the floor. A wooden ladder—protruding up from the hole by several feet—was lashed to the wall by a combination of thick rope and iron spikes.

Puzzled, Rodrigo climbed down, descending past one other floor and then into the earth itself. At the bottom, a large chamber had been carved into the bedrock, with a single tunnel running—as near as he could tell—in the same direction as he had been traveling.

With no other route available to him, Rodrigo wandered into the tunnel. To turn back would be to give up hope. To admit he was not strong enough to carry God's message.

✦✦✦

"There you are. Praise God."

The tunnel had not remained straight, and but for a decided lack of other obvious egresses, Rodrigo might have wandered forever. As it was, he discovered a source of light, and as he approached it, he was met by another man.

The newcomer was taller than Father Rodrigo, forced to stoop by the low ceiling of the tunnel. His face had been weathered by wind and sun—indicating he was no more a permanent resident of this subterranean place than Rodrigo—and his nose had been proud once, but it now canted to the side, and scar tissue knotted the bridge. His white beard was heavy enough that it nearly obscured the larger scar running down his left cheek. His smile, a mouth full of strong teeth, was as welcome as a fire might be to a freezing man.

"Robert said you were awake," the man said.

"Yes," Father Rodrigo replied. "Praise God," he added, bringing his hands up into the traditional prayer position—not knowing what else to add.

"You play the part of a poor priest well." The man wrapped his hands around Father Rodrigo's. Rodrigo tried to extricate himself and supplicate himself in some way, but the taller man resisted his attempts. "But there is no need to continue your charade. You need not hide here."

Part of Robert of Somercotes's conversation came back to him. *Cardinals—the cardinals were all imprisoned in this place, until they could elect a new Pope.* An irrational terror, born of this memory, swept over him: they thought he was a cardinal too. What if, in the slaughter and apocalyptic insanity of the Mongols destroying what had once been Hungary, his beloved superior—and confessor—had fallen and Rodrigo had been appointed his successor? Had Chancellor Báncsa been secretly elevated to one of the cardinal bishoprics, and through some machinations that he, in his feverish state, had forgotten, had that title been accorded to him—not because he deserved it but because there had been nobody left? Or—no less likely—had some agent of the Devil disguised Rodrigo to appear to these good men here as the Provost of Vâcz?

He forced himself to breathe calmly. "Of course," he replied. Hiding his dismay, he extricated his fingers from the other man's grip and more properly grasped the man's hand. "I am Rodrigo," he said, divesting himself of any title—real or imagined. "Rodrigo Bendrito."

He should tell this man that he was nothing more than a simple parish priest, but he held his tongue. Deep in his mind, he felt the spark of the fever and it frightened him, but what frightened him more was the thought his message would go unheard. Would God forgive him if he pretended to be someone other than he was in order to save the Church? Was this deception part of the test put to him by God? Was he supposed to participate in the election of the new Pope in order to ensure that the man who received his message would be strong enough to take on the burden?

"Yes," the other priest said. "And I am Giovanni Colonna." He smiled again, and Rodrigo's confusion was eased by the reassuring expression. "Come," Colonna said, laying a hand on Rodrigo's shoulder, "let me guide you."

Rodrigo let himself be led. "Where are we?" he asked. "Robert—our mutual friend, evidently—said we were in the... Septizodium."

Colonna chuckled. "*In?* No. It's up there somewhere." He reached up and tapped the low ceiling. "The Septizodium is near the base of the Palatine, and if it was ever a real temple, that building has vanished. All that remains is a facade, dedicated to ancient and forgotten gods. Behind that facade is a hollow shell—four walls that have managed to remain standing over the last few hundred years."

He walked slowly, matching Rodrigo's pace, and Rodrigo was thankful for the taller man's patience. He seemed like the sort of man for whom a walk from Rome to Paris would not be a hardship—his stride long enough the miles would vanish effortlessly.

"We are being hidden, you see," Colonna continued. "Even if the enemies of the Church discovered our location, they would not be able to reach us, because there is no way out of the Septizodium—out of that *box* of stone—other than climbing the walls, and the Bear is guarding those walls."

"The Bear?"

"Matteo Rosso Orsini, the Senator of Rome. We are under his care."

"But if we cannot get out, then how did I get in?" Rodrigo asked. "Where did the food I ate earlier come from?"

"Angels," Colonna laughed. "You were brought by angels."

They reached an open chamber and were closer to the source of the light. Rodrigo looked up as they exited the tunnel. Another ladder led out of this pit, and crouching beside the upper end of the ladder was another priest. He was outlined by the light—real daylight—and his long and twisted beard was so illuminated that his face appeared to be floating above a white cloud.

Colonna let him go first, and Rodrigo climbed the ladder, accepting the hand of the other man as he reached the top. Up close, the beard lost some of its mysterious luster, though it was no less strange and exotic. Not only was the beard so long that it nearly reached his waist, but it curled and corkscrewed as well. Strands of white hair were twisted into braids and then fed back into the central mass, and the whole arrangement looked like a tangle of ghostly vines descending from the man's face. His eyes were chips of slate in his face, and his simple cap was pulled low enough on his head that whatever hair he had on his crown was hidden by the black cloth.

"Ah, Rainiero," Colonna said as he stepped off the ladder behind Rodrigo. "God has graced us with another day of sun. I predict today will be the day that you decide to offer that monstrous beard of yours up as an offering to Him."

The man named Rainiero clasped Colonna's offered hand. When he smiled, his beard parted to reveal a pink mouth. "I take comfort that your faith in my weakness, Giovanni, is not nearly as strong as my faith in the reward awaiting me for enduring the trials offered by God's heat." He laid his hands on Rodrigo's shoulders and looked intently into his face. "God bless you, my son. I hope a night of rest has rejuvenated you."

"Rainiero Capocci," Colonna said, introducing the bearded man. "Governor of Viterbo, when he is not busy laying stone and raising walls. Or electing a Pope. Rainiero, this is Rodrigo Bendrito."

Rodrigo nodded and allowed Capocci to clasp one of his hands. His palm was rough and calloused, though warm; his grip was surprisingly gentle for the strength that lay coiled within the man's thick forearms. "God bless you," Rodrigo said somewhat awkwardly. How was he supposed to address these men who insisted on such intense familiarity and who thought he was a peer?

"You've been away for a while, haven't you?" Capocci asked, releasing Rodrigo's hand.

"Yes," Rodrigo admitted, flustered.

Capocci touched his ear. "Yes, you speak like a man who has recently awakened from a long nap. Still not quite sure where you are."

"I'm not," Rodrigo admitted and then actually bit his tongue to keep from speaking further, despite the questions, fear, and confusion whirling within.

A new voice brought a welcome distraction. "Good morning, my fellow brothers in Christ!" The hall, beyond Capocci, which Rodrigo had barely noticed, led to a sunlit opening, a neat and rectangular portal. Approaching them was a tall and lanky priest with a head of thick black hair. As he neared them, Rodrigo examined his face and immediately thought of a fox. His eyes, darting from face to face to Capocci's hand on Rodrigo's arm, missed nothing. "What sort of debate engages you so resolutely this morning?" he asked with a canted, obviously false smile.

Colonna let loose a sharp laugh, like a dog's bark, and quickly interposed himself between Rodrigo and the fox-faced man. "Debate?" he snorted. "Rainiero examines our new friend like he inspects his horses. In a moment, I am sure, he'll pry open his mouth to peer at his teeth."

Capocci jerked Rodrigo closer, and the younger priest stumbled into the bearded man's arms. "Indeed," Capocci said, "the best measure of a man is in the muscles of his jaw." He put a hand under Rodrigo's chin and lifted his head. "Is he a talker or an eater?"

From the corner of his eye—Capocci's extremely firm grip prevented him from actually turning his head—Rodrigo could see the fox-faced man trying to step around the imposing bulk of Colonna. "What have you learned?" the new cardinal asked Capocci, finally relenting to the game the others were playing.

Capocci's fingers dug into Rodrigo's cheeks near the jawline, forcing the priest's mouth open; Capocci put his face close, his whiskers tickling Rodrigo's nose. "It's very dark in there," Capocci announced. He twisted Rodrigo around, ostensibly so that the morning light would better illuminate the back of the priest's throat, but the change in position meant that Capocci now stood with his back to the sharp-faced cardinal. "Whose man are you?" Capocci demanded in a ferocious whisper, right into Rodrigo's ear. "Here all is discord and intrigue. Your vote may well decide the election, so do not make it rashly."

Rodrigo's eyes widened in shock, and a strangled noise rose in his throat. Capocci released his grip and delivered an open-handed slap across the priest's face. Rodrigo staggered, more from surprise than pain.

Colonna, head turned to better watch the antics of his friend, laughed. "He's a talker, that one."

Capocci turned toward the other two men. "Useless as a horse. He'd spend all day trying to convince me that he was no good at the plow, that he couldn't walk in a straight line." He gestured toward Rodrigo. "Listen to him now. Whining already."

Rodrigo hadn't said a word. Holding his hand to his stinging cheek, he was still trying to process what Capocci had whispered. The questions buzzed around in his head, making him dizzy, and when he took a step back, Capocci grabbed his arm and pulled him farther away from the open pit. Shrugging off the bearded man's aid, he wandered forward until he could lean against the wall.

His face was warm. He feared the fever was back.

The fox-faced man stepped around Colonna and approached Rodrigo; he laid one hand on the priest's shoulder, almost sycophantically. "Are you all right? These two are buffoons, unworthy of the robes they wear, and they cannot help themselves. Nothing more than degenerates who play with their own filth."

Behind the fox-faced man's back, Colonna made eye contact with Rodrigo and wagged a finger in caution. The cardinal saw something in Rodrigo's face and spun to look; Colonna immediately shoved the finger up his nose, digging for something hidden in his nasal cavity. Capocci leaned against the opposite wall, twirling the end of his mustache, studying Colonna's exertions with exaggerated gravity.

"It is best to ignore them," the dark-haired cardinal said. As Colonna withdrew the finger and began examining the results of his exploration, the cardinal shook his head and turned Rodrigo toward the brightly lit doorway. "Come, let us find the others and engage in more civil discourse."

"Yes," Rodrigo managed, allowing himself to be led again. "Some civility would be a pleasant change."

"I am Rinaldo," the fox-faced man said as they walked away from the pair. "Conti de Segni. Perhaps you know my family?" *The civility of noble families, of castes where children did not perform like monkeys in front of their parents,* said his tone.

Rodrigo shook his head, more concerned with keeping track of the names of these strange new men. After several months of only Ferenc as his constant companion, he found this sudden deluge of new faces—new names, new voices, new factions—overwhelming.

Deus Pater, orationem mean confirma, et intellectum mum ague et memorial... The prayer came to mind, one of the many lessons offered by Brother Albertus during the journey so long ago—Padua to Cologne—that began his education. *Ad suscipiendum,* he remembered. *Strengthen my understanding and memory.*

Thus, Capocci, the builder of walls, had a capacious beard and was capable with his hands. Capacious capable Capocci. Childish, but it worked; here was one name and one face solidly cemented to each other in Rodrigo's mind. And the first cardinal, the one who had met him in the tunnel—*Colonna.* He was as tall and solid as a column. Columnlike Colonna. Capacious capable Capocci.

It is through humble reflection upon Names and Virtues and Words that a man may understand God, he reflected, recalling more of the memorized lesson.

"Where have you come from?" de Segni asked, mistaking Rodrigo's silence as social awkwardness. "The journey was difficult, yes?"

"Yes," Father Rodrigo agreed. "Very difficult." *Rinaldo,* he decided, finding the business of remembering them much easier now. *Like Rinaldo the fox in children's nursery tales.* Fox-faced Rinaldo.

He stole a glance over his shoulder. Capocci and Colonna watched him go, all humor gone from their faces. Colonna wiped his finger on his robe. Capocci gave him the slightest of nods and, like his taller cohort had moments ago, held up a warning finger.

"I do wish God had provided a different reason for us to gather in Rome, but..." de Segni said, raising his eyes Heavenward. *Who am I to question God's will?* his gaze said; Father Rodrigo, remembering himself, finally, nodded and bowed his head in quiet agreement. "I was with his Eminence," de Segni continued after a moment of contemplation, "while he was a legate in Lombardy. We are—were—related, actually. Our family is still..." He brushed aside the thought with a wave of his hand. "He is with God now and feels no more pain. That is all any of us can ever hope for."

Rodrigo's pain was starting to return, as if someone had removed the spike in his side only to replace it now with a fresh one and was slowly hammering it into his flesh. He had walked too far, too soon, and each step toward the door was more difficult than the last. He couldn't help but wonder if, by dying, Pope Gregory IX had left this world at the right time. *I have so far to go,* Father Rodrigo fretted, *and my burden is too great.*

And then they reached the door and stepped into the light.

CHAPTER 14:

THE QUARTERMASTER'S TONGUE

Rutger's private chamber was austere: four bare walls, one broken by a single high window; an empty hearth, its brick darkened by a layer of soot built up from years of service; and a moldy, crumbling bench that had long since succumbed to the moisture that seeped through the stone tiles of the floor. The room did have a solid door, though, and once closed, Andreas and Rutger had a modicum of privacy.

Rutger moved with a stiffness that could easily be mistaken for formality of bearing, but Andreas knew Rutger suffered from a malady of the joints that sapped his strength. The older brother was like a moribund oak, dried and brittle, and the persistent fog that clung to the trees around Legnica made his hands and feet swell. Growing up, Andreas had seen similar afflictions take hold of craftsmen and laborers in his village. The pain could render a man unable to walk, and at its worst, would steal away his ability to work at his trade, a fate worse than death for many. Rutger, however, still walked straight-backed, with a pained dignity that made him gruff at the best of times, and at the worst, angry and quick to judge.

"What were my orders in regard to the Livonians?" he snapped. He sat down slowly, in painful stages, on the greenish bench. "Do you not recall them?"

Andreas stood before Rutger, hands clasped at his waist. He knew full well what Rutger had said; the others had heard the orders as well, and Maks had even reminded him of them just before the fight at the alehouse. Andreas had made the decision with conscious awareness of the violation. He could have avoided the fight altogether, but he knew he had made the right choice. He had to make Rutger see it as well.

"With respect," Andreas said, lowering his head, "they had interfered with our affairs, and to let them act without consequence would have been to reveal a weakness in our spirits. We will have to contend with them sooner or later, and I thought it best to remind them *now* of the consequences of their arrogance."

Rutger slapped a palm on the wooden bench. "You took this decision upon yourself without consulting me, without asking my permission. Are you an undisciplined mercenary who cannot be trusted to follow his commander's orders? I had not thought to give much credence to the…stories I have heard about your insolence at Petraathen, but I fear I may have endangered all of us by refusing to believe these malicious—"

"Sir," Andreas interrupted. "I…I beg your pardon, Brother Rutger. I speak out of turn, and in doing so perhaps I do give credence to this fancy that my company was so intolerable that I was no longer welcome at Petraathen, but…" He stood tall and proud as he pulled back the right sleeve of his robe to reveal the burned sigil on his forearm. "I passed the Trial of the Shield, I took the Vow, and I earned my sword. I have given myself—body, mind, and soul—to the Virgin. If you wish to doubt my devotion to my oath or my brothers, you had best do so with steel in hand, because that is how I will answer such an accusation."

Rutger raised a hand in a gesture of submission. "Lower your guard, Andreas. I do not attack your obedience to our ideals or your zeal in executing them. Your valor in battle preceded you, and we welcomed the news of your imminent arrival with much joy. Our company is made finer by your presence; do not seek subterfuge in my words on that matter. However, this chapter house was born out of a desperate and unusual necessity. We have not been brothers-in-arms long enough to think as one unit, and until that time, it is all the more imperative that we strive to maintain discipline. There is no doubt in my mind that you are the most astute battlefield strategist we have, but for the sake of our company, I cannot be distracted by wondering if you are following my orders."

Andreas relaxed slightly, and he stared at the floor. He started to reply, but then shook his head and remained silent. No answer was necessary. He had expected such a reminder, and had steeled himself for it, but when it came, he found he had no stomach to counter it. Doing so would strengthen Rutger's concern that he was brash and unfit to lead the others. It would be better to show some humility, to accept the charge as given, and to move on to the larger issue at stake. *Pick your battles*, he had reminded the Livonian *Heermeister*, and it was an excellent platitude for him to remember as well.

"Feronantus's success depends on secrecy," Rutger said, his tone softening, "and it does us no good to be under extra scrutiny by old rivals or to engage in a drawn-out pissing contest with them. What does that gain us?"

"Respect," Andreas replied after a moment.

"Is it part of our ideals that we seek that from other orders?"

"No. But I did not do it to earn *their* respect."

"Whose, then?"

"Our brothers."

Rutger sighed and ran a hand across his short gray hair. Andreas leaped forward to press his point. "They may not have taken up the shield, but our trainees are able. Eilif reacted swiftly when I was faced with two targets. If he had not been there, I would have had to hurt one in order to best them. I told them I was going to engage the Livonians, and they were not to be drawn into the fight unless they sensed my situation was dire. I *trusted* them to guard me, and they did." A big smile broke across his face. "I would wager any one of them could handle at least two Livonians on their own. They're not children anymore.

"And even if the Livonian *Heermeister* suspects we are not at full strength, he cannot be sure; however, wherever he chooses to engage us, his losses will be great. He will be cautious because he has to be; with the Mongols about, he will have to conserve his own strength. He's not going to be thinking about moving against us; he's going to be wondering how many men he will have to take with him to the alehouse whenever he gets thirsty. When he lays down at night, sleep will elude him because he will be worried that his compound is not secure. These are not baseless fears, Rutger, because our men could accomplish any such assault, if there was need."

"I remind you," Rutger retorted, "that there is no such *need*. Our original purpose in coming here was twofold. First, we had to find a way to stop the Mongol hordes from sweeping over all the land from here to the western sea. A task that has already been undertaken by Feronantus and his team." He frowned. "The second half of our duty was to hold the line here and keep our enemies focused on the Circus."

"And how are we doing that by hiding in a ruined church in the woods?" Andreas asked. "We sent one man to the arena, and when he won, the Khan stole him. What has our response been to that insult? We have done nothing. What would Haakon—if he is still alive—think of us? Have we abandoned our brother?"

"No," Rutger growled.

"Then how are we to get him back? We don't even know where he is. Or if he is even still alive." Andreas sighed. "We are too cautious. Yes, Feronantus took many great warriors with him, but to think of our strength as lessened because they are not here is to think of ourselves as too weak to defend our own honor. Rescuing Haakon, holding this line, showing the Livonians that it is not in their interest to prick us just to see if we respond—these are things that we *can* do, that we *have* to do."

Andreas searched the graying quartermaster's face for some hint as to his disposition. He feared he had been overzealous with his words, but such words needed to be given voice. Like Rutger, he had heard stories as well, of a time when Rutger had not been this reticent, when the older man had been a lion and not a caged cub. Speaking with such fiery rhetoric was a gamble, but he saw a glimmer in Rutger's expression that suggested his efforts were not in vain. There was still anger in his eyes, but there was also a hint of spurned pride. *That's right, brother,* Andreas thought, *remember who we are. Our fortunes are writ in steel and sinew, not skulking in shadows and waiting for the end.*

"You have something more on your mind," Rutger said after a long silence.

Andreas nodded. "The Mongols grow bored without the fights, as that is the sole reason they had tarried here and built their arena. Many have left, but the host that remains is still too numerous for us to fight alone. While I did not make contact with the Flower Knight while I was in the village, I think I know how to reach him and, in the process of doing so, how to draw the Mongols out again."

He could feel the excitement building as he talked, the thought of active resistance over passive waiting causing his soul to uncoil its tensed strength. "There is a place called First Field. It is where Haakon earned the right to fight in the arena, and since the Mongols closed the arena, there has been no impetus to stage qualifying fights. We should change that; we should go to this field and challenge all comers. We should raise our standard there and say, 'We have come to prove ourselves, and we will do so here until the Mongol Khan deigns to open the gates to the arena again.' Eventually, he will take notice; perhaps he will even send out one of his champions."

Rutger stared at him intently. "And you think the champion they will send out will be the Flower Knight?" When Andreas nodded, the older man grunted. "There is a great deal of risk in your venture, and I do not believe there is much chance of success. We know nothing about how many champions the Khan has, or if he even cares anymore of what goes on outside his compound." His words were defeatist and cynical, but his tone was much lighter—the voice of a man trying halfheartedly to talk himself out of something his head knew to be foolish, but his gut told him was true.

"Low or not, it is the best option we have," Andreas said. "The Mongol compound is well guarded, and we know too little about its layout and its guards to risk sending men over its walls. We would be better served by earning the trust of a man who resides inside."

Here Andreas paused, aware of the weight of their situation, of the tenuous balance of it. *The edge of the blade.* "It is also our best chance at restarting the Circus," he said. "We must pull the Khan's eyes toward some affair more entertaining than whatever it is he's doing in his tent, sealed away from the rest of this place."

He felt his own smile turn mirthless, reminded once more of the fate that awaited them all. "If we entertain this Khan, then we acquire precious time—not only for our brothers on their dangerous mission, but for our own lives as well. We may not yet be sure what we're going to do with that time, but every moment that we put off the end of this game is a moment we can use to plan and prepare. I would rather face the dark prepared than stand ignorant, caught off guard like some novice stableboy. Ours is the righteous fight, Rutger, the burden of defending the weak and the innocent. We don't hide ourselves from the night; we *drive it back.* It is our duty to stand tall and herald the rising dawn."

Rutger was silent, but his eyes were bright, moving jerkily back and forth as if he had just been shaken from a long sleep. "You're prodding a dragon to keep the lions at bay," he sighed. His sword hand flexed, motions that were doubtless painful, but so ingrained they could not be stopped. Once taken up, and even after it was released, the sword never truly left a knight's hand; even in his dotage, he would remember its weight, and the vows and obligations that came with it.

"In the end, either will devour us," Andreas said. "Wouldn't you rather choose the manner of your death?"

Rutger laughed. "God and the Virgin must love you, boy, to give you such words to stir this old heart."

Watching Rutger's hand open and close and seeing the flicker of pain in the back of his eyes that no training or will could completely hide, Andreas knew that the quartermaster spoke the truth. The Virgin *did* love him, and he, in turn, wanted to share that love with Rutger. *Let us all die as we were meant to,* he prayed, *on a battlefield of our choosing, with a sword in our hands.*

CHAPTER 15:

TÜNDÉR MAGIC

Ferenc burrowed into the hay, pulling the old blanket over his body. First the sun and then the moon had faded, and the temperature in the squalid barn was cool. He had fallen into a stupor at once, indifferent to the heat and drifting dust; ironically, it was the quiet and the comfort of early morning that finally woke him.

When he'd first come to consciousness he'd been terrified, disoriented; then in a dizzying flash, he remembered where he was and how he'd gotten here. Or he almost remembered it. Had he abandoned Father Rodrigo? After that horrible, endless journey, after the holy man's feverish dreams and gibberish, had he stood by him through all of it, just to desert him in the end?

He had not deserted the priest. He *could* not have. He, Ferenc of Buda, son of Mareska, would not do such a thing. Someone on his father's side might, perhaps, but even then, it took many years of constant moral degradation before one was capable of treachery. They were so strict, his people, so diligent in teaching their youth how things must be; it took years to outgrow the fear of disobedience. Only men of his grandfather's age had achieved such indifference to conformity and duty that they could ever abandon someone they were honor-bound to assist.

He hadn't deserted Father Rodrigo, and having reminded himself of this fact, he allowed himself to relax. He had only listened to that bizarre girl. During that moment of utter chaos in the crowded, roiling marketplace, she had appeared on the back of his horse—awkwardly attaching herself to him like a leech. She had never ridden a horse before—that much was clear by the way she clung to him. And she had shouted in his ear, directing him after the running soldier.

His hands crept to the satchel still attached to his belt, exploring the rough outlines of objects within until he found the ring. After the girl had wrested it from the clamped fingers of the downed soldier, she'd given it to him.

Who was she? Did she understand the meaning of the ring? It had caused quite an uproar, and Ferenc still did not know why.

He lay listening to the horses in the stalls below: the steady crunch of the hay between strong teeth, the noisy exhalations, the tails whisking against the warped wood of the stalls, the occasional nickering to one another. The sounds made him feel safe; they were the closest things he had to memories of home.

Ferenc rolled onto his back and stared up at the ceiling. Sunlight bled through a narrow window set high in the wall of the loft. He slid his hand through the dry hay until the tips of his fingers were lit by golden light. Despite the long sleep, he was worn out—the aches in his back and legs reminding him just how tired he was—and it was fine to lie here for a little while. Just a little while.

Especially since he had no idea what to do next. Just thinking about it was almost more exhausting than the actual chase had been yesterday.

His eyelids fluttered, and his breathing eased as he sank deeper into the hay. In a few hours, the light would fall directly on his face from the hatch used to let down hay. He'd wake then. He was sure of it. *A few more hours,* he thought drowsily. His hand jerked up, waving at an imaginary bug, and then his arm relaxed again, flopping against the hay. His head slid to the side, his breathing slow and regular.

Then he heard a sound that was not the horses, and he sat up abruptly, hand reaching for his knife. Someone was in the hayloft.

Right beside him.

"Hey!" he shouted and tried to get to his feet, the knife held out defensively before him. How could he, a hunter, allow someone to get that close to him?

"Shshshsh!" The whisper was distinctly feminine in tone. He huffed in relief and lowered the knife a little. It was the girl. In the morning light, he recognized her pale skin and narrow, bony shoulders.

"Ferenc," she said, pointing to him, as if it were a code word.

"Ocyrhoe," he said, almost apologetically, but still wary, nodding toward her and lowering the knife. But he did not sheathe it.

They had only gotten as far as each other's name in being able to communicate with each other. When she began to jabber, gesticulating with quick, exaggerated movements, he had to shake his head to remind her that he had no idea what she was talking about.

"Father Rodrigo?" he interrupted, trying to slow down the torrent of words coming out of her mouth. "Rodrigo?"

She cocked her head like a dog hearing a strange sound, and frowned.

He repeated the priest's name once more and then pointed to himself. "Ferenc." Then to her, "Ocyrhoe." Then, feeling apologetic for the caricature, he imitated Rodrigo bent over his horse, eyes rolling. "Father Rodrigo," he said definitively.

"Ah," said the girl. She crossed herself several times and hummed something like a Gregorian-style chant, her hands in a praying position. "Father Rodrigo?"

"Father Rodrigo," Ferenc confirmed. Her emphasis was different than his, but clear enough. "Where? Where is he?"

She shook her head and shrugged. Ferenc grunted with frustration. Did that shrug mean *I don't know where he is?* Or *I don't understand what you're asking me?* He couldn't tell, and when she asked him a question, he could only shake his head and shrug in return.

A chill ran up his spine as he considered their inability to communicate. This was not an inconvenience; it was a catastrophe. He knew his own language, and what piecemeal Latin he had gleaned from Father Rodrigo during their long journey, but that was it. Nothing could have prepared him for the trek he'd just completed; never in his life, before the battle at Mohi, could he have imagined himself beyond the boundaries of his native tongue.

She sensed his anxiety, and rather than joining him in it, she very deliberately calmed herself with a gentle, long breath. She put a hand on his arm and repeated the breath, gesturing for him to do the same. He made a face but breathed with her. And he did feel calmer, although perhaps that was just her hand on his arm, a human touch.

Ocyrhoe released him and grabbed a few strands of hay. She twisted them, carefully tying the dry straw into a loose knot. "Father Rodrigo," she said, presenting the twisted strand to him. Glancing around the loft, she spotted a short-handled pitchfork leaning against the wall and scooted across the loft to grab it. Indicating that he should put down the Rodrigo straw man, she put the pitchfork between Ferenc and the knotted strand, and then gazed at him solemnly.

It made no sense to him: if this was meant to graphically display the problem, why didn't Father Rodrigo just slip through the openings of whatever was keeping him, like stray straw between the tines of a pitchfork? She saw the expression on his face, rolled her eyes, and grabbed the piece of straw, which broke under her angry touch.

She moved the pitchfork aside and squatted opposite Ferenc. "Father Rodrigo," she tried again, now pointing to herself, and this time did a very good imitation of a person with hands bound, trying to break free. She pretended she was being dragged away across the loft, her leather sandals dragging a path through the strewn hay. Ferenc gasped, and when Ocyrhoe patted his arm, he let her drag him over to the loft window. She pointed to the right, and when Ferenc looked, he was shocked to realize they were still in the middle of the city, surrounded by far more urbanity than he was used to. There was little to be seen but a spreading sea of other rooftops, russet and brown and gray in the wan morning light.

"What do we do?" he demanded in frustration. If she knew he had been captured—which was obvious to him now, in retrospect—did she know where he had been taken? And if she did, then how was she going to communicate that location to him? "Can you take me there?" he asked.

She gave him an impatient frown, her meaning clear: *Why do you talk to me with words you know I can't understand?* She pointed to herself and to him, clasped her hands together, and said their names rapidly: "FerencOcyrhoe." *Us.*

Which was the best news he had heard yet. She wasn't planning on abandoning him, which, of course, meant his course of action was clear as well. He nodded and echoed her compound word. *FerencOcyrhoe.* Together. A tiny laugh slipped out of him, spurred by an image in his mind. A cool winter's night a dozen years from now, him telling the story of his incredible adventures around the fire pit to his awestruck children and neighbors.

She pointed out the window again, straight in the direction she'd said Father Rodrigo was. Then she indicated both of them—*FerencOcyrhoe*—and then pointed again, looking expectantly at him the entire time.

He blinked, his head snapping backward on his neck like a turtle retreating into its shell. "What?" he said. "Are you crazy? How can we possibly get him? What kind of place is he in? Even if we find him, where will we take him? We can't stay in this loft. We can't—*I* can't—stay in this city—"

He was cut off by a loud, piercing whistle, courtesy of Ocyrhoe's tongue and teeth. A moment of unnatural thunder shook the building as the horses collectively spooked at the sound and thrashed against their ropes. She waited for them to settle, and then began talking again. He held up his hands to slow her down, but she ignored him, and after a few seconds, he realized it wasn't *all* gibberish. Some of it sounded like Latin; he could understand certain words but had no context for them—*bona,* he recognized, and *malus* as well, and *ecclesiam* and *sacerdos* and *Summus Pontifex.*

The Bishop of Rome. Yes, Father Rodrigo's message. The one he hoped to deliver to the Pope.

He watched her face as she spoke. She was a scrappy little thing, younger than he, but he could not guess by how much. She was too bony and petite to have noticeable breasts, even if she was mature. Her hair was a color common enough in these parts, but her skin was at least as pale as a Northerner. In the hazy morning light, she looked like a *tündér,* a fairy of his homeland. Not a *szépasszony,* of course—a fair woman, the most beautiful of supernatural beings—but even the woodland fairies, although prone to mischief, treated you right if you stuck with them.

And this one had certainly already proven her good intentions—as well as, arguably, magic powers. He was not frightened of fairies. If she was, indeed, a *tündér*, she would eventually reveal that she knew a language he understood—the *proper* language of fairies.

She stopped talking and looked at him with a far-too-patient sigh. He realized, sheepishly, that he had been staring at her with a stupidly vacant expression.

She glanced up toward the heavens and muttered something; it struck him as an apology to someone absent. Perhaps someone on high. Her own gods? Then she sighed once more and firmly pressed her small, bony right hand against his sternum. Her fingers were dirty and pale and her nails ragged—more ragged than his own, which was saying something.

He was distracted by her hair. He shook his head as she started to speak, and reached out for a gnarled knot of hair. He had thought it was simply dirty and matted, much like his after weeks of traveling, but that wasn't the case. Her hair had been knotted very specifically, in a way that seemed familiar.

Gasping, he glanced around at the straw, looking vainly for the straw Rodrigo, until he remembered it had fallen apart. He bent and scooped up another long stick of straw and tried to remember the knot she had tied in the hay. It was familiar, of course, because he had seen his mother tie it. It was a basic hitch, used for horses and sacks—the sort of knot one tied unconsciously, when wanting to restrain something momentarily.

Ocyrhoe watched his clumsy fingers with a pitched expression, and as he finished, her eyes widened. She grabbed his hands, holding his wrists tight, and held the knotted straw between them. She squeezed his wrists, several times, her fingers moving in a complex pattern against his skin.

"Yes," he cried when he realized he understood the rhythm of her pressure. *It was* tündér *magic.* "Yes," he said. "Kin-knot."

She smiled like sun breaking through a cloud, showing healthy ivory teeth. Just hearing his tone, she understood that he understood. She laughed and squeezed his wrists again.

I know you.

CHAPTER 16:

EXTERGE LUTUM OCULORUM MEORUM, UT VIDEAM

The cardinals were like the squirrels in the parks in Paris: they pretended indifference, but as soon as there was a hint they might be fed, they grew animated and friendly. The cardinals milled about in the odd, shadowy courtyard of the Septizodium, attempting to warm themselves in the morning air—and not succeeding. The sun, while risen, had not yet climbed to such a height that its face could look down on the trampled grass of the Septizodium's interior.

It was, as Colonna had said, a four-walled chamber, open to the sky, but with no visible means of entrance or exit. Other than the rectangular door cut into one of the walls near the base. Rodrigo understood the nature of their confinement now. The Septizodium was their prison and yet was still nothing more than a facade. The cardinals were seemingly imprisoned in this box, but from their vantage point, the Septizodium was simply the way they communicated with the outside world. Their real *prison* was the confused mass of tunnels and fractured corridors that honeycombed the ruins surrounding the historic facade.

Rinaldo Conti de Segni had sought to lead Rodrigo out to the center of the Septizodium, but Rodrigo had hung back, preferring to remain in the gloom still clinging to the walls. The others were gathered in the open space, and Rodrigo was not quite ready to meet all of them. For the moment, he wanted to assess them without undue influence, without the sort of manhandling that he had suffered at Capocci's hands.

He was uncomfortably aware that the group was aware of his presence and they were also assessing him. *Your vote may well decide the election.*

He did not understand why God had sent him here—on a fool's errand—and the only explanation that made any sense to him was that God was not yet done with him. Perhaps God was giving him direction, even now, through the words of these men. What better way to discover a worthy recipient of God's message than to be instrumental in his elevation?

In the courtyard, the buffoons, as de Segni referred to them—Capocci and Colonna—had met Robert of Somercotes, the man whom Rodrigo had seen first after awakening last night. Somercotes nodded to Rodrigo; Rodrigo, uncomfortably aware of how much he did not know about everything going on around him, thought it must mean something that Somercotes and those two were friendly with each other—but what? He had no idea.

The three of them were sitting on a makeshift stone bench, a slab of granite that had been laid across the ragged caps of several columns, and Rodrigo wondered if Capocci had been responsible for the ad hoc furniture. Once Somercotes sat, it was easy to mistake him for a graying statue, if it weren't for the subtle movement of his head as he tracked the others wandering through the dust-laden sunlight. Capocci, in comparison, was a frenzy of movement. He sat, even though he didn't seem to want to, and even sitting, he couldn't keep his hands still. Beside his end of the bench was a pile of debris. Anxious for activity, Capocci scooped up a handful of stones from the pile. Without looking at them, his fingers sorted and cataloged them. He arranged them, large to small, between the fingers of one hand, like a juggler.

Nearby, a curly haired man, not much older than Rodrigo himself, plucked random notes on a highly ornamented lute. The courtyard was too big—and the man too indifferent—for the sound to carry far, and his song was like scattered rain on a thatched roof. The man's eyes were closed, and his lips curled around a private prayer. Or a ribald stanza. It was hard to tell, though Rodrigo might have guessed the latter from the way the minstrel's lips curved up, as if to punctuate a line of verse.

De Segni followed Rodrigo's eyes to the lutenist. "That is Tommaso da Capua," he said in a disapproving voice.

Da Capua, like the musical term da capo, Rodrigo made the mental note. *Another easy one to remember.*

"As his expression may suggest," de Segni continued, "he is not the holiest of men." He lowered his gravelly voice almost to a whisper. "His vote reflects that, of course." More vulpine than ever, he looked shrewdly at Rodrigo.

Rodrigo tried to make sense of these words. *His vote reflects that, of course.* Disapproval. De Segni and Tommaso were on opposing sides. But who was the candidate, and why was there dissension? How could men of the cloth, leaders of Christendom, adopt an air of near enmity toward others of their kind?

Rodrigo knew what an enemy was. He had learned on the death fields of Mohi. It was impossible for anyone in Rome to truly be an enemy to anyone else in Rome. If any good Christian behaved otherwise—especially men of the Church—there was only one reason for such behavior.

The end times, Rodrigo realized. *The Day of Judgment.* The inevitable approach of his vision—his persistent and perpetual nightmare.

His burden.

He kept staring around at the assembly, as they kept staring at him. On the other side of the courtyard sat a small cluster of cardinals, their heads bent together in quiet conference. Two were advanced in age, faces lined and worn like the stones of the Septizodium. De Segni, still watching Rodrigo without appearing to be doing so, noted where his attention had wandered. "You are interested in our more venerable brethren?" he asked approvingly. It was the first time, Rodrigo realized with a start, that de Segni had expressed approval—of anyone.

One of the pair of elders had a drooping face, as if his skeleton were shrinking inside his skin; the other had a mane of white hair and eyebrows to match. The combination lent his face an antique, leonine aspect. "Romano Bonaventura and Gil Torres," de Segni said, still surreptitiously measuring Rodrigo's response (and he had none, for he did not know these men). "The two with them, the younger ones, are Goffredo Castiglione and my kinsman Stefano de Normandis dei Conti."

These two stood literally in the shadows of their elders, subservient in manner and attention. Rodrigo shook his head, chastising himself for failing to think of mnemonics for this cluster. Collectively, he supposed he could think of them as *the group fox-faced Rinaldo approved of*, but that did not, in itself, tell him anything about them—or about the undercurrent of tension that permeated the gloomy cloister.

A fifth man was listening intently to the elders' debate, a pleasant smile on his face. Of all the cardinals in the room, with the exception of the so-called buffoons, this fellow was the most at ease. His smile was neither beatific nor idiotic, but just the natural expression of a relaxed and comfortable man. "The smiling one is Riccardo Annibaldi," de Segni said, not sharing the relaxed cardinal's expression. "He is a...*free thinker*."

Unreliable, Rodrigo translated, trying to wed the cardinal's name to the word in a way that made sense. *Anni-B, Unreli-B...* It almost worked.

He realized, with a start, there was one more cardinal, haunting the courtyard's doorway. He was watching them all—especially de Segni and Rodrigo—like a predatory beast who, having recently fed, was in no rush to take another victim, but was nonetheless examining the herd for signs of weakness. He met Father Rodrigo's gaze and smiled slightly, but the expression made the priest shiver and look away.

Without meaning to, he locked eyes with de Segni and held them, like a drowning man holds on to a piece of driftwood. De Segni allowed himself a small, private smile. "Someone you recognize?" he asked.

Rodrigo shook his head, returning his attention to the trio of Capocci, Colonna, and Somercotes. "No," he said and stopped himself from saying any more. *Just the face of evil*, he thought, chiding himself for such a foolish reaction. He was just a singular presence, that was all—the sort of man who commanded a room simply by the very indifference he projected upon deigning to enter.

"Sinibaldo Fieschi," de Segni said after looking over his shoulder. "Our late Pontiff's right-hand man. The man who best embodies the spirit of Gregory IX's wishes and desires. Would you like me to introduce you?" Rinaldo's gaze—focused on Rodrigo—was so piercing, so searching, that it made the young priest dizzy.

There was a commotion from above: shouting and the creak of ropes. *Praise God*, Rodrigo thought and used the moment to break away from Rinaldo, pretending he wanted to better see what was happening. At the top of the walls were soldiers, bearing buckets attached to thick ropes. Hidden machinery began to let out the rope, and the soldiers guided the buckets down into the courtyard of the Septizodium. The soldiers worked swiftly, having done this same ritual time and again, their movements efficient and well rehearsed.

A man wearing a helmet with a crest of black feathers waved to the Cardinals below. "Good morning, Your Eminences," he shouted down. "You will be pleased to note that there are lemons and oranges today."

"Very good, Master Constable Alatrinus." De Segni made the sign of the cross for the commanding officer. "May God bless you and your men on this day."

"Thank you, Your Eminence," the master constable shouted. He spotted Rodrigo and threw the young priest a salute. "Your Eminence," he said, "I trust you have been provided with a chamber and a bed."

"Yes," Rodrigo answered, after assuring himself that the soldier was not speaking to anyone else. "I have been made"—he glanced at de Segni—"most welcome."

The soldier laughed and then caught himself. "It will be another hot day," he called to de Segni, "until this afternoon, we fear. Not that you can tell yet, but the weather is about to change." He pointed. "Clouds are building in the east. The soothsayers tell us it will rain heavily." He put up his hands. "I suppose they can look east as well as anybody. I've had the men provide extra portions this morning in case we are prevented from returning this afternoon. Has there been progress?" He let the word hang in the air, with tentative hopefulness.

De Segni shook his head. "We are no closer to a decision than yesterday, my son." The cardinal chuckled. "Believe me, you will know when we have decided."

"I hope it happens soon, Your Eminence," the soldier said. "For all of our sakes."

"Of course," de Segni replied, and though his tone was silky and smooth, it contained a note of rebuke.

The master constable, realizing he had spoken too familiarly, bowed with a grandiose wave and retired—more expediently than necessary, Rodrigo thought. Several of the soldiers retired with him, their buckets lowered. The rest stood around aimlessly, waiting for the cardinals to finish their morning meal.

De Segni strode to the wall where the buckets had been lowered, and examined their contents. "Come," he said, satisfied by what he found. He spread his arms to encompass all of them. "Let us pray before we enjoy this bountiful meal." He bowed his head, brought his hands together, and began to speak a Latin prayer of thanks.

Rodrigo noticed that neither Fieschi nor Somercotes lowered their heads during the prayer. He flushed under their stares, and he quickly bowed his head, but his neck itched during de Segni's benediction. He peeked twice. Neither man had looked away. "Amen," he said—too loudly, perhaps—when de Segni finished, and he dropped his hands and scurried toward the cornucopia contained in the buckets, trying to avoid looking at either of the two cardinals again.

I am one of the squirrels, Rodrigo thought as he bumped against the other men around the buckets. Nervous and fidgety, hyperaware of the possibilities of predators nearby. Scurrying to get food and then rushing back to the sanctuary of a bush or a tree branch to hurriedly eat his snatched meal.

Who was an enemy here, and who a friend? What a ridiculous idea that was—thinking of some of these men as enemies. And all of them, with the exception of Annibaldi the "free thinker," appeared to be very invested in not trusting each other.

Fieschi, he saw, made no move toward the buckets, remaining just inside the doorway. Watching, like a hawk.

✦✦✦

Fieschi watched the cardinals mill about the courtyard, his eyes straying more often than not to the newcomer. The man still looked very weak, possibly still feverish, but his delirium had clearly eased, and he was able to walk. Able to be exposed to the wild ideas of the others.

Or they to his.

There was nothing about him that gave any indication of his identity, and based on the way Somercotes and his lackeys were watching him too, they did not know who he was—or what he represented. By taking the satchel before any of his fellow inmates were sharp enough to notice it, Fieschi had stolen all there was to steal. He had played to Orsini's paranoia and self-doubt, planting the seed that the priest was one of Frederick's pet cardinals, but he wasn't entirely sure himself. The man could be nothing more than a simple priest—one who was inflamed with heretical madness, which may be useful in its own way. But was there a way he could turn the mystery of this man's identity to his advantage?

He had seen the priest be accosted by Colonna and Capocci, the two dangerous clowns who were wiser than they let on; he knew perfectly well what they were doing, even though de Segni did not seem to, a persistent trait of his fellow cardinal. *Fools,* he thought bitterly, *I am surrounded by fools.*

His eyes swept over the radiance of cardinals, disgusted to be reduced to living among them in squalor. Even Castiglione looked appalled and morose, as if he'd give up his position as the Papal candidate in exchange for a bath and a night of sleep on a feather bed.

Castiglione, Fieschi thought coldly, *acting the role of the pious priest, trying to pretend he doesn't know they wouldn't allow him such humility.* The damned agents of the Holy Roman Emperor were immovable in their insistence to endorse him as their candidate for Pope. Of course, it was a complete coincidence that this faction—Colonna, Capocci, da Capua, Castiglione, and especially Robert of Somercotes—had all been given the worst rooms in the makeshift sanctuary they had discovered in the maze of broken passages. Rooms with holes in their ceilings, directly under the location Fieschi had instructed Orsini to encourage the soldiers to relieve themselves. The dankest, most stinking, fetid rooms. Anything to make the cardinals desperate to get out of here. If even one of them could be made miserable enough to throw the vote against Castiglione—breaking this interminable deadlock between the two factions—Orsini would release them all. The *sede vacante* would be over. There would be a new Bishop of Rome—one who had a *proper understanding* of the necessary relationship between Rome and the Holy Roman Emperor, a role that Romano Bonaventura was only too pleased to be considered for—and things could return to normal.

Fieschi himself had the best room, the coolest, snuggest, and most secure, with the most comfortable bed; to encourage their steadfastness, the Cardinals who reliably voted against Castiglione—Bonaventura (naturally, given his nomination by the others), Torres, Stephano dei Conti, and Rinaldo—were given decent lodgings as well.

God looked out for those who had His interests at heart. That was part of Fieschi's job in Rome. They all knew that, and they didn't care to upset that dynamic—one that had worked well enough for them over the last decade.

Then there was Annibaldi, the damned, impudently independent Annibaldi, who had so far refused to vote for either candidate, even though he had been outspoken about the Emperor in the past. For weeks now, he had, pleasantly enough, wanted to engage in actual debate, demanding evidence of either candidate's merit, indifferent to their political alliances. Fieschi respected such integrity when it served his own purposes. When it thwarted them, however, he found it infuriating. Increasingly so.

But he could discount Annibaldi's need for debate now. The new man would be the vote that would change the dynamic; one more for Bonaventura would be enough to convince the others that their resistance was pointless. Even if Colonna and Capocci got to him first—even if Robert of Somercotes had already started to convince him of his righteous duty to bring peace through an alliance with the Holy Roman Emperor—Fieschi was confident in his own abilities to bend the new priest to his will.

He watched the ailing priest fumble with an apple and a leg of some greasy meat. *He will either serve my needs directly or I will use him to sway the others. Either way, he is the perfect tool.*

It was almost as if God had sent him to Fieschi.

CHAPTER 17:

RUMORS OF MY DEMISE

Kim grunted as the masseuse worked his shoulders, her fingers digging into the tense muscles. He lay facedown on a narrow platform, his eyes closed, and the scent of the oils she was using took his mind to other places. Guilt and anguish were not his way, nor dwelling on what was gone, but smells and sounds were powerful things, and in an effort to relax, he let himself fall into the embrace of his memory.

Books, he recalled—halls of learning where golden sunlight poured in through the windows, illuminating courtiers draped in silk. Sweat also, and blood, shared by brothers and friends in times of war and peace, and dark caves in the mountains where secrets of a long-hidden brotherhood were passed from generation to generation. The recollections were sweet, better than the reality had been, but that was the nature of memory: the past turned to silver and polish as time went by. A mercy for most, that the hardships faded in time, but when the memory lost its sting, it became something of a torment.

He grunted as she found a particularly hard knot below his left shoulder blade, the exhalation more agitated than the last. Her hands paused and then vanished, and he heard her sharp, shallow breaths. *Fear,* he thought, fear that her tiny yet muscular hands had injured him.

"Not your hands," he apologized in the Mongol tongue. He opened his eyes and looked at her. "It is my history that pains me." She was not Mongolian, and truth be told, he had no idea what languages the girl spoke, but she seemed to understand.

She was a pretty Chinese woman, brought west with the endless train of wagons that followed the great Mongol Horde. Her long black hair was twisted up and held in a bundle by a pair of lacquered sticks, and her face, though downcast, was soft and young. She wore fine clothes and smelled of the oils of her trade. She was part of the comforts he and his fellow fighters enjoyed, fanciful things that were meant to make it easy to forget where he was and why, but her beauty and her scent had the opposite effect, reminding him of what he had lost. She was just another bar in his cage.

He made no move to rise from the platform, and she shifted from side to side in her kneeling position, unsure of what he wanted of her. "Please," he said, "you need not fear me."

With a look halfway between relief and resignation, she gestured for him to put his head down again. As if taking permission from his statement, she set her fingers into the work harder, and he clenched his teeth. *Some pain is good; some pain is necessary.*

Most of the discoloration from his bruises was gone, but underneath, he was still stiff and sore. The beating he received from Tegusgal's men could have been worse, and the fact that he was allowed the luxury of this massage was a sign of how his punishment had been a matter of formality rather than severity. None of his injuries were permanent or even truly debilitating. It was a warning—a reminder of whom it was that held the key to his cage. *The Khan didn't want his prized dogs made lame. Just disciplined.*

Zug was faring better too. The man's energy was returning, invigorated by recent events. He was not yet ready to fight, but Two Dogs's strength had rebounded to a level whereby, with an earnest blow, he could send an unready man careening into the wall of their practice yard.

Soon, he thought as the woman worked her hands into his hair. Her fingers kneaded the base of his skull. While Zug regained his strength, the burden of their planning fell on his shoulders, but it would not be much longer before the Nipponese man would be ready to take up his *naginata* again.

There had been no word or sign from the Rose Knights. He had sent Hans with both his message and the false one written by the priest, trusting that the boy would relate the events at the bridge to the knights. Whilst his punishment had been light for straying farther than allowed, Tegusgal—Onghwe Khan's senior commander and the man in charge of maintaining the *health* and *safety* of the Khan's violent menagerie—had tightened security around the camp. It was a show of force—mainly for the Khan's benefit, Kim supposed—but the unfortunate side effect of the increased patrols was that it would be more difficult to get a message in or out of the camp. Nor could Kim leave the camp to return to the woodworker he had stolen the staff from and repay him. It was a regrettable situation, as the craftsman might no longer be inclined to finish the staff he had been working on for Kim, but there was no sense in worrying about what could not be changed.

All he could really do was heal, practice, and be patient.

On the other hand, while a locked and guarded gate could keep men in one place, it did little to stop the spread of rumors, and from these, Kim had caught a few things that let him know his excursion into the city had not been for naught. The battering he'd given the other knights near the bridge—the ones who wore the red cross and sword—had apparently been followed by a fight in the street. There were many variations to these rumors, but the majority of them painted the Knights of the Rose as the perpetrators of this second humiliation.

No message yet, but they had come into the sprawling city. For the time being, patience was all that was required of him.

Tentatively, the woman tapped him on the shoulder, indicating that she wanted him to roll over. As he did, she held up a small clay jar and indicated she wanted to put its contents on his face. The bruising on his torso had gone away, but there were still ugly blotches on his cheeks and around his eyes. Again, no permanent damage had been done, but the face always healed more slowly than the body. He nodded and settled more comfortably on the platform, folding his hands across his midsection.

She had just started smearing the cold unguent on his right cheek—the stuff stank of camphor and mint, and it was chilly on his hot skin—when he heard a gust of noise, so like an ocean wave breaking upon the shore that, for a second, he was transported back to the beaches near Byeokrando. He held his breath, listening for the sound to repeat itself, and when it did, he realized it was human voices he heard. *Cheering.*

He gently pushed her hand away from his face and slid from the platform. He stretched as he stood up, feeling with some satisfaction that the persistent knot of frozen muscles in his shoulder had been undone, restoring his full range of motion.

He pushed aside the loose flap of the tent and stepped out in the sun. There were no crowds inside the compound, and the sound could not be coming from the arena, as there were still no matches scheduled. The sound came from somewhere else, somewhere close by. The crowd roared again, and he turned his head toward the sound, listening intently to the noise. It wasn't the roar that was magnified by the walls of the arena, though it had that same sort of swell to it. It was the voice of a smaller crowd, one that gathered in a much more open space.

First Field, he realized. Someone was fighting at the proving grounds.

Since Zug's defeat in the Circus, First Field had fallen fallow, empty but for the occasional group of fighters battering one another all but senseless. Without any true tournament fights, all the Khan's fighters had to sustain themselves was a dismal trickle of rumors. Onghwe Khan was bored, some whispered; this land had been conquered too easily, and the fighters who answered the Khan's call were not good enough for him to even bother throwing them upon the mercy of his Eastern warriors. Other rumors spoke of the main Mongol force at Mohi and how Batu and the other Khans were seizing great storehouses of treasure—jewels and coins and other riches that would never be shared with the dissolute Khan and his men. Others swore that the Khan was more patient than Heaven itself, and he was simply waiting until the Western fighters were in a frenzy to compete, and only then would he start the challenges again. There were other stories, variations of these and even wilder tales; Kim had heard them all, several times over. They were nothing he hadn't heard before when Onghwe had set up his Circus in other cities.

He started to walk toward the main gate of the Mongol encampment, but was brought up short by the masseuse. "Thank you," he said, "but that will be enough for today." His pulse beat heavily beneath the hot skin of his cheek. He should let her finish, but the sound of cheering had infused his blood with too much excitement to lie still.

She shook her head, chattering at him in Chinese. She held out a cloth and mimed wiping her face. She hadn't had a chance to wipe the salve off his cheek, and he gave her a short nod as he accepted the cloth. "My apologies," he said as he rubbed his face clean. "I will speak well of your efforts when I request you again." She bowed deeply as he returned the cloth, murmuring something in Chinese that he took to be a blessing on his magnificence and kindness.

Kim took his leave of her company, his feelings somewhat mixed. She was as much a prisoner as he. Previously, he would not have given much thought to the woman's feelings about his satisfaction with her ministrations—she was, after all, simply doing her job—but here in the camp, they were both trophies belonging to Onghwe Khan. Their shared desire to survive made them compatriots, reliant on one another for basic reminders of their humanity. It was as Zug kept reminding him: how long could they hold out hope of ever being free again, and how much would they have to sacrifice to be so once more?

The guards at the gate were clustered around a runner, a man who had come from outside the Mongol compound. As Kim strolled closer, the runner was waved through the cordon of armed Mongols. One of the guards pointed in his general direction—not *at* him, but at the sprawl of tents behind him where the men charged with watching Onghwe's fighters resided—and Kim came to a stop.

The runner came across the compound, and Kim trailed after him like a scavenger following a predator about to make a kill. The man had news of what was going on at First Field, he sensed.

Tegusgal was not available, and so the runner breathlessly gave his report to Tegusgal's second, a large man whose name was Ashiq-temür. It meant "iron helmet," and while he had probably been given the name as some sort of ancestral reference, he had truly grown into the name. His girth was mainly due to a bulbous paunch that covered a once-muscular frame; he had no hair, and the skin at the base of his skull was rolled and lumpy with fat. Tegusgal was quick-witted and shrewd; Ashiq-temür was short-tempered and eager to dispense discipline with his hands or with a stout stick.

"A Frank has come to the First Field," the messenger reported. "He raised his standard and issued an open challenge to any man who would dare face him. He's knocked down five men already, and he's started shouting that the Khan has no worthy champions."

Ashiq-temür, seated on a broad divan, was unmoved by the news. "Let him shout," he grunted. He idly scratched his broad belly. "The Khan will not answer to the demands of a barbarian fighter." He waved the runner away.

A Frank! Kim stepped forward, thrilled by the possibility that this fighter was a Rose Knight. "Forgive my impertinent interruption, Master," he said, bowing low to his fat jailor, "but I could not help overhear this conversation, and while I see that you speak with the utmost reverence of our most illustrious Khan, might I offer my services?" Tegusgal was the shrewd one, this argument would never work with him, but Ashiq-temür was more easily swayed. His head was thick, after all; there couldn't be much room for a brain.

"What do you want, Kim?" Ashiq-temür asked. He spoke familiarly, as if Kim were nothing more than a servant or a house pet. It was a tone Kim had grown inured to, and he no longer bristled at the man's insulting tone. If anything, the man's disdain only increased Kim's desire to convince his jailor of his plan.

"This Frank is a loud-mouthed upstart, and I have no doubt that his prowess is unworthy of the Khan's attention. Perhaps I could go to the field and engage him." Kim indicated his face, thankful now that the masseuse had not had a chance to fully work the salve into his bruises. "Look at me. I am ugly and malformed. I cannot possibly be a shining champion of the Khan's magnificent collection of fighting men. Am I not the appropriate response to this man's brazen challenge?"

"What if he beats you?"

Kim smiled. "Would I give you the satisfaction of seeing that?"

Ashiq-temür brayed with laughter. "Your arrogance always amuses me, Kim. I will raise a cup in sorrow on the day when it is whipped out of you." He waved over a pair of nearby guards. "Escort this foolish dog to First Field. We apparently didn't beat him enough. Let the Frank do it for us for a while, and then bring him back."

CHAPTER 18:

TO THE PLACE OF THE CLIFF

His mouth against the nape of her neck, Gansukh let his hands slide down Lian's narrow frame to the swell of her hips. He knew he shouldn't be doing this. Not in the narrow alley behind the north storehouse. It was too public; they could be discovered at any time. *Too dangerous.*

Lian pulled his head up and crushed her mouth to his, silencing his mutterings. She leaned back against the shadowed wall of the storehouse, thrusting her pelvis out. He gripped her more tightly as her body pushed against him. He should have let go; he knew he shouldn't be encouraging this behavior, but at the same time, it was exactly how he had imagined it. *No. Not here. Not like this.*

She grabbed one of his wrists and moved his hand around to her backside. Her tongue flicked against his lips, and when he tried to catch it, it curled into his mouth and danced across the tips of his teeth. He moved his other hand too, and giving in to his desires, he lifted her up and shoved her against the wall.

She gasped slightly, turning her surprise into a moan of pleasure, and her legs parted. As he was supporting her weight, she closed her legs around him. Underneath her long tunic, she was wearing thick woolen pants—riding attire—and he ground himself against her in frustration. Too much clothing; so little time. He was wearing leather leggings himself, and while he was well practiced at pulling aside his silk undergarments so that he could piss from the saddle, he found himself fumbling with them now. But even if he could, he still had to get her clothes off too.

Releasing her, he dropped to his knees. He roughly pushed her tunic up, feeling the soft and warm skin of her belly. She growled, deep in her throat, and he felt her stomach rippling beneath his hands. Gripping his hair with both hands, she pulled his face to her, and he licked her belly hungrily as his fingers pulled and tugged at her pants. His right hand began to explore between her legs, pressing at her through the cloth, and she lifted her left leg over his right shoulder. He could smell her now, and his need was overwhelming.

He pulled at the knots of his riding leggings, frustrated at his inability to get the cursed garments off. His desire was evident beneath his fumbling hand, and just as he freed himself, she froze. Her fingers were stiff in his hair, holding him immobile.

He tried to quiet his ragged breathing. She wasn't moving. Was someone coming? If so, then they couldn't be caught in this position. They weren't hidden. He strained against her hands, trying to look around, but she let out a tiny hiss of air and held him tight.

He shrugged her leg off his shoulder and pulled her hands away from his head. He glanced around and saw no one in the alley. The buzz of voices from the main courtyard was the same constant din in the background, and he strained to hear the noise that had startled her. A voice, footsteps, the tiny scrape of metal against metal—anything to indicate they were in danger of imminent discovery.

Lian adjusted her pants and smoothed down her tunic. Her breathing eased as she ran her hands through her hair, combing the errant wisps back into a single black cascade. Her face and neck were still flushed, and Gansukh thought about putting his hands on her again. Finishing what they had started...

She read his desire plainly in his eyes and stepped forward, her face close to his. Her hands dropped to his waist, and he gasped slightly as she took his softening hardness in her hands. Her lips brushed his as she tucked him back into his pants. "The third night," she whispered. "There isn't time now. Let us find each other on the third night after we leave Karakorum. We can take as long as we want."

Gansukh groaned softly, but relented. She was right. Whatever they had started to do in the alley would have been over too quickly. As hard as it was to wait, it would be better. He nodded, and she kissed him fiercely once more and then slipped out of his embrace.

"I'll go first," she said as she glanced around for the satchel she had been carrying when they had met outside the alley and she had dragged him into the midmorning shadows. She spotted the bag, and as she grabbed it by its shoulder strap, a blue silk pouch fell out, hitting the ground with a *clink.* Gansukh picked it up, and he felt its weight and how its contents shifted.

He had divided up the spoils of a conquest enough times to instinctively know what was in the purse.

She was avoiding his gaze, and he hesitated to offer the purse back. He wasn't going to give it up so readily. Not until she looked at him.

She raised her eyes and met his gaze, and he was startled by the mixture of fear and defiance he saw. Her face softened, and he saw something else—a quiet desperation that made his chest tighten.

She needed him.

"We have to go," she said, tugging the purse of coins and jewelry out of his slack hand. She stowed it carefully in her bag and then paused, pushing her hair back behind her ears. She wanted to say something else, and he waited for her to speak, but she changed her mind and flashed him a hopeful smile instead.

Clutching her bag tightly, she strode away, heading toward the crowded courtyard.

He watched her go, lost in thought.

◆◆◆

"Have you seen Gansukh?"

The question frightened Lian. Not because she hadn't seen Master Chucai approach, but for a moment, she panicked, terrified that he knew everything. He had seen them in the alley; he knew what was in the bag she held so protectively. "N…no, no," she stammered. She had been walking alongside the mounted ranks of the Imperial Guard, her head down and eyes averted from the ranks of bored warriors. Trying to be as invisible as possible. "Not since yesterday," she added, trying to shove aside all the memories of the encounter in the alley that were still scampering around in her head. "If I see him," she said, getting herself under more control, "I will tell him you are looking for him." She bowed slightly and made to continue walking.

"Wait." Chucai had her pinned with his unwavering stare, as if he could—by force of his will—read all her secrets. He came to within half a pace and shifted his piercing gaze to the bag in her hands. "I thought we had loaded all of your—"

"Lian!" Gansukh strode up behind Chucai, an angry expression furrowing his brow. "There you are."

Flustered, and not entirely sure why but thankful for the confusion nonetheless, Lian bowed toward the young warrior. "Gansukh," she said, indicating Chucai. "Master Chucai was looking for you."

Gansukh glanced at the *Khagan*'s tall advisor for a second before returning his attention to her. "And I've been looking for you," he said. He pointed at the bag she was carrying. "More lessons on how to act?" he asked. "Aren't we done with all that?"

Lian risked a glance at Chucai and shook her head. "Are you ever done learning how to hunt?" she snapped, suddenly finding herself on much more secure footing. "I told you we would continue going over the lessons until you had mastered them as well as you have the bow." She stamped her foot. "Did you think you could escape me on the steppe?"

"I was really looking forward to staring up at the stars," Gansukh groused, "instead of having my face buried in lessons on courtly manners." He shot Chucai a pleading look, but the tall man only shrugged and stroked his beard. With a heavy sigh, Gansukh reached for Lian's bag, which she handed over without hesitation. "This is never going to end," he snorted as he slung the bag over his shoulder.

"Soon," Chucai assured him. "It will end soon enough." His gaze relented, though Lian was not convinced Chucai's disinterest was entirely genuine.

Gansukh grunted and glanced around at the ranks of Imperial Guard. "Are we ever going to actually leave?" he asked.

"That all depends on the will of the *Khagan*," Chucai said, and Lian bowed her head, a devotional acknowledgment of the *Khagan*'s magnificent being. "We are ready, though, so as soon as he desires to leave for Burqan-qaldun, we shall."

Gansukh nodded smartly. "Good. I am looking forward to getting out of this stifling palace and sleeping under the open sky again." He thumped a fist against the bag, and Lian tried very hard not to flinch, anticipating some sound from the purse of jewelry and coins. "I will not let these become my prison. I am a free man."

He inclined his head to both of them and wandered off. Chucai and Lian watched as Gansukh and the bag disappeared into the crowd in the direction of the *Khagan*'s *ger*. His stride was exaggerated, and he swaggered slightly, as if he had just won a wrestling match.

"Horse boy," Lian chirped. Privately, she wanted to run after him and kiss him—a fierce urge flushing through her blood, the encounter in the alley still fresh in her mind and body. But to openly expose herself in that way would be to destroy the illusion they were attempting to weave for Chucai. If they had even been successful in doing so—Chucai's bland expression made it hard to tell.

"He has learned much about life at court, hasn't he?" Chucai noted. "But for all of our help, he's still a nomad of the steppes." He waved a hand toward the palace walls. "Out there, it's his world."

Lian gave Chucai one of her alluring yet aloof smiles, hoping he would misread her expression as being disdainful of having to credit Gansukh with any intelligence whatsoever.

Secretly, she was counting on it. He had come to her aid so quickly and so effortlessly. *Would it be that easy?*

◆◆◆

Toregene blocked the inner door to Ögedei Khan's quarters, barking orders at anyone who dared to come within earshot—servants, guards, the other wives. Ögedei slumped on an enormous chair near the center of the room. Absently, he toyed with a large bone-handled knife in a leather sheath, oblivious to the chaos around him. Occasionally, a servant would wander close, intending to ask for the *Khagan*'s guidance on the disposition of a piece of furniture or of some robes, but the *Khagan* only grunted inconclusively—if he answered at all. Toregene would quickly snap at the confused servants, sending them scurrying away, smarting from the lash of her tongue.

Ögedei was ready to leave Karakorum. She could sense his indifference was born from frustration. He knew all the preparations were necessary, that to hurry them would only cause them to take longer, but all he yearned for was to begin the long journey to Burqan-qaldun. The *Khagan*, like most men, did not like to wait. It was a trait his father had truly mastered; unfortunately, it had not been passed on to any of his sons.

"We are leaving," she announced in a shrill voice. "If it cannot be readied by the time the *Khagan* leaves this room, it stays here." After a moment of shocked silence, the servants and other wives exploded into a frenzy of activity as they frantically tried to stuff more items into already overstuffed trunks.

Ögedei was looking at her, a small smile playing across his lips. He waved her over, and she crossed the room to sit at his feet, tucking her legs beneath her.

"What would I do without you?" he asked.

Her smile was genuine. "Thankfully, it is a question that will never be answered, my Khan. I am yours now and forever."

Ögedei nodded; then his smile faded. "My wife, I must ask a favor of you."

Toregene turned to face her husband more fully. "Anything, my Khan."

"I want you to stay here."

"What?" She stared at him, unable to fathom the reason for his request. She was First Wife. She was his woman; she was always at his side. That was her right. Why would he not take her with him? His face was impassive; if he suffered any qualms about his request, they did not show.

It is not a request.

"Of…of course, my Khan," she murmured, dropping her gaze. She put her hand on his knee for a moment, and when he did not move, she let it slip off. "If this is what you want," she tried. "If…if this is your wish."

Out of the corner of her eye, Toregene saw that all activity in the room had ceased. The servants were trying to hide behind the trunks they were hauling from the room. The other wives had lost all interest in their final, desperate flurry of packing; Jachin was openly staring at Ögedei and Toregene, and she made no effort to hide her glee.

Toregene couldn't imagine what offense she had given the *Khagan*. She tried to calm her thoughts, but Jachin's delight was only making her angrier.

"Toregene," Ögedei rumbled. He rested his hand on her head, stroking her hair, and his touch quieted some of her anger. "You are First Wife," he said, "and there is no one I would rather have as the head of my household." She leaned against his hand, grasping his arm so that he would not stop touching her hair. He raised his voice so that everyone in the room would hear his words. "I *must* go on this hunt, and to be successful, I must be able to concentrate. If I have to worry about—"

"You will not have to worry about me," Toregene interrupted. She hadn't meant to beg, but the thought of being passed over for Jachin was still too much to bear. "I will be like a shadow at midday. I will—"

He put his hand over her face, his fingers pressing against her mouth. "I need you to stay," he said. "Someone must watch over my affairs. Someone I can trust."

Behind her, Jachin gasped, and Toregene blinked heavily as her vision swam. She sagged as he removed his hand, and she tried to steady herself. "My Khan…" she began, but he was no longer sitting in the chair.

His hand resting on the hilt of his father's knife, Ögedei strode toward the door. "To the hunt," he cried, and all activity in the room resumed. Guards opened the door as the *Khagan* approached, and the remaining servants, tottering under overflowing bags, scampered after him.

Toregene caught sight of Jachin's face as she followed the *Khagan.* Second Wife was still trying to decide if she should be elated or furious, and Toregene gave her no satisfaction either way. She remained slumped over, her body quivering, until the wives and their servants were gone.

She sat upright and waved over one of the remaining guards. "Find my son," she said.

"I'm sure he's with the caravan," the guard replied.

"Find him," she snapped. "And his bags." When the guard hesitated, she explained her desire more plainly. "He isn't going. If I stay, so does he."

The guard nodded and, taking another man with him, departed to find Guyuk.

Toregene smoothed her hair back, running her fingers along the ribbons woven into the thick braids. Her blood was still racing, and her hands shook slightly as she worked. Her mind was no longer frozen in shock; in fact, it felt like there was a river in her head. Her thoughts raced and leaped like a torrent of fresh mountain water, released from the cold captivity of winter.

The *Khagan* had left her in charge. If he didn't come back…

"Guyuk," she whispered. *My son. The* Khagan*'s son.*

None of Genghis's progeny had enough patience. Not like she did.

✦✦✦

Master Chucai met Ögedei as he emerged from the palace. His tall advisor bowed deeply, acknowledging the significance of Ögedei's appearance this morning. The *Khagan* had left his palace, and as soon as he climbed aboard his magnificent wheeled *ger,* he would be leaving Karakorum. "The sun shines brightly this morning, O great *Khagan,*" Chucai said. "It is an auspicious day to begin your journey."

Ögedei nodded absently as he looked out over the assembled caravan. Hundreds of carts and wagons and wheeled tents, thousands of horses, his Imperial Guard, many of his courtiers, and a host of merchants, craftsmen, and nomadic camp followers—all ready to chase after him to the place where the Blue Wolf had lain with the Fallow Doe, the sacred grove where the Mongol race had been born and where his father had been buried. Where he must go to face his destiny. *This is my empire,* he thought, and even though the sun was warm on his face and chest, he shivered slightly. *They will follow me anywhere.*

"Everything is prepared, my Khan," Chucai reminded him. "We are ready to leave at your command."

"It is time," Ögedei said. Chucai nodded, but when no one else seemed to react to his words, he raised his voice to address the entire host. "I am Ögedei, son of Genghis, *Khagan,*" he bellowed, "and I go to Burqan-qaldun, the Place of the Cliff."

He strode down the steps from the palace as the host cheered, and while the roaring sound stunned him, he kept moving. His gait faltered as he approached the seething press of bodies, but they parted before him, opening a path to the wooden steps that had been placed beside his mobile tent. He strode through the gap, buffeted by hands that grasped and pressed against him. He kept his gaze forward and his expression fixed in what he hoped was an appropriately grim scowl. The noise was overwhelming and showed no sign of weakening. He found himself wondering if this was akin to being buried in sand or what it was like to drown in a raging river.

At the top of the steps, two attendants held open the flaps on the *ger,* and he ducked through the opening. The attendants dropped the flaps behind him, and he paused to let his eyes adjust to the dim light inside. The heavy hide of the tent blocked the bulk of the cheering and shouting outside.

The *ger* had been arranged as a replica of his rooms in the palace. Half a dozen people waited to serve him. A fire crackled in a large stone-lined pit, and Ögedei could hear and smell meat cooking. Animal furs lined the floor, and at the back of the *ger* stood his great chair from the main hall in the palace. Borakchin and Mukha lounged on low couches near his chair; they were dressed as if for a court dinner, and the gold threads in their gowns glittered in the candlelight. On his right, Mukha's favorite entertainers, a troop of Chinese acrobats, were juggling a dizzying number of colored balls.

"This is not how my father hunted," Ögedei sighed.

The floor lurched beneath him and then began to rock gently as the *ger*'s driver got the team of oxen moving.

CHAPTER 19:

GRAVE GRAVATAE

Ferenc had willingly followed Ocyrhoe through the city, had even let her hold his hand as they walked, as if they were young lovers; in the passing throngs, they risked being separated, and she was concerned that the wide-eyed country boy could be carried away in the current of people. The initial fear he had expressed about standing out as clearly Other was soothed within a quarter hour, once she showed him that half the city was made of people from foreign lands: priests, pilgrims, merchants, and travelers of all hues and costumes.

Eventually, Ocyrhoe turned them from a major thoroughfare down a smaller, almost empty side street. They followed this, unpaved and dusty, for the length of a bowshot. The buildings to either side were stone and old; they were not decorated and had few, if any, windows. She turned again into a narrow alley to the right, between two high buildings with no windows at all. It was cool in here; the sun never peeked between those walls except perhaps at noon in high summer, and then briefly.

The alley dead-ended where the buildings did, against a third building. It was like being in a deep, deep canyon: a narrow slot of sky above, shadow below, and no escape except back the way they'd come. There were no doors, no smaller alleys, nothing. Ocyrhoe approached the crumbling stone and brick of the dead-end wall and began to examine it, as if for cracks. After a few fruitless moments, she turned and faced Ferenc expectantly. He gave her a blank, confused look and shook his head.

Ocyrhoe was sure she had explained this to him in the outpouring of their first "conversation," when they suddenly realized they could communicate through the silent language she had learned from her kin-sisters, and known to them in some ancient tongue as *Rankos Kalba,* or *Rankalba.* She was still confused that he, a male, could know this code, but there was no time to wonder about that now.

Perhaps he had not really understood what she'd said before. Admittedly, she had simplified it; it would be exhausting and very time-consuming to try to explain the Septizodium and the elections and Orsini and Fieschi and too many other things. She sent a silent prayer to the Bind-Mother. *Oh, please, let him understand me.*

She slapped the cool stone wall, then took Ferenc's wrists and tapped her fingers on the bony flesh in alternating singles, pairs, threes, fours, *grip,* then three, then one, and so on—variations signing out the basic message, as if she were leaving notches in a long piece of wood or on a cornice, or tying knots in a cord or her own hair: "Fatherrodrigo is inside. Prisoner." Ferenc blinked, then nodded. "Many rooms, in many buildings," she continued. "Different rooms with tunnels connecting all. We are close. We must get in." She noticed confusion in Ferenc's expression. *Too fast,* she thought. *Whoever taught him* Rankalba *didn't finish the lesson.* "Understand?" she asked, signing more slowly against his inner arm and wrist.

He mused on that for a moment, then nodded, though his expression suggested he was still unsure. She chewed her lower lip, looked up, then down, then decided to try drawing a map on the dust of the ground. She held out her hand. "*Pugio*?" she asked, using the Latin word. At his blank look, she mimed holding the weapon and stabbing the air with it, then again held out her hand.

"*Pugio*," he said, and he repeated it once more as he gave her his knife. He was, she realized, learning the Latin word.

In the dirt of the alley, Ocyrhoe crouched and drew a bird's-eye view of this alley and the immediate surrounding streets and buildings. She placed the facade of the Septizodium in the center of it and then drew the surrounding structures; these she knew by rumor were connected via tunnels, but after she drew in the streets, she was not sure how to designate tunnels. When she was finished, she looked up at him. "*Mappa*?" she said, again using the Latin word.

He nodded agreeably as he squatted next to her. She made a little *X* on the map beside one of the scratched-in buildings. "FerencOcyrhoe," she declared, pointing to it. She patted the stone wall again, then etched in deeper the line representing it on the map.

Ferenc nodded. He pointed, on the map, to the interior of the building. "Father Rodrigo?" he said.

Ocyrhoe touched his wrist. "Maybe," she squeezed, then shook her head. It would take far too long to explain that the Septizodium was a temple that wasn't really a temple, just an ornamental wall on an otherwise nondescript building. Instead, she pointed to various other buildings on the map, each time signing "maybe here," until Ferenc nodded that he understood: the priest was somewhere nearby, and they had to find him.

"Hidden door," Ocyrhoe added, and then he understood why she had been staring at the wall when they first came here. He stood up, anxious to continue their search, but she shook her head and pulled his arm to return his attention to her crude map.

"Priest," she said, pointing to each of the smaller buildings in turn. "Priest, priest, priest, priest, priest."

Ferenc's eyes popped wide open. He babbled something in his native tongue and then, grabbing her wrist, hesitatingly fingered out, "More. More. And more." He frowned, then firmly amended, "*Many.* Prisoners?" Rendering a question in *Rankalba* was not easy. She took his point by the lifting of his brows and general plaintive expression.

Ocyrhoe nodded. "Many prisoners," she signed. It wasn't quite accurate, but at least it gave him a vague understanding of what they were up against. He blinked and held his hands out wide, shrugging—a universal gesture of confusion, wanting to understand, not knowing. Ocyrhoe winced. There was no time to explain to him who Senator Orsini was or that he was keeping the cardinals captive until they voted in a new Pope. Even if she could somehow find a simple way to tell him, it would not help him understand her plan to reach his companion.

Not that she really had a plan to reach Father Rodrigo. Just an idea. And probably a very feeble one.

Ferenc patted her arm to get her attention and made a brushing-aside gesture; the bevy of imprisoned priests could await explanation. "Father Rodrigo," he said gently.

She nodded, relieved that he was willing to stay focused on the task at hand, without a lot of explanation. When he stood this time, she let him.

Ferenc patted the wall and imitated what she had been doing earlier: searching out a secret door. He glanced at her; she nodded. He began to scan the wall himself, one cheek pressed against it as he pressed the opposite hand in front of him against the stone, examining. He did this for about as long as it might take to cross through the green market at midday. Then he shook his head and stepped away from the wall.

He held his hand out, and Ocyrhoe offered her wrist. "Not here. Look other walls," he signaled. It was slow and awkward; he lacked her fluidity in gesture and movement, but he clearly understood what had to happen. "Where look now?" he asked.

She pursed her lips and, after a moment, pointed toward two other places on the map. He sat beside her again and followed her finger. "Underground," she signed, trying to communicate the idea that all these buildings were connected by underground tunnels.

Ferenc nodded. "Like rabbits," he signed.

She offered him a tiny smile. Perhaps it was better that he didn't know the full extent of the task before him. He had a simple determination about him. It wasn't that he was feeble or slow minded, but that he didn't worry about anything else.

She led him out of the alley, back into the beating heat, and into another alley on the far side of the main road. She was sure it was from one of these two alleys that Fieschi must have escaped the maze of rooms and tunnels, but the actual egress remained a mystery.

Ferenc's patience, she realized, was exactly the sort of trait required to find a hidden door in a featureless stone wall. The cracks, even under her careful prodding, would have seemed to be nothing but cracks to her. Ferenc's hand somehow recognized them as something else. He pushed in one spot; nothing happened. He moved half a pace to his left and pushed another spot.

Suddenly, and with an eerie silence, an entire arm's-width slab of the wall moved, pivoting under his touch; the musty smell of subterranean air hit her nose.

✦✦✦

Some part of Rodrigo knew he had fallen into nightmare again, that he had slipped away from the real world. He knew there was no hope in trying to run from what was to come, even though it was to worse to relive it, over and over again, knowing what would come, than to have lived through it the first time. He knew he had to suffer the nightmare. That was part of his trial, part of his burden.

He sat on the mud-caked rim of an upended wagon wheel and looked out over what had been, just weeks before, a thriving village. The river had supplied fish; nearby fields had supplied corn; gardens around the farmsteads had brought in root vegetables of all sorts. Honey merchants had catered their sweet clay jars to mercenaries hired by King Béla massing on the drier margins of the muddy fields, excluded by their lowly status from Béla's fortified camp, grumbling as they paid for food, mead, beer—grumbling more as they moved their own makeshift settlements away from the advancing river. The marshes had swarmed with biting gnats and flies, like white-hot lancets as they supped, as now they swarmed with carrion flies. Even before the battle, to Rodrigo, it seemed Hell itself held no match.

The battle had been another kind of flood, this one comprised of blood and disintegrating humanity. He could not recall all the logistics and the plans, the victorious sweep across the bridge, the later repulse and encirclement, the fleeing of selected units, followed by rains of stones, exploding pots, arrows. The screaming of the horses and men, confusion, escape, and then the endless press of the Mongols plowing into the roiling flocks of disheartened mercenaries, having already dispatched many of the main ranks of Teutonic

Knights in their white riding coats emblazoned with black crosses—the flowing banners weaving back and forth through the slaughter, some ablaze, others leaning, vanishing to be trampled into the bloody muck as the standard bearers fell victim to an arrow or a saber. Mongol raiders plunging in and out, shouting and grinning and sweeping their sabers as the soldiers of Béla and Archbishop Csák tried to flee the burning, bombarded fortifications—dying by the hundreds on the ramparts, dozens of riders and horses at a time knocked over by flying, bouncing, cart-wheel-size stones. Or being caught in the fiery wash of those smoking, blazing, exploding jars that fell along with the stones.

So many dead. Vultures wheeling overhead were not the only beneficiaries. During the day, the fields of battle hosted thousands of darting, swooping swallows, feasting on the flies that, in turn, plagued both living and dead. And at night came the bats, leathery wings whispering through the fetid air, feasting on mosquitoes that had the grace to plague only the living.

Rodrigo remembered his own attempted flight as a series of vignettes, one horse after another dying beneath him of wounds or exhaustion, then on foot, wearily avoiding the clusters of fleeing knights—many having shed their armor and crosses, stumbling as fast as they could through the carnage, heading south and west, where they would loot farms and murder farmers and their families and servants in panicked desperation.

How different were the knights from the Mongols? Little different, in practice. Even before the battle, or in their brief days of victory, they had drunk deep and sallied forth from the fortress and their shifting lines of tent camps to rape villagers' wives and daughters, even aging crones. In defeat, they returned to rape and then kill, loot and then burn, practicing the last desperation of destroying the land so that the

Mongols themselves would have no benefit. The knights of the black cross had turned on their own with a ferocity that shook Rodrigo's faith and overturned all his youthful views of righteous Crusades, Christian good, and Mongol evil.

The savagery proved, to Rodrigo, the end of human civilization. No emotion, no interaction between two living people, could ever mean anything real now; it was all a feint, a gauzy veil of deceitful civility over the true color and timbre of mankind, which was becoming unadulterated evil. There was nothing decent or good or truly Christian left under the sun. The stink of hellfire spewed up from narrow fissures in the earth. Even if he could have died, Hell would not have taken him; there were worse torments, and they would come seeking him.

He rose from the wagon wheel now and stumbled through the mud, retching, trying to tear away his clothes, which sickened him with their filth, but he was too weak even to manage that. The rain was torrential. If he could inhale mud, that might quench the fire of his lungs, his heart, his liver. The mud was the only simple thing left, and now even that was running with the blood of infidels and Christians alike. No, it was all the blood of infidels; there were no Christians left. He was the only Christian left at Mohi, and if he did not turn the tides of fate, he would be the only Christian left anywhere on earth.

He trudged on blindly, no idea where he was going. Despite the pain and the exhaustion, his soul was in such a panic that he needed to keep walking; he would have run, but the mud sucked at his feet and ankles.

A battlefield is never silent, even when the battle has been decided. The sounds of the dying men and horses, the cries of the carrion birds circling and then settling, and here, the sound of rain. But somehow, through all these noises, Rodrigo heard a single human voice cry out plaintively to him: "Holy man, help me." That was all it said.

He stopped and turned automatically in the direction of the voice, as if compelled by an invisible force. Among the piles of corpses he did not see any sign of life. *Oh God, there was a boy, alive.* A local youth, not a soldier. He recognized him. *Ferenc,* that was his name. Ferenc. He was from Buda, survived as a hunter. His mother had been a wisewoman, an herbalist, a healer.

Just after the battle, two days or so ago, Rodrigo had held Ferenc back, with a strength now almost gone, and the boy had tried to fight him off, to throw himself at a group of six Mongols who were taking turns raping Ferenc's bloodied, dying mother. Two eternal sunrises ago, Rodrigo had had the strength to wrestle with the boy and drag him away from the horror, into the shelter of some battered bushes and behind a wolf-chewed horse. Somehow Rodrigo had managed to pin the boy to the ground until the atrocities were over. The woman was dead; the attackers had moved on. Then he had allowed Ferenc to shove and kick him away, even punch him. Fallen back on the mud and filth, he had watched the boy run to his mother's corpse.

That was the last he'd seen of Ferenc until this moment.

The boy lay face up, pinned between a layer of mangled dead and a single Mongol. One of the corpse's eyes stared without interest at the wheeling birds above; the other was gone, gouged out by a knife. The boy was pale and still, his breathing labored.

Rodrigo stared at him for a moment, working idly through what he could do, what he could not do, making the gray, soulless calculations of a weary, overburdened man.

It would be best for the boy, he finally decided, to die now, to escape from current and future misery. Before the gates of Heaven slammed closed against this entire generation of human beings, perhaps young Ferenc would be allowed to enter. Even if those gates slammed in his face, and he spent eternity in Purgatory, that would be infinitely better than what awaited him here on Earth.

Rodrigo closed his eyes and began to turn away. But then he heard a whisper, cool and certain. He looked over his shoulder, wondering if the boy had spoken, but no, Ferenc was simply watching him, the fingers of one hand slowly opening and closing—listless, resigned.

A sensation at once warm and chill came next, and Rodrigo reached back to feel at his cloak and shirt, wondering if blood was seeping from an unknown wound, if his spine had been pierced. No, he was sound enough—no arrow, no unexpected gash.

He turned slowly again, eyes leveling with the distant horizon, words of impossible greeting frozen on his lips.

What came next staggered him. He lurched across the field and nearly fell over another tangle of corpses. The sky blinded him. The cascade of light was without color, without depth, but not without sound: in the middle of his searing vision, that unexpected blinding brightness, millions of unvoiced words hollered and echoed through his mind, speaking of infinities, impossibilities, revealing all the truths in the forms of endlessly detailed wheels of entities, histories, implications, connections—sucking his soul up and out like whirlpools.

Rodrigo's knees gave way, and he fell. For a time, he forgot everything and felt nothing, not the mud on his hands or knees, not the rain on his head and back, not the diminishing sounds of the battlefield. His relief was as intense as his confusion; here at last was divine rescue from all the gruesome realities around him, all the unsolvable dilemmas of his life.

Then, in the place of here and now, doors opened, and through those doors he saw vistas limned in infinite detail with grim and gorgeous details. The images rearranged and merged, and now he saw all too clearly how the world might end, all life and hope and sin and travail ground away by more spinning wheels of history, infinite clouds of implication and fiery storms of devilish conspiracy, and it was worse than anything any prophet of doom had ever uttered. He was being filled with awful, sublime, eternal thoughts and teachings—and *instruction*! With a horrible, paralyzing clarity, Rodrigo understood he was being forced to *absorb* these commands, brutally but masterfully stuffed like a sausage with all the things he needed to understand, all the places he needed to be and acts he needed to make flesh—all that he had to do.

Then the flood slowed, became a trickle again, and vanished into the mud and ash of his physical body. He forced himself to open his eyes, forced himself to stand.

The wheels became dust motes, spinning up and away into the clouds. As if in exchange, a feather dropped from the sky, wafting back and forth before him, inches from his nose. Like a child, he reached up with filthy, callused fingers to grab it, study it—but it eluded him and landed at his feet.

The feather of a buzzard, not a dove.

Terrified, relieved, he was nevertheless grieving at a great loss—the loss of that connection, those truths, like the sudden damming of a great torrent. For a moment, he had been part of the timeless. Now, part of mastery and creation.

Once again, he was just a man, just mud and ash, no longer filled with lightning and sun.

But now he had things to do, and they lay before him in reasonably clear order, all decisions made. He turned back toward the boy. Rodrigo's eye fell again on that slowly clasping hand, the skinny body pinned forever beneath the all-seeing dead Mongol.

Rodrigo now needed human company the way he needed air to breathe. To be alone would be to remember his loss, and that he could hardly bear. Ferenc was the only soul he knew still living in Mohi.

He reached a hand toward the boy. "My salvation," he muttered, then looked away, face racked by a pained grimace, and tried to remember that this battlefield, these corpses, the boy himself, were all part of an extended dream, that he was not actually living it but merely being *reminded* of it—to sharpen his heretofore blunted purpose.

If he could look more closely at those wheels again, he might comprehend. But no matter. The wheels of vultures, the wheels of hungry swallows and bats, the fluttering, chanting wheels of angelic wings…

No different. No matter.

With all the empathy and sorrow and compassion and fury in the world printed on his soul, he understood how all of this must end. He understood, with a divine-wrought clarity that he thought was reserved only for saints, what needed to happen for this worldly evil to be stopped. He shuddered at the enormity of it. He wanted to hide from his own understanding. But there was no escape; he, Father Rodrigo Bendrito, a humble priest, *he* was the one assigned by the Lord to end this madness. He did not want this burden—his aversion to it was emotionally violent—but he had no choice but to surrender to it.

He would take the necessary wickedness, the awfulness, the blame, and the sin on his own shoulders, attempt however miserably to follow in the footsteps of the Lord; Rodrigo's suffering would be great, but it would be nothing compared to the suffering of Christ, and ultimately, this would all be in service to Him, whose nature Rodrigo alone now truly understood. The world was ending in fire, and soon. He knew it in his soul; it was more vivid to him than waking life: he could feel the heat, smell the scorching, hear the roar of it. The world was ending in fire, and he, and only he, was responsible for what must happen.

He could never tell anyone else about his vision. They would mock him, imprison him, torture him for a heretic. The very thought of confessing this moment shifted his nightmare away from Mohi and turned it instead to an inquisitor's dreaded chamber of smoke and heat and screws and steel. Implements of horrific construction surrounded him: some with ropes and pulleys, some with spikes, racks and presses and nooses and chains. A robed figure with long, bony hands reached for his arm, and as the stranger's cold flesh touched his, he screamed fiercely.

Memory and the hideous nightmare of his past merged in a shuddering rush with a higher awareness, a waking awareness of life and being. *Praise God.* He raised his head painfully and looked around, awake and drenched in sweat, his breath loud and raspy. A scorpion scuttled across the empty bed on the far side of the room and vanished into a crack between stone wall and stone floor. There was only one bed in this room—whose was that?

He raised his head in confusion, blinking as sweat from his scalp dripped into his eyes. Yes, he was in his own room, but in the hectic, unconscious thrash of his nightmare, he had actually dragged himself off his bed and into this cooler corner of the chamber. A wave of nausea overwhelmed him as he realized that scorpion could have been scuttling over him as he thrashed, and he would now be dying from the sting. Perhaps he had been stung, and that explained the memory of his vision. Perversely, he wanted to pull aside the plaster and stone and find that scorpion, poke it, taunt it to arch its awful dun-colored tail; death was welcome compared to the dread responsibility he'd been given by the furious, wheeling angels watching over him at Mohi.

He laid his head back on the stone floor. The scorpion was far less terrifying than the burden of his nightmare. Were there more scorpions in this room? In another? Did a scorpion's bite always mean death? Would a scorpion attack a human on instinct, or did it need to be provoked?

An older voice inside him—it sounded like the Archbishop, though Rodrigo knew that it wasn't—rebuked him. *Quoniam iniquitates meae supergressae sunt caput meum.* The burden of one's sins was a heavy weight to bear. *Grave gravatae,* he thought, remembering the next line of the Psalm. He had come to believe, over the course of the journey to Rome, that if he delivered his message, his prophecy, to the Pope, then he himself would be relieved of it, and he would have earned a peaceful death, in the city of his youth. All he wanted was rest. Surely the furious angels would let him rest once he had turned over his fearsome message to Christ's representative on Earth.

But Gregory was dead, and no one had been chosen to replace him, and that required Rodrigo to remain alive, the only soul who knew the future, the only one who knew what had to happen, what had to be done. God had killed Gregory to keep Rodrigo on the hook. He should have been honored and humbled that he was singled out for this momentous job, but he felt none of those emotions. He only felt hollow, as if Rodrigo the man was steadily being devoured by the burden.

All that remained was the burning fervor of the message.

CHAPTER 20:

A SIMPLE PLAN

During the night, Raphael feared that Vera—like Alena—was taking a turn for the worse. Her wounds seemed to be winning; her fever spiked, her skin grew pale and damp, and her eyes fluttered whenever she managed to come up out of a sleep very near to death itself. The change in Vera saddened Raphael greatly. He knew he should not allow himself to be so troubled by her condition. This was not the first bedside vigil he had kept, and he knew the danger of the bond that could be created between two people. Death was seldom just or predictable when it came to loved ones.

Still, he remained, renewing candles as they guttered and died, and fading in and out of his own napping reverie, but with a hand always on her wrist and another at her forehead. To his surprise, as night merged into early dawn, there came a scuffling noise before the door of the drafty old house—then, a mouse-gentle knock. Feronantus answered and led in a group of men and women—Khazars who lived in the neighborhood. They brought in two generous bowls draped with woven cloths and containing rich broth and gruel, which Raphael gratefully accepted. Feronantus thanked them for their help and led the curious group of five back to the door, managing to persuade them through signs that it was best if Vera was not disturbed.

Raphael found their visit remarkable. A much safer course would have been for the Khazars to turn them over to the Mongols, for Graymane's *jaghun* would not have stopped at the Volga. They likely had crossed at the nearest convenient ford and even now were hunting them, or else preparing another ambush.

Raphael fed broth in measured spoonfuls to the Shield-Maiden. Her lips opened, and by slow degrees, she consumed a third of the bowl, but when he tried some gruel, she swung her head aside and almost knocked the bowl from his hand—a sign he found encouraging. He put aside both bowls and resumed his vigil, until a thin shaft of sun through a far window struck his eye—and simultaneously, the woman stirred and spoke.

"Graymane's Mongols must have guessed our plan," Vera said. With his aid, she sat up, looked around with half-focused eyes, and then motioned with a raised hand not for broth this time, he determined, but gruel. "They scouted the ground and laid their ambush well." She ate sparingly of the pasty mixture, then turned her full attention to him. "I *thought* it was you. Always..."

Feronantus, straddling a stool beside the cot, folded his arms and looked at Raphael with a slight smile.

"It is my duty," Raphael said, and immediately felt awkward. Both Vera and Feronantus knew otherwise; straightforward and direct, she possessed neither the guiles nor the protections of Raphael's own civil manners.

"We changed course to avoid their first patrol and rode directly into a canyon with no exit," she continued. "We should have seen it coming, but they had already slain Sister Sofiya, our forward scout..." Her voice trailed off, and she devoted a few moments to staring dully into empty space—something she did whenever she spoke of her sisters who had fallen in battle.

Which now meant all of them, for during the early hours of the night, the red lines creeping up Alena's arm from her infected wound had reached her armpit and then, Raphael guessed, her heart. She had died in a series of backbreaking convulsions so terrible that Raphael knew he would replay them in nightmares for weeks to come. Lockjaw was not such a bad way to die if it affected only the muscles of the jaw; what horrified Raphael was its effect on the great sinews of the spine.

"The details are unimportant…I cannot recite them anyway without turning this conversation into a funeral mass… and that would last the whole day long," Vera finally said.

Feronantus and Percival exchanged a look. Raphael knew what they were thinking: *Good, the poor woman is coming around; she understands the danger and the need for haste.*

Vera took more broth and a little more gruel. Her face recovered some of its color, and her hands took up the wooden spoon so she could feed herself, but Raphael leaned in close so that she did not have to raise her voice to be heard.

"Rather than let ourselves be cut to pieces at the Mongols' leisure, we mounted a charge into what seemed the weakest part of their force," she said.

Raphael found himself wishing he could have been there to witness the foolish and beautiful glory of that charge.

"Once we made contact," she said, oblivious to his gaze, "we were able to cut our way through, killing perhaps a dozen. Escape to the west was impossible. They could retreat at will and shoot arrows at us. Only by confining them against the river could we fight at close quarters. So we continued making that way, losing Shield-Maidens one after another, and defeated all who stood between us and the water. It was an effective way—the only way—to inflict losses upon Mongols.

"But they were too many. In time, it became clear we would not be able to scatter them completely. The river, then, became our only hope. We broke through their line once more and made a leapfrogging retreat to a place where trees and shrubs grew dense along the bank. Toward the end...all became confused. There were six of us, then four..." Her eyes closed. "My Shield-Maidens submitted to the sword of a sister, who then cut her own throat, rather than be harried and tormented by prancing, grimacing Mongols."

She lay back and stared up at the ceiling. Bowl and spoon clattered to the floor before Raphael could catch them. "At the end, it was just Alena and me, concealed in the bushes. We stripped off our armor. Darkness came, a mercy. We slipped quietly into the Volga and swam. The current carried us miles downstream before we could cross and fetched us up near a village. The adventure that brought us from there to here would make for another interesting story, but—"

"But the only part of it that matters," Feronantus said, "is whether you were able to cover your traces. Graymane would have crossed the river at first light yesterday." He glanced toward a rude hole in the wall where a window had once stood. The pink light of dawn was warming to gold. The Mongols had been on this bank of the Volga for twenty-four hours. "His blood is up, and having gained the *Vor*, he is not the sort of man to release it until he has put us all in the ground."

"I would say we took reasonable precautions to cover our tracks," Vera said, "but we had to get bandages. Those we obtained from village women going down to the river in the morning to draw water and wash clothes. And so all depends on whether Graymane is interrogating those people."

"We must move as soon as you are able," Feronantus concluded.

"I will only delay you," Vera returned. "You must go without me."

"That is noble of you," Feronantus said, "but you are assuming that the Khazars will allow you to stay."

Here Feronantus was alluding to developments that Vera could not have known about.

Since the startling arrival of Vera and Alena yesterday afternoon, the behavior of the Khazars had been complicated enough to arouse Raphael's curiosity. No people could have been more hospitable in bringing all sorts of aid and succor to the wounded Shield-Maidens. But it would be a mistake to draw too many conclusions from this alone, for these were mountain tribesmen, and such people always extended hospitality toward guests. More telling had been the behavior of the rabbi, Aaron, and the merchant, Benjamin, with whom they had been talking when Vera and Alena had arrived. Aaron seemed greatly troubled by the news that the two wounded Shield-Maidens might have led a Mongol unit directly here. Which only proved that Aaron was an intelligent man.

No visible crack had yet appeared in his facade of hospitality, but his anxiety was obvious. To judge from the lights in the windows of his home, he had spent much of the night awake, talking to Benjamin, who, at first light, had begun making preparations to leave.

Finding himself somewhat useless for the time being—since Vera seemed on the mend and there was nothing to do in her case but wait—Raphael excused himself from the tumbledown house and strolled through the half-abandoned village to the more modest but better-maintained structure, less than a bowshot away, where Rabbi Aaron dwelled.

Benjamin was pacing about restlessly in the stable yard, keeping an eye on a pair of servants loading goods and luggage onto a short train of packhorses. Benjamin saw Raphael approaching, and guessed his intentions. But he was polite enough to begin the conversation by expressing condolences over the death of Alena and inquiring after the state of Vera's health.

They were speaking in the *lingua franca,* which Benjamin knew well. In his younger days, he had lived in Byzantium, and there had transacted a considerable amount of business with merchants from the great trading cities of Italy. Speaking it seemed to remind Benjamin of more pleasant and prosperous times, and so he and Raphael tended to use it instead of Hebrew.

At their introduction, Raphael had assessed Benjamin as too old and fat to accompany them on such adventures. At each subsequent encounter, however, he had lowered his estimate of the Khazar's age and finally saw that what he had at first taken for fat was just an uncommonly stocky build padded by heavy clothing. Benjamin had probably not yet reached the age of fifty. He carried himself well and was as capable as any man of undertaking the journey they now contemplated.

Raphael badly wanted not to lose him.

"You could be thinking," Raphael ventured, with a nod toward the packhorses, "that the obvious attractions of doing business with us might not make up for being hunted across the steppe by a force of joyless Mongols."

Benjamin did not laugh—he was far too reserved and formal for that—but he did reveal a bare trace of dry amusement. "Perhaps if we knew each other better," he said, "I would be willing to partner under such ominous circumstances. Or perhaps, if I could make any kind of sense out of your errand…

I would find some way to align our interests. But neither condition pertains."

Before Raphael could respond, they were interrupted by the voice of Percival, rising over the wooden fence that surrounded the stable yard. He was but a few yards away.

"Allow me to help settle both matters with a few words," he said. A moment later, he appeared in the gate and entered the yard.

Reacting to the annoyance on Raphael's face, Percival continued. "I was following Cnán—not eavesdropping. But I'm afraid I've lost her."

"What is she up to?" Raphael asked, with a glance at Benjamin.

"At the end of Vera's narration, she slipped away."

"I was unaware of that."

"As no doubt she intended. But I was not so distracted and happened to catch sight of her borrowing one of our ponies."

"Or stealing it."

"No, she will return," Percival said, with that placid confidence which alternately fascinated and infuriated Raphael.

During the side conversation about Cnán, the Shield-Brethren had veered into Latin, and Benjamin might have understood a few words. But Benjamin was not interested in Cnán. He was far more intrigued by Percival's first remark.

"What did you mean," Benjamin said, returning to the *lingua franca*, "when you spoke of *settling* both matters with a few words?"

"In order that you should better know us and see how our interests align, it is simplest for me to tell you what we are doing," Percival said.

Raphael naturally assumed that Percival had come up, on the spur of the moment, with some clever stratagem. The Frank was going to tell Benjamin some plausible-sounding cock-and-bull story about their errand, innocuous enough to assuage all the Khazars' fears.

And so it was with a light heart and giddy expectation of quick success that Raphael now rounded up Feronantus and Rabbi Aaron and got them all together in the latter's little house, with Percival standing before them, ready to spring his clever tale.

As soon as Percival opened his mouth, however, Raphael saw it had been a terrible mistake. He knew this even before Percival uttered a word. He knew it because of the look on Percival's face: the utterly open, childlike guilelessness—and that weird effulgence that surrounded him whenever he was seized by whatever angel or demon took delight in toying with him.

"Weeks ago, I had a vision," Percival announced, "that we should set our course for Kiev, where we would find something of inestimable value, without which our quest was doomed."

Benjamin shifted and threw Raphael an irritable look. His instincts were clearly telling him to run away. The packhorses were neighing restlessly in the stable yard. Yet here they were, trapped in a conversation with a Frank who suffered from supernatural visions.

Feronantus had little choice but to play the role of the dignified leader and see this through as if he had expected it all along.

All unaware of this prickly dynamic, Percival continued. "I assumed, at first, that this benison would be some sort of holy relic. And when Vera told us of the tunnels and catacombs below the city, filled with treasures, I naturally assumed that what I sought would be found there. Instead, we uncovered nothing but a few odds and ends, and I lost my best friend in battle."

Percival's face darkened—literally. The effulgence took on a grayish hue, which Raphael observed with both alarm and deep curiosity. He threw a glance at Benjamin, who had cocked his head to one side, mouth open a little, eyes searching. Their gazes met. Raphael gave the merest shrug.

"In the weeks since," Percival said, "I have prayed and meditated upon these events, imploring God to send me understanding. This morning, God answered my prayers. The object of our quest to Kiev was not some artifact, but the Shield-Maidens themselves. Vera's return to our group is confirmation of God's will. She was destined all along to join us and ride with us into the East."

Benjamin seemed embarrassed. "You have too many quests for me to keep track of," he muttered.

Percival shook his head forbearingly. "For us, there is only one," he said.

"The one that takes you into the East, following the caravan trails?"

"The same."

"And what, pray tell, might be the object of that quest?"

"Don't!" Feronantus sat forward and stretched out an arm toward Percival. But it was too late.

"We will ride into the heartland of the Mongols' empire. We will find the Great Khan, and we will slay him."

Feronantus burst out with a long oath in his native Gothic, not at all becoming of a monk. Raphael was able to make out the names of at least two pagan gods.

The little meeting had become a Tower of Babel. Benjamin spoke to the nonplussed rabbi in Khazar Turkic, presumably translating Percival's words, and they went on to conduct an agonizingly long discussion in that tongue, perfectly opaque to Raphael.

Finally, as Feronantus buried his head in his hands and sank back in gloom, Benjamin looked at Raphael. His cloudy scowl faded, he lifted his shoulders, held out his hands—and smiled.

"Why not just tell us that in the first place? I cannot speak on behalf of my cousins who dwell in this little village, of course. But as far as I'm concerned, anyone as determined as you seem to be to kill the Great Khan, and throw his empire into disarray, is brethren to us all in this terrible time foretold by the *Nevi'im*, and there is almost nothing I won't do to help further your quest."

The rabbi ran his fingers through his beard, as was his habit when deep in thought.

"I felt confident you'd see it that way," Percival said, breaking into an amazed silence.

"This all came to you in a vision?" Benjamin asked.

Percival looked up and smiled. The light on his face was again apparent. Raphael was almost certain the others saw it as well. There were so many reasons for living, breathing, sinful men to feel uncomfortable around Percival.

"You are indeed a holy fool," said Benjamin, "for I am a strange man, and not one merchant in a thousand would respond as I have." Benjamin now turned to address Raphael in Hebrew. "Please say to the others that I commend you all for your bravery and wish you the best of luck on your quest. But we who must remain here are in grave danger. We can only assume that the Mongols will search tirelessly for the surviving Shield-Maidens." Raphael quickly translated.

Feronantus's response was immediate and simple. "We will draw them away from you," he said, "and destroy them."

CHAPTER 21:

QUOD DEBUIMUS FACERE, FECIMUS

"Why did you let him go, you idiot?" Fieschi snarled, whirling away from de Segni in frustration. "He was *right there*, he was standing next to you, you were befriending him...and then what? I looked away for one moment, and suddenly, Robert of Somercotes is practically *embracing* him!"

Fieschi seldom lost his temper; when he did, months of controlled, pent-up anger erupted from him at once. And in this moment, when he could not raise his voice as he wanted to, the fury came hissing out of him like scalding steam. Rinaldo Conti de Segni winced. Although they were standing in his bedchamber, it was clear he wanted to flee; Fieschi owned the space entirely with his wrath. "At least I made an opening gambit," de Segni said, trying to look disdainful rather than chastened. "I approached him. You have not done that much. Consider that before you accuse me of not taking sufficient action."

Fieschi made a disgusted sound and turned back toward de Segni. "I approached him when he was delirious. I took his satchel from him. What little we know about the man we know because of me. If I had walked across the courtyard to get close to him today, it would have been obvious, *even to him*, that I was up to something. Somercotes and I would have gotten into a veritable tug-of-war and torn his arms off. Whereas you had managed to approach him as if in innocent greeting, welcoming him to our special little hell, offering assistance and introduction. And then you handed him over to the enemy!" He shook his head. "I can't believe I ever considered putting you forward as a candidate."

De Segni stiffened. "I would have made a better choice than your precious Bonaventura."

Fieschi's nostrils flared, and the whites of his eyes flashed in the torchlight. "I swear, if you waver in your support of Bonaventura, you will find a scorpion in your bed."

De Segni held up his hands as if warding off a blow. "Of course he'll get my vote, Fieschi. That doesn't mean I approve of him." More bitterly, and softer, he added, "At least it isn't *you* I have to vote for."

Fieschi's face, which had been florid with anger until that moment, was suddenly unreadable. Incompetency distressed him; insults did not touch him. "You have just demonstrated why you would have made a poor candidate for Pontiff," he said, almost triumphantly. "It takes a selfish, petty man to choose a Bishop of Rome according to the candidate's *personality*. There are important issues at stake, and we cannot afford to indulge our egos or our personal preferences. I am not fond of Bonaventura myself—"

"You're not fond of anyone, Fieschi," de Segni interrupted, in full control of his disdain now, "except yourself."

Fieschi shook his head slightly, slowly. "This is precisely the petty bickering that Frederick's men want us to devolve to. Rise above it, Rinaldo. *Now*."

He turned on his heel and stalked out of de Segni's room.

As much as he despised Robert of Somercotes, he respected him, as an able enemy ought to be respected. Somercotes had snatched a quick and easy victory away from Bonaventura; the Englishman had quickly mustered the necessary voices to put Castiglione forward as a challenging candidate, and now the two factions were deadlocked. It enraged Fieschi that so many cardinals would consider voting for a man whose will would bend not to the Church, but to the Holy Roman Emperor—somehow Somercotes had intellectually seduced them into it. One candidate or the other would need a two-thirds majority to become the next leader of the Catholic Church. That meant eight votes, now that this mysterious priest brought their number to an even dozen. The new arrival was the fulcrum upon which to rest the necessary lever to pry loose the undecided cardinals. But damned Robert of Somercotes knew that as well, and had clung to the priest like a leech, seldom out of his company and never out of his sight.

✦✦✦

"I heard you cry out in your sleep," Somercotes said gently, sliding the damp cloth from Rodrigo's forehead to the back of his neck. "I have some knowledge of physics, but the guards will not allow my medicines to be brought in. Fieschi is afraid I will drug my fellow cardinals to bring them under my sway." He laughed bitterly. "At this point, I admit, I would be sorely tempted to do so if my simples really had such power."

Rodrigo shook his head. His hair was drenched in sweat, and he still trembled from his nightmare. Somercotes's voice was soothing, but the words rolled over him with as much meaning as a gentle surf. "I don't understand," he managed to say.

"And you are the luckier for it," Somercotes said peaceably. "Here, try to sit up. We have nothing to give you but water, until they bring the next meal, but try at least to sip a little more." He held out the wooden cup to the priest. Rodrigo looked at it warily, uncertain he could hold it without spilling all the contents.

"I'll help you," Somercotes said at once, understanding his expression. The cardinal solicitously held the cup up to Rodrigo's dry lips, and the priest parted them to let the water slosh over his tongue. He swallowed quickly and, on reflex, inclined his head toward the cup, wanting more. Somercotes tipped it slightly higher, his free hand behind Rodrigo's head for steadiness. Rodrigo swallowed again, then shivered and sagged back against the stone wall. He was glad the nightmare was over, but he would rather have been dead than awake.

"I must understand," he said, his voice harsh and ragged.

"Are you unfamiliar with the means by which a new Pope is elected?" Somercotes asked, leaning forward. He set the cup on the floor. Rodrigo, glancing at it, remembered the scorpion that had scuttled across that same part of the floor moments earlier. He wondered if he should tell Somercotes.

"The *sede vacante*," Somercotes continued.

"Yes," Rodrigo said, stirring out of his reverie. "There is no Bishop of Rome. We must elect another one. I understand this process."

"We are deadlocked," Somercotes said. He regarded Rodrigo warily still, as if there were questions he wanted to ask but was not sure if he wanted to hear the answers. "Neither candidate has enough votes. We are imprisoned here until one of the two—Castiglione or Bonaventura—is elected."

"And then that one is Pope," Rodrigo said to himself. "And to that man I may deliver my message."

"What message is that?" Somercotes demanded, his voice suddenly sharper.

Rodrigo, eyes glassy, kept staring at the floor. "It is not for your ears, and you should rejoice at that mercy."

"From whom does it come?" Somercotes pressed, in a more careful tone.

Rodrigo shook his head, exhausted.

"Is it from the Emperor or Orsini?" Somercotes asked. He used an either-or inflection that confused Rodrigo, so Rodrigo ignored the question.

But then he sat up a little straighter as a thought struck him. "I want to meet the two candidates," he announced. Surely given the momentous message he carried, the unspeakable significance of it, the angry angels from Mohi would show him which was meant to be the true Bishop of Rome, and he could unburden himself at once, without waiting for the technicalities of investiture. There was no time for such trivial rituals now.

Somercotes cleared his throat. "The candidates themselves are mere men. What matters is the values they embody, their devotion to the divine Will."

Rodrigo nodded, his eyes suddenly clearing. "That's why I must meet them," he said. "I must see which one the divine Will has chosen."

Somercotes opened his mouth to argue with the logic of this, then shut it again quickly. "How can you see that before it has happened?" he asked, trying a different tactic.

Suddenly, finally, Rodrigo met his gaze. "I will be able to see it. You cannot imagine what I...see."

Somercotes relented. "Very well," he said. "Afterward, perhaps, you can tell me more of your message and how you came to be here."

"Perhaps," Rodrigo whispered. And then his eyes turned away again, the glassiness returning.

✦✦✦

Ocyrhoe always kept a stub of candle rolled in her belt, but she had no way to light it, so the first hundred yards or so had been in total blackness. Now that they had finally descended the steep stairway—thirty-two steps, she counted—it was a little easier. They had gripped hands, harder than they needed to, and with Ferenc in front, they felt their way along the left-hand rock wall, cool and musty.

He stopped suddenly where a passage opened up. The air moved slightly toward them, and his sharp nose picked up human scents. He let go of Ocyrhoe's hand, grabbed her wrist, and signaled, "This way." They grasped hands again and, still in absolute darkness and silence, moved slowly forward.

Ocyrhoe wondered if Ferenc realized how unprepared she was for this so-called rescue attempt. She hoped he was not relying on her to know some secret trick. She had none. He now knew as much as she did about where they were—more, perhaps, with his tracking skills. She knew only the myths and hearsay of the city and of history; he knew what his heightened senses told him, and she trusted them more than the whispered rumors of ignorant locals.

After some twenty paces, Ferenc stopped suddenly and released her hand, only to take her wrist and move swift fingers over her skin. She had difficulty counting the fingers in the dark, but context supplied some of the words. "Two men ahead," he informed her. She was surprised; she could not hear a thing. "Around the corner. Light."

She jerked her head aside to look past him and saw the slightest, faintest hint of a blackness less absolute than the blackness they'd been walking through. "Follow," Ferenc signed, then took her fingers again. She followed him, step for step, ashamed to be relieved he was in front of her.

As they sidled forward along the wall, the patch ahead grew gray, and then a grayish amber. Soon she could hear sounds, but not voices. The sounds confused her; they were the blunt noises of construction, or perhaps of mining, a rhythmic, soft percussive sound, like someone digging. And then voices, but not speaking—the occasional grunt of effort, a heavy sigh.

Soon it was clear to her what Ferenc must have realized when he first stopped: just ahead of them, on the right side of this tunnel, there was a corner turning off to another tunnel, and it was from there the sound and soft light came. Ferenc paused again and then let go of the wall, pulling her gently over toward the far side of the subterranean corridor. She reached out her free hand until it touched the rock to her right—but here it was not rock. It smelled earthier and felt more like hard-packed clay or soil. Again, she followed Ferenc step for step as they approached the corner.

He stopped just before they reached it, and turned toward her. She could barely make out his silhouette as the light from down the tunnel spilled out weakly behind him. He resumed signing along her wrist. "Two men. Large. Not young. Twenty-five paces away," he spelled out laboriously. "Dangerous?"

Now she took his wrist. "I don't know," she replied. She felt him stiffen. He must be realizing only now that, despite her impetuosity, she was not the expert here. "Maybe priest prisoners," she signed. "Maybe."

After a hesitation, he fingered, "Let's go," and turned back toward the corner.

He stepped around it. She followed him.

Ahead of them were two large men in ragged cloaks or gowns—ruined finery, she guessed, so possibly two of the imprisoned cardinals. The burlier one, with a huge beard, was attacking the wall. At the moment she saw him, he seemed to have just shoved a spike into the compacted earth, and then he dropped the spike and began to claw his way into the small hole it had made with his bare hands so that flakes and clumps of dirt fell away. He stood on a pile of debris that rose above his ankles. The other man, thinner but taller, stood on the far side of him, holding the torch. His face was more visible than the bearded man's; he looked not only relaxed but actually delighted by his partner's progress.

"Go?" Ferenc asked on Ocyrhoe's wrist.

She had no idea; she was almost annoyed with him for making her decide. "Yes," she tapped back finally. They were here to find the priest; they would not find him by avoiding people who probably knew where he was.

Ocyrhoe and Ferenc were both so soft of foot, and the two men ahead of them so intent on their activity, that they crept very close before the one holding the torch glanced up and noticed them. They froze. He blinked, frowned in confusion, and then grinned.

"Capocci," he said amiably. "Soft. We have an audience." He spoke in Italian.

The one named Capocci grunted, "Eh? What?" and straightened up from his labor. The torchbearer gestured into the fading light. As Capocci's shadowed face turned toward them, Ocyrhoe said quickly, in the same dialect the torchbearer had used, "We are friends, seeking another friend."

Capocci chuckled. "Did you hear that, Colonna? They're only friends."

"Friends of whom?" Colonna asked, as if this were a casual afternoon chat with fellow passersby at a market.

"Father Rodrigo," Ocyrhoe said, a hint of defiance in her voice.

The two men sobered immediately. Capocci took a step back, staggering over the pile of dirt he'd amassed around his feet. Now he was level with Colonna, and four dark, searching eyes glistened in the torchlight at the young duo.

"*Father Rodrigo?* How interesting," Colonna said after an appraising pause. "Well, you certainly look the part; you're both even more ragged than he was when he got here."

"Is he alive?" Ocyrhoe asked, forcing her voice to remain dispassionate. "Is he well?"

"Alive but not well," Capocci answered. "We're curious about your curiosity."

Ferenc grabbed her wrist. "What are they saying?" he demanded. She brushed his hand away.

"Can you take us to him?" Ocyrhoe asked. "In exchange, we will show you a way out of here so you do not have to dig yourselves out."

The two men exchanged glances, and then their faces softened with mirth. "What, this?" Capocci said, gesturing with his filthy hands to his destruction. "I do this for exercise."

"We've already dug two others," Colonna explained. "And we know about Fieschi's exit. Is that how you got in here? It's only guarded after sundown."

"No surprise you have nothing to offer us," Capocci concluded cheerfully. "But don't let that stop you from trying to convince us to help you. I could certainly use a new distraction, couldn't you?"

"Absolutely," said Colonna heartily. "In fact, I personally thank God you've come. What is it you want, exactly?"

◆◆◆

It was spectacularly ill-advised to go to Orsini's home in broad daylight. Fieschi knew that. But he also knew that Robert of Somercotes had let himself into the new priest's room and blocked the door behind him. He knew from listening at the crack of the door that they were talking, or at least that Somercotes was; the sick priest sounded perhaps delirious again, or at least deeply distracted. Fieschi knew exactly what he wanted to do, but he knew better than to undertake it without first consulting Orsini. Waiting until darkness might be safer—but Somercotes moved fast. There was no way to ensure the Englishman would not have rallied the priest, and by extension the entire swing vote of the College of Cardinals, before sunset. *Damn Rinaldo for letting Somercotes steal him,* he said to himself for the thirtieth time in an hour. A vital opportunity had been thrown away because de Segni wanted to be the first to get his morning meal. *Fool. Selfish, lazy, shortsighted fool. Like all the rest of them.*

He decided to risk being recognized. After he stalked away from de Segni's room, he pulled off his cardinal's robe and hurled it into his own chamber as he walked past; underneath, he wore a simple priest's robe, so perhaps he could disappear into the midday market crowds, anonymous. He grabbed the torch outside his room, which demarked the limits of habitation along this particular tunnel.

He walked on into the darkness, to the second empty room along the corridor, which had a broken beam blocking most of the door. With practiced efficiency, he twisted his body and the torch around the beam and slipped into the small chamber. It was empty, but on the far side was a dark gash in the wall. He crossed and moved into this narrow opening; turning sideways for ease of movement, the torch held in his forward hand, he navigated the tight, zigzagging tunnel some thirty paces as it sloped gently upward. Then it opened onto a broader tunnel, which, if Fieschi took to the left, would lead eventually to his convenient freedom.

But above his torch's hissing, he heard a sound. He stopped moving. He stepped out into the tunnel but saw nothing. He could not tell from which direction the sound had come. Another sound—a voice. Voices. He glanced in the direction of the tunnel egress. If there was anyone between him and the exit, he should be able to see them, at least the faintest trace of them, in the outer reaches of his torchlight. There was nobody there.

So he turned to the right and began a slow trek. Now another voice, and unexpected—a girl's voice. *A girl's voice.*

Could it be the young woman from the marketplace? The one who'd fled on horseback with the wild young man?

He wanted to rush toward the voices but constrained himself. One slow step at a time. The voices continued.

Laughter. He stopped short again, briefly; he knew that laughter. Capocci and Colonna. They leaned toward Castiglione, Somercotes's choice. Fieschi fought off a sudden, enormous wave of dread. Was Somercotes carrying out a full-sprung conspiracy right under his nose, without Fieschi realizing? Was that toady of the Unholy Roman Emperor truly that efficient?

He saw the light now, coming from around the corner to the right; he hesitated, wondering if he should douse his own torch and try to approach in stealth. That would not work; they'd smell the smoke. And he would be at the mercy of whatever they decided to do with their own torchlight.

Cursing the entire enterprise—especially de Segni, who could have prevented it coming to this—he took a broad stride forward, putting himself in the middle of the tunnel that branched off to the right.

"Good afternoon," he said loudly. "What an interesting situation we find ourselves in."

Capocci and Colonna, he recognized, of course. He had not seen the girl or the youth before, but they fit the description from the market very neatly.

All four of them froze and stared at him. He smiled smugly and took a few slow, almost cocky steps toward them. "There is something unsavory about subterranean assignations," he said, lazing over the words. He directed his words toward the bone-thin girl, memorizing her face with his keen stare. "I hope, young lady, that they are paying you well for these abominations?"

"Not as well as you would, since unlike you, we don't live in Orsini's pocket," Capocci growled.

Suddenly, the two large cardinals, without warning or conference, but in nearly perfect unison, lurched over the debris; Colonna dropped his torch, which was snuffed at once in the damp earth. Each man grabbed one of the newcomers: Colonna almost effortlessly tossed the woman onto his back; Capocci huffed a little from the effort, but he had the young man up and over his broad shoulders in a trice. And then the two of them, again as if it had been rehearsed, turned and fled into the absolute darkness of the tunnels.

Astonished, Fieschi ran after them, with a shout that was as fruitless as it was ignored. Colonna's laughter bounced off the walls but then evaporated into the darkness.

◆◆◆

The moment the youth appeared in the doorway, Somercotes saw a softening come over the stranger's face, expressing a humanity that he did not know the man had in him. Rodrigo's eyes opened wide, and his jaw went slack, but he managed to scramble to his feet without assistance. The wild-haired young man stood just inside the doorway, unsure of the situation, and regarded the ailing priest with caninelike devotion.

"Ferenc?" Rodrigo whispered and then automatically switched to a tongue the newcomer seemed to know. He staggered across the stone floor, and the young man leaped to catch him, grabbing him under the arms, both to hold him up and to embrace him. Somercotes had no difficulty imagining some great moment of bonding in their past—a battle, perhaps? He studied the interaction closely.

The youth—Ferenc, Somercotes assumed that was his name—said something to Rodrigo, his tone and body language suggesting that he was rebuking the priest for standing.

Capocci and Colonna, who had brought these strangers to Rodrigo's chamber, exchanged astonished looks. "What bastard tongue is that?" demanded Capocci.

"It is Magyar, from Mohi," said the other, a young girl, doubtless a ragged child of Rome. She stared at the two men with a strangely motherly expression. "Ferenc helped Father Rodrigo get to Rome—"

"To deliver a message to the Pope," Somercotes concluded. He glanced briefly at his fellow cardinals, but they were both agreeably preoccupied with listening to the torrent of words that now came out as the boy—*Ferenc,* he reminded himself, noting she had said his name as well—solicitously helped the priest return to a sitting position.

"An ugly language," Capocci observed pleasantly.

"Too many *ka*'s and *shka*'s," Colonna said in agreement.

"What are they saying to each other?" Somercotes asked the girl.

She shook her head. "I don't know Magyar," she said.

"Then how do you know the boy's story?"

"He told me," she said and lifted her hand, wriggling her fingers without thinking. To their puzzled reaction, she lowered the hand, then pressed her lips closed.

Other than the rapidly muttered conversation between Rodrigo and the boy, there was a pause. Somercotes looked hard at the girl, who pretended not to notice. "Does the young man speak Italian?" he asked. "Latin?"

She glanced away and shook her head.

"Tell me, how do you communicate with him?" Somercotes pressed.

She clearly wished she could take back what she had said, and if Capocci hadn't been casually blocking the door—though Somercotes knew the wily cardinal was anything but nonchalant—she might have fled the room.

Ferenc answered Somercotes's question before she could stop him. He finished his conversation with Rodrigo, turned eagerly to the girl, and took her arm. Before she could slap his hand away, he began to squeeze and touch her wrist.

"An unusual way to communicate," Somercotes said, bemused. She shrank back under his close scrutiny. He took a step and quickly reached to the side of her head. Ferenc's eyes widened as the cardinal gently took hold of a long lock of the girl's hair, which had been interwoven with thread into an irregular series of knots. "I've seen this before," he said. He glanced at Ferenc, then back to the girl, and let go of her hair, his fingers curling like snakes and then thrusting out in ones, twos, threes. He looked pointedly at Ferenc—and smiled. "I did not realize males spoke such a language."

"He doesn't know it well," the girl said brusquely, still not meeting his look, "and I don't know how he learned it."

Somercotes took a deep breath and let it out slowly. By keeping these two intruders here in secret, he could quite possibly ferret out more information about this Father Rodrigo, something more definite than the muddling ravings the priest supplied in plenty. But Somercotes felt certain he knew *what* the girl was and might learn soon enough who had sent her—and with that knowledge, he could think of far better uses for her.

Before he could speak, Ferenc let out a cry of delight and reached for a small bag hanging from his belt. He began to jabber away again in his native tongue, and Rodrigo—who had again slumped into a glassy-eyed stare—suddenly sat up straighter, blinked, and looked alert. As Somercotes watched, the boy reached into his satchel and pulled out a small metal object—a ring. A signet ring. An ecclesiastic signet ring—which meant the delirious priest really was a cardinal.

Ferenc handed it to Rodrigo, who took it between thumb and forefinger, staring at it as if he could not understand its significance.

The three cardinals exchanged looks; even Capocci understood now that this was serious.

"May I see that?" Somercotes asked Rodrigo, holding out his hand.

Rodrigo, confused, held it up toward Somercotes without relinquishing his hold of it.

"That is *not* a cardinal's ring," Somercotes announced, examining it. He made this pronouncement in a pleasant, casual voice, as if complimenting Rodrigo, but the words were meant for Colonna and Capocci, who nodded sagely as if they already knew this wisdom. "It is an Archbishop's ring," he added. "There is some story here, no doubt fascinating. Perhaps"—and here he straightened and peered at the girl again—"perhaps you can help us by filling in the details by signing to your friend there in *Rankalba*."

The girl was plainly shaken by the fact he knew the esoteric name, and her instinct to flee was plain on her face, but to her credit, she mastered her fear and nodded. "He has already told me everything he knows," she replied. "He does not know very much."

"Tell me what he does know," Somercotes persisted, smiling at her in a way he thought might inflict a small chill. "Something significant, worthy of an Archbishop's ring."

The girl swallowed hard. "Only that the priest has a message to deliver."

"Of course, there is nobody to deliver it *to*," Rodrigo said, speaking in Italian for the first time since the foursome had pounded on the door for entrance. "I am a word lost in the empty air. I am a seed thrown on stones."

"Ah," Somercotes said appreciatively. "A messenger stuck forever with his message and no one to receive it."

Somercotes turned his attention back to the pale, narrow-shouldered girl. "Speaking of messengers..." he said and lifted his eyebrows. The girl looked away, then back, with a faint but noticeable spark of defiance. In reward for this show of character, he gave her a reassuring smile. "If you are what I think you are," he said in a low, confident tone, "then I have an assignment for you. A true message to deliver. A message that will definitely be heard."

She lowered her gaze. Somercotes waited patiently for her to answer.

"Give me the message," she said finally, looking him squarely in the eye.

Capocci and Colonna watched them both with mild curiosity. Ferenc's attention was on Rodrigo, who was slipping once again into a fog of confusion. "The word who spins in the air, the dove who is a buzzard who is a dove..." Rodrigo muttered. "The flies that buzz God's song, mosquitoes humming along..."

"The recipient of this message," Somercotes said delicately, crossing himself, "is His Majesty King Frederick, the Holy Roman Emperor. If you cannot gain an audience, you may deliver it to any commander in his army, which is camped just outside the walls of Rome."

The girl kept her face calm. "And what is the message?" she asked.

"The message is quite literally *this*," Somercotes said, with a sweeping gesture all around them. "This *place*. The fact of this imprisonment by Senator Orsini, the location of the Septizodium. Whatever route you took to break in here, show someone, and bring them back here with you."

"As is...my duty," she said, pressing both hands over her heart and bowing her head slightly. "I go at once."

Somercotes held up a hand to stop her. "Do you know who I am?" he asked. When she shook her head, he smiled at her. "It will be difficult to inform the message's recipient as to who sent it if you do not know my name, don't you think?"

She blushed, though the expression in her eyes said she was more angry than embarrassed.

"I am Robert of Somercotes," he said, "a cardinal of the Church." He placed a hand on the top of her head. "And I offer you all my blessings for your journey. *In nomine Patris, et Filii, et Spiritus Sancti.*" He felt her flinch as he said the Latin words, but she held still until he finished.

"I...I am Ocyrhoe," she said, and though she seemed to want to add something, she clamped her mouth shut and shook her head slightly.

"Well met, Ocyrhoe. We are *bound* together now by our message, yes?" The fact she had not offered the ritual exchange did not concern him overmuch. She knew what he asked of her; he didn't care that she seemed too young to fully understand. The message itself was what mattered. "Go and deliver it." He gestured toward Ferenc. "Take the young man with you. You seem to work together well." *And it will be less complicated for us to explain his presence here.*

✦✦✦

Outside the door, Fieschi suppressed a sigh of satisfaction. He straightened, glanced around the corridor to make sure nobody saw him, and walked swiftly back down the corridor toward the tunnel that would lead him to free air and Orsini.

There was so much for he and the Bear to talk about.

CHAPTER 22:

AN AFTERNOON AT FIRST FIELD

The crowd swarmed across the wooden planks of the scaffolds like a ferocious colony of termites, a writhing mass of humanity that twitched and leaped and shouted in response to the two combatants. First Field had three fighting grounds, and as only the center one was in use, the audience had repositioned the scaffolds to more tightly embrace it. In between the scaffolds, crates and wooden beams and chunks of rock made for makeshift platforms from which still more of the commoners could watch. There were patches of color in the otherwise uniform sea of dirty brown, tiny clusters of men in finer robes, surrounded by their mailled guard.

A standard stood next to the ring; Kim caught glimpses of it through the throng. Every time the crowd parted slightly, affording him a brief view of a corner, his desire to see it fully only increased.

His Mongol guards hung back, milling about on the periphery of the excitement. They were outnumbered, and the crush of people was too great, too uncontrolled, and they were hesitant to force a gap through which Kim could reach the fighting ground. Unwilling to wait for them to decide how best to approach the crowd, Kim walked to the back edge of the scaffolding and leaped, reaching for a bracing bar. He pulled himself up, feeling the muscles stretch and pop in his shoulders, and he hung there, a few feet off the ground, face pressed up close to the back of a Westerner. He pulled up a leg, got it hooked on the long plank, and pulled himself over the bracing bar, barreling into the top row of spectators.

They were not amused, and several turned angrily on him as he shoved his way into their midst. Below them, his Mongol guards shouted up at him to come down, and the Western men, hearing these strident voices, suddenly lost interest in pushing Kim off the scaffolding.

Kim ignored the men around him. He was too busy examining the fighter in the ring.

Down below, a tall, powerfully built man in a quilted coat—apparently the Frank—stood near an equally sized, heavier-set man who was lying on his back. The Frank held a wooden sword, and though he was breathing heavily, he did not appear to be overly tired. His brow was damp with sweat, matting his blond hair to his head, and he had a broad smile on his bearded face. As the man on the ground rolled away, the Frank planted the tip of his weapon in the ground and raised one hand in a salute to the crowd.

They reacted in kind, yelling and screaming their adoration of his martial prowess. The Frank turned slightly and bowed to the flag standing in the triskelion beside the ring. Kim could not help but smile. It was the symbol of the Rose Knights, just as Zug had drawn for him in the dirt.

The Rose Knight's opponent crawled from the ring to a thunder of booing and catcalls. Another man stepped forward, ducking under the ropes. This one was shorter, though no less strong than the previous combatant, judging by the thickness of his arms and legs. He was also a Westerner, darker in skin and hair than the Rose Knight, but his beard was trimmed in a similar style, and his clothing was equally unadorned. In one hand, he carried a thick shield, and in the other hand, a wooden cudgel. He spun his weapon a few times, and the crowd fell silent, leaning forward with intense fascination to listen to the sound the heavy club made as it whirled through the air.

The Frank nodded, acknowledging the man's right to enter the ring. Holding his blade in a low, close guard, he eased into a ready stance. Kim watched intently, his mind already starting to catalog the Frank's fighting style, comparing it to his own. Looking for ways it could be beaten. The Frank's sword was shorter than the staff Kim preferred, but the way the Frank held his weapon suggested such proficiency that to think the Rose Knight would be disadvantaged in matters of reach would be foolish. There was patience in his stance as well, a placid calm not shared by his opponent.

They had not even crossed weapons, and already Kim knew who was going to win the fight. Nevertheless, *how* the battle played out would be useful knowledge.

The Frank thrust, the tip of the blade driving at his opponent. It was a surprising move, as his stance had seemed more suited for defense, but that was part of the illusion. He had wanted the club-wielder to think he was ceding the timing of the first blow. The other man turned the thrust aside on his shield, stepping forward as he did to bull-rush the Frank. The Frank responded, moving so fluidly that he seemed to have been waiting for that very response from the club-wielder. Kim considered the possibility that the thrust, like the stance, was part of the lure to which the club-wielder had fallen prey. The Frank's weapon rotated in his hands, the tip arcing away, and the club-wielder found himself rushing toward the hard pommel of the wooden sword.

The pommel slammed into his head, and as the stunned fighter attempted to recover, he stumbled and swung his cudgel and shield as one in the Frank's direction. The Frank hadn't stood still. As soon as his pommel strike had landed, he was stepping past the staggering fighter. In the confusion following the strike, his sword had somehow managed to slide past the man's guard, parallel to his body. The Frank, behind his opponent now, pulled the wooden blade tight against the man's neck, choking him. His opponent struggled and grunted, dropping both his weapons as he attempted to free himself, but he could neither reach the Frank nor get any leverage against the blade pulled tight against his throat since the Frank's hip was also at his back, pushing it forward and putting him hopelessly off balance. It was an interesting technique, extremely useful in this situation where the Frank was using a wooden sword, but Kim wondered about its efficacy in combat with a sharp weapon.

By the time the man yielded, the crowd had exploded into noise again. Their voices echoed loudly amid the ruins of Hünern, and Kim knew this was the sound he had heard back at the compound. As the Frank slapped his opponent on the back, sending him staggering toward the rope, Kim lightly slipped under the bracing bar and dropped back to the ground.

His Mongolian escort crowded him, and the one in charge started to berate him for leaving their side. Kim cut him off with a wave of his hand. "I am ready to fight," he said. "Make a path for me."

This was his chance to make contact with the Rose Knights.

✦✦✦

The man with the shield and club made five, and Andreas had yet to be touched by any of his opponents' weapons. His arms and legs tingled a bit from the exertion, but mostly he felt warm and loose. The exultation of the crowd fed him as well, their noise a fire that roared through his veins. Virgin forgive him, but he was starting to enjoy himself.

During the first fight, he had been distracted, and his opponent might have landed a blow had he been a better fighter. Rutger had admonished him about the stolen Livonian horses, directing him to return them before he came to the field to offer the open challenge. The command had rankled him, even though he knew the aged quartermaster was right. The Shield-Brethren were not horse thieves, nor were they in open conflict with the Livonians (regardless of how Andreas felt about their machinations); to keep the horses was tantamount to starting a feud that would descend into open violence. The Livonians were still Christian soldiers, and the greater enemy was the Mongol force; for the time being, the Shield-Brethren fought to uphold the honor of *all* of Christendom.

Andreas, Styg, and Eilif had brought the horses back to Hünern, abandoning them at the first sight of a Livonian patrol (which had taken longer to find than they had anticipated). The Livonians had pursued them for a brief while, but quickly gave up when they realized they had *stolen* back the same horses. Being able to return to their *Heermeister* with this news seemed to be victory enough that chasing a trio of Shield-Brethren through the ragged streets of Hünern lost its luster.

Which hadn't quite been what Rutger had meant when he told Andreas to return the horses, but all in all, it seemed like a good solution.

However, Andreas had taken a liking to the *Heermeister*'s bay stallion, and returning it to a man who did not seem to appreciate it overmuch had put him in a foul mood. A mood that had been quickly driven away by martial exertion, the best remedy for the confusion and consternation that could plague a fighting man.

While the crowd madly cheered his latest conquest, Styg leaned over the ropes and offered him a waterskin. Andreas took it gratefully, the cool taste a merciful respite from the sweltering heat of his gambeson.

"How many more?" Styg asked, partially in jest, but there was enough concern in the young man's face that his question demanded a serious answer.

"As many as it takes." Andreas wiped the sweat from his forehead. "We are here to make contact, and I will fight until he shows." No mention of what might happen should someone manage to best Andreas. Better to not give credence to such a thought.

"You've not said a word to any of them since this began," Styg said. "How do you know you've not missed him?"

"Firstly, he is not from Christendom, as most of the previous fighters have been," Andreas answered, reminding Styg of the obvious reason. "Secondly, our man single-handedly beat a pair of Livonians, each of them on horseback, with a *stick*." Andreas took another drink from the skin. "I would hope the Livonians are more skilled than the men I have fought so far. Otherwise, I weep for the future of Christendom." He grinned at Styg. "Did you not see the runner sprint off for the Mongol camp after I beat the second man? By now, they know we are here. They must be curious, and I am sure their fighters are as bored as we are. The mere suggestion of a decent fight will draw them out. They'll come."

Styg was about to reply when a commotion between two of the scaffolds caught his attention. People were scrambling out of the way; a few even slipped under the ropes, using the open space of the ring to more readily avoid the press of bodies being forced to part. "Someone comes," the young Shield-Brother noted. "You may be right. I think you have caught their attention."

They could see the source of the chaos in the crowd now. Several Mongol guards were forcing the crowd back with the butts and shafts of their spears, opening a way for a man to approach the arena. He was smaller than the previous opponents, with black hair and almond eyes set in an intent, hard face whose age was difficult for him to assess. He wore loose-fitting clothes that gave him an easy freedom of movement, and by the way he walked, Andreas could see the sort of grace in him that came only from an impressive amount of strength. His face, however, was mottled, with bruises and cuts that had not yet healed, lending him somewhat of a horrific appearance that belied this quiet strength.

A silence settled over the First Field as the newcomer reached the rope. He glanced up at the standard of the Shield-Brethren as it fluttered gently in the afternoon breeze, and he offered Andreas a flash of white teeth before placing his hands together at his chest and bowing.

"Ah, now we are getting somewhere," Andreas murmured to Styg, passing back the skin. Andreas had eschewed a longsword in favor of his waster—a wooden sword that squires and knights alike would use for practice bouts in the training yards. It would be insufficient to cut or perforate flesh, but it was as good for leaving bruises and breaking bones as any wood stave, and killing was the last thing he wished here and now. He faced the newcomer and raised his wooden sword until the hilt was before his eyes, a salute that he hoped his new opponent would recognize.

The smaller man regarded him a long moment, then gave a nod of his head. He held out an open hand, and Andreas realized he carried no weapon. He watched with some incredulity as one of the Mongol guards stepped forward and offered the fighter a short hardwood staff. It was an exchange much like the sort of request a knight makes of his squire for his sword, but Andreas realized the reason the Mongol had held onto the weapon was that they did not trust their fighter to walk around armed.

Yes, Andreas thought. *This one is different.*

His opponent ducked under the rope and entered the ring. The crowd remained silent, breathlessly awaiting the commencement of the fight. Andreas stood ready, his wooden sword held loosely in both hands, waiting to see what would happen next. Waiting to see how much patience the other man could muster.

His opponent snapped into motion with a flourish of explosive movement, the stave whistling through the air as the smaller man whirled and leaped. Despite the strangeness, there was something familiar in it that pulled at Andreas's memory, reminding him of the flourishes he had seen in his training days as a squire. His opponent was out of measure, and his flourishes were more ornamental than aggressive, a range of motion that was good for fitness, for driving away fear. They were hardly fitting for fully adult men, fighting in earnest. Andreas felt his impression of the man changing, his assumptions about this man's skill bleeding away. The kicks were head height, exposing all sorts of targets, and surely, what was the point of kicking a man when you had a weapon in hand?

Andreas relaxed into his guard. In his hands, the weight of the wooden sword was a comforting reminder of the years of training drills, both at Petraathen and Týrshammar. *This shouldn't take too—*

Without warning, a foot slammed into his center, past his unmoving weapon, and drove his stomach against his spine.

He went down; as he fell, his body instinctively reacted, transforming the fall into a backward roll. Months and years of practicing falls just like this one had built muscle memory that reacted automatically. He cursed himself for failing to see the blow coming and cast forth a silent prayer of thanks to the Virgin for both the padded weight of his gambeson and the years of breathing training. It was because of both of those that he could go without air for a short time while his lungs recovered from the kick. Dimly, he was aware of his opponent's staff pounding the ground where he would have been had he not managed to turn his fall into a roll.

He was wrong. This fighter was *good.*

◆◆◆

The Frank raised his blade in a salute, and while Kim did not know the exact meaning of the gesture, it was clearly a respectful response to his own acknowledgment of the Frank's prowess. They had exchanged all the pleasantries necessary, and Kim held out his hand for his weapon. His escorts had insisted on carrying it for him, and he had had to hide his amusement that they thought him so helpless without his staff. While it was a fine piece of hardwood, it was just a stick, and he could have entered the fighting ground with no weapon at all, especially given the Frank's wooden sword. But since they had brought it, and they expected him to use it, it seemed prudent to keep up appearances. Staff in hand, Kim ducked under the rope and entered the ring.

He appraised his opponent for a moment, eyeing the man's restful guard. It was the same stance the Frank had taken with the club-wielder. Having seen that fight, Kim knew the lack of aggressiveness in the stance was meant to lull him into making the first move. If that was the Frank's opening gambit, then Kim could respond in kind. He too could lull his opponent into thinking he wasn't ready to attack.

He began walking forward, his staff held in his right hand, parallel with the ground. Drawing closer, he swept it into circling arcs, his hand gripping it at the center. The spin moved left, right, then left again before his right hand moved as far left as it would go. Then his left flew into motion, and he took a two-handed grip at half-staff.

Moving forward and leading with the butt, he executed three rapid stabs with the end at shoulder level, then three kicks from low, to middle, to high with his left leg, never once letting his foot touch the ground. As his left leg kicked, his right arm drew the staff back, keeping the butt focused upon his opponent. He planted his left leg and launched his right into a rounding kick as high as he could, his hips rotating with a powerful snap that launched him into a spinning leap, his right leg flowing into a crescent kick from outside to inside. Right foot and staff butt met the ground in the same motion. The Frank had slid into a low guard, and his gaze was guarded, as if he were struggling to hide his reaction to Kim's opening flourish. *Was he disappointed that I did not attack him outright?*

Kim stalked forward, the stave whipping across his body, but ending always with either point or butt aimed squarely at the Frank. His movements were a variation of his previous actions, and while the Frank watched him intently, he could see the big man was not taking in the subtle differences in the motion of his body. *Closer, closer.*

He reached a distance a mere length of the staff from his opponent. His stance shifted, the right leg now forward, and the point of his staff swept through the dirt, then whipped upward to face level as he skipped forward with a one-step side kick to his opponent's middle, deeper than the earlier three, with the full force of his turning hips and left heel driving it in. He made contact with the Frank, folding him in half and knocking him to the ground.

Kim was surprised that the kick had landed, and more so that the Frank had managed to take the blow without crumpling completely. His astonishment slowed his response, and the following jab of his staff struck the ground, missing the Frank as he turned the backward fall into a roll. The larger man was surprisingly fast, and though he'd been taken off guard by the blow to his middle, the speed with which he recovered was a measure of his skill. Kim had seen men gasp for breath like fish out of water after receiving such a hit.

But the Frank was already moving again, and Kim tightened his grip on the staff.

◆◆◆

Andreas kept moving, launching himself backward until he regained his feet, where he at least looked like a warrior. In the back of his mind, shame warred with excitement: he should have seen the kick coming; this fighter was not like the others.

His eyes narrowed on the Easterner's hands. This shortened grip on the longer weapon made no sense; surely it would be better to hold it by the end, to take advantage of its greater reach. The pain in his midsection told a different story. Perhaps this Eastern warrior preferred the close fight. *Very well.*

He darted to his right, snapping his point forward as he moved. It was not the most powerful of strikes and would not be terribly effective against a man in armor, but against an unarmored opponent's arm, it would be enough to disable the limb. In his mind, he could hear his own shouted commands during the training sessions at the chapter house. *Hit first; hit fast!*

His blow connected a little off center—so as not to break his opponent's arm—and the other man's hand let go of the staff. His opponent whirled away, and Andreas stayed close, intent on pressing his advantage.

The staff whirled toward his head, a one-handed swing that caught him off guard. He beat it down, stepping out of line, and snapped the point of his wooden sword back up. The butt of the staff intercepted his strike, preventing him from landing a second blow on the already bruised arm. With a flick of his wrist, he slid his point along the staff, down into his opponent's fingers. It would be painful but not debilitating, as pain alone was never enough to stop a well-trained man in the throes of the battle rush.

Even as Andreas's tip struck the Easterner's fingers, the staff was already rotating, and the end he'd beaten down slammed with an awful force into his bruised midsection. He clenched his teeth, flashing a grim smile. It would have driven the breath from him a second time, but for the fact that his lungs were already empty. He was leading with his left side, and his gambeson was well padded. The blow hurt, but it did not slow him overmuch.

✦✦✦

The force of the Frank's strike jarred Kim's arm from wrist to shoulder. His left hand reflexively opened, releasing the staff. Surprised, Kim retreated, flexing his fingers and moving his wrist. His arm was not broken. Curious, as this man seemed skilled enough that had he wanted the limb broken, he might have done so with the opening he'd taken. *Mercy? Or foolishness…?* The latter Kim doubted. In his experience, foolish men were less likely by far to live long enough to become skilled warriors. *Or perhaps these barbarians are merely too stubborn to fall.*

The Frank stayed close, pressing in on perceived weakness. Seeking to break his opponent's momentum, Kim brought his staff about in a one-handed strike aimed at the Frank's head. The blow did not connect, but by battering it aside, the Frank had to change his direction. He stepped away, bringing his tip up in an attempt to strike the arm again. This time, Kim was ready, and the butt of his staff turned aside the Frank's point before it could land. The Frank was resourceful, however, and Kim felt pain blossom across the backs of his fingers as the tip of the wooden blade slid down his staff and struck them a blow that was not as hard as it might have been, but painful nonetheless.

He didn't let go, though, as his opponent had just given him an opening. Kim kept the staff moving, rotating the weapon about and whipping up the end the Frank had beaten aside. With satisfaction, Kim felt it solidly connect, but the Frank was moving away already, acting neither winded nor broken. Leaping back, Kim endeavored to give himself space.

Instead of retreating out of reach as well, resetting their fight, the Frank chased after Kim with serpentine speed. A gloved hand shot out, seizing Kim by the wrist, and he was jerked off balance. The point of the Frank's wooden blade snapped forward in a sudden thrust. *Bend in the wind,* Kim thought, letting his body arc away from the point, not quickly enough to avoid it altogether, but far enough to avoid the worst of it. The point loomed in his field of vision, and he struggled to bend farther. He felt the impact more than he heard it—a loud crunching noise that resonated throughout his skull—and he found himself unable to breathe through his nose. He fought against blurring eyes as tears reflexively came.

The Frank had broken his nose.

Through the haze of his vision, he saw the sword whipping around to finish him with a blow to the left side of his head. Disoriented, his stance wobbly and not stable, he was in danger of being knocked senseless. If he let the blow land. Blocking out the pain in his face, he concentrated on his hands, forcing them to respond to his demands. The staff swung up—agonizingly slowly, it seemed—and the two wooden weapons loudly crashed against one another as he fought to remain on his feet.

✦✦✦

It was like sparring with Taran, Andreas realized. Getting his hand on the Easterner's wrist had opened the other man's defenses, and the strike to the nose—with the commensurate flow of blood—had evened the score. But the fight was far from over. *It's not truly a fight until both are bleeding.*

The nose? Taran had laughed once when Andreas had landed a lucky strike. *That barely counts.* And he had swiftly demonstrated to the younger Andreas just how little a broken nose slowed down a resourceful and practiced fighter.

Andreas kept up the pressure on the Easterner, striking from both sides. Each attack was parried, but he could sense his opponent's increasing desperation. His opponent's balance had been direly shaken; Andreas could feel how unstable his stance was in how the staff bounced against the wooden sword. With each strike, the Easterner's balance slipped a little further. *He will have to yield soon,* he thought. *One of my blows will get through, and then—*

The Easterner didn't try to block the next jab, and his left hand snaked out—the arm he had hit with the staff!—and grabbed the tip of his sword. It was a move that would be dangerous, if not outright deadly, to try with a real sword, but with wood, it was a sneaky, but clever, trick.

Andreas could be clever too, and instead of getting into a tug-of-war for his weapon, he let go of his waster, leaving his opponent holding two long weapons by their ends. His hands free, Andreas made to finish the fight with a grappling move.

As he'd been taught, and had done hundreds of times, his left hand reached toward his opponent's throat, and his right came up for a hammer blow to the temple. His vision flashed, and his hands were suddenly not where he wanted them to be; his head rang, and rippling lines of agony ran down his frame. Dimly, he realized what had happened: as he had closed to grapple, the Easterner's thumb had darted out and jammed itself into one of the energy points in his neck.

Again, his conditioning and training saved him, and he reacted with a knee strike, which only slid off his opponent's thigh, expertly moved to protect the groin. His left hand was over the Easterner's shoulder, so Andreas shifted to grab his opponent's neck. He braced the other man as he threw his head forward, trying to smash his forehead against the other man's broken nose.

But the Easterner wasn't there; he'd slipped around to Andreas's left. Andreas was still throwing his weight forward, and combined with the lock the man now had on his left arm, he was hurled off his feet, face-first into the dusty ground.

Spitting out dirt, he rolled to the side, getting his feet under him again. He had fallen on top of his sword, and his hands had unconsciously grabbed the weapon. As he came to his feet, he discovered two things: the first being that his right hand was on the pommel of his wooden sword; the second was that his left arm refused to work. Dislocated, but not broken, he hoped.

His opponent had taken advantage of the throw to go for his own weapon. He held his staff in that shortened two-handed grip Andreas was coming to be wary of, and his face—not very pretty before—was a mass of blood and swollen flesh now.

Andreas turned his body slightly, angling his right shoulder toward the man, moving his sword behind his body to hide it from his opponent. No use trying to do anything with the left arm anymore. He was a single-handed opponent now. His choices were fewer; his tactical options much less complicated.

He had no doubt this was the man who had beaten the Livonians at the bridge. This had to be the Flower Knight. The fight was coming to its inevitable conclusion. One more pass would probably be all it would take. One more chance to deliver his message.

Andreas smiled. If his plan worked, then losing this fight would be worth the reward…

Come at me, then. Let's finish this.

◆◆◆

Kim was surprised at the failure of his thumb strike to the Frank's energy point. A secret technique of the Flower Knights, the strike should have paralyzed the man's entire body, but instead, the Frank had only lost the use of his left arm. In any other situation, Kim would have been fascinated by this revelation, for it suggested the Rose Knights had access to esoteric fighting styles, techniques that relied on a man's understanding of his opponent's energy centers. As it was, not only was the Frank still standing, but he had retrieved his sword and had adopted a truly defensive stance. It looked almost coy, the way he was hiding behind his own body, but Kim was wary of the fact he could barely see the other man's weapon.

It was a good stance, probably one that was very effective against another edged weapon, but the staff worked better as a thrusting and jabbing weapon, and after a few weak parries on the part of the Frank, both men realized the staff was ultimately going to win. With one hand, the Frank beat each of his attacks back, but he was forced to give ground with each parry.

Kim recovered badly from a wild sweep of the sword after a parry, exposing his left shoulder, and the Frank took the bait, sensing this was his one hope to regain the fight. Kim was ready, though, as the recovery had been a feint, and the butt of his staff effortlessly pushed the wooden sword aside as it came toward him. Kim surged into the opening and, with a sharp snap of his wrist, clipped the Frank on the temple with the staff. The Frank stumbled, grunting in pain, and then crumpled to the ground of the proving field.

The roar of the crowd came back to him, shut out before by the all-consuming focus of the fight. Kim was breathing heavily, and out of the corner of his eye, he could already see an enormous confusion on the other side of the ropes as his Mongol guards tried to calm the surrounding crowd.

A hand grabbed his ankle, and he looked down, surprised. Didn't the Frank realize he had lost? The Rose Knight was squinting up at him, his mouth moving. Was he praying?

No. He's trying to tell me something.

He would not be able to celebrate his victory for long. The Mongols would drag him out of the ring in a few seconds. He had so little time.

Kim knelt beside the fallen man, slipping his hand behind the Frank's head. The man's gaze was fierce and unwavering, in spite of the blow to the head, and he hissed one word, loud enough for Kim to hear over the roar of the crowd.

"Hans."

The boy's name.

In a flash, Kim understood. He and the Rose Knights did not share a common language; it would be difficult for them to communicate effectively. But they did share one thing in common: the friendship of the boy. "Hans," he repeated.

"Hans," the Frank said the boy's name one last time, as if to seal the understanding that had passed between them. The boy would carry their messages. The two of them stared at one another for a moment that stretched longer and longer, until Kim abruptly realized that the guards hadn't yet come to retrieve him.

The crowd had grown silent, and he saw that the man's eyes were now fixed on something behind him with a sudden, alert intensity. Kim glanced over his shoulder, and his guts tightened at what he saw: the crowd was vanishing, slipping away like the tide gone suddenly in reverse, rushing away from the shore. They were fleeing before the arrival of heavily armored Mongol warriors, men with plumed helmets and long pole-arms with wickedly curved blades.

The Mongols scattered the crowd, flowing around the ring until the dusty brown of the audience had been replaced with the black armor of the Khan's personal guard. Within seconds, the two fighters were surrounded by a tight cordon of armed men, their deadly pole-axes lowered ominously toward the ring.

After a few seconds, the ring parted to allow a burly Mongol with a beard twisted into an ornate braid to approach the ring. He wore polished lamellar armor that shone in the sun, and his helm was topped with a horsetail plume that danced in the wind. It was Tegusgal, wearing his ceremonial armor—the armor he only wore when he was attending to the Khan. "Your weapon," he demanded of Kim, pointing at the staff.

Kim glared at Tegusgal, his cultivated calm dangerously close to breaking. He should have known Tegusgal would have learned of his trickery to come out to First Field, and he should have equally prepared for the man's personal involvement in retrieving him. But the elation of the victory over the Frank and the subsequent success at making contact had driven all those thoughts from him, and to be so unexpectedly confronted with the vicious and shrewd captain of the prison guards was to be caught off guard. Fighting to keep his face impassive, Kim relinquished his staff, pushing it toward the Khan's man. Tegusgal picked it up and strode forward, swinging it heavily down on the back of Kim's leg. "On your knees, dog."

Kim collapsed forward, his hands clawing at the dry ground of First Field. Out of the corner of his eye, he saw the Frank looking at him, an expression of something not quite sympathy, not quite anger on his face. Kim turned his head slightly and held the Frank's gaze, drawing strength and serenity from the Rose Knight's expression. But then another commotion drew his attention back to the scaffolding again.

The Mongol guards parted, falling away from the edge of the ring, and their retreat pushed the crowd even farther back so that, in a few seconds, the area around the ring was deserted but for Kim, the Frank, and Tegusgal. Kim swallowed heavily, his mouth suddenly dry, as he spotted the reason why.

Ten broad-backed slaves, bearing a red-curtained palanquin, slowly came to a halt next to Tegusgal, who dropped to his knees as well, holding Kim's staff in front of him like an offering to a god.

Beside him, the Frank pushed himself up to a sitting position with his good arm.

The bearers knelt as one in perfect synchronization, laying their burden upon the ground. The palanquin was enormous, draped with dark silk, edged in gold ornamentation. A pair of snarling wolf heads, made from gold wire and sporting ivory teeth and flashing rubies for eyes, adorned each of the forward corners. A curtain parted on one side, and Tegusgal jerked as he heard the voice issuing from within. The words were too softly spoken for Kim to hear, but he could guess as to their import from Tegusgal's reaction.

The captain of the guard stepped forward and delicately raised one of the curtains on the front of the palanquin, keeping his face downturned the entire time. He stared at his boots as a thick-bodied figure ducked under the edge of the palanquin's roof and stood upon the dry earth of the proving ground.

Kim felt the Frank stiffen next to him, and he did not fault the man's reaction. Here was Onghwe Khan, the man responsible for all their misery. He was dressed in fine silks inlaid with cloth of gold. His beard was thick and oiled, and but for the ostentatious garments, he was a surprisingly unassuming man. *But for his eyes,* Kim thought, wondering if the Frank saw the man's eyes as he did. *The eyes are like hungry tigers.*

The master of the Circus had come.

"What is this?" the Khan demanded.

Tegusgal snapped to attention and, in a quiet voice, began to explain what had transpired, even though he had witnessed none of it. As the Khan's attention passed from them—they were two dirty and bloody men, sitting in the dirt, not worth his attention—Kim turned his head slowly until he could once more meet the eyes of the Rose Knight. *A message,* he thought. *He must understand.*

He raised one hand surreptitiously from the ground, no more than the height of one finger's width, and with his index finger, he pointed at the Khan. The Frank saw the motion of his hand, and though his brow creased with confusion for a brief second, he gave the tiniest of nods.

Kim raised his hand farther off the ground, making no effort to hide the motion now, and he tentatively touched at his bloody face, as if suddenly aware of how much his broken nose pained him. He slid his hand down to his throat, letting the bulk of his hand hide the motion of his middle finger. He drew it across his neck in a small, but unmistakable, cutting motion.

The Frank stared at him for a long moment, and Kim was afraid Tegusgal would finish his explanation before the Frank understood. He didn't dare risk making the motion a second time. *Please understand,* he silently implored the other man.

Something flickered in the Frank's eyes, a deep-seated and mischievous gleam. Then, with a tiny curl starting at the edge of his mouth, he tipped his head fractionally.

I understand and agree.

They were of one mind: they had to find a way to kill Onghwe Khan.

CHAPTER 23:

SERVUS SERVORUM DEI

The guard outside Orsini's palazzo held up his hand as Cardinal Sinibaldo Fieschi approached. "Good day, Father. Please state your business with the Senator."

Fieschi, lost in the turmoil of his thoughts, stopped abruptly and stared at the man's hand. He had been thinking about the gates of Rome, about which one the pair of ragged messengers would probably use to escape the city, and he hadn't been paying much attention to his surroundings. Walking through Rome during the day, dressed as a priest—even a simple one, without any of the usual finery he or the other cardinals wore—was much less dangerous than the hurried and somewhat stealthy pace he typically adopted during his nocturnal visits.

"*Servus Dei,* bringing urgent news to Senator Orsini," he growled at the guard. "Let me pass."

The guard blinked but did not move aside. Fieschi, on the other hand, did not blink, pinning the man with a stony glare that worked so often on the weak willed. "The Senator wants to see me immediately."

The guard shrugged and sucked on the inside of his cheek. "The Senator is a busy man, Father. Why don't you tell me what's so important and I'll have someone inform the Senator?"

The man didn't recognize him. The nighttime guards knew him, having been informed that he would occasionally show up unannounced; after a few visits, they had simply turned a blind eye when he arrived at the palazzo's gates, indifferent veterans to the secret machinations in which their master was involved. The daytime guards, though, were another matter; their purview was less complicated: keep the palazzo safe; don't let anyone disturb the Senator.

Fieschi stepped close. "Listen to me very carefully, you son of a poxy bitch," he said. The guard jerked to attention, surprised by such language coming from a priest's mouth. "The news I carry is of vital importance to the Senator and to the safety of Rome itself. If your stubborn ignorance causes harm to befall the Senator, he will—I am certain—have you flayed alive with less ceremony than he would take in picking his crusty, noble nose. You will—immediately—escort me, Cardinal Sinibaldo Fieschi of the Holy Church, to the Senator's chambers, or not only will your skin be ripped from your body and thrown to the dogs, but the hands of your wife, your mistress, your daughter—if you have managed to breed—will be nailed to the headboard of your favorite whore's bed."

The guard had more spine than Fieschi credited him for, and he held his ground until Fieschi raised his left hand as if he were going to deliver a backhanded slap. The guard caught sight of the large ring on the cardinal's hand, and the blood drained from his tawny face.

He fled, running for the palazzo, and Fieschi allowed himself a tiny smile before he followed.

◆◆◆

"Threatening my staff now, are you, Sinibaldo?" Orsini asked as Fieschi entered the Senator's sitting room.

"He did not recognize me," Fieschi said with sullen irritation. "He mistook me for a common parish priest—"

"I thought humility was one of the traits holy men sought to embrace. A reminder of one's insignificance before God, no?" Orsini observed with a trace of a smile. "Besides, do you really expect my entire domestic staff to know you on sight? That would suggest both of us are atrocious at keeping secrets." He drew back his smile and his face turned cold. "Why have you come in the middle of the day? What has happened? Did someone die?"

"Not yet," said Fieschi and repeated with emphasis, "not *yet.* There is a more alarming crisis that you must address. At this very moment, a messenger is heading to alert Frederick of the cardinals' imprisonment."

Orsini's face darkened. "What messenger?"

"That's the worst of it. A Binder." Fieschi threw him an accusing stare. "So much for your successful eradication of that witch network."

"How do you know this?" Orsini demanded.

"Oh, my friend, my friend," Fieschi clucked. "You would not believe the excitement we've had in our little prison. I will tell you all that has happened, but first, you must immediately lock the gates; the guards must be on full alert, not only at the gates, but the rooftops of any building within jumping distance of the walls."

"Are you serious?"

"Have you ever heard of a Binder-carried message not being delivered?"

Orsini frowned. "What you are proposing is costly and difficult; I want to know that this is a genuine threat."

With visible effort, Fieschi controlled his temper. It was no wonder the palazzo guards were so disrespectful and arrogant—they took their cues from their master. While it would be satisfying to wash his hands of this disaster and let Orsini discover the danger of doubting his words, the messenger could disrupt everything. "I heard—with these very ears," he said with some forced patience, "I heard Somercotes give the message to the Binder girl. Simply, it asks for Frederick to assault the Septizodium and tells him that she knows of the secret passages."

"And you let her go?" Orsini snorted.

"Someone half my size who has been trained in the arts of concealment and stealth just might be able to slip past me in a pitch-black tunnel," Fieschi shot back. "However, she will have a harder time evading your guards in broad daylight—that is, if you could be bothered to actually alert them to that necessity." He gestured ferociously at the door behind him. "For every second you sit there, staring at me like a clod, she gets closer to one of the gates. Why would I dare leaving the Septizodium during the day if it were not for a crisis such as this? Damn your indolence, man. I am certain of this. If she is fleet, she could already have reached the Porta Appia or the Porta Latina. We have no time. You must act now!"

Orsini narrowed his eyes. "Very well, Sinibaldo. I will send out an alert," he said, rising to his feet and striding toward the door, "but then you must tell me exactly what you know and what has happened."

"Of course," Fieschi replied. He stared at the door after the Bear had left the room, his mind tumbling over the possibilities. If Orsini was too late, and the girl managed to slip out of the city, how long would it take for her to reach Frederick's pickets? How long would Frederick ponder her message before responding?

The election of the next Pope had to happen soon. He couldn't wait. He had to force the cardinals to vote. He had to find a way to break their deadlock. Appealing to their avarice and their self-serving natures hadn't worked so far. He recalled the look on the guard's face when he threatened the man's family. *Perhaps,* he thought, *it is time to find a different incentive.*

◆◆◆

Blinking even in the shaded sunlight of the alley, Ocyrhoe helped Ferenc pivot the stone back into place. It slid with remarkable ease, and she was amazed at how invisible the crack was, how solid the wall, when the door was properly closed. She would never have found it without Ferenc.

He was blinking in the shade too. With his eyes, he gestured behind her, back out toward the main street. He held out his forearm with a questioning expression. When she did not take it, he grabbed her wrist and played his fingers across her skin. "What way?"

Ocyrhoe had been thinking about their route out of Rome since they had left the company of cardinals deep inside the tunnels. Porta Appia and Porta Latina were closest, but since Fieschi knew they were here, she worried their presence would become known—perhaps it was already known—and Orsini would be alerted. The Bear's men would be watching for them, both around the Septizodium and, quite possibly, at the gates.

If they moved quickly, they might be able to get to the gate before the guards had it closed. But if they were too late, all would be lost. It would take too long to cross the city to a different gate. By that time, the city would be crawling with the

Bear's men, much like it had been when her sisters were first taken, and it would be difficult to escape.

No, one of the other gates was a smarter plan. Even with the guidance of the other two cardinals—Capocci and Colonna—they had stumbled through the tunnels for some time, and since they had met no resistance, she could assume Fieschi had gone to Orsini. *How long will it take him to reach the Bear?* she wondered, trying to remember the night she had followed the cardinal to the palazzo. Orsini would have to send messengers to close the gates—if that was his first reaction—and so the best gate would be one which it would take his messengers a long time to reach; they would have more time to reach it themselves before an edict arrived to close the city. It might be possible…

She traced the route in her head: north, to the Coliseum and past the Basilica di Santa Maria Maggiore; east along the Via Tiburtina, all the way to the gate. *The same one Ferenc and Father Rodrigo came through when they arrived in Rome.* She shivered slightly as a chill touched the back of her neck. Even if Fieschi ran to the Porta Appia himself and dispatched messengers from there, the Porta Tiburtina was far enough away to be a good choice. That was what she told herself. There was no other reason to choose that gate…

"Follow me," she signed back. "Hand-holding."

They interlaced fingers, grimy palm against grimy palm, and walked quickly toward the main street.

Walking was always a pleasure for Ocyrhoe, no matter where she was going, and it was so even now when there was so much to worry about. Ferenc might be more acute of hearing and of vision, but she apprehended the patterns of life in a holistic, intuitive way, and even a brisk walk—almost a run, if they could sustain it—would reveal much to her about the mood and temperament of her city.

As they walked, she wondered about this Robert of Somercotes who had known the name of her sisterhood's secret language; she wondered too about Ferenc. How could a male come to know a language that had only ever been used by Binders—who were, as far as she knew, always female? *If only I had had more training,* she lamented, *perhaps these mysteries would not be mysteries.* If only she'd had more of an interest in history and philosophy before the Bear's men had come for her sisters.

They stopped at a small turn in the road, just around the corner from the marketplace that sprawled in the shadow of the Coliseum. Ferenc pulled up short next to a wagon maker's shop, not to avoid a slow-moving cart trundling by, but for some other reason entirely.

Ocyrhoe gave him a questioning look, and he released her hand to tap on her arm: "Listen."

Embarrassed that this stranger to her native city had better ears than she did, Ocyrhoe took a deep breath and held it, willing her senses to move beyond their immediate surroundings. Ahead of them—on the far side of the marketplace—there was some commotion. Through the general roar, men's voices shouted in anger; women wailed beseechingly.

A riot. There were any number of explanations why the beleaguered people of Rome might flare into anger, but the tight knot in Ocyrhoe's stomach warned her it was for the reason she feared most.

Her fingers danced rapidly along his arm. "The guards have been alerted," Ocyrhoe signed.

He was startled. "They are looking for us," he signed, looking for her confirmation that he read the situation correctly—that they were the cause of the riot up ahead. "The angry tunnel priest did this." He punctuated his statement with a quizzical look.

She shrugged, then nodded and tapped his wrist twice with two fingers—total agreement. "I will tell you more later," she fingered. "Angry tunnel priest is F-i-e-s-c-h-i." Then, aloud, she said, "Fieschi."

"Fieschi," Ferenc repeated. His quizzical expression remained.

Ocyrhoe realized that he didn't understand how a priest could command the city guard. He wouldn't understand the word *Senator,* and to explain what a Senator was would take too long. "He works for a Rome leader named Orsini." As an afterthought, she added, "Orsini imprisons priests."

Ferenc's mouth dropped open, and he touched her upper forearm in the simple *Rankalba* gesture: "Why?"

"Too long to tell now," she signed again. "Later. Must move quickly now. Must hurry to gate."

Before it was too late.

CHAPTER 24:

THE KNIFE EDGE

It was the fourth night before Gansukh had an opportunity to do more than take care of his horse, throw his gear on the ground, and collapse into a restless sleep—sleep that was blissfully free of memories of the encounter with Lian in the alley. It was a secret, much like the green sprig he kept hidden in his *deel*—an impossibility that was somehow true, but which he feared would vanish if examined too closely.

Instead, he sought to lose himself in the steppe—the fresh air, the open sky—but that joy was overshadowed by the ponderous and constant needs of the *Khagan*'s caravan. Each evening, the call to halt came a half hour before sunset, and it always took until well after nightfall before the last cart came to a complete stop. So many of Ögedei's retinue were completely unprepared for living on the steppes that Gansukh was kept busy each night sharing his experience at starting fires, setting up tents, assisting in securing the numerous horses and oxen, and otherwise preparing for the chill air that came down from the mountains. Finally, he was able to slip away from the general chaos and set up his *ger* on a shallow rise that looked down over the main supply train. He could see the rounded dome of the *Khagan*'s *ger* where it sat in the center of the camp.

Once he laced up the flaps of his *ger*, he finally felt confident that he would have a few minutes to himself, and he laid out the contents of Lian's bag: stiff leather shoes; dried meat and fruit; an empty waterskin; the purse, which was filled with rings, necklaces, and a few coins; and a short knife in a leather sheath.

The knife gave Gansukh pause. In the alley, when he had felt the purse, he had known what it contained. He had tried to think of other reasons she might have it, but he kept coming back to the simplest answer: she was going to try to escape during the trip to Burqan-qaldun.

During the last few days, he had wondered about the contents of the bag, but there had been little time for more than a passing thought here and there. As long as he had her bag, she couldn't realize her plan to escape.

What had bothered him was the nagging idea to never look. If he didn't know, then it couldn't possibly be true. But on seeing the contents, he found himself both saddened and surprised. And the latter depressed his mood even more, and he wasn't sure why.

Lian was, after all, a Chinese prisoner, regardless of how much freedom she had at court. Why wouldn't she desire to escape? He was a free Mongol warrior, and court had nearly stifled him. He had, in fact, been eager to start this journey to the sacred grove, as it meant some freedom for him too.

He realized it was the presence of the knife that bothered him so much. It was possible that she was only planning on using it for killing and skinning game, but that was to perpetuate an illusion. She wasn't a hunter. Was it for self-defense? He took the knife out of its sheath and tested its edge. If someone got in her way while she was trying to escape, would she use the knife?

"Master Gansukh?" A servant, outside his tent.

Gansukh tossed his riding coat over the scattered contents of Lian's bag and unlaced the top of the tent flaps. "Yes?" he asked, suddenly glad for the interruption.

The man was one of Chucai's runners. "Master Chucai requests your presence at the evening meal. Outside the *Khagan*'s *ger.*"

Gansukh nodded and let the tent flap fall closed. He stared at the lumpy pile beneath his riding coat. Dinner was an opportunity to talk with Lian. He hadn't seen her since they had left Karakorum; he had wanted to ignore her dictum that they wait three days and seek her out immediately, but he had been too busy and too tired. And there was the issue with the contents of the bag as well. Regardless of the other reasons he wanted to see her, he had to deal with the bag, and having seen the knife and the rest, he knew he it was past time to seek her out. He had to try to convince her of the futility of escape. Munokhoi's men patrolled all around the caravan. He had watched them set up their patrols when the caravan had halted. If she were lucky, they'd only catch her and return her to the camp; more likely, she'd be mistaken for a Chinese rebel and ridden down.

Trying not to think about the sight of her lying in the dust—her body broken and bloody, pierced with arrows and cut by swords—he swept everything but the knife back into her bag. Shoving the sheathed knife into his sash and cradling the bag under his arm, he unlaced his tent flaps and went down to the *Khagan*'s *ger.*

The question that kept gnawing at him was whether she would use the knife if he were the one who tried to stop her.

✦✦✦

A wide circle of torches surrounded the *Khagan*'s *ger*, and carpets had been laid out on the ground in ragged arcs inside the ring of torches. The *Khagan*'s private cooks had been working steadily since dusk, and the aroma from their cooking fires made Gansukh's mouth water and his stomach grumble as he approached. Three long tables were set up beside the wheeled *ger*, and they overflowed with food.

The *Khagan* slumped in an ornate chair behind a fourth table, and seated around him on low benches were his advisors and special guests. Gansukh spotted Master Chucai on the *Khagan*'s right side. He was listening to something the *Khagan* was telling him, his fingers idly picking at the breast meat of a cooked duck.

Not wanting to be seen by either man, Gansukh wandered along the row of torches, looking at the other guests scattered on the carpets. He found Lian sitting by herself, and as soon as he spotted her, she noticed him. For a second, he reconsidered his decision. It was not too late to approach the main table and present himself to the *Khagan* and Chucai, but the weight of the bag in his hands made his mind up for him. Why had he brought his lessons with him? He did not have a good answer.

He walked over to Lian and sat down. He set the bag down between them and gently pushed it toward her.

"I missed you last night," she said, glancing down at the bag. Her voice was almost too soft to be heard over the noisy gathering.

"I was busy," he said awkwardly.

Her hands crept toward the bag and gently pulled it into her lap. "Did you look inside?"

"I did." Gansukh tapped the knife stuck in his sash.

She remained still, clutching the bag tightly to her stomach. "What are you going to do?"

There was no sign of the fiery woman who had accosted him in the alley. She was resigned to some fate she had already decided upon in her head, some judgment she assumed he was going to pass.

What was he to do? The contents of the bag suggested she was going to escape, and he should tell Chucai what he knew. It would reflect poorly on him if she ran, as rumors of their relationship would surface. Munokhoi, the ambitious and vindictive *Torguud* captain, would especially relish the opportunity to turn the *Khagan* against him. Would the bond he had with Ögedei be enough to convince them that he had nothing to do with Lian's flight?

But he had not expected her to be so complacent, to give up so readily. He had thought her mind was made up—she would be free or she would die trying. "I don't know," he replied honestly.

She started to stand, and he grabbed her arm, holding her back. "Listen to me…" She tried to pull free, and he tightened his grip. "Listen," he said. He glanced around, checking to see if their conversation had caught anyone's attention. Too much *arkhi* had been drunk already; no one showed any interest in their conversation. "This is the worst time to escape," he said. "There are too many patrols, and they're all still eager to prove themselves. You'll never make it."

While he spoke, she had been staring at his hand, but she raised her head now and looked up at him. "The worst time…" she said. "Is there a better time, Gansukh?"

He let go. "That's not what I meant."

"What did you mean?"

"Lian, you can't—"

"I have to, Gansukh. I cannot spend the rest of my life as a prisoner." It was her turn to grab him. "Help me."

Her words paralyzed him. His tongue would not move, nor could he pull away from her. Help her? It wasn't the question that had struck him senseless, but the sudden realization that he *wanted* to. But at the same time, he was confounded by the realization that doing so would mean either never seeing her again or going with her—two choices that had been swimming in the back of his mind for the last few days, but that he had studiously avoided thinking about. Until this very moment, when she spoke those two words.

"The Mongol Empire is on the brink of disaster, Gansukh," Lian whispered. "Ögedei Khan will drink himself to death—despite everything—and what happens then? The Empire will fall apart as his wives and his brothers fight amongst themselves over who will be the next *Khagan*. What happens to me during that time? To us?"

Gansukh found his voice. "Ögedei Khan knows what he must do," he said. He removed her hand from his arm. "I know what my duty is." Something fluttered in his chest, like a tiny bird caught in a bramble, and he exhaled slowly, letting his chest collapse. Whatever he felt became more frantic, fighting the crushing weight of his denial, and then it went limp. He was very tired all of a sudden, and all his appetite was gone. All he wanted to do was go back to his tent and sleep. He didn't want to have to make this choice.

"Please give me the knife back," Lian asked softly.

He shook his head. "If you are caught with it, you will be punished," he said dully.

"If I'm caught with any of this, I'll be punished." Lian pounded her fist against the bag. Some of her fiery independence was returning, and Gansukh felt a brief spasm in his chest, one final flutter of affection.

"Lian—" he started.

She shook her head, refusing to listen to him, and leaped up. Clutching the bag, she rushed out of the ring of torches. Gansukh got to his feet, meaning to follow her. *To what end?* The thought made him indecisive, and he staggered slightly as he tried to sit back down and go after Lian at the same time.

"The horse rider has had too much to drink already."

Munokhoi and a pair of *Torguud* guards had come up behind him. He hadn't seen them coming, and he held his tongue, unsure how much of the conversation with Lian they had seen. Munokhoi came too close to Gansukh, a leer stretching his face. "Your pretty bird has flown," he chuckled. His breath stank of *arkhi*, and his eyes were black holes that seemed to suck the torchlight into them. "If she flies too far away, the giant bear won't be the only thing we hunt." He glanced at his companions and laughed with them. "What soft skin she has..."

Gansukh stood firm on the sandy ground. Before he had come to court, his reaction to Munokhoi's words would have been physical. He would have drawn his knife and demanded the other man do the same. But after all the lessons with Lian, he knew that was the reaction of a wild animal—one wolf responding to another. Munokhoi had come looking for a fight; why give him that satisfaction? Did he not have better weapons at his disposal now?

I am a better man because of her, he realized, and the dead thing in his heart started fluttering again.

"There are no walls out here, *city boy*," he said with a hint of a smile. "How are you going to catch something that can fly out of the range of your Chinese toys?"

Munokhoi jabbed Gansukh in the chest with a stiff finger. "You know nothing about—" he growled.

"Captain Munokhoi." One of his companions interrupted Munokhoi, and when he whirled on the man, the guard redirected his anger with a gesture.

A guard was running toward them. "Captain Munokhoi," he shouted, scattering a trio of concubines and a minor ambassador as he dashed across their carpet. "The patrols are late, and horses—without riders—"

Munokhoi didn't wait for the man to finish. He shoved Gansukh aside and sprinted toward the main table. "The *Khagan*," he screamed. "We are under attack. Protect the *Khagan*!" His *Torguud* guards drew their swords and followed, shoving their way through the suddenly panicked crowd.

Gansukh hesitated, torn between his duty and what was caught in his heart. *Lian*...

CHAPTER 25:

DECIPIES, ET PRÆVALEBIS

"Even by your standards, that is rather childish, don't you think?" There was an impish gleam in Colonna's eyes that belied his tone.

After the messengers had left their impromptu conclave, the cardinals had dispersed as well, not wishing their meeting to be stumbled upon by the others. He and Capocci had intended to lead the girl and the young man back to Fieschi's secret entrance, and once they had passed the Old Scar—the name Capocci had given to the savage break in the foundation of the ancient temple in which they were housed—the roughly hewn cardinal had taken his leave. *I have souls to rescue,* he had said as he vanished into the dark tunnels. *These two, I leave in your care.*

Once the messengers had departed the confines of the Septizodium tunnels, shutting the secret panel and sealing Colonna in darkness once more, he had returned to the haunts of the captive cardinals. Capocci had not been that hard to find; Colonna suspected he knew what the other man was up to.

Capocci was seated in a dusty antechamber, a narrow room with tall arched doorways. Of the four thresholds, three were filled with rubble, hiding whatever grand hall this chamber abutted, and the fourth led back to the rest of the areas more commonly used by the cardinals. A pair of small lanterns kept the seated cardinal company, along with a few other objects.

The heavily bearded cardinal glanced up when he heard Colonna's voice. "Most children know better than to play with poisonous insects." His beard seemed to flap like a bird's wing as he smiled. Something small squirmed in his leather-clad grip, and he dropped it into a clay jar sitting on the floor in front of him. "You may be right, however. This new hobby may qualify as infantile behavior, but for something so infantile, I must say I'm pretty good at it." His smile broadened, his bearded wings lifting. "Want to try it?" He gestured to a wooden box beside him; out of the tiny airholes in the top came the furtive scratching of half a dozen furious scorpions, clawing and crawling over one another. "There is another glove." A heavy leather gauntlet, left-handed, lay on the floor beside the box.

Colonna shook his head as he lowered himself to the floor. He leaned back against the wall of the dusty chamber. "I rest content merely abetting your follies, without actually participating."

"Follies!" Capocci cried out in mock outrage. "I do not consider this a folly! In a den of vipers, it is a marvelous thing to have all possible tricks up one's sleeve." He slid open the lid of the box—just enough—and thrust his hand inside. After a moment of concentrated groping, he grinned with satisfaction and drew his hand out. Quickly, in a motion that ran counter to his air of relaxed insouciance, his bare left hand slid the lid home again.

Pinched between his right thumb and forefinger, an angry scorpion wriggled. "Hello, my little angel of death," Capocci cooed. "I am the great and powerful Cardinal Capocci, and I offer you a chance at redemption. Will you mend your ways and become a harmless plaything? Will you cast off your poison and be born again in the name of Christ? What's that?" He lowered his head and nodded as if he understood the clicks and snaps of the scorpion's pincers—the secret language of arachnids. "Yes, you say? Oh, blessed by the Lord on high! Well then, let me assist you in your *resurrection.*" Adjusting his grip on the squirming scorpion, Capocci reached for the stinger with his bare left hand. "This won't hurt a bit, my innocent child."

Colonna, despite himself, leaned closer to watch. This was not the first time he had seen Capocci perform this trick, and as much as he pretended otherwise, he could not help but be fascinated by what came next.

With a magnificent finesse of movement that one would have not thought possible in a man with such thick and rough fingers, Capocci expertly gripped the stinger—at the base of the last of the six segments that made up the tail—and gave it a quick, firm jerk. Though he knew it was a fanciful notion, Colonna imagined he could hear a yowl of outrage from the scorpion as it was parted from its deadly weapon.

Capocci held up the tiny dagger, squinting at it for a moment in the dim light of the lanterns, and then he smiled at Colonna. "Sing Hosanna," he told the scorpion and dropped this one too into the clay pot.

"Are they well away?" he asked Colonna, referring not to the scorpions, but to the others most recently in their care.

Colonna nodded. "They are."

Capocci sighed. "What do you think of Robert's plan, then?"

"As good as any. Naught will come of it, I fear. Or at the worst, we will emerge from this purgatory to find a city filled with corpses—Orsini and Frederick having killed themselves and everyone else in their frenzy to keep us *safe*. What sort of world will we thrust the next Bishop of Rome into?"

"God only knows, my dear Giovanni," Capocci sighed. "God only knows."

"Speaking of God, He will forgive me—I hope—when I say this, but I like your idea of dropping them on Fieschi in his sleep." Colonna leaned forward to peer into the clay jar. "Though, I am not sure the fellow ever actually does sleep. He's out most nights—all night—at Orsini's, and he has never, to my watchful eye, dozed off once during the daylight hours."

"De Segni, then," Capocci said offhandedly. "Or Bonaventura!"

Colonna grinned. "A marvelous choice. The good man will shit himself, probably in front of us. Ho, he will surely lose some votes that way." He laughed until a thought struck him. "Or when they appear to sting him, and then he doesn't die, Fieschi will use that to imply Bonaventura is some sort of holy man."

"Ah, excellent point. That sort of foolishness would clinch the election. Some of the others are rather prone to such superstitious nonsense." Capocci deftly retrieved another scorpion. "In that case, perhaps we suggest to Somercotes that he use them on Castiglione, to the same end."

Colonna shook his head ruefully. "Fieschi is well practiced in law and rhetoric, remember? He will use this as the basis for an argument that Castiglione is an agent of the Devil, as is clearly demonstrated by his unnatural affinity to the demonic sort of creatures that scorpions are."

"That's true," Capocci sighed. He plucked the stinger from the scorpion, then dropped the angered arachnid into the clay jar and flicked the now useless stinger into the room's far shadows. "Let's just throw them on Fieschi anyway. For the fun of it. God will forgive us this infantile transgression, don't you think?"

Colonna leaned his head back against the cool stone wall. "I would think so, my friend. He has had little enough to say these past years about an endless parade of monstrous cruelties."

◆◆◆

The chaos in the marketplace at the Porta Tiburtina confirmed Ocyrhoe's fears. Wagons were lined up for the gate, but none of them would be moving anytime soon. A dense mob swirled and surged around the wagons like surf raging upon broken rocks. Ocyrhoe spotted a lanky thief boldly lifting a crate of fruit off the back of a sagging wagon, then darting away with his prize—no one the wiser. Most of the merchants had already packed up their stalls, even the farmers who wouldn't be able to get out of the city until the guards decided to start letting people through. It was better to have their wares and goods safely stowed than stolen or ruined in the crush.

A line of guards, pole-axes lowered and wavering in the general direction of the mob, like the rippling ridge of hairs on the back of a nervous caterpillar, stood fast before the gate. More than a few looked distinctly unhappy—nervous, fearful. They didn't know how long they were supposed to stand there or under what circumstances they could begin allowing people to pass through the gate.

Once Ocyrhoe realized she and Ferenc couldn't simply walk out of the city, she examined the mob and the guards more carefully, listening and looking for some opening, a gap, a weakness through which they might pass. *Not out. Not through...ah, yes...*

"We can use this," she signed to Ferenc, dragging him away from the edge of the mob. They slipped into the back alleys, winding ever closer to the wall of Rome itself. Gradually, the district became more and more residential, more quiet and deserted, but the guards who might otherwise have been patrolling were absent—no doubt called to the gate as reinforcements against the riot that would eventually erupt. Whatever had stricken the marketplace near the Coliseum would sweep through the crowd at the gate, sooner rather than later. Judging by the number of guards and their somewhat fearful presentation, they were well aware of the oncoming storm.

Eventually, she found what she was looking for—the wall itself. Maybe three stories high, the wall around Rome had been built to keep people out, not in. In some places, it was possible to clamber to the top by way of dirt that had been piled against the inner side. They weren't so lucky here, and they didn't have the time to find such an easy method of escape. The wall was made of rough volcanic rock, knotted and twisted with all manner of hand and toeholds. It shouldn't be too hard to climb—as long as they weren't seen.

Ferenc said something to her in his tongue, but she shook her head and pantomimed climbing the wall. When he still hesitated, she shoved him at the wall, and he finally relented. He grabbed at several knobs, lifting himself up easily, and proceeded to climb the wall, as if he had spent many hours in his youth climbing such barriers. *He probably had*, Ocyrhoe thought, *or trees, even*. She hesitated, hand on the nearest knob of rock. *Trees*. She was about to leave Rome, the only home she had ever known. Outside the city was...*outside*. There were no walls, no houses, and no streets. Just forest and swamp and plain and...what else? She held her breath. Was she doing the right thing? Was she ready for this?

"Halt!"

Behind them, a man ran toward them, fumbling to pull his sword out of its scabbard. Ocyrhoe recognized the colors of his garb. *One of the Bear's men.*

She glanced up at Ferenc. He was halfway up, far enough that the guard couldn't reach him, but not far enough to quickly reach the top. There would be no time to finish the ascent before the guard reached them, and if they were on the wall, they'd both be easy pickings.

Ferenc looked down, and there was an agonized moment when they stared at each other. If she ran, would the guard chase her? Or would he go after Ferenc? What would they do if they split up?

She shook her head. She didn't know. She hadn't thought through their plan that far.

"Get down from there!"

The guard was nearly upon them.

✦✦✦

Fieschi pushed the door closed and waited for his eyes to adjust to the darkness. With a hand lightly brushing the wall, he walked carefully into the tunnels. He knew where he had to go, and what he had to do; it would not take him long to reach the common areas where the cardinals resided. As his feet retraced the steps he had taken earlier, back toward the room where he had eavesdropped on Somercotes and the others, he banked the remainder of his long-burning frustration with Orsini. *He had reacted too slowly. It would be hours—possibly days, even—before they could be sure the city had been sealed in time.*

He had to force the vote. He couldn't wait to find out if Orsini had been successful or not. Besides, even if they were caught, there would be no way to know to whom in the city they might have spoken. He had to assume the secrets of the Septizodium would not remain secret much longer.

When he reached Somercotes's chamber, it was empty, and it took him several minutes of wandering through the narrow, dimly lit halls before he found his quarry. Somercotes was in one of the rooms that had natural light, and when he entered the chamber without announcing himself, the room was too bright for his dark-accustomed eyes, and he stood in the doorway, blinking.

When his eyes had adjusted, he saw Somercotes watching him with a bland expression. His Bible lay open, in his lap, as if he were sharing a passage with his companion. On the bench beside him sat the new arrival—the *madman*—still filthy and disheveled.

"Cardinal Somercotes," said Fieschi without preamble, "a word in private, if you please."

"Certainly, Cardinal Fieschi," said Somercotes pleasantly, completely unruffled by Fieschi's tone. He closed his Bible and turned to the priest. "Father, if you have need, do not hesitate to seek me in my chamber." The priest looked up vacantly, his sweaty face shining with reflected sunlight.

Fieschi was surprised to find himself contemplating a desire to smash that beatific expression with a rock. Like one of the many shards of stone, lying within easy reach—

Somercotes now laid his hand on Fieschi's arm, fingers digging into flesh, drawing his attention from the smiling priest. "Let us go to my chamber, Cardinal," Somercotes said. His gaze was steady and his grip strong, but Fieschi tore himself loose, refusing to let the other man lead him, and stalked from the room.

Fieschi's own hands shook slightly, and he clenched his fingers before him as he walked so that Somercotes would not see how close to the surface his rage was.

When they reached his chamber, Somercotes closed the door behind them, a polite smile stuck on his face. As he braced the door with a loose timber—affording them some privacy—the smile vanished.

"I have little to say to you, Sinibaldo," he said tightly, "and even less tolerance for your company. So speak concisely, and then remove yourself from my presence."

"You have been entertaining unauthorized guests," Fieschi said. "You have been engaging in covert activities with the aim of destabilizing our work here."

Somercotes stared at him for a second and then let loose a snort of laughter. "Who are you to lodge such a complaint, Sinibaldo? I know where you go at night, and why, and I am not the only one who smells meat on your breath when you return. Your dining habits alone *destabilize our work,* if you can even call the hellish farce we are subjected to here *work.*"

"You have engaged a messenger to seek aid from the Holy Roman Emperor," Fieschi said. "A man whom you know to be no friend of the Church."

"*Your* Church," Somercotes said. "I count Frederick to be one of the most learned and enlightened men of our age. I would celebrate any effort on his part to aid us in our trying time. But that should be no mystery to you. I have never hidden my admiration and respect for the man. Why would I not seek his assistance?"

"So you do not deny sending a messenger?"

Somercotes shrugged. "I have sent many messages to the Holy Roman Emperor, and would have continued to do so had we not been sequestered in this hellish dungeon."

Fieschi gaped, his words caught in his throat. "No," he started, suddenly flustered, "earlier today. You sent a message earlier today."

Somercotes said nothing, and there was nothing in his expression that gave Fieschi any clue as to what the man was thinking. Eventually, the Englishman shrugged. "Today?" he drawled, seeming to give the matter great thought. He shifted the book in his hands as if he were about to open it and start reflecting on a passage from the Bible. "I'm not sure what you are talking about, Sinibaldo. You are the only one who wanders in and out of this place. How could I have sent a message?"

Fieschi snapped his mouth shut with an audible click. Mentally staggered, he held himself as rigid as possible, trying to ascertain how to extricate himself from the error he had just made. *He knows that I know. I have just given myself away, and he pretends otherwise.* He needed to shift his attention away from the messenger, as well as the implication of what Fieschi might have done in response to such knowledge.

"This new man is not who he appears to be," he said.

"No?" Somercotes raised an eyebrow. "Who is he?" Daring him to open his mouth, to reveal some secret knowledge that he could not—should not—know.

Fieschi ground his teeth. Somercotes was toying with him, this upstart from that damp and tiny island so far from Rome. Somercotes had been the confessor to the English king. His name didn't matter; he was nothing more than a barbarian who had converted to Christianity to save his own head. Did Somercotes actually think hearing the confessions of an uneducated savage and offering absolution made him a peer? *He* had studied canonical law at Bologna, under Accursio, and been awarded *maestro* for his studies. He was Vice Chancellor of the Holy Roman Church; he had been the Pope's voice during the last few months of His Eminence's life.

"He's a charlatan," he heard himself say. "A spy for the Emperor."

"And you aren't a lapdog for Orsini?" Somercotes snorted.

"Orsini is the Senator of Rome and, as such, has a vested interest in the next Bishop of Rome," Fieschi retorted, still struggling to find his tongue.

"And Frederick doesn't?" Somercotes inquired. "I think your logic is overly convoluted, dear Sinibaldo. The man who rules over most of Christendom has more of a stake in who is elevated to become the next Pope than a self-appointed upstart who acts like he has read too much Tacitus."

Somercotes stepped away from Fieschi, slowing the rise in tension between them. "It is too late for your ill-conceived and unfounded accusations, Sinibaldo. This new man cannot be swayed or bullied by you, nor even by the Bear himself. He has a genuine religious zeal to him that I find refreshing, if a trifle alarming. The only thing that can move him will be the spirit of the candidate, and you know as well as I do that Bonaventura is as charming as cold porridge. Rodrigo's vote will go to Castiglione. He will be the only man here who casts a vote based on whom he thinks the better man, not for any political factions. Well, perhaps he and Annibaldi...but Rodrigo comes from a place of genuine innocence."

"Ignorance, you mean," Fieschi spat back, regaining some of his composure. His blood pounded in his temples, and the edges of his vision wavered and shook. He had to be careful. Somercotes had a way of getting under his skin, making him irrational and prone to responding too quickly, too emotionally. *Gregory warned you...* He shoved the thought aside. "He will fall for whoever has the most charisma."

"And we both know that is Castiglione," Somercotes said calmly. "Really, Sinibaldo, I do not see what it is that you needed to talk so urgently about. It is time for me to pray now; please let me do so."

"Do not assume," Fieschi said through clenched teeth, "that I cannot persuade him of the wonders of Bonaventura's character."

"If he casts his vote for Bonaventura, I will reveal him as the *spy* you think he is, and you will lose the vote," Somercotes said with a sigh, sounding indulgently sympathetic.

"Well then, if he casts his vote for Castiglione, I shall do likewise," Fieschi retorted.

"Will you? And how will you prove it?" Somercotes asked, as if catechizing a young child.

"How will you prove he isn't?" Fieschi replied, his ears burning like he was a young child, and loathing Somercotes all the more for it.

"Well," Somercotes said, drawing the word out, "I do have his ring. His *cardinal*'s ring. And you do not." He smiled at Fieschi then, the smile of a man who thought he had been granted a decisive victory.

"Which I do not have *yet*," Fieschi argued and made a lunge for Somercotes.

Somercotes was caught off guard by the sudden escalation from argument to action, but only needed to take a half step back to avoid Fieschi's somewhat spastic lunge. As he did so, he dropped his heavy book. Likewise, Fieschi—unprepared to have missed—stumbled forward and had to brace himself against the chamber's wall to avoid falling on his face entirely.

But then Somercotes was behind him and, now alert, wasted no time in leaping on Fieschi's back. Reaching forward with his left arm, Somercotes began to choke him.

The weight of the other man on his back made Fieschi lurch to one side, but his hands found the wall again and he pushed back, then reached up to grab the arm around his neck, before finishing the fall. The motion pulled Somercotes forward, off balance, and tumbled him over Fieschi and onto his back on the chamber's cold stone floor.

Not a trained brawler, Somercotes hadn't braced himself against the throw, and even before his head hit the ground, he was confused about what was happening. He had lost his chokehold on Fieschi, and his arms hung limp. Fieschi cast about and, spotting Somercotes's book, grabbed it up and struck the English cardinal in the head. The spine of the book gave under the impact and Fieschi shifted his grip, using the stiff and stone-encrusted cover instead. He struck Somercotes several more times, until the boards shattered.

"Frederick's help will mean nothing to you now," Fieschi said as he threw aside the ruined book. He was calm, for the first time since they'd entered the room, for the first time since he had been accosted by that churlish guard outside Orsini's palazzo. He had no more doubt about what he had to do, about what must be done. *There must be a vote; a Pope must be elected. The Church must prevail.*

Somercotes, his face bloodied from Fieschi's blows, was still conscious. His eyes fluttered, and a sluggish moan slipped from his slack lips.

Fieschi scrabbled at Somercotes's robe, reaching for the braided rope the other man wore around his waist. A symbol of his austerity and piety, it was the sort of rope a sheepherder would use. Stout and strong. Fieschi gathered up the long strand that hung unencumbered and wrapped it once about Somercotes's neck. Bracing his knee against the struggling cardinal's shoulder, he leaned back, pulling the rope taut. The heavy weave burned in his hands as Somercotes thrashed.

Somercotes got his hands on Fieschi's robes and tried to pull himself closer, but Fieschi's knee kept him at bay. The Englishman's hands became more frantic—at first like talons and then like the wings of a frightened bird. He gurgled and spat, each breath shorter and more desperate than the last.

Fieschi held on. He breathed evenly—in, out, again and again—and kept the rope tight.

The Church must prevail. *I must prevail.*

CHAPTER 26:

RÆDWULF 'S BOW

"It is a *jaghun*," Cnán said, "which is to say a unit of one hundred, made up of ten *arbans* of ten men each. The man you call Graymane is named Alchiq. He is new to them. About a week ago, he rode in out of nowhere to a Mongol garrison west of the Volga, where this *jaghun* and two others were encamped, and simply commandeered it."

"So he is a man of high rank," Feronantus said.

Cnán shrugged. "They know little about him, other than what I have just told you."

As soon as Vera had been able to ride, they had moved beyond the eastern limit of the Khazars' territory. A few hours before, Cnán had arrived at their camp—proving once again her extraordinary tracking skills.

She had been absent for four days.

Following a wash, a nap, and a bowl of antelope stew, she had gathered the others to convey all she had learned.

She went on now to say a few words about where Alchiq's *jaghun* had crossed the Volga and where they had subsequently gone, though as everyone understood, this information was no longer of much use; she had broken contact two days ago, and the Mongols could have covered much distance since then. "Alchiq dispatched an *arban* up into those hills where the Khazars live," she said, nodding toward the dark crests rising from the steppe to the west.

"Too small to perpetrate a massacre," Raphael remarked. "This Alchiq has a light touch, when it suits his purposes."

Some around the council looked as if they were about to raise objections, but they were silenced by a look from Cnán. *She has her own commanding presence, doesn't she?* Raphael thought.

"The *arban* in question is made up of Turkoman recruits from Kiwa, not all that far from here as distances on the steppe go, and they speak a similar language. They were sent to parley, not to kill. They took no casualties during the action against the Shield-Maidens and do not hunger for revenge, as some of the others do."

"You have information about casualties?" Vera said. Unlike the others, she had not grown accustomed to Cnán's ability to move about Mongol-held countryside and gather intelligence.

If Cnán was offended by the skepticism in Vera's voice, she hid it well. "The brunt of your charge was taken by an *arban* of men from Barchkenda, which was all but destroyed. Six were killed outright, two died later of wounds, one is permanently disabled, the last has been absorbed into another *arban* that also took casualties during the fight on the riverbank. The total strength of the *jaghun* has been reduced to a little more than eighty, now organized in eight *arbans*. Some of these are unchanged; others are thrown together from survivors."

"How does that work, in an army where *arbans* are recruited from specific clans and villages?" Percival asked. Perhaps not so much out of practical curiosity as because he enjoyed watching Cnán's mind work.

"It depends on everything—language, clan rivalries, customs. Sometimes it goes smoothly; in other cases, the *arban* is thrown into disarray or even outright conflict."

"Then, since we are outnumbered, let us make *conflict* our ally," Feronantus said.

This was one of these gnomic utterances that threw the group into silence as all waited for Feronantus to make himself clear. Raphael studied their leader during that silence, looking for clues as to the old warrior's state of mind.

Feronantus's outburst of rage when Percival had revealed their plan to the Khazars had been replaced by a kind of sullen embarrassment when Percival's gambit had worked. After that, for a day or two, he had been pensive and withdrawn, but the need to prepare for battle seemed to have focused his mind and pushed into the shadows whatever was troubling him.

"You said earlier," Feronantus went on, "that Barchkenda lost nine men to the Shield-Maidens. Now, I know nothing of Barchkenda, but I shall hazard a guess that it is not a large place."

To this, Cnán responded with a smirk.

"I see from your face that it is even smaller than I imagined," Feronantus said. "The loss of nine of its young men must be a disaster for them. The men in the surviving *arbans*, having seen the devastation wreaked upon these soldiers in a brief melee, will be thinking of their own homes and families. Let us so arrange our tactics as to give them even more to brood upon."

◆◆◆

Cnán was flat on her belly, making the most of a scraggly tuft of wormwood scarcely big enough to provide cover for a dog.

She had learned that if she lay perfectly still and avoided raising her head from the ground, distant observers would read the silhouette of her rumpled, ragged clothes as a pile of leaves or a scattering of rocks. She might have found better concealment in the tall grass growing out of the lee slope below and to her right, but to go down that way would take her out of view of the small party of Mongols patiently following her trail across the grass to her left.

As usual, she had gone to the Mongol camp before dawn to spy on them. But then she had gone against all her instincts—and not at all to her liking—by leaving an obvious trail for them to follow.

Alchiq, or perhaps one of his commanders, had dispatched a group of seven warriors to investigate. For the last hour, they had been gaining on her. They could have caught her quickly, of course, had they chosen to ride hard. But they knew that they were following a mere pedestrian in wide-open country and that time was on their side, and so they had proceeded at a measured and cautious pace, scanning the country ahead for ambushes and other perils.

Cnán would be in a terrible spot just now, were it not for the fact that, two hundred paces away and down the slope to her right, at the bottom of a dry gully, Rædwulf was patiently waiting in a scatter of stunted trees.

Unaware of her scrutiny, the Briton stretched and let his eyes wander. The sun was warm; the late morning was comfortable. She hoped he wasn't planning to take a nap.

Cnán had spent most of her life in parts of the world that were not known for producing persons of large stature. She had long been vaguely aware that if one traveled north and west long enough, one would reach a part of the world inhabited by persons with pale skin and strangely colored hair, often taller than other peoples of the world.

The men of the steppes were like their ponies: low to the ground, stocky, agile, hard to kill. Like any other human population, they would from time to time yield a man of unusual height. But this conferred no advantage in the Mongol way of war, which was all about mobility, quickness, and maneuvering. When hand-to-hand combat occurred, it was probably because something had gone awry. The Mongols did have formations of armored cavalry, employed in special circumstances. A big man might find a place in such a unit. But wrestling was the martial art that they held in the highest esteem, and since size, weight, and strength so often determined the outcome of wrestling matches, this was what big, strong Mongols tended to do for a living. The Khans used them as executioners.

The Northmen did not know or practice the steppe way of war; instead, being ignorant of the art of maneuvering, they preferred to fight in big, lumbering formations that clashed head-on in open fields. It was to be expected that the largest men of such societies would cover themselves in armor and ride out on oversized horses to engage their foes in personal combat with heavy weapons. In this respect, Percival had met her expectations precisely.

Percival, however, was not the biggest and strongest man in their party. That distinction fell to Rædwulf. He was two inches taller than Percival, with a rugged, homely face, and—as she'd come to notice—covered all over with muscles. Among the Mongols, he'd have been their greatest wrestler. Among the Franks, he'd have become a cataphract—a mounted soldier in full armor. But Rædwulf came from an island off the northwestern extremity of the world where the warriors were skilled at a peculiar form of archery.

Compared to the bows of the Mongols, Rædwulf's weapon was huge and primitive, far too unwieldy to be used on horseback. No other man in the party could draw it except for Percival, who could pull the taut, hempen, three-stranded bowstring only partway.

Rædwulf drew his weapon in a peculiar style, not so much pulling the string back as shoving the bow forward. And when he practiced during warm weather, shirtless on the steppe, it was spectacularly obvious to Cnán that every muscle in his huge body was straining to the limit. This apparently was the highest and best use for a Briton of exceptional size and strength: not wrestling, not sword fighting, but drawing a crude bow of unbelievable stiffness, then holding it at full draw long enough to loose a massive arrow, tipped with an iron warhead, into the body of a foe.

His warheads came in various shapes, some made for piercing armor, others with broad heads for slashing through vessels and organs as they passed through the victim's body. All of them were heavy, which, as Cnán understood, gave them greater range than the lighter and more numerous shafts of the Mongols. But in order to take advantage of that range, it was necessary to shoot them from a bow that could only be handled by the likes of Rædwulf.

The seven Mongols had drawn close enough to make Cnán worried about her choice of cover. Soon, she would have to move, lest some sharp-eyed rider spy her lying at the base of the wormwood shrubs. If she tarried, she might die here.

Writhing on her belly like a snake, keeping her head low to the ground, she crawled down the slope until the top of the rise came between her and the Mongols. Then she pushed herself up and brought her knees below her chin, rising to a squat. Rædwulf, pacing slowly back and forth along a row of ten arrows that he had shoved into the ground, didn't notice her dark head pop above the ripe seed heads of the grass. But he did hear the whistle of a marmot, or something like it, from farther back in the gully. Finn had been amusing himself by learning to mimic the sounds of the (to him) exotic creatures that lived in these parts. Cnán watched in amusement as the huge Briton's head swiveled toward Finn, then turned back a moment later, finally seeing Cnán on the slope above him. Moving quickly, for she did not know how long they had before the Mongols came in view, she held up a hand with all five fingers splayed, then made a fist of it, then extended only the thumb and index finger.

Rædwulf nodded and unslung his bow from his shoulder. Then he glanced up past Cnán. Something drew his eyes to the ridgeline behind her.

She rotated on her haunches and followed his line of sight to the Mongols, lance tips and helmets bobbing slowly as they came, their ponies at a walk. Cnán rolled and pressed herself flat against the earth, nestling in the grass. She could hear the soft tread of hooves on turf, Mongol voices calling out to one another.

The trackers were spreading apart, some following her visible trail, others moving to the sides to block any escape and drive her into the center.

She risked pushing up on her elbows and raised her head to look down the slope and watch Rædwulf. She was certain she had brought the Mongols within his range; they had paced it out yesterday when reconnoitering. But this would not save her if his aim was bad.

The archer was breathing deeply, expanding his great chest, flexing his arms. He glanced down at the ten arrows lined up before him, points embedded in the soft soil, ready to grab.

He reached for one, and Cnán tensed, but rather than pulling it up and nocking it, he merely brushed the fletches, smoothing out some irregularity in the alignment of the goose feathers. His eyes flashed white, rolling up in their sockets to peer at the approaching Mongols. The closest was perhaps thirty paces from Cnán.

She sank back down into the cover of the grass and peered at his face through the golden stalks.

The Mongol leader's eyes wandered over the landscape that had just come into their view, following Cnán's trail down toward the little copse of trees in the gully. And there his attention locked.

In the open space of the steppes, the Mongols could ride circles around maille-clad Westerners, to either escape or pepper them with arrows. A gully choked with gnarled trees was precisely where he would expect his quarry to hide.

Satisfied, the Mongol muttered to his pony and began to ride ahead at a walking gait along the broken and trampled grass of Cnán's trail. His men took his cue and followed in a loose gaggle, with the exception of two outriders dividing into parallel courses that would eventually bracket the gully.

Their faces were alert, but it was the alertness of hunters pursuing birds or other innocuous prey. Even had they suspected an ambush waiting in the trees, all their training and experience would tell them they were safe at such a distance.

The waiting made her twitch, then sweat, and finally, knot up all over. Cnán had never imagined that Rædwulf would allow them to come so close to her. She remembered, as a child, sneaking up on a marmot she had spied gathering seeds among a jumble of stones. By the time the marmot had realized that Cnán was stalking her, Cnán had drawn so close that the animal's instinctive reaction was to freeze rather than run away, and yet freezing only made it possible for Cnán to draw closer.

At some point, the only thing for it was to turn and run. But she didn't dare stretch her cramping leg.

The riders were within twenty paces, then ten. The only thing that kept them from spotting her was the intent fix of their gazes on the trees below, and the only thing that prevented Cnán from jumping to her feet and bolting like a terrified marmot was the knowledge that it would only earn her a Mongol arrow, or several, in her back.

One of the riders trotted forward to draw abreast of their leader, and the breeze brought her his casual remark, words that at first made no sense to Cnán—a reference, perhaps, to some place they had visited that reminded him of this one, years past.

Without taking his eyes off the trees, the leader smiled and nodded, and in that moment, he looked almost identical to the one who was speaking. They were brothers, she realized—brothers or cousins, reminiscing about past hunts back in their home territories, still far to the east.

Cnán felt a sudden electric quiver, as if all the years and distances were suddenly collapsing around them—destinies joining, death stalking all at once, the last and most perfect of hunters preparing to string all of their skulls on a gore-clotted rope.

At the same moment, the leader—as though sensing her emotions from a distance—glanced down and looked directly into her eyes.

He opened his mouth to raise an alarm, but his eyes flicked up again, drawn by a distant, barely audible *twung* and an impossible, gently arcing flash of gray and yellow.

In the same instant, his brother, or his cousin, gave a deep, final grunt and fell back over the butt of his horse, as though struck in the middle of his chest by a giant's invisible mace.

The leader's expression turned icy cold. *Admirable calm,* she thought—or the stunned response of a marmot. He let out his breath in a low groan and sidled his pony a few feet, then flicked his eyes between Cnán, the trees in the gully below, and his fallen comrade.

The cause of this sudden death was not obvious. No arrow projected from the fallen man's chest. Rædwulf's long shaft had passed right through his body and out the back, leaving only a slot with blood welling out.

The same sound again. On the leader's opposite side, a Mongol turned his mount toward his fallen comrade, then lurched as a fat arrow buried itself in his shoulder all the way to the fletching. He reached around to claw at the shaft, grimaced, and then looked in stunned dismay at the leader, mouth open. When he decided to scream, the sound was buried in a gargling cough. As if suddenly sleepy, his eyes closed. His head slumped back and he toppled sideways out of the saddle, hitting the ground with a solid thump.

The leader now understood. His head snapped around toward Cnán, and a murderous look came over his face. He lifted his lance and pivoted his pony to ride toward her, but a third arrow hissed past his ear.

Cnán heard a muffled curse from below—Rædwulf deploring his aim. The leader heard as well, and it sharply focused his attention; throwing a vicious look at Cnán, as if to say, *I shall hunt you down and deal with you later*, he took off at a gallop down the hill, followed closely by one Mongol and paralleled, off to his right, by a third.

Meanwhile, the two outriders had gained some faint understanding of what was happening and began to ride down toward the verge of the trees, more slowly and uncertainly, as they had to pick their way down the sloping gully walls.

In the time it took Cnán to gather these impressions, Rædwulf had shot the leader out of his saddle. His companion veered to one side, hoping to ride around the little grove, and this forced Rædwulf to step out from cover, draw his bow, and stand his ground, tracking the horseman's progress and judging how much to lead him.

This one took the arrow near his hip socket but kept riding, keeping stiffly upright. The horse shrieked—the arrow had passed through and embedded in its flank, pinning the rider in place. In agony, neither horse nor rider seemed to know what to do next.

Then, a pause in the action as Rædwulf returned to the trees for more arrows.

The fifth and last Mongol from the central group had made it into those same trees, a dozen yards off, and was thrashing around on his horse between the close-packed trunks, making it impossible for Rædwulf to get a clear shot.

The archer stalked out from cover, pivoting to and fro with a nocked and half-drawn arrow, trying to make out where his foe was.

The Mongol broke free, vigorously kicking his horse, and galloped into the open with his own bow fully drawn and aimed, but drew up and faltered before loosing his arrow. Cnán thought she knew why: he had seen Rædwulf for the first time and was astonished by the man's outlandish appearance, his incredible size and coloration.

The Mongol's arrow sang harmlessly over Rædwulf 's head. Immediately after, the Englishman loosed a shaft that buried itself in the horse's chest. Screaming, the pony reared—and died, head straight out, falling over as a deadweight. The Mongol dismounted adroitly, landing on his feet, but dropping his bow. He quickly hid himself in a stubble of scrubby bushes that might, in a few years, grow up into more trees.

Rædwulf calmly returned to his arrows and grabbed another. Then he seemed to think better of it. The brush might deflect his shot. And the Mongol, with saber in hand, would be a serious problem if all Rædwulf had was a bow.

He set the bow down, undid his belt, and before dropping the scabbard, drew out his sword.

Just in time. In a crackling of sticks and brush, the Mongol burst forth into the small, cleared space and swung a scything blow at Rædwulf. Rædwulf stepped forward and deflected the Mongol's saber to his right, then crashed his left fist into the Mongol's nose, spraying blood all over and planting him on his arse. Before the Mongol could recover, Rædwulf moved in and with a quick, sidewise cut, slashed the man's throat, producing a fountain of dark stuff from which Cnán averted her eyes. Just as well. She needed to think about getting out of there.

Only a few paces away, the pony of the first Mongol to die had moved to a clear patch of grass and begun nosing around for forage.

The plan, she knew, called for Rædwulf to recover all of the arrows he could. They were too valuable to waste. But she could not bring herself to approach the bleeding corpse that, only a few moments ago, had been riding with a grin on his face, sharing memories with his brother or cousin—who was dead now as well.

She walked up to the pony instead, speaking to it in the language of the Mongols, making the sounds and saying the words that they used when they wished to put a horse at ease.

This task was not made any easier by terrible noises emanating from the gully below. Finn was harrying the two outriders through the scrub with his bloody lance.

But by the time she had reached the pony, and made friends with it, then clambered up onto its back, Finn and Rædwulf had finished their work in the gully and were riding up the slope on the mounts they had tethered back in the trees. They were coming to collect Rædwulf's arrows, speaking to each other in low conversational tones. Their calmness had the opposite effect on Cnán.

As they approached, Rædwulf intercepted her piercing glare. He slung his bow over his shoulder and returned her look. "What?" he asked, then glanced at Finn, who was equally puzzled. Finn wiped streaks of blood from his face and hands. "We'll need a quick sluice," he observed.

With great difficulty, Cnán managed to bridle her urge to scream.

CHAPTER 27:

COME BLOOD AND FIRE

The sky over Hünern was overcast and gray, but no less hot for that.

Kim experimentally flexed the hand that had taken Andreas's blow a week ago. The fingers still ached. That he could move them at all was fortunate. They would take a little longer to heal completely, and he hoped he would not have to fight before then.

Slavery could be endured, but slavery with no chance of escape—due to his own mistakes—was more than he wanted to think about right now.

He stood in the shadow of a canvas awning propped up on two wooden stakes, watching as Two Dogs sat opposite a massive, heavily scarred wrestler with dusky skin and thickly callused hands. The pair was too far away for Kim to hear what they were saying, but their intent expressions and nods said that at least Zug had managed to find a way to speak to the man most of the camp referred to as Madhukar.

The large, dark-skinned wrestler abruptly raised his thick hands and gesticulated wildly. Zug neither flinched nor fled in alarm when the giant of a man began flailing about. *Few have seen as many violent men as Two Dogs,* Kim thought with a tiny smile.

The progress of their plan had been slow. Onghwe was sharp-eyed as a tiger, and evading his notice took meticulous care. Each person they approached was carefully considered beforehand. If the group was sufficiently large, they could tip the Circus into chaos and rouse the complacent to fight with them. If the conspirators were few, they would be put down like dogs before the others even noticed. The fighters of the Circus were a varied lot, and some of them were more comfortable in their captivity than others. Worse, some had learned long ago that being spies for their master was a quick way to gain extra comforts.

So far, their judgment had held; their choices were solid. None of the fighters they approached languished in the comforts of the Khan's graces. Every one of them longed for freedom—better yet, for revenge.

Leaning against the post, Kim averted his eyes from the conversation, not to be seen paying too much attention to the exchange. Tegusgal had expressed his displeasure once again in the aftermath of the fight on the First Field, and Kim knew it was a lucky thing he was still able to fight at all. Silently, and not for the first time, Kim vowed that he would live to see Onghwe's henchman scream and squirm in a muck of dirt and his own blood. Few men so deserved a miserable death as that one.

Deep down, he knew that the plan was itself a sign of madness; they would all be killed. But if their defiance was great enough, their sacrifice might mean something. At least, it might bring the arena crashing down on Onghwe's sick games of murder and slavery.

Letting his eyes flicker back to where Zug and Madhukar talked, Kim wondered if Two Dogs's own enthusiasm hadn't infected him at last. *Or perhaps we have all been asleep, our souls driven into slumber by the oppression of our slavery,* Kim thought, *and only now are we awakening.*

But unlike a first breath drawn at dawn, this waking would not be pleasant. It would be bloody and horrific, and likely their last. Somehow that realization did not sadden him. Far better to die on your feet than waste away on your knees.

Zug rose from where he sat, and the other man waved him off. First glances often lied, but their parting looked congenial enough. Straightening, Kim waited for Zug to walk past his tent and remained there for several moments before taking a different route back to where they had agreed to meet.

In the shadow of the camp wall, they sat and shared a jug of water.

"Success?" Kim asked.

"I understood his barbarian tongue as well as any here," Zug said. "He is eager to fight the Mongols, and if we rise up, he will join us." He paused, snorted, and then looked aside, smirking. "Or he thinks I am a gardener and wishes to share my love for this land's exotic spices." Kim was often unable to tell when the fighter was joking. "But I think it went well. Who is next?"

"There are many," Kim answered. "Nearly all are discouraged. They may not believe what we plan is even possible."

"They lack courage," Zug spat. "When the day comes, if a man has no bravery, I will give him some of mine."

"They'll only join us if they think we can win," Kim said. He took up the waterskin and drank deep. His arms still ached from the exercises he'd made himself do after his fight.

Cheers rose from the arena as two fighters threw themselves at one another in a wrestling match. The prowess of the Rose Knights had intrigued the Khan, and now the proving fights were again underway. The arena's gates were open, attracting crowds, and the blood sports had once again commenced.

Any one of the plotters might die out there before they could act against Onghwe. The victories that had made all this possible had also doubled the risk.

They watched the gray clouds roll on, struggling to hold back their rain. Kim's eyes were drawn to where a small cluster of flowers grew wild, not yet trampled by the many feet that trod paths between the tents of the camp.

"You're certain we can trust Madhukar to stand with us?" he asked.

"I am certain," Zug said, as if addressing the gloomy heavens. "I didn't understand everything he said, but the anger in his eyes was unmistakable. He is like us—glad to die fighting."

A gleam appeared in Two Dogs's eyes, a faint stirring of the courage absent or deeply hidden in the man when they had first met. Perhaps a warrior still dwelled within, waiting for the right moment. Kim wondered if any of them would live long enough to see what that inner spirit was now capable of.

And what of me? he wondered. Living so close to death for so long, forcibly made aware that each day might be their last…strange to see how, given sufficient leisure to dwell on things, to imagine over and over what he could lose in any attempt to be free, fear could corrode great holes inside a man.

It was not the thought of this world and the people he might be leaving behind that unnerved him. Kim had known he was living on borrowed time since the death of his brothers. But once the possibility of the Khan's death became real to him, all the old pain of his buried longing for freedom rushed forward—even while he had to maintain total control, keep his accustomed demeanor, or risk arousing suspicion.

Watch the birds take wing, he thought. *Let that be enough. Perhaps some will survive and live new lives out there, away from this hell.*

He stood and walked over to the cluster of flowers. Reaching with a callused hand, he plucked one from the dirt and held it high to the slate-gray clouds, like an offering, but the storm did not listen.

The hot grayness continued.

◆◆◆

Dietrich von Grüningen stood beneath the barn's thatched roof and fumed at the insult he had been forced to endure. He certainly knew mockery when he saw it—in his own way, he was a master of that art—and the *kindness* of leaving the horses for his men to run after like fools sent a message worse in its own way even than the humiliation he had endured outside The Frogs.

We give back what is yours, out of charity, since you are obviously too weak to take it back by force or guile.

Burchard had been run nearly in circles attempting to recover their mounts. One more black mark against a Livonian legacy that had already been hideously battered at Schaulen.

Would Volquin ever have allowed such petty affronts to their honor? Dietrich thought not. He suspected his men had made the same judgment, though they had the sense to keep it to themselves. Order required unquestioned power vested in authority, and in an ideal world, every man knew his place in that chain of command that passed from God to the Pope and down, down, down in every direction from there. And in reverse, from the lowliest cur slinking through the muck and mire to peasant to Pope—to God Himself.

In the service to the Pope, Dietrich was technically the highest Christian authority in this wasteland of decay rucked up around the bones of Legnica. Yet the Shield-Brethren had defied him once and insulted him twice. They had taken these offenses to the very border of what might be allowed to pass without calling down a distracting and violent response.

Dietrich could not himself shed the blood he felt was owed for these indignities. Had these arrogant sons of demon spew kept the horses, had they been foolish enough to kill one of his men—had they done this or done that, he might have been granted satisfaction. But now, instead of revenge, he had only the taste of ash in his mouth.

Ash not at all diluted by bad ale.

As with the aftermath of Schaulen, all Dietrich could truly call his own was this seething anger, and so he held it close to his breast like a disappointed lover clinging to a wilted flower, hoarding it to keep the flame of an all-too-often hopeless passion alive. He was God's servant, selected by his highest-chosen emissary, and his task was holy in the eyes of the Almighty. Vengeance taken against those who defied God was justified in every sense of the word. He had merely to deduce how to accomplish it without risking his own sacred task. *They've left me precious few options, but there is always something one may do.*

He'd only finished drilling against Burchard and Sigeberht a short time ago. Training against two men at once was a habit he'd maintained from his early years in the order, and it had benefited him both in the skills it had granted him as well as the understanding of how to balance two conflicts in one field of vision. Even so, all he felt now was a weak spark of discouraged anger—not the flame he needed.

And tired. So very tired.

He took off his gambeson alone as his squire saw to the maintenance of his maille. The water he splashed on his face was as warm as the rest of this damnably hot place and brought little refreshment. Resting his hands on both sides of the raised trough that served as the basin, he breathed in and out, filling his lungs with fuel for the fires.

It was not a question of whether he would make them pay, but of how and when. To that task, he turned his mind to a long-accustomed meditation of strategy, arranging his key plans in verse and ordering those verses in an elegant, memorable sequence—then analyzing and parsing both structure and logic, to find deeper meaning, alternate interpretations—treating the vengeance he and his brothers were owed as he would a piece of the Holy Scripture.

Necessity demanded subtlety, or at least something that would not provoke an obvious response from them. He could not very well raid their chapter house, and one of his men knifing one of theirs was out of the question; bodies had a way of turning up.

No, the formalities had to be observed in doing God's work, and this *was* the work of the Almighty. Of that, he had reassured himself countless times.

Dietrich seated himself on a long bench against the back wall of the barn. The smell of animal feces and straw was overpoweringly pronounced, even this far back, and the crowding of his brothers around and inside the ramshackle structure had made him ever more grateful that his rank afforded him the right to demand a private space to call his own. Heaven's hierarchies served his purposes well. He could not attack the men of Petraathen overtly, which forced him now to contemplate the options available to him. *They took something of value from me—my dignity. Returning pilfered horses does not begin to wash away their crimes. Prudence dictates that I take something of greater value from them. And that would doubtless be their own self-regard—the greater, more shining, infinitely precious pride of a glorious and damnable arrogance.*

His stomach twisted unhappily within. Strategizing and hating always knotted his innards. He was hoping for a silent way to release some pent-up gas when the door opened. Clenching his buttocks, Dietrich raised his eyes to see one of his knights standing in the door, an initiate named Gelther.

"I gave instructions I was to be left undisturbed," Dietrich growled.

"Forgive me, *Heermeister*," Gelther murmured, "but a runner has arrived, and I thought you should know—the arena has been reopened. The Circus has begun anew."

◆◆◆

"What about the Persian with the club?" Zug suggested. "He's immense and dangerous, and the guards are afraid of him."

Kim sat across from him in the tent, face set with a frown.

"He's also been a beneficiary of the Khan's favoritism before," Kim said.

Zug thought the Flower Knight was far too picky, too discerning in his opinions of whom they should and should not approach in their endeavor. Zug feared that if his friend had his way, when the time came, their group would not be nearly large enough.

"As was I," Zug said, his expression drawn into a tight grimace. "It is a cage, and a trap, and I would have been glad to be rid of it at any time."

The Flower Knight looked haggard in a way Zug had not seen him appear since the early days of their captivity, before acceptance of their situation had settled in and allowed him to keep the calm for which he'd become known since. "Different favoritism, and you know that," Kim murmured.

"You don't like his fury," Zug added. "It's no different from my own." He smiled wryly. Every so often he couldn't resist the opportunity to poke at his friend's peculiar sense of honor.

Kim was a good man—a better one than him, perhaps—but he had also not endured the shame that Zug had carried since even before Onghwe Khan had taken them.

"Fair enough," the Flower Knight murmured. "I don't like it. Too much fervor is a risk, even if the heart behind it is loyal and longs for freedom."

"There is the one who fights with the hatchets and the knives," Zug said, letting the previous remark slide. "He has more than enough calm to balance a fiery temper. And thanks to you, we have enough hotheads already."

"Will he talk to us?" Kim asked, lifting his brows.

"Not to me. Our fight was painful. Honor. Strength and youth…skill." The world had taken some time to come into focus as the lasting effects of the liquor departed from Zug's body. He mulled all these points while prodding a broken tooth with his tongue. "But he might speak with you."

"He doesn't know me," Kim said with a shrug.

The splitting pain in Zug's head that had racked his every waking moment in the aftermath of the loss to the Rose Knight had dulled weeks ago to a low ache that was finally fading in the warming prospect light of the task he and Kim had set for themselves. "That's exactly why you stand a better chance than I do," he grunted irritably. "I'm not convinced he likes anybody."

Kim raised an eyebrow. The bruises on his face had not completely faded, and they gave it a motley look. "I didn't know he detested others that much. But I will talk to him. Quiet is good, and he's one of the best at that. I wonder how the Khan managed to take him in the first place?"

"Carefully," Zug replied. "We shouldn't waste time, so we'll do it like last time. You find him, bring him, and I will wait."

To hold at bay, for now at least, the false solace of wine required that he focus every moment on the task at hand. The instant that focus was lost, the longing for the wine and the memories he'd used it to suppress would return like an angry, winged spirit clawing at his heart, shrieking in his dreams, tugging at him to seek out the old ways of forgetting past shame, long-ago failure.

"Agreed?" he asked.

"Agreed." The Flower Knight rose and exited into the gray day.

◆◆◆

Dietrich had armored himself and now sat astride his recaptured horse with a new sense of purpose. The reactivation of the Circus was a development that had slowly but surely filled his thoughts, outlining a path to greater successes—and ultimately to the vengeance he craved.

When the news had first arrived, his reaction had been the familiar indignation borne of Mongols pitting captured Christians, even heretics, against pagan warriors, but that had rapidly cooled as he saw the possibilities. He would soon set about the task of choosing one of his better fighters for assignment to the lists.

First, however, he had to see where the other soldiers of Christendom stood.

Riding through Hünern, Dietrich took only passing note of the city's sad state. He took care to ride past The Frogs en route to his destination. There, he paused and regarded the site of his embarrassment with cold, heavy-lidded eyes, searing this miserable place into his memory. Another marker in a long list.

It helped to remind oneself of the tally of foes in need of punishing.

Then he swiveled the horse aside and trotted ahead, Burchard and Sigeberht coming up swiftly behind to keep pace with him. People dashed out of his way, throwing themselves to the side of the road to avoid the pounding crush of hooves. Dietrich paid them no more heed than he would ants beneath his boot, glad only that they at least remembered the respect that was appropriate for one of higher station.

They passed out of Hünern and rode across open lands toward where the Weidlache wound through the landscape. There was an old estate near the riverbank that dated back to Roman times. The Mongols had put the entire place to the torch when they passed through, after killing the occupants, whoever they had been—doubtless wealthy nobles who refused to join or cooperate with them.

This estate had stood gray and mostly empty—there were always half-starved squatters around—and no doubt haunted, until another order had moved in and made it their chapter house.

It was here that Dietrich and his men rode to find the commander of the Knights Templar.

The Templars had made good their fortifications, Dietrich reflected as they approached the makeshift stronghold. It was not a castle and could not repel a siege, but of all those orders that had staked out compounds around the ruins of Hünern, the Templars had made the most of their position and would perhaps evoke at least some hesitation in the mind of an ambitious brigand or tax collector.

A pair of sergeants stood guard at the gate, spear tips gleaming and prominent. They glowered as Dietrich and his small group approached.

"I am Dietrich von Grüningen, *Heermeister* of the *Fratres Militiae Christi Livoniae*," he said, his voice friendly, calm, and casual, rather than demanding or threatening. *Let them think we are equals.* "Who commands here?"

The guards inspected them and decided they were no immediate threat. "Leuthere de Montfort commands our brothers," the leftmost guard said. "He is currently in conference with Emmeran of the Knights of St. John. Pass, sirs, but watch your arms, that you be not mistaken for goads or agents. You will be met."

Dietrich smiled, nodded, and then sucked in a breath and rode through, Burchard and Sigeberht keeping pace. The two guards watched them closely, and Dietrich saw one call over a squire and send him running toward the compound.

Shortly thereafter, other squires took their horses and they were escorted inside.

The interior of the place gave testament to the fires that had gutted it, but here and there amid the blackened stones, bits of old finery could be seen, like rare flowers poking through the floor of a burned forest. Dietrich and his men waited quietly just inside the entryway in the company of a stern-faced knight in the unmarred white surcoat and red cross of the Templars. So close, Dietrich felt the old bitterness rising in him once more. His own order had it in them to be as great, if not mightier, than the holders of this ruined house.

After Schaulen, who could say how far back that ascendancy had been pushed?

Burchard was also watching the Templar, calm assessment in his eyes. God's hierarchies demanded a certain competitiveness, Dietrich reflected, and even allies sharing his great cloak could feel a certain animosity. At least his bodyguard was paying attention now. That was encouraging.

Dietrich's contemplation was aborted by the approach of another Templar, this one older and harder faced. "Leuthere will see you now," he said and gestured for Dietrich to follow.

Leuthere de Montfort was known to Dietrich only by reputation, but that was sufficiently lively and widespread to merit respect. He came from nobility, though in lieu of dedicating himself to the family name, he had opted instead to devote himself to the martial orders in the service of Christ. He was known for courage, zealousness, and an almost holy imperturbability in the face of adversity.

Sitting opposite him now, after having seen him but a handful of times at a distance, the man up close was precisely what Dietrich had expected.

"I am honored to meet you in person, Leuthere de Montfort," Dietrich said, all casualness subdued, lowering his voice and deliberately intoning respect. *As this man obviously warrants.*

"Dietrich von Grüningen," Leuthere replied, his face as stolid and almost as gray as a chunk of battered stone. "The honor is mine."

They sat upon wood stools before the fire-blackened stones of a large hearth, its once-fine carvings now reduced to charred, grotesque mockeries. The whole interior was redolent of recent scouring fires, and perhaps even burned bodies. The Templars did not seem to mind—or even to notice.

Dietrich was directly opposite Leuthere. The third point of the triad they formed was occupied by Emmeran, commander of the contingent of Hospitallers in Legnica. He was of taller stature than Leuthere, but projected less strength. In the present company, whose devotion was supposed to be absolute, Emmeran seemed strangely removed from the affairs at hand.

"We were discussing the matter of the Circus of Swords when you arrived," Emmeran said more quietly. "You have heard the news?"

"I have just assigned one of my best fighters to the lists," Dietrich replied. "I had hoped to speak with you both on the subject." He paused and folded his hands in his lap. "What do you believe our purpose is in being here?"

"Something I myself have wondered," Leuthere said with impenetrable calm. "When we came here, it was with the understanding that our swords were needed to keep this accursed Khan from laying waste to Christendom. Until the Shield-Brethren of Petraathen had the audacity to challenge the silence of the arena, my brothers and I were contemplating departure. After all, we are not sufficiently strong to lay siege to the Mongol encampments, and without the arena, we have had little reason to remain."

Was that a faint hint of admiration in Leuthere's voice for the Shield-Brethren—or consternation at their actions? Dietrich could not tell. *Damn the man's calm! Medusa herself could not render him more unreadable.*

In the absence of certainty, he tried to steer their opinions toward concern, perhaps even alarm.

"The Shield-Brethren are not to be trusted," he said. "They have already committed assault against my own order, and their actions at the First Field were rash—exceedingly rash. They have given us an opportunity to stall this Khan through bloodshed in his arenas, true enough, but that does not mean they are deserving of our support."

"The matter of the horses, I had heard of that," Leuthere said and looked aside placidly, as if discussing a matter of hounds and hares. "They were returned to you, were they not?"

This man is a veritable wall, Dietrich thought. *I cannot tell what wheels turn behind his words. Is he a friend or a foe?*

"Yes," Dietrich replied. "Albeit in a manner that did little to demonstrate common courtesy, much less respect. There is also the matter of my battered men. But I am more concerned with the immediate matter of the Circus of Swords and knowing where the other orders stand than with seeking restitution for a possible insult," Dietrich lied. "My words should be taken as caution against putting too much trust in the overly impulsive. It would behoove those of us who prefer a more disciplined plan to show solidarity rather than follow a trail left by the rash and the audacious, don't you think?"

"Fairly asserted," Leuthere said. He turned his cold eyes to Emmeran, seeking his counsel.

"I am not convinced this ordeal is more than a mummer's farce," Emmeran told them in softer tones. The Hospitaller seemed in all ways a man possessed of less verve than Dietrich and Leuthere.

God in Heaven, Dietrich thought, *you are a warrior in the service of the Almighty. Where is your passion?*

"We cannot leave now," Dietrich replied more sharply than he'd intended. "The Pope has called upon us to be here. We cannot back down from such a command and such a charge."

Emmeran raised his eyebrows. Leuthere was silent. "Forgive me, *Heermeister* Dietrich," Emmeran said, "but I would have thought that, of all of us, you would understand the value of discretion and caution, given the tragedy that befell your predecessor."

Schaulen. It is always about Schaulen. Dietrich felt the rage building inside like boiling water over an open hearth. "That was different," he said. He could not, *must* not, lose control in front of these two men. He had several leaders yet to see, and if word should get around that he was rattled and could not hide his anger, he would find himself truly without allies in a place that was already unfriendly to his order.

"Nevertheless, your point is well taken," Dietrich said, laying his gaze on Emmeran. *Coward. Sit and contemplate, if you like. Muse on the weak and the sick, while the Mongol host rolls over Europe and the Shield-Brethren bring our efforts to naught. I and mine will be doing something about it.*

He cleared his throat. "Caution and discretion are not without their place."

"You and yours mean to stay, then?" Leuthere asked. Whatever motivated Leuthere de Montfort, try as he might, Dietrich could not see behind the Templar's mask.

"Yes. Somebody must encourage a different direction than that taken by our rash, so-called knights of the Virgin Defender. If others will not step up to that task, then I and mine will fill the void. If God wills it, others will then follow. It is a blessed path, and righteous."

Whom God favored was not even a question in Dietrich's mind. The Shield-Brethren had not, he strongly suspected, abandoned their pagan roots. A weed with beautiful branches was still a weed. Pull it from the earth and the roots would appear the same. Somehow, someway, Dietrich would do just that.

"I encourage you to speak to the other orders," Leuthere said, indirectly indicating that the conversation had reached its conclusion. He extended a hand to Dietrich. His grip was powerful. "I thank you, Dietrich, for conveying what information you have. You have given me much to consider. I pray you find the way you seek. If God favors you, others will surely follow in your track."

"Go with God," Emmeran murmured and extended his own hand. This grip was also surprisingly strong.

"His will is always foremost in my thoughts," Dietrich added, bidding both men farewell. Burchard and Sigeberht awaited him in the fire-blackened entryway, faces lighting with curiosity as he approached. He dismissed it with a wave of his hand as their horses were retrieved. His mood had sobered somewhat as he climbed into the saddle, but the humiliations continued to rankle, and the relative lack of progress here was unsettling.

Still, it had not been without its benefits. If he could show the worth of his own course, Leuthere had implied, the Templars might follow, and they would be a great strength to have at his back. Nevertheless, the battlefield could change rapidly in a short time, taking away one's advantages and handing them to his enemies.

Dietrich remembered Emmeran's words, much as they galled him, and now took them to heart.

As they rode out of the compound and headed back to their own chapter house, he silently vowed under the eyes of God that here and now would *not* be another Schaulen.

Come blood and fire, disaster or storm, he would triumph.

CHAPTER 28:

PILLOW FIGHT

Fire rained from the sky.

Munokhoi's alarm had created a chaotic surge around the *Khagan*'s *ger* as guards tried to push their way through the confusion of concubines, ambassadors, and other guests. Many of those gathered at the feast were too stunned to do anything more than stand with mouths agape, like herds of simple-minded oxen. As the burning arrows began to fall, they began to react, but for many, it was too late. Munokhoi's voice was quickly drowned out by the shrieks and screams of the injured and dying.

A courtier with a flaming arrow jutting from his left eye grabbed at Gansukh as the young warrior fought against the buffeting panic of the crowd. The courtier gibbered at Gansukh, his words lost in the sizzling cackle of the fire devouring his face and hair. Gansukh shoved the man away before the fire could leap to his own robes, and the courtier spun away, scattering flecks of flame.

In the distance, a tiny spray of orange light leaped into the sky. *The hill,* Gansukh realized, his pulse hammering in his ears. The enemy was on higher ground, using the difference in elevation to increase the range of their archers. Not too far from where he had set up his tent. His shoulders tightened, and he cast about for some shelter as the lights in the sky grew brighter.

Hissing, the fiery rain fell again, but the arrows landed among the vast sea of tents that lay behind the open area where the feast had been arranged. The archers had shifted their assault, and Gansukh grimly noted their efficiency. The fire arrows were meant to cause confusion and to divert the efforts of the *Khagan*'s guards toward saving the tents and supplies. *Split your enemy*, he thought, *divide his strength.*

A trio of concubines ran from a nearby tent, the hems of their robes on fire, and they stamped a frantic dance in an effort to put the flames out. Guards were still streaming past Gansukh, jangling and clattering as they jostled one another in their rush to protect the *Khagan.* Munokhoi's alarm was now being carried by many voices, counterpoint to the crackling roar of a half dozen fires. Gansukh spied a few soldiers wrestling barrels of water toward the burning tents.

At this point, it was closer to a riot than to a camp.

Gansukh found himself looking for Lian. Munokhoi and his men were surrounding the *Khagan,* and he had no place with them; the rest of the Imperial Guard would either be protecting the *Khagan*'s entourage or taking the battle to their attackers. He might be useful in helping stem the spread of the fires, but that sort of threat could be dealt with by anyone who could lift a bucket of water. His duty lay to the task given upon him by Chagatai and Master Chucai. Part of that duty was...*Lian.*

He thought he saw her, a flash of that long black hair he often dreamed about. Shouting her name—even though part of him knew there was no hope of her hearing him—he started to run after her, but a large tent nearby erupted in a billowing column of fire. The heat was intense; coughing, he retreated from the inferno of the great tent, his arm raised as a desperate and pathetic shield against the heat.

The leather walls of the tent cracked and shriveled, pulling back to reveal the glowing shafts of the wooden framework. Several of the poles had already begun to crumble, leaving only bright coals that hadn't yet fallen into ash. The grass around the tent that hadn't been trampled was starting to burn, tiny crawlers of fire eagerly seeking out other tents. A lost ox, confused and terrified, balked at the burning grass. It stood still, lowing plaintively, and waited for the fire to claim it.

Gansukh veered away from the raging bonfire of the tent, tasting the acrid smoke on the back of his tongue. Nearby, horses—tied along a picket line—whickered fearfully and pulled against one another as they tried to flee in different directions. Gansukh caught sight of someone moving among them—the flash of a silk robe—and he stumbled as quickly as he could toward the terrified beasts.

Lian was trying to untie one of the horses from the picket, a sturdy chestnut mare. Her hair was wild about her, a spray of blackness against the muted colors of her robe. The horse's reins were tied tightly to the leather strap snaking across the ground, and Lian fought to keep the line under control so that she could undo the reins. Each time the mare bucked and strained, all her work was undone.

"What are you doing?" he shouted. "We're under attack."

She ignored him, though she had clearly heard him, as she left off trying to undo the knot. Instead, she caught the reins and tried to control the frantic mare.

Gansukh put his hand on her shoulder. "Lian—"

"I'm trying to escape, you idiot!" She whirled on him, her hair whipping fiercely around her head.

"It's too dangerous—" he started.

"It will always be dangerous," she snapped. "Why can't you understand that? I'm a slave. A *good* time to escape doesn't exist. I have to take the chances I'm given, and this one is *good enough.*" Her eyes reflected the fires surrounding them. "The guards are distracted," she said. "By the time they think to look for me, I'll have vanished into the night."

She let go of the horse's tether with one hand, placing it on his chest. "Please, Gansukh. I have to go," she said, staring at him.

Gansukh glanced around, his gaze sweeping across the tumult of the camp: tents on fire; horsemen thundering by; men screaming, some in anger, some in fear, some in pain. "I don't know who's attacking or why, but they're organized. They're going to shoot at anyone on horseback."

"It's dark," she countered, taking a step closer to him, her hand drifting down his chest. "Everything is in turmoil. They're focused on the *Khagan.* They won't notice me."

He shook his head. "It's too risky."

"Gansukh," Lian said, "I have to try." She drew in a deep breath and bit her lower lip. "If you care for me at all, you'll help me." Her eyes darted down, and for a second, she was so demure and fragile that he was overcome with a tremendous urge to crush her in his arms. "Let me go."

"Lian—" He raised his hand to touch her face, but she ducked under his arm. Her hand grabbed at the knife he had taken from her earlier—the one he had shoved in his belt. He grabbed for her, feeling her hair slip through his grasp, feeling the slippery silk of her gown against his fingertips.

She sliced through the reins, and the mare reared back, flailing with its front hooves. Gansukh had to take a step back to avoid getting kicked, and Lian slipped beyond his reach. The mare spooked, no longer tethered to the picket, and Lian got both hands in its mane and hauled herself onto its back with a grace that surprised Gansukh. In a second, the horse and its rider were lost in the smoky pall that covered the camp.

Gansukh spotted the knife lying on the ground, and with a curse, he scooped it up. He sawed through the first set of reins he could get his hands on. Unlike Lian, he kept his grip on the slippery reins, and after he had shoved the blade back into his belt, he swung up onto the horse. Slapping its rump, he set off after Lian at a gallop.

◆◆◆

It was a privilege to protect the *Khagan.* Munokhoi's entire adult life had been spent in that service, working diligently to be noticed for his courage and bravery; he was the fist of the *Khagan,* hard and ready to be used in the service of the Empire. It was his command that had been chosen to be the Imperial Guard accompanying Ögedei on his trip to the Burqan-qaldun, and he was given two more *jaghun* to command as well. Once they reached Burqan-qaldun, the *Khagan* would reward him with the silver *paitze*—the slim tablet that gave him command of a thousand men. He would be *noyon*—a general of the *Khagan*'s army—and he would no longer be shackled to court life. He would be allowed to excel at what he truly knew was his purpose: to actively hunt the *Khagan*'s enemies. He would not show them mercy; he would never stop pursuing them until every last man who dared to defy the *Khagan* was dead.

The fires were no longer spreading. The *Khagan* was safe in his tent, surrounded by three *arbans* of armored soldiers. His patrols had circled around and disrupted the archers who had been pouring waves of fiery arrows on the camp.

It was time to take the battle to the enemy. It was time to show them the wrath of the *Khagan.*

He and his men jogged through the firelit camp. They were his handpicked elite, nine men who had each killed as many as he—men who would not balk or hesitate at his slightest command. Like him, they understood their duty—they were as defined by it as he was. They were Mongols.

Camp followers and other soldiers scurried past Munokhoi's *arban* as they fought the scattered fires: tamping down blazes with thick blankets, pouring protective circles of water or sour milk (any liquid they could get their hands on) around burning tents, hauling cargo and livestock to safer locations. Ash hung in the heated air; what little wind there was this night spent itself in confusion, blown back and forth by the small fires.

The heat felt good on Munokhoi's bare head. His sword glistened orange-red in the ruddy light as if it were already covered in blood. He held his buckler loosely in his left hand, almost unconscious of its presence. He did not expect to need it.

Whoever the attackers were, they may have been bold and clever, but he knew they were cowards. They had sown panic and fear with their aerial bombardment, and might even be using the confusion and darkness to cover their assault, but these tactics were the refuge of frightened men. They did not have the superiority of numbers or skill; otherwise, they would not have hidden behind such tactics. They knew they were attacking the *Khagan*'s Imperial Guard—warriors without peers across the steppes—and they had already shown their fear.

They knew they were going to die, and Munokhoi was only too happy to help them meet their end. There would be no glory for these craven ambushers. They would all die in the night; by morning, the only thing left would be leaking corpses. Carrion feed.

He couldn't help but hope that he might run across Gansukh. He had seen the bastard whelp run off to chase after the scheming Chinese bitch. He knew those two were plotting something—he had had men watching them both, but had not learned anything useful enough to warrant alerting the *Khagan* or Master Chucai. It would be better if some accident befell them. In the aftermath of this battle, no one would question two more dead bodies. Unfortunate victims of the nighttime raid.

His hand tightened on his sword, and a wicked smile crossed his face. He'd prefer to kill them himself, of course, and the fantasy of cutting either or both of their heads off only fueled his bloodlust.

They passed beyond the last row of tents, and as one, Munokhoi's *arban* picked up speed. They were in open terrain now, and like wolves who had spotted their prey, they were eager to bring the battle to the enemy.

An enemy that was coming to meet them too.

The fires behind them scattered light across the armor of the approaching warriors. Chinese soldiers, Munokhoi noted, their armor ragged and mismatched. Only a few had plumes atop their pointed helmets. *Far from home and so desperate in their attempt on the* Khagan*'s life,* he thought as he pointed his sword. *None of their families will ever know where they died.* When he shouted the command to attack, his voice almost broke with laughter.

The Chinese were charging too, a lumbering line of spears and swords that seemed no more threatening than an annoyingly thorny hedge. Baring his teeth, Munokhoi ran ahead of his *arban,* exulting in the lust for battle. As he closed with the line of soldiers, he saw isolated faces more clearly: faces twisted with desperation, eyes wide with barely contained panic, mouths already flopping and panting, like tired hounds.

He swung his sword and felt it slide off a shoulder guard and bite deep into the flesh beneath. As the Chinese man stumbled, Munokhoi kicked him in the leg. He screamed with delight as the man fell to the dirt, and after he wrenched his sword free, he stomped on the flailing soldier until he felt bones break under his heel.

Another soldier came at him, and he raised his buckler to block the man's wild swing. The impact jarred his arm, and he swept his buckler wide to brush his assailant's sword away. But there was no need. His assailant was staring dumbly at the spurting stump of his own arm. One of Munokhoi's men had severed the arm with a massive stroke, leaving the Chinese man shocked and defenseless. His last moment was spent vainly trying to find his missing arm before Munokhoi's sword sliced through his throat and ended the search.

Munokhoi caught his man's eye and nodded in recognition. The Mongol grinned back, pleased to have both served and been acknowledged by his master; in the next second, his expression changed as a great thunder shattered the night air.

The Mongol was wrenched off his feet, his upper body snapping backward as if he had been struck by the fist of a vengeful spirit. He sprawled on the ground, dead, his chest a shattered mess of leather, bone, and steaming fragments of some black material. The air was heavy with an acrid smoke, something fouler than the smoke stench from the burning tents. It was a stink Munokhoi knew, but it took him a few seconds to place it.

Chinese black powder.

They would fill clay pots with the powder, as well as rocks and shards of metal. Coupled with a fuse, these pots were smoking bombs that exploded, hurling their contents into a mass of attackers with devastating effects. Many a Chinese citadel required more effort—and more men—than expected due to these Chinese firebombs.

It hadn't been a pot that had killed his man, but something else. Something that threw metal and black powder, almost like a catapult but not unlike a crossbow.

Munokhoi adjusted his grip on his sword, swallowing the tiny glob of fear in the back of his throat. He sucked air in through his nose, taking the metallic stink of the Chinese weapon deep into his chest. *Death can come quickly*, he thought. Better to die with his sword red with Chinese blood than to stand dumbly like a stupid cow.

He charged toward the fighting, swinging his sword heavily as if he were butchering an ox for a feast. A Chinese soldier parried him weakly, stepping back under the force of the blow, and Munokhoi smashed his sword down again, breaking the man's guard and feeling the heavy shock of impact. The soldier groaned and collapsed; Munokhoi tried to pull his sword free of the dying man, but the blade was caught in the bones of the man's chest.

Nearby, a Mongol fell to his knees, clutching at his stomach. His Chinese attacker raised his sword to deliver a killing blow, his face alight with triumph, and Munokhoi quickly drew his dagger as he charged. He got his shoulder under the man's sword arm, forcing the weapon away from the downed soldier, and he stabbed upward with his dagger, finding the soft spot beneath the chin. The man choked, spitting blood, and more blood gushed from the hole in his neck as Munokhoi pulled the dagger free.

The blood was hot on his arm and chin. Some of the blood splashed on his lips, and he touched it with his tongue, savoring the sweet taste.

The fear fell away. This was all that he needed. "For the *Khagan*!" he screamed, wrenching the sword from the dying Chinese soldier's hands.

As if in answer, the thunder sounded again, and the strength of its breath threw both one of his Mongol warriors and his Chinese opponent to the ground. *Wildly inaccurate,* he thought, sniffing the air for its tangy scent, *but still quite dangerous.*

He wanted it. There was a sensation in his groin not unlike what he had felt when he had first put his hands on the tiered crossbow made by the Chinese or when he had first seen Chucai's new whore. This was something he did not possess, that he was not the master of, and the thrill of conquest coursed through his body.

He would not be denied.

"For the *Khagan*!" he screamed again. *For my glory,* he thought.

✦✦✦

The walls of Ögedei's *ger* were draped in shiny panels of embroidered blue silk, masking the rough leather of the outer layer. An iron brazier, its top twisted into an intricate array of blooming flowers, sat on a thick Persian carpet. It was filled with glowing coals, and it heated the room evenly against the chill of the night air. Furs and pillows were scattered near the brazier, transforming the floor into a soft terrain that extended almost to the silk-draped walls. The intent was to create a space not unlike his rooms at Karakorum, a refuge from the less hospitable reality of traveling, but this luxury was nothing more than a prison to Ögedei, a blatant reminder that he was isolated from what was happening.

"Do you not hear the sounds of battle?" he growled at the two men who stood near the laced flap of the *ger*. "I should be out there—fighting! I should be leading my men into battle." He raised his hands at the men, clawing at the air. "My hands should be covered in the blood of my enemies."

The slimmer of the two men stroked his long black mustache. "It would be fine sport, my Khan," he offered. "But—"

Ögedei snarled and stepped closer to the man, the muscles in his neck straining. Daring him to continue.

The guard fell silent, and his hand dropped to his side. His mustache drooped.

The other guard, broad in the chest and arm, cleared his throat nervously. "They have come to kill you, my Khan, and for that, they are fools. If you were to step outside of this tent, would you not be giving these fools what they seek?"

Ögedei stormed over to stand too close to the second guard. He loomed over the shorter man, breathing heavily on the crest of his helmet like an old bull challenging a young rival. Daring the man to look up at him, to give him an excuse…

The guard stared at his boots.

"Pah." Ögedei spat on the carpet, and he rudely shoved the man with his shoulder as he returned his attention to the first guard. "What is your name?" he demanded.

"Chaagan, my Khan," the first guard said, dropping to his knee and bowing his head. The second man, recovering from the *Khagan*'s shove, did the same. "And I am Alagh," he said.

"Selected by Munokhoi for your obstinacy and allegiance to his command, no doubt," Ögedei continued. He started to pace around the tent, the hem of his cloak stirring up a tiny cloud of dust in his wake. The coals in the brazier seemed to wink at the three men.

"Yes, my Khan," Chaagan replied.

Ögedei caught himself clenching and unclenching his hand. He wanted the security of his giant cup—wanted the strength that the wine would give him—and his hands could not hide his desire for the drink. *I am weak.* He squeezed his fist tightly, as if he could crush that thought into dust.

Was this not the purpose of his journey? To cast off the shackles of the wine and regain his dignity and honor. To have his subjects look upon him with faces filled with devotion and respect. Not the way they refused to look at him now, embarrassed by his drunkenness. By his *weakness.*

He kicked at a pillow, and his foot met little resistance against feather stuffing. The action was so unrewarding that he kicked another one, harder. The results were similar, and instead of kicking a third cushion, he scooped it up and tore at it with his hands. The silken fabric resisted his efforts, taunting him with its soft resilience, and growling deep in his throat, he pulled his dagger free of its sheath and stabbed the pillow instead. Cutting and tearing, he released a cloud of goose feathers, an explosion of white snow that filled the tent with yet more reminders of how soft he had become. Whirling, he stabbed and slashed at the floating feathers, striking at invisible enemies—laughing phantoms that darted and hid behind the screen of floating feathers.

Eventually—his arms aching, his chest heaving—he relented. Leaning over, one hand propped against his thigh, he glared at the insolent feather clinging to the shining blade of his dagger. All of his effort amounted to nothing: his blade was clean, and his enemies were still there, floating just out of reach.

Ögedei glanced at the two soldiers standing guard, examining their faces for any reaction. Chaagan and Alagh stared at the opposite wall, their expressions blank and stoic; judging by their unblinking fascination with the tent wall, they had seen nothing at all of what had transpired over the last few minutes.

"I am the *Khagan*," Ögedei sighed, flicking the feather off the blade and sliding his dagger back into its sheath. He walked over and stood directly in front of Chaagan. "Would you die for me?" he asked.

"Yes, my Khan," Chaagan answered.

"Would you fall on your sword right now if I asked you to?"

A muscle twitched in the guard's jaw, and he hesitated briefly before barking out his answer. "Yes, my Khan."

"Would it be a good death?" Ögedei asked.

Chaagan looked away and did not answer.

Ögedei stepped closer to the guard and put his hand on the man's shoulder. He felt Chaagan twitch under his hand, and a flicker of fear twisted the guard's lips. "I think," Ögedei said, his voice dropping to a conspiratorial whisper, "that if I were to run out of this tent and engage the enemy—an enemy that wants nothing more than for me to present myself in that fashion—that I would be doing something very similar to falling on my own sword." His grip tightened on Chaagan's shoulder. "Do you agree?"

Chaagan nodded. "Yes, my Khan."

"That would not be a very good death."

"No, my Khan."

"I should let men like you—and Alagh, as well—fight for me, because that is your duty. That is all that you want to do for me—to fight in my name, to fight for the glory of the Empire."

Chaagan stood up slightly under Ögedei's hand. "Yes, my Khan."

"And yet, you are here with me now. Inside this damned tent, watching your *Khagan* fight with a...pillow. There is little glory in that, is there?" Ögedei chuckled at Chaagan's bleak expression. He released his grip and patted the man's shoulder—the way a father absently reassures a confused child. "Let us watch the fight outside this tent," he said, nodding toward the straps that held the tent flap closed. "I want to witness my fierce warriors in combat. I want to behold the glory of their actions."

The wine would always fill him with bravado, but without the brittle bluster it provided, all that was left was a squirming nakedness, a raw awareness of the prisoner he had become. He had been a warrior of the steppes once, but now he was the *Khagan,* and that title was nothing more than a golden chain crushing the life out of him. He could not participate in the glory of the Mongol Empire; he could only bear witness to it.

CHAPTER 29:

DEUS IUDEX IUSTUS

"What are you doing up there?" the guard demanded, fumbling for his sword.

Ferenc hung halfway to the top of the old Roman wall, frozen with indecision, fingers of one hand clinging to the gap between two blocks of tufa, and the other scrabbling for purchase on a brick-and-mortar facing.

Left behind on the path below the wall, Ocyrhoe backed away from the guard, who was focusing his attention on the one most likely to escape—the youth clinging to the wall.

"Get down!" The guard raised his sword—with little effect, since Ferenc's feet were at least two yards over his head.

Bits of grout and decaying brick sifted down from Ferenc's fingers and broke away from his questing toes. Should he keep going? Was Ocyrhoe going to run?

Comically, the guard now began to jump, waving his blade in an attempt to close the distance. Ferenc arched his back and raised his feet. More grout broke free. Some of it sifted into the guard's face, and he swore, backing off to rub his eyes.

Ferenc and Ocyrhoe hadn't planned well, that was obvious—run ragged by their mission and the environment of fear that was sweeping Rome. If they were split up, where would they find one another again? Ferenc found it strange that he and this tiny girl had become so inseparable, as if they had been running together, struggling to survive, since they were children.

His mother's secret language had helped, of course. She had never openly taught it to him, as he was not one of *them*, the *szépasszony* who wove the kin-knots, but he had learned it regardless, absorbing the signs and gestures and codes by being attentive in her presence, and by remembering how she had touched and tickled him when he was a baby. The *tündér* magic all children know when they are born and then forget as they learn to be human.

The guard, frustrated by Ferenc's inaccessibility, now turned his attention to Ocyrhoe. He extended his blade and lumbered toward her.

With a small yelp, she leaped onto the wall and scrabbled up along the brickwork, grabbing frantically at higher handholds in an effort to climb out of the guard's reach.

Looking up and to her left, she shouted at Ferenc, "*Ascende!*"

The guard grunted and stretched up, reaching for her dangling foot. She yelled, jerking and kicking her leg.

The guard got a grip on her ankle and yanked, pulling her off balance. Her legs swung free, and as Ferenc watched, her right hand slipped.

"*Ascende!*" she cried, oblivious to her precarious hold on the wall.

And leave her behind? Where was he supposed to go? What was the message they were supposed to deliver? The old man in the Septizodium—the one with the kind face and the *presence*—had sent them out of the city on a secret mission, but he had described that mission only in the language Ocyrhoe knew. If Ferenc kept climbing, he would be leaving Ocyrhoe behind, and that meant abandoning the mission.

Ocyrhoe swung her free hand up and managed to grab a loose brick. The brick slid sideways but held. The guard, just a few feet below her, let loose a stream of frustrated curses.

The boy gauged the distance between Ocyrhoe and her pursuer, who had given up trying to grab her from the ground and had started climbing the wall himself.

She flattened against the wall, sucking in a breath, then planted her feet and resumed her climb, as quickly as the crumbling wall allowed. She was a good climber, but she didn't have Ferenc's experience or the guard's strength.

The guard's searching hand was now just inches below her heel. *She wasn't going to make it.*

Ferenc shuffled laterally to his right. *Just a little farther.* He glanced down, checking his position, and then took a deep breath. Ocyrhoe looked up and to the left, her face screwed up in panic and confusion as she tried to figure out what he was doing.

He met her gaze and nodded once. *Without you, there is no mission.*

Ferenc let go of the wall.

✦ ✦ ✦

Cardinal Sinibaldo Fieschi kept his eyes squeezed tightly shut as he whispered the seventh Psalm. "…*Iudica me, Domine, secundum iustitiam meam et secundum innocentiam meam, quae est in me…*" The rope burned across his palm and his knuckles ached, but he could not let his grip loosen. Not yet. "… *Consumatur nequitia peccatorum; et iustem confirma; scrutans corda et renes Deus iustus…*"

The body trapped in the rope—already he was no longer thinking about it as a living person—had stopped thrashing and clawing. As Fieschi continued to pray, he felt the man's hands loosen and the deadweight increase. *God strengthens my armor,* he thought, *for I am virtuous and upright in my heart.* He heard a rattling noise, like sand being scattered across a stone floor, and the muscles in his hands cramped from exertion.

His prayer was cut short by a sound that escaped from his chest—part sob, part exclamation—and his hands opened without his willing the action. It was as if one of God's angels had touched his wrists, and the ethereal touch of the divine messenger had broken his grip. He fell back and sprawled on the floor, gasping for breath. A weight lay against his legs. A heavy, *still* weight.

When he finally noticed the stink of death—the expelled shit and piss from the dead man's bowels, mixed with the faint tang of blood—he opened his eyes. He shuddered slightly at the sight of Somercotes's face—the bulging eyes decorated with a lacework of blood; the tongue protruding from the agonized mouth, a copious smear of blood across his lips and beard from his broken nose; dark shadows around the cardinal's neck, a rope burn under his jaw.

"*Convertetur dolor eius in caput eius,*" Fieschi whispered, making the sign of the cross, "*et in verticem ipsius iniquitas eius descendet.*" *He brought it upon himself.*

He pushed Somercotes's body away and, legs trembling, got to his feet. His hands ached, and his right palm was raw from the rope, but he was standing, he was alive. Somercotes was not. The distinction was very clear in Fieschi's mind, uncluttered by remorse or guilt.

This was not his victory, his personal triumph. By garroting this *heretic,* he had saved the Holy Roman Church.

The ring. He remembered what they had been arguing about before the Will of God—*Deus iudex iustus*—had flowed into him and guided his hand. The ring that supposedly belonged to that charlatan—a cardinal's ring. It was a symbol that would allow him to participate in the election of the next Bishop of Rome—a potentially key vote. He had to find that ring.

He crouched over Somercotes's body and, trying to ignore the stench, pulled and poked through the simple robes, feeling for the ring. There were few places to hide anything in the cardinal's garment, but he checked the seams for unusual bulges or gathers that would suggest a hidden pocket; after a few minutes of fruitless searching, he turned his attention to the dead man's shoes. Without Somercotes's feet in them, they were just old leather scraps—worn thin in the heels, the stitching unraveling along the outer edges.

Would he have hidden the ring in his chamber? Fieschi crawled toward one corner to begin, on his knees, feeling the stones in the wall for fit, trying to shift or pry each one out to reveal a hiding place. No success. He then stood and ripped the heavy mattress cloth, flinging away handfuls of the straw stuffing. From the pegs on the wall, he ripped down Somercotes's cloak and extra robe, pawing through the cloth for the hard shape of a ring. He even tore apart the cardinal's damaged Bible, though part of his brain knew there was no way to hid a ring within the pages of the book.

Nothing.

Fieschi glared at the body. Even in death, the man confounded him. Could he have secured it somewhere in the tunnels? No, that would be even more risky than hiding it in the room; he would have to keep it where he could find it quickly, and such a place would have to be nearby, familiar. Somercotes's chamber was the only place where he could be afforded some privacy, where he could be assured he would not be disturbed while he hid the ring or retrieved it.

Did he even have it? Fieschi had to admit the possibility that Somercotes had been lying to him. His breath caught in his throat as he recalled the conversation he had overheard between Somercotes and the messengers. They had brought the ring back to the mad priest. He had heard them talking about it; he could distinctly remember the tone of Somercotes's voice as he had examined it. *An Archbishop's ring...*

"You fool." He savagely kicked Somercotes's body. "You lied to me." It wasn't a cardinal's ring at all; it was the ring of an Archbishop.

Fieschi's mind raced, sorting back through the letters and documents that he had read to the Pope in His Holiness's final days. He had been so caught up in the speculation of who this stranger was and the effect his presence was going to have on the election of the new Pope that he hadn't given enough thought to why the man was *here* or who he was.

There had been reports from Hungary, following the battle at Mohi. Reports of who had been lost at that battle. *An Archbishop...*

Fieschi needed time to think. He needed to figure out what to do next. Time to pray, even, if that would help. He looked at the room—the dead body, the torn clothes, the scattered straw from the ripped mattress—and realized, as if seeing it all for the first time, that he couldn't simply walk away from the room as if nothing had happened. Bits of straw clung to his robes. His right hand was red and raw. No one could connect his appearance with what had happened here. Had anyone seem him with Somercotes?

The mad priest.

He could deal with him later. Right now, he had to get out of Somercotes's room. He had to get rid of the robe he was wearing—the same plain vestment he had worn when he snuck into the city. It smelled too much like sweat and piss and shit. Like violent death.

His gaze was drawn to the small metal lantern that provided the illumination for the room, the flickering flame like a single, blinking eye. More of a wink, in fact, as if it knew some deadly secret it would impart to him if he would only pick it up.

Stepping around Somercotes's body, he scooped up the lantern and went to the door. Placing the lantern on the floor, he lifted and removed the door's timber bar, then carefully opened the door a few inches to check the hallway. Satisfied it was empty, he bent over and delicately plucked the small stub of candle from the lantern's metal shell. The candle's flame danced eagerly.

Fieschi tossed the candle into the scattered straw. The candle bounced once, then lay on its side. The flame grew brighter as it spread into the straw.

With a grim smile, he left the room, pulling the door shut behind him. No one would know of his handiwork, not until it was too late.

Omnis arbor, quae non facit fructum bonum, excidetur, he thought as he walked, *and thrown to the fire…*

✦✦✦

Ferenc twisted and angled his body as he fell. He saw, out of the corner of his eye, Ocyrhoe's open mouth and wide eyes as he flashed by her, but there was no time to tell her his plan. There was no time to do anything but pull his arms and legs in before he collided with the guard. He felt the guard's head against his arm and side, and then the two of them were falling, a mass of flailing arms and legs.

They hit the ground, Ferenc on top, and the impact drove the air out of his lungs. He rolled off, then stood, wincing as he tried to put weight on his left leg. He had twisted his ankle. It wasn't a bad sprain—he could walk, albeit it with a bit of a limp, and if he was careful, it would stop hurting in a day or so.

The guard groaned, eyelids fluttering, and his arms and legs jerked in uncoordinated spasms. He was stunned but not senseless. In a few moments, he would regain his wits.

Ocyrhoe landed lightly nearby and started jabbering at Ferenc. Ferenc shook his head and tried to grip her arm, but she yanked it from his grasp, poked his chest with an angry finger, and then pointed to the wall. Ferenc shook his head again and touched his left leg, took a limping step. "I can't climb," he said. "Not quickly." He grabbed at her arm again, with both hands this time, and held her fast while he signed. "We have to go. Unless you want to kill this guard."

She snapped her mouth shut and glared at him. Her eyes darted back and forth like the tiny swallows Ferenc had once watched hunt and swoop across the flower meadows in the spring, and then she nodded. "*Sequere,*" she said, disengaging her arm from his grip. She took his hand and pressed her fingers against the top of his wrist. "We'll find another spot to climb," she signed.

He began to walk as fast as his rapidly swelling ankle allowed. He reversed their hands—now holding her—and began to sign. "Hard to climb now. Harder to jump. Can climb this side, but how to get down?"

She shrugged and shook her head, clearly not understanding his question.

Just before they turned a corner, he glanced over his shoulder. The guard was still on his back, feebly waving his arms and kicking his legs. He looked like a bug. In a moment, they would be out of his sight.

"Wall keeps people out," Ferenc signed. "Have you ever been outside?"

She blushed and looked away, and he could feel her arm tense as she thought about pulling away. He had embarrassed her and was surprised at his reaction to her pain. He squeezed her arm, trying to tell her he did not mean to cause distress with the question. But he knew the answer.

Ocyrhoe had never been outside of Rome. She didn't know what the other side of the wall looked like, much less the world beyond—but judging by her reaction, she understood why he had asked.

It didn't matter how easy it was to climb the inside of the walls of Rome; the inside might be left to decay, but the outward-facing rampart must be kept reasonably strong and smooth, or it would not be any sort of barrier against enemies.

He had injured himself falling not much more than three times the height of a man. Jumping from three stories? Neither of them would survive.

"Need different route," Ferenc signed. He thought of the dark places they had recently visited, the tunnels under the old temples of the city. His fingers curled and tapped her forearm. "Underground. Can you find a way?"

CHAPTER 30:

WAITING FOR THE STORM

Andreas sat on his pallet with a grunt of pain. The stone walls were a mercy during the rain and the wind, but in the murderous heat of summer, they made little difference, especially when it was a gray heat—a steaming, sunless heat. There was no breeze without or within, and little for him to do other than sweat.

In all the stories singers told of heroics and of battle, they rarely, if ever, spoke of the waiting or the coming down afterward. Unless it served the story, they didn't speak of the wounds either. He tried to straighten his aching back and felt muscles move beneath skin so tight from exertion that he wanted only to fall into a deep slumber and never move again.

The bruises he had received on the First Field overlaid their own dull throbbing upon previous layers of older pains. Battle rush and focus on opponents permitted a man to ignore these irritations, but after battle, they came rushing back with an angry vengeance.

At Petraathen, Taran had taught them numerous exercises designed to drive away fatigue, as well as stretches that kept abused muscles and ligaments from seizing up, and he would need to do more of those soon or else suffer the consequences.

Still, Andreas sat, feeling the sweat pour down his face, acutely aware of his own mortality.

The fight against the Flower Knight a week ago had taken more out of him than it should have, and now he was staring at his sword hand, listening with a grimace as the finger bones clicked uncomfortably as he opened and closed his fist. *That's new*, he thought.

"You look like hell," Rutger said from the doorway. Even against the gray of the outside, the quartermaster was a dark silhouette. "I warned you this was dangerous."

"Someone has to reap what I sowed," Andreas replied with a rueful attempt at a smile, quickly distorted by a grunt of pain. Unless he got up and did his exercises, come morning he would barely be able to move at all. "Better the consequences fall on my head," he said.

"You sound like Percival," Rutger chuckled, pulling up a chair.

"Percival? God and the Virgin, I hope not," Andreas laughed in return. It hurt the tensed muscles in his midsection. Everything hurt just then. "Was he here before I arrived? Did he go with the others?"

Rutger nodded.

"Ach, I am sorry to have missed him," Andreas said, "more so because we could use his sword arm right about now." He leaned back and raised his own sword arm experimentally. The knuckles clicked again. Cracking roasted pigs' feet—that's what his knuckles sounded like. "At least now I can rest for a little while."

Rutger shifted in his seat. His worn expression immediately told Andreas that something was wrong. "I don't like that look, Rutger," he said. "That look says no sleep and no food for a week, or worse. What's happened?"

"We've just had word from Hünern," Rutger sighed. "Your show of audacity has sufficed to intrigue the Khan. The gates to the arena open tomorrow." He paused. "Your name is on the lists—high on the lists."

The news hit Andreas like a fresh punch to the stomach. He stared blankly for a moment. He'd known in the back of his mind that this might happen, but somehow it hadn't occurred to him that it could happen before he'd had the opportunity to get any real rest.

Andreas started to laugh. That hurt as well, and for a moment, he tried to hold it back, but to no avail. His shoulders quaked, and his abdomen spasmed as he shook with grim mirth at his circumstances. Then he threw his head back and laughed at the ceiling. Tears flowed from his eyes before he mastered himself and wiped them away. "God indeed pays the foolish their due," he said after he regained control of his voice. Now he took a deep breath, and that hurt as well. "So be it."

"You damn fool." Rutger shook his head. "You're in no shape to fight."

"I'll be the judge of that," he said, pushing himself once more to his feet and stepping around like a drunken crane. His legs burned, but if there was real need, he could fight—perhaps even manage a burst or two of speed, if danger pressed. He'd regret it afterward, but this was no time for conserving strength. He had attracted the Khan's attention, and if he was in the ring, perhaps those tiger eyes would not look so sharply upon the rest of his order.

"You're pushing yourself too hard," Rutger said again, more quietly. "You're one of our best, but even the best can be broken and beaten. Be careful in the lists, Andreas. We can't afford to lose anyone."

Andreas flashed a rueful smile. "We'll all be putting everything on one line of battle or another, sooner or later…I just need to live long enough to see it." He laughed and felt a cough travel upward, doubling him over, which hurt even more. The injuries were piling up. He'd yet to break any bones or rip out hamstrings or sinews, however, which was a godsend.

"Look on the bright side," Andreas went on. "Our plan worked. The arena is open and the bouts will begin anew. All eyes will be on the Circus." *And I will fight again, and harder, against opponents as dangerous as the Flower Knight—and he didn't even want to kill me.*

Rutger seemed to guess his thoughts. "I warned you about this," he said. "Be cautious."

"Caution won't get us victory or success." Andreas dropped forward onto his hands and flung his legs out behind him. He began his exercises against the protest of every muscle in his aching limbs and torso. Bruises cried out, innards rebelled at the sudden upset of their brief, cherished balance.

But his arm went beyond complaining and nearly folded under him. It had still not recovered enough. *Don't grumble. Plug on,* he thought.

Rutger watched him for a long moment in silence.

He could feel the older man's eyes on his back.

"There is a difference, Andreas," he said, "between walking on the edge of a blade and dancing merrily across it like some caperer in a great hall. Do not mistake foolishness for courage."

Andreas didn't pause in his exercises. "I'll keep that in mind."

When he had finished, and his body was aflame all over, he sat back down gingerly on the pallet. Rutger handed him a cup of water. He downed it, thirsty as if he might never drink again.

"There is a boy called Hans who passes messages back and forth between myself and the Flower Knight," Andreas said after a moment. Normally, he wouldn't pass this on, as there was no need for anyone but himself to know. "Whatever happens here, I want him taken to Petraathen when this is over by whoever amongst us survives." It was a grim thought, but he wanted the boy to have the chance, if that was what he wanted.

"You have my word," Rutger said quietly.

✦✦✦

In Hünern, the rats went unnoticed, and that was their strength. In the streets, Hans was invisible, and so he was left to his own devices. He was waiting right now at the base of the tree, the one place he knew would grant him a momentary sense of safety. It wasn't much, but beneath these branches there was peace.

Hans had shown Andreas this tree, and the big knight's reaction had confirmed its importance in a way that he had suspected on some level, but not understood, truly, until then.

Several other children were sleeping nearby, and Hans had taken care not to wake them. One of them was the last boy he had sent running to the fighter's camp. The boy had taken a bad clout on the ear that had left the ear swollen like a vegetable, surrounded by a green, brown, and reddish bruise.

Hans watched him as he rested. He felt guilty about the boy's injury, but getting the messages back and forth was important. Brother Andreas had told him so, and he was a good man.

The plan was actually very simple and was based on how Hans and the other children had gone about making sure they all had food during the bad times: send a different boy each time, each with a different story, bring the prize back, and divide it among all of them. While the Mongols closely watched the gate to their camp, they seldom interrogated the children who went in and out, running this or that little errand for the people inside. Sometimes they brought ale; other times they delivered something purchased from the local craftsmen.

Making sure that the boys knew which tent they were supposed to find, and remembered the words they were supposed to say, was not hard, because each boy didn't have much to remember. "How many flowers?" they would ask, and Kim would tell them. The boy would return and tell Hans, and he would pass the news on to Andreas. It was simple, and so far, it had worked, but there was always the chance of something going wrong, and so Hans waited nervously beneath the tree, trying to comfort himself in its presence.

When Andreas had bid him run off behind the alehouse, he'd also worried and had come here, like now, to comfort himself. It was only later that the sounds of the fight at First Field had summoned him to witness Andreas's duel with the Flower Knight.

It was after that that Andreas had asked him to organize the boys and run these messages—but not without obvious reluctance. *He is afraid for me,* Hans had thought with an unexpected glow of pride. *But I am not the one facing the swords. Fearless for oneself, fear for others—that must be what it means to be a hero.*

Knowing that he would have soon aroused suspicion if he did all the delivering himself, Hans had turned to the other rats of Hünern to help him, creating the system they used now. It had held up for a week, so far—and none of the boys had gotten hurt or captured.

It had occurred to Hans every time he worried for one of the children that they were safer than most of the adults, if only because they were beneath notice, but that did not make him worry less. *I made them do dangerous things. If any of them gets hurt or killed, it will be my fault.*

The sound of footsteps. Someone was coming. He shifted.

A boy stepped out of the shadows cast by the overhanging roofs. He was shorter than Hans, with sun-darkened skin and brown hair.

"Tamas went into the camp. I saw him walk past the guards," the boy said, grinning. Usually, Hans asked at least one other boy to watch and make sure the messenger got through. This doubled as assurance that any obstacle could be related back to him and as a dry run where the boy who watched could see how it was done. The next time, the watcher would become the messenger.

"Did you see how he did it?" Hans asked. The boy nodded.

"Do you think you can do it next time?" He tried to keep the urgency from showing. The rats had to learn everything the hard way. Rats rarely got a second chance if they made a mistake.

After a moment's pause, the boy looked at him with narrow honesty and eagerness. "Yes."

Hans stood. There was a difference between thinking you were ready and knowing it. The boy knew it. He gave a slow nod. "In two days, you'll go."

The boy grinned again and folded his arms around himself, and Hans saw the mix of pride and fear in his eyes that he himself felt. Next time, the youth would risk everything so that the channel of communication could stay open, and Hans would wait for news and worry again beneath the tree.

Rats so seldom knew love. These boys knew his love, but not his guilt.

◆◆◆

Kim sat outside his tent, listening as a singer performed in a language he didn't understand. Still, the song stirred him. A man did not need to understand the words to know what was being said. Music, like violence, crossed all languages. These were the oldest and most complete ways of communicating that people possessed.

Kim was waiting for the boy. He credited the youth named Hans for devising a means to pass their messages back and forth, and also felt gratitude and admiration for the courageous youths who came to him every few days to inquire of his progress, to pass on information, and to take his own messages back.

He always knew a messenger; the same phrase was used, and Hans sent only boys who spoke the Mongol tongue. Hans was a most discerning and clever lad, wiser than Kim had initially given him credit for.

He raised a cup of water to his lips and drank, taking a mental tally of those they'd managed to bring into the fold since the last time he'd sent a message. When he lowered it, a dark-haired youth stood before him. He smiled nervously.

"Do you enjoy the shade?" the boy asked.

Kim smiled. "Even on gray days it is a relief, like the branches of a tree."

The youth took a breath and asked, "Have you found any flowers today?" The boy's grasp of Mongol speech was not exceptional but would not arouse suspicion.

Kim reached for a small wrapped bundle of cloth beside him and unwrapped it, revealing four blossoms. He put them in the boy's hand. "Four, this time. Next time, there will be more." He hoped.

The boy smiled. “I will take them back, thank you.” He turned to go, and Kim moved his attention back to the empty cloth in his hand. There had been no breeze, which reflected his own sense of stagnation, even as events began to move forward.

But then he felt the first stirrings in the air. Looking to the grass beyond the edge of his tent, he saw that the blades were bending back and forth as the first cool breath of wind whispered through the camp. Above came a distant groan and then a roar of thunder.

The storm was finally coming. As he rose and turned to enter his tent, the first drops of rain began to fall.

CHAPTER 31:

FREEDOM LOST

She was free.

She clenched the horse's mane tightly, her fingers aching from the strain of holding on. She had no memory of getting on the horse: one moment she had been crouched among the panicked horses tied to the picket line, her breath fluttering in her throat; then she had been flying, her feet lightly skipping off the ground as she let the horse drag her away from Gansukh.

Part of her wept at leaving him behind, but she had had no choice. If she was going to escape from the *Khagan*'s camp, this was her only chance. She couldn't be afraid of the ambushers—they couldn't be worse than the Mongols. They might even be her own countrymen, and while Lian didn't hold any illusions that men bold enough to attack the *Khagan*'s caravan would be any less cruel than the *Khagan* himself, she was still heartened by the fact that there were still people who fought back against Mongol tyranny.

She bent over her horse's back, trying to make as small a target as possible. The white blur of tents rushed by as the horse ran. She didn't try to guide the animal; she let it find its own way, urging it on by beating her heels against its ribs. *Run,* she pleaded, *run as fast as you can.*

"Lian!"

She glanced back and spotted another horse and rider pursuing her. Her hair whipped around her face, and she risked letting go to rake her hair out of her eyes. *Gansukh.* Why couldn't he let her go?

Or was he coming with her?

Her horse veered to the right, and she grabbed on with both hands, tightening her legs around the horse. She lashed out with her heels, driving the horse faster. *Don't be a fool,* she thought. *He's trying to stop you.*

Distantly, she heard a rumble of thunder, and she glanced up at the sky. Behind her, the smoke from the burning tents was making the stars blink like fireflies, but up ahead, the sky was filled with a constant sea of stars. *Where was the storm?* she wondered, looking for some patch of darkness that would indicate clouds. Rain would slow her down, but it would obscure her trail.

On her right, she heard men shouting, and her heart quickened at the voices. They were speaking Chinese! Her horse blew air noisily from its nose and veered away from the voices, panicked enough that it wanted to shy away from any living creature.

Gansukh shouted her name again, and when she looked, he was closer. His horse was bigger and stronger—he was gaining on her.

Her horse stumbled, grunting deep in its chest. Lian tensed her body, clinging tightly to its mane. When the horse stumbled a second time, her heart skipped a beat. It twisted its head to the side, and she saw foam and blood on its mouth, and then it collapsed. For a brief second, she had time to stare at the thin shaft of the arrow jutting from the horse's neck—if it had been a little higher, it would have struck her instead—and then she was flying again. The sensation was not the same, though, as she clawed and flailed at the air in an effort to grab onto anything.

She hit the ground shoulder first, and she cried out as her momentum flipped her over the point of impact and slammed her hard on her back. She slid and tumbled, and every rock on the ground hit her like a fist—in the small of her back, on the arms and legs, on the cheek. She tried to curl up into a ball—the same way she had when the Mongol soldiers had first beaten her when they had taken her captive—but her arms and legs wouldn't work.

Her horse screamed nearby, having broken a leg as it had fallen, and the sound was made worse by the bubbling wetness of its pierced throat.

When she stopped tumbling, Lian lay in a heap. She didn't know if she had broken any bones in the fall, but it didn't matter. She had failed. Even if she could stand, she was too bruised to run. Her right hand pawed at her face, a motion she couldn't understand the genesis of, and there was a strange keening noise coming from her throat.

Hooves thundered past her head, and she felt the impact of a heavy weight against the ground nearby. "Lian!" Gansukh tried to put his arms around her, and her right hand—still wriggling like an agitated snake—vainly pushed him away. "It's me." He tried to pin her arm, and finding some unknown reserve of strength, she fought him all the harder.

Somehow she extricated herself from his embrace, even though she didn't think she had the strength to stand. She could crawl, though, and on bloodied knees, she tottered away from him. Her hair was twisted and matted against her face, and she spat out a mouthful.

She meant to scream at him, but her voice died in her throat.

A line of strange soldiers stood in front of her. They wore haphazard armor, some more complete than others, and the scattered markings on their shoulders and chests were Chinese. Several of the soldiers carried spears, and having spotted both Gansukh and Lian, they lowered their spears.

Gansukh had grabbed her ankle, and he hissed at her as she struggled, but she ignored him. *Chinese!* A new opportunity had presented itself to her, a sudden and unexpected path to freedom.

"I am a prisoner," she said in Chinese. She raised her hands, showing them her scraped and bloody palms. "Please don't kill me."

"What are you saying?" Gansukh hissed in her ear.

She jerked her leg free of his grip and crawled closer to the line of soldiers. Several of the Chinese soldiers lowered their spears slightly, but their general apprehension did not lessen.

"Please," she whined, making eye contact with the nearest man. "I am captive of the *Khagan.* I beg you to free me."

Two of the soldiers exchanged glances, chattering to one another too quickly for her to follow. The one on the left wanted to continue their mission; the one on the right was considering her request. Prisoners were always useful, he argued.

"Is this man your master?" asked the curious one. His helmet had a plume of dark feathers, and there was a precision to his words that spoke of formal education.

She nodded, letting a small sob escape from her throat.

The soldiers surged forward, their spears focusing now on Gansukh, who muttered an oath under his breath. Lian glanced over her shoulder and tried to catch Gansukh's eye, but he was too focused on the spears to notice her effort.

A hand grabbed her arm, jerking her forward, and she gasped as the Chinese leader dragged her forward. Gansukh edged forward and then stopped, eyeing the threatening spears. She knew that look in his eye, the same sort of frantic stare a cornered animal has, one that knows what comes next but is powerless to stop it.

"Wait!"

The Chinese man wound a hand in her hair and jerked her back. She struggled in his grip, winding herself toward him, while trying to keep the soldiers from thrusting their spears into Gansukh. "He's…he's a special advisor to the *Khagan*," she cried to the man holding her hair. "He has value."

The first Chinese man, the one concerned about his mission, grunted and spat. "He doesn't look like much." He nodded his head toward the camp. "We don't have time."

"No, wait," Lian said, frantically thinking how to convince these Chinese men without revealing too much. "They don't look like much," she said hurriedly, adopting a more haughty tone. "These steppe warriors are all barely one bath away from being animals, but this one is…special."

"We don't have time for hostages," the first man repeated.

The man who held her hair wound his hand another revolution, pulling her closely to him. "Go," he said to his companion. "A hostage could be useful…" He scratched his chin thoughtfully for a moment and then barked a command at his men: "Tie him up."

"They want to take you—" Lian started to explain to Gansukh in Mongolian, but the Chinese man jerked her head back, and she cried out in pain.

Gansukh surged forward. The Chinese spears came up, and Gansukh stopped just short of the points. One of the soldiers jabbered at him to back away, lightly flicking his spear point at Gansukh's chest to make his command clear. Glowering at the man who held Lian's hair, Gansukh took a step back. His hand remained on the hilt of his sword.

"What were you saying to him?" Lian's captor demanded.

"I was trying to tell him to not fight," she insisted, trying to lessen the tension on her hair. "He is a proud man. He will not just lay down his sword because you ask him to."

Another boom of thunder rolled across the camp, and Lian realized the sound was too slight to be real thunder. It was the concussive sound of Chinese explosives, and she swallowed the lump of fear that had risen in her throat. *Fire arrows and explosives,* she wondered. *What sort of attack is this?*

The first man made a cutting motion with his hand. "We did not come for hostages," he said, and he called to the spearmen. Half of the circle surrounding Gansukh pulled back their spears and made to follow their squad commander. "Kill them both" was his final assessment. His men falling in behind him, he ran toward the tents of the Mongol camp.

Lian's captor hesitated as Gansukh shrewdly eyed the soldiers still holding their spears on him. He remained still, but Lian could read the subtle change in his breathing. He thought they were going to kill him, and he was readying himself.

"Tell him to lie down," Lian's captor hissed in her ear. "Tell him to do it quickly, or my men will kill him." She heard the sound of a knife being drawn from a sheath, and then the cold touch of blade eased against her throat. "And then I'll kill you."

She nodded, trying not to pull away from the man or the knife. "Lie down," she said to Gansukh in Mongolian. "They want to take you prisoner."

"Why?" he growled. His face was like a mask—only his eyes moved, tracking back and forth between the soldiers threatening him.

"I'm trying to save your life," she insisted.

He glanced at her, and she flinched at the wounded look in his eyes—the naked accusation of betrayal.

"Please," she whispered. "Trust me. If you don't, we're both dead."

Gansukh didn't reply, but his hand moved slowly away from the hilt of his sword. Putting both hands out in front of him, palms forward, he knelt on the ground. One of the soldiers reversed his spear and hit Gansukh in the lower back with the butt of his weapon. He collapsed on the ground, and as a soldier put a knee in his back and grabbed at his hands to bind them, he kept staring at Lian. He didn't look away as the Chinese men hauled him up and, with a nod from their leader, dragged him into the darkness of the night.

◆◆◆

As soon as the *Khagan* sat down to eat, Master Chucai made his excuses and left the feast for the solitude of his tent. He had been working nonstop for nearly a week by the time the caravan had left Karakorum, and with the camp established and the *Khagan* and his entourage seated for the nighttime meal, he was no longer needed. For a few hours, he could meditate or read—he had brought along a new edition of Zhu Xi's commentary on the Four Books that he had been looking forward to examining for some time. He found, more and more, that it was not sleep that truly recharged his vitality, but more spiritual activities. When he lay down at night, parts of his mind churned over the matters of the Empire, and while he found new solutions to problems waiting for him when he awoke, sleep was never particularly restful. Meditation and reflection were his most treasured activities, and there had been a scarcity of both in the last few weeks.

The shouting of the guards stirred him from his meditation, and his eyes snapped open. His *ger* had been dark but for a single flame in a small brazier and the ambient light from the camp that slipped through the space he had left open at the top of the tent flaps, but there was more light spilling into his *ger* than he had expected to see. Not sunlight. *Firelight.*

Master Chucai leaped to his feet and raced to the entrance of the *ger.* He clawed open the flaps and rushed out. His primary concern was the *Khagan*'s *ger,* and he quickly ascertained that it was undamaged and that the figures milling around it were the Imperial Guard. He was too far away to make out individuals among the clustered guards, but he assumed Munokhoi would not tarry long at the *Khagan*'s *ger. He will take the fight to the enemy,* Chucai thought as he strode through the maze of tents and wagons. *The men guarding the* Khagan *will be diligent, but they won't be imaginative.*

He had had some reservations about putting the hotheaded *jaghun* captain in charge of the entire Imperial Guard that was accompanying the caravan to Burqan-qaldun, but Ögedei had ignored his concerns. While he had no doubt Munokhoi would ruthlessly deal with the fools who had mistakenly thought they had stumbled upon a wealthy caravan, it would probably be best to ensure that the *Khagan* remained safe during the fracas.

Chucai came to a sudden halt. He stared at a nearby tent, watching as a trio of overdressed courtiers struggled to douse the flames slithering across the tent's roof. Blinking his eyes clear of the dust and ash floating in the air, he slowly turned his head and carefully examined the spread of the fires throughout the camp. An idea swam in the depth of his brain, like an enormous koi in a murky pond, and he tried to remain still so as to not spook it, so that it would come to the surface where he could fully apprehend it. There was a pattern to the fires. They weren't randomly scattered throughout the camp.

Archers, he noted, *firing from an elevated position.* He scanned the horizon, trying to spot some sign of where the attack had come from, but the smoke from the fires dirtied the air too much to spot any such sign. *This isn't an accident,* he realized, discarding the idea that this attack had been a case of mistaken identity.

Initially, the *Khagan* had wanted to travel with a smaller entourage—none of his wives, a minimum of supply wagons, and only a single *jaghun* to protect him. The idea had been ridiculous, and Chucai had dismissed it outright, arguing that the *Khagan* could travel with no less than a *minghan*—one thousand men—as his personal security force. And, of course, a thousand men would have required a commensurate increase in supplies, which would have, in turn, increased the amount of time it would take to assemble the caravan. While Chucai thought the desire to travel to Burqan-qaldun was more than a passing fancy on the part of the *Khagan,* he wasn't the sort of eager sycophant who would fail to question the ramifications of an idle whim. While the Empire was fairly safe to travel—especially in the heart of territory that had been under Mongol rule for several generations—it didn't mean that the *Khagan*'s personal safety wasn't still of paramount importance. There was always the possibility of attacks by roving bandits—clanless men who would prey on an insufficiently protected caravan or a group of nomadic herders.

But bandits didn't announce themselves with a volley of flaming arrows. Fire would destroy the very cargo they were hoping to steal.

His own reaction to the attack had been mindless. He had leaped to a conclusion that wasn't supported by what was actually happening around him. Wasn't that one of the very lessons Zhu Xi sought to impart in his commentary? This attack was directed at the *Khagan*; the raiders knew whose caravan they were attacking. The true question—the one he should have been asking earlier—was why?

Chucai heard a distant crump of noise, and he knew at once that it was the sound of black powder igniting. Grimly, he nodded to himself as he began to walk toward the *Khagan*'s *ger* again. He wasn't hurried. He took his time, his gaze sweeping back and forth across the chaos. His height gave him an advantage; while he couldn't see over the tents, the scurrying frenzy of panicked courtiers and concubines and shouting soldiers did little to block his field of view. Chucai walked and watched, looking for the real reason the camp had been attacked.

If the goal of the attack was to assassinate the *Khagan*, then why hadn't they set fire to the *Khagan*'s *ger*? Were their archers that unskilled? Chucai doubted that was true. In which case, the fires were a distraction, a means of splitting the Imperial Guard. But why?

Chucai cut to his right, no longer moving directly toward the *Khagan*'s *ger*. Something had caught his eye. He wasn't sure what he had seen, and it was possible he was chasing a ghost, a writhing smoke shadow cast by firelight.

The koi was surfacing in the pond in his mind.

He caught sight of the movement again, and the feeble phantom coalesced into the dim shapes of three men, dressed in dark clothing, skulking between tents. They carried long sticks—spears, though one was longer than the other two.

"Hai!" Chucai shouted, curious to see if these phantoms would bolt like startled rabbits.

The three men froze, dark blots against the dull leather of a tent. If he hadn't been staring right at them, he might have not seen them. During the day, they would have stood out quite plainly, but in the night—with the haze of the smoke—they were nearly invisible. *Which is exactly what the fires were for,* Chucai realized. *Cover.*

"Hai! Men of the Imperial Guard," he bellowed, directing his voice toward the *Khagan*'s *ger*. "To me! There are assassins among us."

The men moved, two of them sprinting off between the tents; the other man lowered his spear and charged Chucai, hoping to silence the alarm that had given them away.

Master Chucai had but a moment to ready himself. He had no weapon, and briefly he chided himself again for reacting without thinking, but then the man was upon him, screaming at him in Chinese as he thrust the spear.

Chucai flowed like a wisp of smoke, the thick sleeve of his robe sweeping up and around like a fan. Angling his body so that he became a thin reed, he felt his sleeve tug as the spear pierced the silk fabric. His hand kept moving, inscribing the course a bird makes as it dives down on a lake and scoops up an unwary fish. The bird then rises back into the sky, burdened by what it has clutched in its talons. Chucai brought his hand up and turned, feeling the Chinese man struggle to pull the spear out of his sleeve. He clenched his other hand into a fist.

The spearman looked up, a realization dawning on his face that he had underestimated the length of his opponent's reach, and then Chucai's fist smashed into his nose. He cried out and fell back, his hands rising to stem the sudden rush of blood.

Simultaneously with the strike to the man's face, Chucai had closed his other hand around the shaft of the spear and yanked it free of the man's grip. Dropping his left hand to the spear, he stepped back, whipping the spear around to catch the man under the left arm. As soon as he felt the spear bite into leather, he pulled it back. The man lowered his arms, staggering from the slice, and Chucai stabbed him in the throat.

The other two had vanished among the tents, but Chucai heard shouts coming from up ahead. His alarm had been heard. Pulling the dead man's spear free, he ran toward the voices.

Soon enough, he caught up with the Imperial Guard. Several had bows, and their arrows had brought down one of the two skulkers. The surviving one stood near the body of his companion, an arrow jutting out of his leg. He held the approaching Mongols at bay with his long spear, and as Chucai approached, he realized the man was holding the *Khagan*'s spirit banner. The horsehair tassels were matted with blood and dirt, and the point of the shaft was more ornamental than deadly. What stopped the Mongols from attacking the man was a reluctance to damage the spirit banner.

Chucai hurled the spear he had taken from the Chinese man, and it struck the last Chinese man in the hip with such force that he was knocked off his feet. He landed with a thump, and when he struggled to sit up, he was immediately hit by a handful of arrows.

Chucai barked at the guards and they paused, uncertain as to the cause of his anger. Chucai approached the two Chinese men, and a quick glance verified they were both dead. "Look for others," he snapped at the guards, shaking his head. "Try to capture one alive."

Dead men were useless to him.

Chucai picked up the spirit banner and ran his fingers through its tassels, trying to untangle them. *What did they want with it?* he wondered. *Why sacrifice themselves for a piece of wood covered with old horsehair?*

He had never held the banner, much less examined it closely. It was just an old stick that Genghis had started tying horsehair to. *We are horse people,* he had explained to Chucai, *and wherever we are, the wind will be with us too.* Over time, the *Khagan* had added more strands to it, and Chucai had always marveled at how this simple thing had become symbolic of the prosperity of the Empire.

When he ran his hands over the banner, he noticed the texture of the wood. It felt both rough and resilient, as if it were an intricately carved piece of freshly harvested wood. He raised the staff, trying to get a better glimpse of its surface in the flickering light from the fires. His thumb encountered a rough spot, and he peered more closely at the bump.

It was a tiny scar, scabbed over with dried resin, not unlike the sort of growth that forms after a sprig has been cut from a living branch.

◆◆◆

In a narrow depression to the east of the *Khagan*'s great caravan, Lian and her captor reunited with Gansukh and a few other battered Chinese soldiers. Her Chinese captor left her for a moment as he huddled together with the other soldiers, their voices low and clipped. Gansukh lay nearby, on his side, his hands bound tightly behind his back. His face was a mass of shadows and bruises, and to not look at him, Lian turned toward the *Khagan*'s camp. All that she could see of the great caravan were the lights of the torches and still-burning fires. The sparse grasses of the gentle slope were limned in orange-and-yellow light, like the edge of an enormous and empty stage.

"What is your name?"

Lian turned her head. The Chinese man who had held her hair was done conferring with the others, and they stood nearby, awaiting further instruction. "Lian," she said. She inclined her head and raised an eyebrow, an imperious look that had worked well on many a sweaty and nervous official. *And you are…?*

"Luo Xi," he replied. His lips pulled into a thin smile, fleeting amusement at her airs. Under the dirt and soot, he appeared to have a strong face—handsome, even, in a Southern way that Lian hadn't seen in years, with strong cheekbones, piercing eyes, and a complexion unmarred by constant exposure to the sun and wind—the opposite of anyone from the steppes. He took off his helmet, revealing a head of thick black hair, and tucked the cap under his arm. He was trying to appear relaxed, but the way his shoulders remained stiff and hunched forward, and the restlessness of his eyes, betrayed his uncertainty.

What was he waiting for?

"I'm from Qingyuan, originally," said Lian, sensing an opportunity to distract him. "When the Mongols came, they burned the city and took every woman and child as a slave. Many of them"—she swayed slightly, feigning dismay with little effort—"mercifully died soon thereafter. Others…lingered. I was…fortunate. I had *useful* skills." She paused, knowing his eyes were on her body. "I had to teach them about Song culture."

Luo tore his eyes away from Lian's body and looked over at Gansukh. The captive Mongol had managed to sit up, and he looked like a hungry wolf that had been caught in a snare. Resentful, tense, and ready for any chance he got. "Did they learn?" Luo snorted.

"I would have made better progress teaching pigs." She laughed derisively and hoped it didn't sound forced.

"Pigs are already more civilized than these mongrels."

Lian turned to the Chinese commander and bowed from the waist. "You have my endless gratitude for rescuing me."

Luo acknowledged the bow with a nod and a slight, formal smile. "A lady in distress is always worth saving."

"You are far from home, even for the sake of rescuing a lady. Or am I simply an added surprise to your glorious efforts at striking the *Khagan* down?"

Luo stroked his chin in an effort to hide a secret smile that wanted to spread across his face. "What is the point of killing a single Khan?" he asked. "Will these mongrels not elect another one?"

"Ah, I see you are a clever man, Commander Luo. Your actions are much too sublime and hidden for a simple girl such as myself."

"And you are much too silver-tongued to be mistaken as such a simpleton, my lady," Luo replied.

Lian laughed. An unexpected thrill ran through her body, making her shiver. She was very much in danger, as were these Chinese men, and yet the two of them tarried long enough to engage in trivial wordplay. Gansukh would never dream of participating in such an exchange, and it had been so long since she had been around a *civilized* man that she had forgotten how pleasant such company was. There was a nobility in Luo's bearing that was unmistakably refreshing.

Luo turned away. He may have sensed the change in their conversation, and unlike Lian, he was not so starved for such talk—or perhaps the reality of their situation pressed more firmly on him than on her. "This filthy mutt," he said, waving a hand at Gansukh, "he is a special advisor to the *Khagan*?"

"Indeed," Lian replied, showing no sign of disappointment, though she felt a tiny panic in her chest. "The *Khagan* values him highly."

"Why?"

"He reminds the *Khagan* of what he once was."

"And what is that?"

"A man of the steppe."

Luo laughed. "And why would the *Khagan* want to be reminded of that?"

Lian shrugged. "I do not know. They value all manner of strange things."

Luo nodded, his attention turning toward the camp. "Yes," he said, "they certainly do." His face grew troubled, and he strode past Lian to get a better view of the camp. He turned back after a moment, and the softness in his face was gone, replaced by a hard certainty, a look Lian knew all too well.

"They have been gone too long," he snapped at the other Chinese men. "I do not like this." He gestured at Gansukh. "If she speaks true, then he may be of use to us. Otherwise"—he glanced at Lian—"we are all dead and our efforts have been for naught." And the look in his eye told Lian that he would not die alone.

Gansukh saw the apprehension in Luo's eye too, and a low chuckle rumbled out of his throat. One of the other Chinese soldiers smacked Gansukh with the butt of his spear, and the Mongol warrior fell forward, his face driving into the dirt. He rolled over onto his side, and his teeth were bared, a grimace of both pain and joy.

Lian's heart pounded in her chest. This wasn't the way it was supposed to happen. The Chinese would free her and keep Gansukh as a hostage. Given time, she was certain she could convince Luo that the young Mongol would be useful. She knew she was being naive and foolish, but despite everything—the years of captivity, the degradation of being Chucai's slave, of being forced to teach this savage manners—she found herself reluctant to turn her back on Gansukh. He was something different in an otherwise cruel and barbaric world. She hadn't lied to Luo; Ögedei did respect Gansukh and might even consider ransoming his return.

Luo roughly grabbed her arm, all pretense of civility gone. "Take her," he said, shoving Lian toward his men. "And if this dog looks like it might bite, kill it."

CHAPTER 32:

THE NIGHT OF STEEL AND FIRE

Two days later, Cnán was sitting in camp when she heard approaching hooves—a party of perhaps half a dozen. "Approaching hooves" was generally not a welcome sound in Mongol-held territory. Nevertheless, she did not even bother to look up from her mending. It would be the war party that Feronantus had sent out before dawn. They would be returning in high spirits. Rædwulf, Finn, Vera, and Istvan, accompanied by Eleázar or Percival, or whichever sentry had first detected their approach and ridden out to greet them. It was always thus. The Shield-Brethren were never surprised, never caught off guard. She was as safe in this camp as an emperor within the walls of the Forbidden City. *Perhaps safer.*

Which meant that she was useless, bored, and irritable.

The war party's tale told around the cook fire was, in many respects, a repeat of the fight in the gully in which Cnán had taken part. This time, Istvan had lured the Mongol party into the ambush. Alchiq had increased the size of such parties to a full *arban* and had changed their tactics.

There was no more leisurely tracking of quarry across the plain: when they had seen Istvan against the skyline, they had sent one of their number galloping straight back toward their main camp, while the other nine had come for him. But only eight had pursued the Hungarian in earnest; one other had trailed along deep in their rear. As soon as Rædwulf's first arrow had taken the leader of the *arban* out of his saddle, this other had wheeled his pony and ridden for the main Mongol party.

Beyond that, it sounded not unlike the engagement Cnán had witnessed. Rædwulf 's bow still had the power to surprise the Mongols with its range, and so he had killed a few. Vera, left without weapons, had been given a crossbow by Feronantus from a pack whose contents Cnán found wondrous indeed.

The other Mongols had tried to circle and penetrate the screen of brush in which Rædwulf had concealed himself, but Vera had killed one with a single, silent boltshot. Two more were killed at close quarters by Finn and Rædwulf while Vera went through the tedious process of redrawing and loading her weapon. A bolt in the back had taken down one horseman who had decided to flee, and Istvan had pursued the last two survivors in a running archery battle across the steppe, eventually killing one with an arrow and the other with his scimitar. Immensely pleased with himself, the Hungarian had returned trailing a short string of ponies and sporting three Mongol arrows that had embedded themselves in various parts of his armor.

Meanwhile, Rædwulf had recovered all but one of his arrows. One, still lost, had missed and likely lay buried in the grass, and he might have been able to find it had they more leisure to search. But many more Mongols would be coming after them soon, and so they dispersed, flying in all directions as fast as they could ride, driving the spare ponies across the grass to lay false trails and then picking their way down into streambeds to complicate the work of those who would soon be tracking them.

As Cnán knew perfectly well, there would be no rest until the *thing* was finished. For there was nowhere to hide on the steppe, and childish tactics like running down streambeds could only delay the moment when Alchiq and his remaining threescore and seven Mongols would descend upon them in force.

Without being instructed to, she got ready to ride through the night.

◆◆◆

What she had not expected—but, in retrospect, should have guessed—was that Feronantus would order them to seek out the main body of the *jaghun* and hunt it down as if it were nothing more than a wounded antelope leaving a blood trail across the steppe. Of course, it made sense. What Feronantus did always made sense in some or other insane way. The Shield-Brethren were supposed to be fleeing; the only way, then, to obtain the advantage of surprise was to turn around and attack.

It might have miscarried had the *jaghun* made its camp in the open. Instead, after a day and a half of hunting the Shield-Brethren across the steppe, the remaining *arbans* converged on a shambling market town that had grown up on the bank of a river.

The river meandered ten leagues in every direction for every one that it actually moved south. But its overall course was decidedly southbound as it flowed toward the Khazar Sea. Raphael was of the opinion that the river might be the one known as the Yaik, originating in a mountain range that might be the fabled Riphean Mountains that were spoken of by the ancient Greeks. If so, it was a boundary, and everything beyond was unknown territory—past the *end of the world,* as

Alexander had conquered it. This detail wreaked a depressing effect on the other members of the party, who had hoped that, after so much hard traveling, they might at least have escaped, months ago, the boundaries of their known world.

In any case, the town had grown up at a place where it was possible to ford the river during the driest part of the year—which was now. Viewing it from a safe distance in the flat, golden light of the late afternoon, Raphael and Vera—huddled a bit closer together than was really called for, as far as Cnán was concerned—discussed it at some length and seemed to agree on something, which Raphael then passed on to the rest of the group.

"The place is far too small to be Saray-Jük, which is fortunate for us."

Cnán had actually heard of Saray-Jük. "A garrison town of the Mongols, located somewhere on this same river, where it is crossed by the Silk Road," she explained. "There, Alchiq would be able to summon as many *jaghun* as he pleased."

Feronantus nodded. "Then we shall proceed as planned," he said, "before Alchiq has had time to send messengers down to the place you named." Wisely, he did not attempt to pronounce it. "Alchiq's decision to make his camp in a settled place will favor us; the unfamiliar noises and smells of the town will conceal our advance."

Our advance.

Cnán's part in the advance was to sneak around in the dark with Yasper, who had gone ahead of them into the market town in search of Cathayan merchants. The time of year favored them. This part of the world was, as a rule, too dry for growing grain and other thirsty crops. But it seemed that some farmers and orchardists had found ways of coaxing food from the ground, perhaps along the windings of the river or in scattered dells watered by streams flowing down from the mountains that Vera claimed lay many leagues to the north. Where this was not possible, they took advantage of the infinite supply of grass to breed ponies. At any rate, this seemed to be the time of year when such people brought their produce here for sale, and so a warren of stalls and wagons had sprung up on a stretch of floodplain nearly surrounded by a loop of the river. It lay between the riverbank and the village proper, which had been prudently situated on slightly higher ground. The Mongols, having no particular interest in the river or the market, had made their camp farther yet from the riverbank, generally west and north of the village.

Yasper seemed to have spent a stimulating afternoon wandering about the makeshift market, which had attracted an assortment of outlandish-looking sorts from various parts of the continent that stretched before them on the opposing bank, as well as a few Westerners—even a Khazar or two. They had come to trade silver money and valuable goods from faraway places for the produce of the local farms, which they loaded onto river barges or oxcarts. Cnán, infiltrating the place after nightfall, smelled what was unquestionably Cathayan food being cooked and was ambushed by something like homesickness. Not a useful emotion for a Binder.

Rather later—an hour or two past midnight, she guessed—she and Yasper hiked up a gentle sandy slope toward the village, which was tiny and despicable compared to the seasonal market. In doing so, they left the savory smells of the cooking behind them. Certain odors, however, seemed to follow them wherever they went: the fruity aroma of alcohol on Yasper's breath and a sharper tang that reminded her a bit of rotten eggs, but sharper, like pepper. The latter emanated from a capacious wicker basket filled with rustling objects—but apparently not too heavy—that Yasper kept slung over his shoulder. He patted it nervously from time to time.

The village was an oval compound of small thatch-roofed houses up on stilts, surrounded by a wooden stockade. They circumvented it, taking care not to expose themselves to the view of the Cuman standing guard at its gate, and made their way through a strip of scrub brush and tall grass to the verge of the field that Alchiq had claimed for the night's camping place.

The Mongols' ponies, numbering well over a hundred, had been staked out in a wide belt surrounding an inner core speckled with small campfires and the indistinct forms of Mongols lying asleep on the ground, rolled up in their blankets. Cnán had learned that there tended to be about one campfire per *arban*, and the rule seemed to hold true here, since there were seven such fires. Most were only smoldering since no one was awake to feed them, and the night was warm enough that their heat was not needed.

She numbered the sentries at half a dozen, and as usual in a well-ordered camp, they were all on their feet, moving about, only rarely gathering to converse.

Feronantus had said that nothing would happen until the moon's crescent touched the western horizon. It was two fingers away from doing so, and so Cnán left Yasper to his preparations, and stole away from the camp back toward the river along the route she expected to retrace later. She had studied the way hastily before sundown, but it seemed prudent to reconnoiter it once in the dark.

North of the village, a screen of trees—the tallest they had seen in weeks—grew between the Mongols' camp and the bank of the river. It was only ten paces in breadth, but its undergrowth was dense enough for Cnán to become lost in it for a few moments, and she made enough noise passing through to alert Eleázar, who was lurking nearby, almost completely invisible in armor that had been blackened with a mixture of grease and char.

Thinking about that overlong sword of his, Cnán did her best to simulate the sweet song of a lark, which they had chosen as a sort of password. A moment later, she heard the call echoed from the branches of a tree over her head. Her call hadn't been convincing enough to fool a real bird; this was Vera, perched somewhere nearby, no doubt with her crossbow. Rædwulf and Rafael would be up in other trees, ensconced in shooting positions with clear views of the ground between here and the Mongols' camp.

Having been thus announced and heralded, she passed out of the tree belt and into open, sandy ground beyond to find Feronantus and Percival, fully armed and armored, standing silently next to their horses and brooding over the river, which ran shallow, and hence rather noisily, through a channel about twenty paces away. This was not its main branch. It divided around a long, slender island, a sandbar that had been colonized and reinforced by leggy trees that thrust from the water and sand like bristles in a brush. The fork they looked over now was the inferior branch, easily forded this time of year. On the opposite side of the little island, it ran deeper. Much of its breadth was suitable for wading, but the middle stretch would require swimming or a boat. A boat ought to be drawn up on that shore. Feronantus had paid for it and offered to pay the same amount again after the boatman delivered them to the far bank—to Asia.

"What news, *Vaetha*?" asked Feronantus, using the false name that Cnán had given him the first time they had met—this had become a perverse, affectionate habit.

"None," she said. "Yet."

"Where does the moon stand?"

"One finger to go."

"Yasper found what he wanted?"

"The market seems to have satisfied him in many ways."

Feronantus enjoyed this, but Percival threw her a wounded look.

"One day, your skills as an observer will get you into trouble," Feronantus said.

"If this is not trouble," Cnán returned, "then what is?"

Feronantus considered it, then shrugged. "It is what we do."

"Attacking sleeping, unarmed men?"

"This undertaking is difficult enough to begin with," Feronantus said. "You yourself have told us many times that it is nothing more than a slow form of suicide. If we were to forgo the use of stealth and surprise, and restrict ourselves to frontal assaults in broad daylight..." He shook his head. "They will all be awake soon enough," he said, "and making them so is your responsibility; if you are so concerned with making it a fair fight, then go and do your job."

With a parting glance at Percival—who declined to meet her eye—she turned back into the belt of woods and slipped through it as quietly as she could. Emerging from its western side, she got a clear view of the moon, just now touching the horizon, and felt shame for being late, followed by annoyance that these men had the power to make her feel shame.

The breeze was light, but unquestionably out of the west, and this told her where to find Yasper—near the eastern edge of the broad oval where the Mongols had staked out their ponies. Downwind, in other words, so that the ponies would not scent him and whinny in alarm. He was expecting her, glancing back nervously in her direction as she scurried among the moon shadows of shrubs and low trees. As she drew closer, her nose detected a new stink: Yasper had put fire to something that was smoldering rather than burning, and spinning out a long braided thread of smoke.

As she crouched next to him, he gripped her upper arm and pointed toward the Mongols' camp. It was difficult to see much, given that it was dark and that she was peering through numerous ponies. Some of these had lain down so that they could sleep deeply, while others dozed standing up. But her eye was drawn by a flickering in the nearest of the campfires. This, she realized, was caused by the movement of at least one person who was on his feet and stealing toward it. Either Finn or Istvan.

Yasper began huffing and puffing on a twist of some fibrous material, causing the feeble wax to glow bright orange. He was working with a punk that burned slowly once lit. As she watched, he touched another punk to it and blew some more, igniting the second one, which he handed to Cnán. He then set his punk on the ground at a safe remove from his basket, into which he reached with both hands and pulled out a stack of flat packages wrapped in paper. This occasioned a lot of rustling and drew the attention of a nearby pony, but Yasper did not seem to care. He handed the packages to Cnán. "Remember, wait until you hear me—what I'll do," he whispered and then stood up in the moonlight and began to walk openly among the ponies, bending from time to time to sever a rope with a knife. This created minor commotion among the horses, which swung about and pawed the ground, snorting, but none bolted.

As Yasper ambled along, he began to hum an aimless sort of tune and then to sing in the slurred diction of the profoundly drunk. This drew the attention of one, and then another, of the Mongol sentries, who converged on him briskly, telling him to get lost. Yasper called back to them in an obsequious, apologetic tone, speaking in his native tongue, a

Germanic dialect. More horses began to wake up and clamber to their feet. Now there was whinnying. It all sounded incredibly loud to Cnán, and she reckoned that it must have grabbed the attention of all of the sentries in the Mongol camp, which, after all, was not that large.

Consequently, when some of the formerly sleeping Mongols began to cry out in agony, terror, or rage, the sentries' response was not as purposeful as it might have been. She saw one of the sentries running toward that sound, only to double over with an arrow in his belly, and reckoned that Istvan must have sheathed his bloody dagger and gotten out his bow. Depending on how much time Finn and Istvan had had to accomplish their task, they might have wiped out an entire *arban*—and their plan, quite specifically, had been to focus all of their attentions on one *arban* rather than spread the pain around.

By now, it was obvious that whatever was happening back in the camp was much more important than ejecting a wandering nocturnal drunk, and so the sentries who had been converging on Yasper faltered and turned their backs on him. He took advantage of this to wheel about and slip away. A noise happened, shockingly loud. Soon, ten more—and then a hundred.

Cnán had spent enough time among Cathayans to know what firecrackers sounded like, and so she would have recognized the sound even if she hadn't spent the whole day preparing for this moment. But the first time she had heard one, as a young girl, she had been stunned by the intensity of the noise—like nothing she had experienced in her life—and had been frozen in bewilderment for several moments. Now, during the interval when she hoped that every Mongol in the camp was in the same condition, she touched the coal at the end of her punk to the paper fuse projecting from one of

Yasper's packages, then threw it into the midst of the horses. As soon as the fuse began to spark and burn, she jumped back and ran, lighted another fuse, and hurled a second packet just as the first began a string of detonations.

The amount of chaos in this place now seemed well beyond anything that they could have hoped for. The few horses that Yasper had had time to cut loose veered to and fro across the camp, starting at each new burst of explosions. Others strained at their lead ropes, some managing to pull their stakes from the ground and gallop off for the wild steppes. Other ponies that were free tripped over the taut ropes of ones still tied. Mongols rolled up to their feet, stumbling over blankets, groping for weapons, converging on the place where Finn and Istvan had been at work.

Still, Cnán felt it would be bad form to return with unused firecrackers, and so she lit the last two packets at the same time and threw them in opposite directions, even while backing away from the scene and toward the shelter of the tree line. Her instinct was simply to turn and run, but she had learned it was sometimes better to know what was chasing you. What she saw, therefore, was Finn and Istvan making a fighting retreat from the camp, pursued by several Mongols who'd had the time and the presence of mind to arm themselves. The melee was eclipsed for a moment by a black shape, impossible to make out in the moonlight. But Cnán understood that Eleázar had moved out of the woods and positioned himself so that Finn and Istvan would lead their pursuers directly toward him. The long blade of his sword glinted like a line of sparks with the flashing bursts of firecrackers. Cnán had seen before what the weapon could do against lightly armed Mongols, and so she did now finally turn her back and make for the shelter of the trees, hoping that the archers would recognize her as a friend.

She reached the tree line without collecting any arrows or crossbow bolts and then could not resist the urge to turn back and look. What she saw, as best as she could make out, was a triangular formation with Eleázar at its apex, facing directly a growing Mongol onslaught, like the prow of a ship beating upstream. Arrayed behind him, protecting his flanks and rear, were Istvan, shooting arrows from a range so close that he could hardly miss, and Finn, wielding his lance. Both kept a wary distance from the blade of Eleázar's sword, which was describing huge looping arcs; its momentum was too great to be stopped, and so each cut had to be joined to the next like the inward turnings of a Chinese knot. Whenever he felt as though he had the leisure to move, he would call out to the others, who would move back several paces, take new positions, and call back to him; he would then back up until he was told to stop. In this manner, the triad made its way back toward the tree line at a brisk but controlled pace, soon coming within range of the three archers posted in the trees. These began to pick off Mongols who were now trying to outflank Finn and Istvan.

All that had happened thus far was apparently demoralizing enough to bring this phase of their operation to an end. Orders were being called out that Cnán translated for the others: "They're saying, 'Fall back into the camp,'" she told them, "'and regroup by *arban*.'"

All eyes turned to the Mongol camp, which was now brightly illuminated. The Mongols seemed to have understood that darkness was not their friend, and so fuel had been heaped on the fires and was blazing up, producing, through the shadows of men and horses, a wavering, tossing pool of illuminated ground.

In the center of this, Alchiq stood up in his stirrups, bellowing commands, rallying his troops around him, gesturing.

Cnán could not make out his words, but she sensed his impatience. She knew what he was telling them: *This is not a bandit raid. Stop treating it as one. This is a military operation. Let us show them what we are made of.*

Almost directly above her, she heard the distinctive *ker-whack* of a crossbow being discharged.

Alchiq's horse reared up and fell over dead. The leader tumbled roughly to the ground. For a moment, he could not be seen as his men rushed in to surround him. Then he was up on his feet, being dusted off, his teeth gleaming in the firelight as he made some humorous remark that elicited nervous laughter from those around him.

Vera, who had fired the bolt, lowered herself from her tree perch by sliding down a rope. She landed awkwardly, still hampered by her wounds, and paused with hands on knees, breathing deeply.

"I almost had him," she said.

"It was a great shot," Cnán said.

"Let's go," Vera said, standing. "You shouldn't even be here."

None of us should be here, Cnán wanted to say, but she followed Vera through the trees and out toward the riverbank.

Looking to her left, upstream, she saw Percival on his horse with his back to her. Nearby, Rædwulf stalked out of the trees with his bow over his shoulder. Swiveling to look right, downstream, she saw the same thing roughly mirrored by Feronantus and Raphael. All three of the archers were making directly for the riverbank; they entered the stream without breaking stride and headed for the sandbar, a stone's throw away. Meanwhile, Eleázar and Istvan had emerged from the woods behind Cnán. Istvan headed for the water, following a few strides behind Vera.

Eleázar stood his ground.

A long time passed before Finn emerged. Cnán had decided to get across the river. She heard his voice call out when she was halfway to the island: "Double flanking maneuver," he said, "probably about one *arban* to either end." He waved his hands alternately to the ground in front of Percival and of Feronantus. "Followed by some more up the middle." He nodded to Eleázar.

"Get to the island," Feronantus called, "and string your bow, hunter."

◆◆◆

While the others had been making their own preparations, Percival and Feronantus had been setting up trip ropes between the trees and the riverbank. At least, that was the only explanation Cnán could imagine for the way the *arbans,* charging at the same moment around the ends of the stand of trees, fell apart and went down in an avalanche of tumbling horseflesh and shouting men.

Percival and Feronantus charged at the same moment, riding opposite ways toward the stalled flankers. Eleázar stood his ground in the middle, waiting for anyone who might try to thrash through the woods.

Cnán froze up, caught between wanting to stare at Percival's headlong ride into the midst of ten foes, and the need to avert her eyes from the same.

One of her feet came down wrong, and she fell on her arse in the middle of the stream. The water scarcely came up to her navel and was not all that cold, but it shocked her back into the here and now; she turned her back on the scene, planted both hands on the river bottom, and pushed herself up onto her feet, then without looking back, made her way onto the island and into concealment before turning around to see what was happening behind her.

The picture had changed quite a bit. She had expected to see Percival dead, all of the Mongols dead, or both. Instead, Percival was alive, and most of the Mongols were simply *gone.* Seeing the Frankish knight charging toward them in full armor, the unhorsed ones had apparently darted into the trees, while those lucky enough to stay mounted had wheeled around and retreated.

Percival was wise enough not to pursue them. Shield slung over his back to collect any arrows flying out of the trees, he galloped his mount across the stream toward the little island, leaving showers of silvery hoof splashes.

Feronantus, meanwhile, had found himself in more of a fight. Perhaps he simply wasn't impressive enough to scare off the Mongols with a mere bluff charge, or perhaps the members of that *arban* had been more high-spirited. Whatever the cause, several of the attackers now lay dead, and Feronantus had abandoned his wounded horse to slog across the river on foot. A few arrows still whicked through the air around him. He hunched and raised his arm as if to bat at insects, then brought it down in a shooing sweep, stood tall, and scowled defiantly over his shoulder.

Eleázar had staged a fighting retreat from the woods and thereby drawn out a few Mongols who had immediately come under heavy attack from the five archers—Vera, Rædwulf, Raphael, Istvan, and now Finn—directly across the channel from him. The arrows had felled a few and driven the rest back into the woods, and Eleázar was now backing across the stream, his giant sword resting across his shoulder as if he had not a worry in the world. He had been hit by a few Mongol arrows, but they hung loosely in his maille, unable to penetrate deep enough to wound him.

Thus covered by the five archers, all of the members of the party made their way to the eastern shore of the little island, which was only a few paces distant, and boarded the little riverboat that waited for them there. During his visit to the market, Yasper had made arrangements for a string of ponies to also be waiting for them—on the far bank.

Percival had formed something of an attachment to the big pony he had just ridden through this engagement, and managed to swim it across the short stretch of river that was too deep for wading.

And so the entire party reached the opposite side of the Yaik River—and the threshold of the steppe land of the Mongols proper—in good order and with Alchiq's *jaghun* in such disarray as to be incapable of following them.

Earlier, Feronantus had said something to the effect that the *jaghun* must be "destroyed and, if necessary, killed," which had made no sense to Cnán at the time. Now, though, she understood. She could only guess how many men under Alchiq's command had been killed tonight. Probably many more were wounded than slain. But that was not important.

What was important was that they had been reduced to a demoralized remnant and that, when the sun rose and the bodies and the injuries were tallied, Alchiq, if he tried to drive the survivors east over the river in pursuit of the Franks, could be facing something like a mutiny.

Feronantus seemed to be of the same view. Of course, his first desire—once they had reached the east bank in good order and paid the boatman—was to put some distance between them and the Mongols, just in case Alchiq did manage to prod some of his surviving *arbans* over the river. So they rode until dawn, heading generally east, but also bending their course south.

Benjamin had explained to them that the Silk Road was not a single highway but a loose skein of routes taken at different times by different peoples, depending on all manner of contingencies. Most of those routes passed well to the south of them. Many converged on the garrison town of Saray-Jük, which, from here, was several days' hard riding downriver. But Benjamin knew of one path that wandered north of the main bundle to cross the river near the market where Yasper had bought the firecrackers. It was their plan to find that road and to meet Benjamin there, at a certain remote, woebegone caravanserai on the steppe.

If the directions he had given them were to be credited, then they could expect to reach it by sundown of the second day.

The night had been long and exhausting, and almost all of them were suffering from minor wounds of one kind or another, and they were hungry. So at first light, they stopped and made a little camp on the east slope of a low hill from whose top it was possible to keep an eye back along the way they had just come.

Within moments, several of them were asleep. Raphael and Yasper made the rounds of those who had been injured, cleaning, stitching, and bandaging their wounds. Percival, who had not suffered so much as a scratch, went to the hilltop to take the first watch. Feronantus got a little fire going. Finn, who claimed he could smell water, draped himself with every waterskin and bottle they had and set out on foot—for he was sick of riding—toward the faint suggestion of a gully that was visible a few bowshots to the north of them.

A bit of time—perhaps the better part of an hour—slipped by as they drowsed, mended, or just sat quietly watching the sun rise.

Then the calm was broken by a cry from Vera. They did not understand the words, since she was speaking in her native tongue, but no one could mistake her tone. She had jumped to her feet and was gazing in alarm to the north. She turned her head toward the top of the hill, and Cnán followed her gaze to see Percival leaning back comfortably against the body of his horse, which had lain down to sleep. Percival, gazing fixedly at the sky, looked no more alert than the horse. His movements were those of a man just stirring awake—or coming out of a trance.

Soon enough, they were all awake and on their feet. Feronantus and Istvan, closest to the ponies, snatched up weapons and mounted.

A lone rider had come across the steppe and achieved the difficult feat of sneaking up on Finn.

From Percival's vantage point, this interloper ought to have been visible from miles away, but Percival had fallen asleep—or what amounted to the same thing, fallen into one of his visions.

Finn, toiling down in the depths of an overgrown gully, filling his water bottles, had been unaware he was being stalked and had clambered up into the open to find himself confronted by the lone Mongol rider, helmeted and armored, with a bladed lance couched under his arm.

Finn, as always, had his own lance; he'd been using it as a sort of hiking staff as he clambered up out of the gully. Startled by the rider—who came right at him—and encumbered by a heavy load of water, he managed to step back and swing the weapon's tip down, knocking the tip of the Mongol's lance down and aside just a moment before it would have penetrated his rib cage. The Mongol rode past him. Finn's body jerked hard and twisted around awkwardly. He was pulled off his feet and dragged for a couple of yards before the Mongol's horse stumbled to a halt.

The attacker's lance had missed Finn's body but became involved in the tangle of straps and ropes by which the water vessels were slung over Finn's shoulders.

With the horse stopped, Finn might have had his opportunity to regain his footing and to disengage himself. But his foe was already in motion. The Mongol swung down out of his saddle. As he did, his long mane of gray hair billowed around him in the morning sun. For a moment, he was on the opposite side of the horse from Finn, but he ducked under the horse's neck and came up behind Finn and wrapped him in a wrestling hold with the speed of a striking snake. Finn's brothers and sisters on the hill above let out a cry of horror, shame, and grief.

Alchiq's massive arms scissored, then relaxed. Finn's corpse bounced on the ground at Alchiq's feet.

Alchiq then turned and gazed up calmly toward Feronantus and Istvan, who were headed for him at a full gallop, both bellowing with rage and pain. He reached down and pulled his lance free, then was up on his pony's back and galloping north with the adroitness that only a veteran Mongol warrior was capable of.

North across the steppe, he was pursued by the vengeful Shield-Brethren, but the only thing swift enough to catch up with him were the wrenching cries of Finn's companions.

CHAPTER 33:

LUCERNA CORPORIS EST OCULUS

"Do you smell something burning?" Colonna asked, rousing from the meditative mood he had fallen into.

Capocci dropped his latest de-stingered scorpion into the clay jar and raised his head to sniff at the musty air of their underground prison. When they had first arrived in the tunnels and broken corridors beneath the Septizodium, the air had been stale and still, a stagnant miasma undisturbed for many years. The effect of their presence, initially, had stirred up the dust and decay of old Rome, clogging the air with tiny particles that caked the insides of their noses.

Da Capua had sneezed nearly constantly for several days before Colonna had offered to cut off the offending part of his face. He had then started to complain that the stench was eating at his soul—presumably, an item more difficult to remove. Since then, the ambient aroma of the tunnels had settled into a faint but unavoidable effluvium of sweat and charcoal.

But Colonna was correct. There was now a pungent scent of burning matter.

"It troubles me to agree with you, my dear Giovanni," Capocci said. He fit a plug into the top of his clay jar, trapping the unhappy but harmless scorpions inside, and then stripped the leather glove off his hand. "I think we should go see if someone has set his beard on fire."

"Oh," Colonna raised his eyes toward the roof and clutched his hands theatrically to his chest, "*please* let it be Fieschi."

Capocci chuckled as he scooped up the other glove. "As amusing as I would find such a sight, I pray God is not inclined to listen to you today." He put the gloves and the clay jar into a leather satchel. "The theological ramifications would be even more distressing than the sight of our good cardinal, slightly charred."

As they walked through the halls, not only did the singed odor increase, but wispy tendrils of smoke sluggishly curled along the tunnel's ceiling. And when they heard shouting, they broke into a run.

The central corridor from which branched several of the cardinals' chambers was filled with greasy, gray smoke. It billowed along the ceiling, crawling and fuming like a living creature, and farther down the hall, a sullen, smoky red maw gaped and snapped, like a yawning, demonic mouth. The air burned Capocci's throat, and the disturbingly appetizing taste of charred meat filled his mouth. In the haze, someone was coughing and spitting, trying vainly to clear his lungs of the foul air.

Ducking to keep his head out of the smoke, Capocci waddled toward the distressed man. His fingers touched cloth, and he gathered the fabric into his fist. The man felt Capocci pulling on him and staggered into the cardinal's arms, as if he were throwing himself on Capocci's mercy. Capocci fell back, dropping his satchel, and tried to lift up and orient the choking man. Who was he?

It was the new one, the strange one—Rodrigo—his face streaked by soot and tears. His eyes were bright, wide and staring, the whites tinted orange and red in the firelit gloom.

"I have you," Capocci said, hugging the man tightly. He was surprised how frail the priest felt in his arms. Beneath the heavy robe, there was not much to the man, almost like he was a spirit who had animated a bundle of sticks into a simulacrum of a human body. "Is there anyone else?"

Rodrigo hesitated, and then shook his head. "S-s-somer… c-c…" he stuttered.

Capocci peered toward the ruddy light farther down the hall, flicking tongues leaping and cavorting inside the red mouth. He pushed Rodrigo into Colonna's waiting arms and knelt to locate his satchel. "Go," he snapped over his shoulder. "Take him to safety. Through Fieschi's secret exit." He found his bag and pulled out his heavy gloves.

"There is no hope," Colonna replied, a tight grip on Rodrigo's shoulder. "No one could bear that flame."

Capocci tucked his bag into his belt, securing it so he didn't lose it a second time. "There is always hope," he said.

Colonna shook his head grimly and then thrust his chin toward the roaring fire. "God be with you, my friend." He retreated, dragging the dazed priest with him.

"*Custodi animam meam, quoniam sanctus sum,*" Capocci muttered as he pulled on his leather gloves. "*Salvum fac servum tuum, Deus meus, sperantem in te.*" He punctuated his plea to God by touching his head, his heart, and the two points of his shoulders.

Anointed with prayer, he walked toward the burning mouth of Hell.

◆◆◆

The fever had him.

Rodrigo wanted to believe that sustenance and sanctuary had driven out the worst of the spiritual poison that lay siege to him, but now he knew it was not gone entirely. It lurked inside, within the walls of his personal citadel, like a demonic army hiding in his gut, waiting for a chance to break loose and pollute both his body and his soul.

And when that cardinal—the one who had fixed him with his eyes, just as a hawk stares at its terrified prey—came into the chamber where he and Somercotes were quietly discussing scripture, Rodrigo felt the walls inside crack again. A small fracture, but a breach nonetheless, and the poison started to ooze out once again.

After Fieschi and Somercotes had left, Rodrigo had tried to calm himself. If only he could sequester the poison, keep the venom from spreading. The last time, it had eaten almost all of his spirit, and only a fortuitous arrival in Rome—in the company of the waif, Ferenc—had saved him. That, and the presence of the kindly ones in the quorum of cardinals trapped under the city.

They—Somercotes and the two white-haired giants, Capocci and Colona—had treated him with civility and dignity. An image of the four of them formed in his mind. Arm in arm, they walked along a slowly meandering river, a row of silver-leaved trees on their left. The trees swayed and whispered in the light spring breeze.

It was a perfectly lovely fantasy, marred only by the suspiciously generous sun. At first, it cast down on him a most heavenly light, dappling the leaves of the slender trees, but the light reddened, then grew warmer—then hot. And the sun grew larger too, swelling from a tiny dot in the blue-white heavens to an angry red sphere, like a gigantic blot of blood. Flames crawled and leaped across the sun's mottled surface like dancing imps, and long snake tongues of fire flicked out at random, threatening to span the sky, threatening to drop down to Earth—and *touch* him. If they did, they would ignite the poison inside, and he and all around him would be blasted to vapor, spreading out over the land to merge with the heat.

Rodrigo turned his head to ask Somercotes if the heat was unbearable, and found himself hand in hand with a charred skeleton. A tongue of fire had lanced down, missing him, but torching his companion instead. Rodrigo tried to pull away, but the skeleton leaned in, eyes dripping clotted gore, while its bony grip painfully squeezed his fingers. When Rodrigo struggled to break free, the skeleton's jaw fell open, and a stream of gray smoke shot out in a sooty plume, stinging his eyes, blacking his face.

Within a few seconds, the sun was blotted out by the smoke-spewing skull, and Rodrigo began to hack up black spittle, his throat and lungs rejecting the filthy air.

He had fallen to his knees—surrounded by intersecting wheels of sparks, flames, and embers circling on the edges of vision—when hands roughly grabbed him. He had fought at first—valiantly, but foolishly—thinking he had been grabbed again by the skeleton, but when the fleshy hands roughly shook him and a voice called his name, he realized he was no longer dreaming.

He was wide-awake. The corridor was filled with smoke from a fire that had been started in one of the narrow rooms used by the cardinals. Rodrigo stared at the black billows, agape with horror and wonder.

He knew in which room the fire burned.

Somercotes.

"Do not struggle so," a voice growled in his ear, and he twisted his head to see Colonna, the tall one. "There is nothing more we can do."

No! What about Somercotes? He struggled in the cardinal's grip, trying to break free so that he could run to the aid of the warmhearted old man. *He can't be dead.*

A shape eclipsed the orange-shot gloom in the corridor, and for a second, through a break in the stinking wave of smoke flowing along the ceiling of the hall, he caught sight of Capocci, in the doorway of the burning room, his white beard spread out around his face like a splash of white sea foam.

Rodrigo broke free of Colonna and fell, banging his knees against the hard floor. Ignoring the pain, he scrambled toward the door. He had to help Capocci. He had to help save Somercotes.

In his mind, he saw the younger version of Somercotes—the one from his dream—pointing toward the door of the hut. The doorway was filled with light. *It was happening again…*

Save us, the angel whispered, and Rodrigo began to scream and gibber and beg as Colonna grabbed his leg and hauled him away from the glowing portal.

✦✦✦

Ferenc and Ocyrhoe rested in the shadow of the niche, further obscured from the road by the thick trunk of the tree that had forced itself, obstinately and resolutely, between several of the large foundation stones of the nymphaeum. The ten-sided building, like many of the older temples built far from the center of Rome, had lost its luster and allure, though its marble facing was mostly intact. No one worshipped there now—a fact she had verified while Ferenc dozed—though, in her heart, Ocyrhoe suspected rites and ceremonies dedicated to Minerva had taken place beneath its rounded dome.

She felt safe here, her back against the sun-warmed stones. The goddess had resided here once, and much as a child instinctively knows—and remembers—its mother's embrace, Ocyrhoe drew courage from the faded memory of that divine presence.

They had walked as quickly as Ferenc's ankle had allowed; though she feared their pace would draw attention, she had been surprised and relieved to discover how easy it had been for them to slip along the edges of the restless crowds. The Bear's guards were watching for runners, and as the citizens of Rome became more frantic, there became too many targets to watch effectively. Made invisible by their more temperate pace, they trailed in the wake of the crowds, letting the mob pull them along, until she spotted the rounded dome of the nymphaeum.

Ferenc was propped up in the corner of the niche, eyes closed, head against the wall. He was worn out—as was she—and as they had walked, she could tell his ankle pained him. Ocyrhoe had insisted on taking a rest—ignoring his persistent protests that he could keep going—and shortly after they had found this hiding place, he had wedged himself into the corner and dozed off.

Such a stupid thing, that jump! At first, she had wanted to scream at him; he had thrown away their one chance to slip out of the city undetected. Instead, he had foolishly injured himself while saving her, without even considering the possibility that she hadn't *needed* saving. She could have outclimbed that guard. She was smaller and faster; he would not have been able to keep up. And then they would have both made it to the top of the wall.

But what then? Where would they have gone from there?

She was still angry, and not just because he had doubted her plan, but also because he had been right to question it. What stung most had been the embarrassment of his clumsily signed question: *Have you ever been out?*

She hadn't even considered how they would have descended from the wall. She was a child of the city; it was all she had ever known, and all she ever wanted to master. She had wanted to be a part of the city the way the other kin-sisters were: both slave and master of the temples, the plazas, the roads, the aqueducts, the gardens, the walls. She had wanted to learn every bump and rock of the seven hills, to know them well enough to walk across them barefoot and know where she was by the texture of the ground beneath her feet. Her world was Rome, and what made her heart ache was the realization of how small and insignificant her dream was. She could walk across the entirety of Rome in a day; outside the walls, she could walk for days—weeks, years, her whole life, even—and not reach the edge of the world.

Her fingers touched and affectionately scraped at the warm stone of the nymphaeum. She was an ant, dreaming the tiny dream of an ant, in a world erected by and for giants. *I am frightened*, she thought, praying to a goddess she did not know how to summon. *I am just one small girl, and I am not very strong.*

Ferenc stirred, his eyelids fluttering. As his senses returned, he sat up sharply. Ocyrhoe laid a hand on his arm, and he calmed at once. Her fingers began to tap and squeeze. "We are safe for now," she signed. "No one is paying attention. They are looking for people who are fleeing."

He nodded as he looked at the wall behind and above them. "Where are we?" he queried.

"Near one of the big gates," she replied. "Two roads, two waterways."

In some ways, it was the worst gate for them to pick, as it straddled two roads—the Via Praenestina and the Via Labicana—and would have the largest contingent of Orsini's men. But at this same location, two of the ancient aqueducts that serviced Rome also entered the city—the Aqua Claudia and Anio Novus. The great wall that encircled Rome, built long ago by a man named Aurelian, was erected *after* the city had been founded. For many generations, Rome had not needed its walls, and when Aurelian had the fortifications built, he did not dare tear down the parts of the city that stood where he wanted the wall to go. Here, at the Porta Maggiore, the wall wrapped itself around road and waterway.

The walls embraced Rome's history; they did not split or block the old temples and mausoleums. And as she had discovered during her brief exploration of the nymphaeum while Ferenc had slept, some of these buildings were built on top of older structures, and some of *those* were riddled with crypts and underground chambers.

◆◆◆

Coughing and choking, Capocci stumbled against the rough panel that was the secret exit from the Septizodium. It moved beneath him, and caught off guard, he flailed to keep his balance as the door swung out and spilled him into the alley. He fell to his knees, cradling his blistered hands against his chest. His tangled beard was a wild array of soot-blackened hair, sweat-shiny knots and curls rising about his face like a spiny bush that had been drained of life and color.

Smoke and gray ash leaked out of the door behind him, a thin flurry lifted by the heat into a clear-blue sky. Capocci crumpled to the ground, landing on his side and rolling onto his back. His chest heaved, gulping great draughts of clean air. He had seen the sky only earlier that morning—during the communal meal the cardinals shared at the slop buckets—but now it seemed so different, so much vaster. He marveled at the smooth emptiness, at the plain purity, a blue unsullied, unblemished, as if it knew itself to be the only true color known to God and man.

Something clouded his view—a round blur that, when he focused his eyes, resolved into a man's face. Capocci frowned, wanting to push the man back.

Not now. I want to see the sky. My breath, my salvation…

"Cardinal Capocci," the man said, "can you hear me?"

Capocci squinted at the man's face, trying to place it. He wasn't one of the other cardinals, but he seemed familiar. The shape of his nose, the width of his mouth, the neat beard—these all belonged to someone he knew. "Master Constable," he croaked, finally remembering—the man in charge of watching over the cardinals in the Septizodium. There were other guards nearby, as well as the tall figure of Cardinal Colonna, his face puckered with concern and dread.

"Cardinal," the master constable continued, "is there anyone else? Is there anyone else inside?"

Capocci raised his hands to cover his face, but paused at the sight of their raw and blistered skin. He dropped them back to his chest and closed his eyes, shaking his head from side to side.

God had sheltered him from the fire. He had seen the writhing *thing* that hissed and spat in the center of the inferno; he had even tried to grab hold and pull it out. But the arm had come away. It was no longer human; the Devil had taken the man's soul and burned away everything that had been good and pure of the man; all that was left was sizzling fat and overdone meat.

"No," he wheezed in response to the master constable's question. "There is no one else."

✦✦✦

The tomb was simple, and yet unlike any other monument in Rome. A freedman's tomb, built for a baker. Also, it was *outside* the Aurelian Wall. Ocyrhoe squinted up at the large, round holes that perforated the side of the building—a series of open, unblinking eyes that looked away from Rome.

They were a stone's throw from the Porta Maggiore, and she would not have dared to stand this close to the gate of Rome had she been on the other side. But the Bear's guards were not looking in this direction; all their attention was on the crowd pressing against them from within the city. The crowd on this side was smaller—more confused than angry. Several merchants, in fact, were selling their wares directly out of their carts, taking advantage of the press of people milling about.

She had been right about the crypt under the nymphaeum. It had connected to older tunnels, and though they had wandered aimlessly for what seemed like days, it had only been a few hours. Ocyrhoe didn't want to think about their fortune—they could have gotten lost for a long time underground—but the path had seemed obvious to them. Perhaps it had been the lack of dust in certain passages, or the smoothness of the stone underfoot, or even the persistent vibration of the water in the Aqua Claudia overhead: these clues and others had guided them well.

They had escaped the city.

Ferenc took her hand, pulling her away from the tomb of Eurysaces, the baker, coaxing her into the wide world beyond Rome. She squeezed his fingers, giddily flashing him a grin. She was glad he was with her. Together, they would find the army of the Holy Roman Emperor and deliver Somercotes's message.

She laughed. She was really doing it. She was delivering a Binder message. She was going to save them all.

Here Ends The Mongoliad:

Book Two

ACKNOWLEDGMENTS

ERIK BEAR
Thanks to my family, to my friends, and to everyone who's fought alongside me on this book both metaphorically and literally. Thanks to all the other writers, especially Mark, for working harder than any one person should. Thanks to my dad and my grandpa, for guiding me down the path of writing.

GREG BEAR
It's been terrific working with all of these fine writers, clashing steel in the mornings under Neal's guidance, then quaffing coffee and breakfasting out of pink boxes of muffins while plotting at a mad pace…watching Mark outline and organize chapters on our blackboard while Joe and Cooper paced and swung and flashed their blades, shooting ideas back and forth with Neal across our writers' table, talking across the continent with E.D. (and wickedly offering her virtual muffins), collaborating with son Erik on both fight strategies and chapters…while we all ventured on foot and horse through untold carnage and across wide plains of rippling grass, straight into the fabulous territories of Harold Lamb, Talbot Mundy, and Robert E. Howard… Thanks to all for the amazing experience!

NICOLE GALLAND

Much gratitude to Mark, Neal, Greg, Cooper, Joe, and Erik for the lively trip we've all taken together—especially for keeping the Skype signal open over the miles, even with all those crickets. A special thank you to Liz Darhansoff. And a nod to everyone involved in the brief, ineffable existence of E. D. deBirmingham.

JOSEPH BRASSEY

To Neal Stephenson, who gave me my shot—I hope I've made you proud. To Mark Teppo, who beat my prose with a stick until it was pretty. To Greg, Erik, Cooper, E.D., and everyone else at Subutai. To Tinker, who taught me to always add violence and put my feet on the path. To Ken and Rob at Fort Lewis, for opening my mind to new possibilities. To my lovely wife and my patient parents, who always supported me. To my little sister and every friend I've had along the way who believed this could happen. Dreams come true. This is for you.

COOPER MOO

Heartfelt thanks to my family for their support: my wife, Mary; our children, Keagan, Connor, and Haven; and my parents, Jan and Greg Moo. A debt of gratitude is owed every member of the writing team, particularly Neal for his leadership and Mark for his editorial guidance. I raise a bowl of *airag* to you all!

NEAL STEPHENSON

Thanks to Mark Teppo, the centripetal force.

MARK TEPPO

This project began when someone asked that eternal question that every storyteller loves to hear: "So what happened next?" I don't think any of us imagined where the answer would take us, but I am exceptionally grateful to have had this creative team—Erik, Greg, Cooper, E.D., Joseph, and Neal—during this journey. I'd also like to thank Karen Laur, Jason Norgaar, and Neal Von Flue for the character portraits they provided, as well as the entire Mongoliad.com community who ventured into the shiny future with us. Jeremy Bornstein and Lenny Raymond took care of us in that eternally unrecognized way that infrastructure people do; thank you, gentlemen. Fleetwood Robbins provided a keen editorial eye, offering a great perspective on the final arrangement of these words. Also, a nod to Emm, whose constant and unflagging support matters. So very much.

Tinker Pierce, Gus Trim, and Guy Windsor provided a great deal of useful insight and instruction as to the Western martial arts. Additionally, Ellis Amdur and Aaron Fields offered fantastic commentary on all matters relating to the martial arts of thirteenth-century Japan. These five gentlemen are true scholars in their fields, and any creative license taken with the arts they study is entirely our own.

ABOUT THE AUTHORS

Neal Stephenson is primarily a fiction author and has received several awards for his works in speculative fiction. His more popular books include *Snow Crash, The Diamond Age, Cryptonomicon, The Baroque Cycle,* and *Anathem.*

Greg Bear is the author of more than thirty books, spanning the thriller, science fiction, and fantasy genres, including *Blood Music, Eon, The Forge of God, Darwin's Radio, City at the End of Time,* and *Hull Zero Three.* His books have won numerous international prizes, have been translated into more than twenty-two languages, and have sold millions of copies worldwide.

Nicole Galland studied comparative religion and theatre at Harvard University and believes they are pretty much the same thing. She has written historical fiction and screenplays under various pseudonyms, much to the dismay of her mother, who wishes hers was a household name. She lives in rural Massachusetts with her husband and the world's best dog.

Mark Teppo is the author of the Codex of Souls urban fantasy series as well as the hypertext dream narrative *The Potemkin Mosaic.*

Joseph Brassey lives in the Pacific Northwest with his wife and two cats. He teaches medieval fighting techniques to members of the armed forces. *The Mongoliad* is his first published fiction.

Erik Bear lives and writes in Seattle, Washington. He has written for a bestselling video game and is currently working on several comic book series.

Cooper Moo spent five minutes in Mongolia in 1986 before he had to get back on the train—he never expected to be channeling Mongolian warriors. In 2007 Cooper fought a Chinese long-sword instructor on a Hong Kong rooftop—he never thought the experience would help him write battle scenes. In addition to being a member of The Mongoliad writing team, Cooper has written articles for various magazines. His autobiographical piece "Growing Up Black and White," published in *Seattle Weekly,* was awarded Social Issues Reporting Article of the Year by the Society of Professional Journalists. He lives in Issaquah, Washington, with his wife, three children, and numerous bladed weapons.